YEAR OF THE RABBIT

A MALCOLM CHAUCER THRILLER

T.D. DONNELLY

THUNDER ROAD PRESS

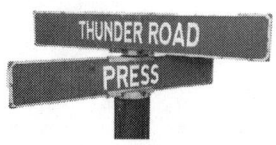

First published by Thunder Road Press in 2024
Copyright © T.D. Donnelly 2024
All rights reserved

ISBN 978-1-965247-00-6 (Paperback)

No part of this publication may be reproduced, stored, or transmitted in any form or by any means, electronic, mechanical, photocopying, recording, scanning, or otherwise without written permission from the publisher. It is illegal to copy this book, post it to a website, or distribute it by any other means without permission. Names, characters, businesses, places, events, and incidents are either the products of the author's imagination or used in a purely fictitious manner. Any resemblance to actual persons, living or dead, or actual events is purely coincidental.

Cover art designed by Miblart

Interior formatting by Rebecca Millar

For my mother, Joan Donnelly.
To live a creative life requires
holding the world lightly,
caring deeply,
and wondering grandly.
I learned all that from you.

Download the free prequel to YEAR OF THE RABBIT at tddonnelly.com

There's a Black Sheep incident at the Korean DMZ.
An emaciated Caucasian man crosses from the North to the South.
He says his name is ... Malcolm Chaucer.

CHAPTER 1

The sniper knew the second this easy assignment became difficult. It came down to an air sensor that wasn't on the building's plans. She breached the NYU biology labs from the roof, through an air filter that gave her access to the narrow crawl space between the roof and the ceiling of the labs on the top floor. She heard a faint click and saw a sensor panel turn from green to red.

She figured that the sensor could tell the air filter was breached. What she didn't know was what the response would be, if any. She picked up the pace of her crawling, crossing sixty feet to a hatch that led into the rafters above the top floor labs.

Click. It was faint, but unmistakable. She saw another sensor just five feet away. It too went from green to red. She saw something in the sensor's digital readout: CO2.

Great. These sensors were set to alert someone when carbon dioxide levels rose even a little. And the sniper was exhaling carbon dioxide with every breath.

Click. Another sensor went red. This was bad. This was very bad. She sped up her crawl even faster, making it to the hatch and slipping into the space below.

She lowered herself onto a cool steel beam that crossed beneath the arched ceiling forty feet above the floor. The arch above was painted black, as was the beam. Once she closed the hatch behind her, she became practically invisible. Her tight-fitting tactical clothing matched the shade perfectly.

The space had once been a gymnasium, she figured. One that spanned the entire top floor of the pre-war building. Now, it hosted a series of laboratories.

The labs themselves were separated by walls, maybe fifteen feet high. But from the sniper's perch, she saw into each and every one.

The door below burst open. In came two armed security guards. One of them held some kind of scientific device in his hand, a scanner of some sort. The other quickly moved from lab to lab, checking with everyone who was here.

And then they started looking up at the ceiling. And suddenly the sniper no longer felt quite so invisible. She needed to locate her target immediately, shuffle him off this mortal coil, and race back the way she came for an expedited exfil.

Her target's name was Sim Ju Won, but he went by Tajo. "Tajo" was Korean for "ostrich," and looking at the slight, quite tall twenty-year-old, with most of that height carried in his legs, she could see why they'd call him that. She was shocked, however, by his appearance. She was told he was a virologist, but she stared down at a boy. He did not look to be twenty. He barely looked sixteen.

He worked feverishly in the farthest lab. The distance wasn't a problem. He was sixty-five yards away. For her Tikka T3 rifle, that was slapping distance.

Tajo was agitated. He was rushing between two pieces of lab equipment. What the equipment was, she had no idea. But she got the sense that whatever he was doing, he was racing against time.

He would never know how true that was.

She checked the security guards. One of them was still searching skyward. She had to be exceedingly careful as she slipped her Tikka around to line up the shot. And suddenly she realized the problem. The box. The box was the problem, because Tajo was inside it.

The box was some kind of containment chamber for biological experiments; a room within the room. It had a small airlock entryway, its own air supply, filters, UV sterilization, and walls of two different layers of inch-thick clear … what? The briefing was silent on the box. Was it plastic? Was it plexiglass? All she could tell was that the box was serious business.

The sniper had tracked his movements, her crosshairs locked on the lower-rear quadrant of his skull. The medulla oblongata. Or as her instructor called it so many years ago, "the off-switch." Instant death. Not so much as a twitch or spasm anywhere in the body. Just the gentle yielding of an inanimate object to the insistent pull of gravity.

If she pulled the trigger now, she was sure she'd miss him entirely. The deflection angle was a problem. A math problem.

If the two layers of the box were ballistic in nature, that would be a challenge, but at least they would be a known factor. She knew how to punch through bulletproof glass. She trained for that scenario. But this? This was virgin territory. She knew she was getting caught up in the numbers, and that was a mistake. *Simplify. Turn it into a word problem.*

The guards below grew agitated. They knew something was wrong. Now they were both looking at the ceiling. The sniper was out of time.

She settled deeper into her firing position, feeling her bones sink and become one with the beam. She visualized the shot two ways, impacting two different materials. Then she split the difference. The high angle of attack and the thickness of the medium between them made the deflection extreme.

Suddenly she realized why she got this particular job. Of course. She knew the shot. She knew full well she was maybe one of twelve people on the planet who could pull it off.

She lowered her aim. Down to the researcher's shirt-pocket protector. She felt it in her bones. It was right. Tajo moved again, to the other machine. If she had to guess, he was deleting data.

Her finger tightened up the slack between it and the trigger. The trigger on her Tikka was altered to be soft and loose. Less than a pound of pressure would be enough to draw it to its release point—a gnat could land on it and fire a round—which meant that the rifle barrel would remain perfectly still throughout her careful, methodical firing sequence.

She felt her heart beat, her lungs intake and expel air. She brought their timing together, like a conductor bringing an unruly orchestra into unison. Time elongated, an eternity of milliseconds between each beat and breath. She brought the stillness that made her a perfect instrument of death.

That was when the security guard spotted her. He yelled something. She didn't dare to break her concentration. For all she knew, he was drawing his pistol as she lay there.

The researcher returned to the other machine. She had three seconds, minimum.

An eternity in her current consciousness.

She lowered her aim more, now at the bottom of the pocket protector. She let the last doubt dissolve away as she waited for her next heartbeat. Atrium. Ventricle. A rush of blood coursed its way on a round-trip journey. She sunk into the stillness that followed. Her right index finger curled ever so slightly.

An explosion interrupted the perfect moment, punching a hole in both layers of transparent material and catching a generally unremarkable NYU grad student in the lower-rear quadrant of his skull.

A blaring biohazard alarm erupted an instant later as air pressure sensors inside the glass box discovered an imbalance. But the researcher did not hear the first note.

The sniper found his off-switch.

By the time the guards drew their pistols, the sniper was gone.

CHAPTER 2

Malcolm Chaucer knew there were seventeen people on the subway car. Ten women and seven men. Three of those seventeen people were armed. He also knew vomit had been cleaned from this car within the last hour, that three of the women were undocumented immigrants, that one man was drunk and another high on a psychedelic, that the woman nearest him was in the process of separating from her husband, and that no one recognized him or viewed him as a threat. He knew all this and more within the first minute of boarding the train.

Turning inward, Chaucer knew his pulse was racing at over 170 beats per minute, that his skin pinpricked with sweat, that his peripheral vision was growing ever more acute, and even his sense of smell was heightened. All of these conditions, and several more, were part of a cascade of reactions born of a deep, instinctual mammalian response to threats, when the brain's "danger tripwire" was set off. The doctors called it hypervigilance, and it was a symptom of CPTSD—complex post-traumatic stress disorder. There were techniques many people used to deal with it: breath-control exercises, cognitive behavioral scripts, and eye movement desensitization, to name just a few.

But Chaucer was not many people. Those techniques did not

work for him. He tried them all. Just a hint that a methodology might treat his condition and Chaucer was all in. He wanted more than anything to cure himself of his affliction, despite becoming more certain with each passing year that no such relief was in the cards. No, Malcolm Chaucer knew a lot of things, but above all, he knew that he was broken; the kind of broken that would likely never be fixed.

A man crossed a street. A man crossed a street and Chaucer read it as a threat, one that mirrored the threat that changed his life forever. That's all it took to send Chaucer's life dancing on the edge of disaster, to induce a panic attack that Chaucer was still fighting to control.

He sat in the nearest available seat and adjusted the noise-canceling headphones on his head, comforted by the sensory-dampening blanket they provided. The G train car was relatively new, giving Chaucer lots of polished aluminum and steel reflective surfaces he could use to assess threats without directly staring. Of the three armed men on the subway, one was a burly man at the far end of the car in an ill-fitting suit and long gray coat that did nothing to camouflage the hip holster or the gun inside it. This man was not using reflections to check out the rest of the train. He took no one and nothing in, beyond the ratty, dog-eared paperback he held in one pale hand. *Private investigator or private security: nothing to worry about.*

The second and third threats were armed with knives. Threat number two was a kid, sixteen at most, in baggy black cargo pants and a white Hanes T-shirt. His head bobbed rhythmically to the sounds in his Beats headphones. He paid no mind to the rest of the car either.

The third threat sat across from Chaucer. To assess him, Chaucer would have to look his way. Luckily, this threat paid no attention to him. His focus was entirely on the young girl seated next to him.

"You are my everything!" Chaucer heard it clearly, above the white noise in his headphones. *Lie.* Sonny lied easily as he pawed the exposed thigh of the young woman next to him. His other arm was around her back, a meaty claw holding her arm tightly.

Chaucer knew his name was Sonny because of the generous neck tattoo across his Adam's apple. Sonny was paler than Chaucer, which was to say quite pale; that particularly pale shade of white that suggested either a creature of the night or a young man who equated skin color with value. Everything else about Sonny said "street-tough." He was in his late twenties, with sleeve tattoos of nubile women on full display, snaking forth from under his Nets jersey. Snaking. That's what his arm was doing, wrapping itself around the young Latina seated next to him. She was thin and pale and uncomfortable with his touch in this public space. But when she looked at him, her eyes searched for signs of love. Signs she did not easily find. She tried to wriggle free from his grasp, but to no avail.

Chaucer looked at the floor. Five stops. *Just breathe and make it five stops.*

"Why are you being such a bitch?! Don't you know what we got is, like, special? You an' me? We can rule this world, baby."

Lie. Lie. Lie. Chaucer had heard Sonny's patter before. It had a quality he recognized. *Rehearsed.* Sonny was not simply a young man looking to exert power and control over an object of beauty. No, Chaucer could smell it in the air. *Agenda.*

The Latina squirmed, trying to disentangle herself from Sonny. Chaucer caught a glimpse of bruises on her arm and waist. Fresh bruises.

"Stop it." She said it, but she didn't mean it. Not entirely. A hundred different micro-expressions told Chaucer the story. She wanted to love this man. She wanted to believe what he was saying, despite a voice deep inside warning her to run. She was conflicted.

And he was persistent.

The train braked hard as it pulled into the next stop. *Ding.* The doors opened. No one moved. No one boarded or left. None of the other passengers paid Sonny or the girl any mind. Help would not be coming for her.

Ding. The doors closed.

Four stops. Just stare at the floor. Just focus on your breath. That would be the smart thing to do. The safe thing. Chaucer's hypervigilance was always in danger of escalating to something more dangerous. Three times in the last six years Chaucer had ended up with a mental-health hold in a hospital in the city. Two of those times, he was released within two days. Once, his stay extended to three weeks. Chaucer knew that one day he would enter such a place and never emerge.

But that day did not need to be today. All he had to do was wait four stops.

Chaucer made it two.

Don't do anything stupid, Sonny. Just don't hurt her in front of me —

Sonny put his hands on her again. She whispered something and pulled away, and he grabbed her bruised wrist, causing her to gasp in pain.

Sonny shouldn't have done that.

Chaucer's life was filled with fear and pain. He had daily questions about why he even continued living, and the reason he kept coming back to, the main reason he made himself persist through pain, and fear, and trauma was that he could help. He could help the helpless. He could help people in the way he once wished someone would help him.

And if that resulted in the psychotic break that ended him, so be it.

So fucking be it.

"Sonny's lying. About everything." Chaucer's voice rang out, interrupting the back and forth between the two. The woman glanced up, surprised. She locked eyes with Chaucer and became instantly mesmerized. Chaucer had the eyes of a hypnotist.

Sonny looked up, enraged. What he saw in front of him didn't exactly inspire fear. Chaucer was six foot two, but he sat hunched over in visible pain. He had roughly tousled dark hair, pale skin, and sharp features that would've been seen as handsome if not for his eyes. Chaucer's eyes were arresting to be sure, but they gave most people the uncomfortable feeling they were being x-rayed. But Sonny was not threatened by them. In them, Sonny saw hostility. He saw menace. And he ignored it all.

"What'd you say, asshole?"

"I told her you're lying. About loving her mainly. But also about who you are. Everything about who you are." Chaucer turned to speak directly to the woman. "He has three main tells when he's lying. The first is his eye contact. It'll be strong, but when he glances away, it will be down and to the right. That's where he looks when he's lying."

"Hey, fuck you, asshole!"

Chaucer ignored Sonny's contribution. He pressed on. "The second is his breathing. He holds his breath a moment before he lies. It's subtle, but you can notice it if you try."

Sonny leaped to his feet, hands balling into fists. Chaucer was pleased to see that the knife in his jeans pocket went untouched. Evidently, Chaucer didn't pose enough of a threat. "Hey, bitch! Fuck you! You wanna talk shit to my girl?!"

Chaucer maintained eye contact with the girl. She wasn't convinced, but she wanted to be. "The third is his neck. His head will jut forward when he's trying to convince you of a lie. Now that he knows about his tells, he's going to try and hide them, but he won't be able to hide all three."

"You wanna get fucked up, asshole?"

Chaucer finally turned to look at Sonny again. "No. I don't. I experience any physical touch as pain." It was a simple truth. The same trauma that caused Chaucer's PTSD yielded other eccentricities, such as a hypersensitivity to physical touch.

The comment stopped Sonny. He wasn't used to this kind of conversation. He wasn't used to truth. Not the way Chaucer was. Chaucer saw him working through what to do next. He saw his fists clench, his chin drop.

"Then you shouldn'a run your mouth, bitch."

Chaucer looked up at the flexing man, trying to project menace. "You're getting ready to attack me, because it's the only way you'll keep the girl under your control. And because you think I'm an easy target. But Sonny? I am not an easy target."

Sonny made his move, just as Chaucer knew he would. A jab with his right, fast and hard. His dominant arm. A mistake. He was also punching down at a seated victim. Another mistake. It gave his body downward momentum, difficult to redirect.

At the last moment, Chaucer dodged to his right, the punch passing harmlessly by his left ear.

Chaucer grabbed Sonny's extended arm with both hands, wincing at the pain physical contact gave him, and he pushed, hard. Sonny tried to pull it back, but Chaucer's momentum forced his arm into the vertical steel pole next to him. Sonny's elbow slammed into the pole, the force causing it to bend the one way it was designed not to bend.

The snap echoed. The entire car heard it. Sonny screamed, his forearm dangling from his body at an angle that was all wrong. All eyes were on Chaucer. Amazement mostly. From their perspective, Chaucer hardly did anything. It didn't even look like he had hit his aggressor, but now Sonny was on the floor of the train car, yelling in agony.

Chaucer stood up and returned his gaze to the girl. She stared back at him with a hearty mixture of fear and awe. "Some lies are spontaneous. Some are rehearsed. Sonny's are well rehearsed. It means he's done this before. Many times before. He wants to use you. He wants to pimp you out. And again, he has done this many times before."

"How do you know?"

"I know when people lie."

Suddenly, Sonny flicked out the switchblade from his belt in his left hand. "Die asshole!"

Chaucer didn't even turn his eyes down to meet Sonny's. He delivered a single kick that connected with Sonny's head, knocking it back into the very same metal pole that broke his arm. The switchblade skittered across the floor and out of sight. Sonny was out cold.

Chaucer said, "Don't. This is over. You don't need to get involved."

The girl looked at Chaucer, but he wasn't talking to her. Only then did Chaucer glance over his shoulder at the private investigator at the other end of the train car, his hand on the gun in his waistband holster. He locked eyes with Chaucer for a brief second, took his hand away, and sat back down.

The girl bit her lip, looking down at Sonny's unconscious form. "You said you know when people lie. I don't. So how do I know that you're not lying?"

Chaucer offered the hint of a smile. "Because I never lie. Ever."

CHAPTER 3

The water off Oyster Bay was as smooth as mirrored glass. James Fitzgerald stared out at it as he often did at this hour, the last rays of the sun glinting off the bay, turning it into a kaleidoscope of soft hues. No matter how bad things got, this view grounded him.

Fitz, as he was mostly known, was about to turn seventy-five, and today he was feeling it. He struggled to lower himself into a white, weathered Adirondack chair and settle in for the sunset.

Chaucer approached slowly, realizing Fitz had yet to register his presence. "Is it your L2 again?"

Fitz spun, startled. *On edge.* "Stop sneaking up on old men, Mal. In some states, that's intent to kill."

"Next time I'll wear a bell." Chaucer crossed the twenty feet between them over the immaculate green lawn separating the bay from Fitzgerald's two-story colonial home. Fitz grimaced as he stood up to greet him. *Pain. Worry—and something else. Unclear.*

Chaucer could see every ache in the man's body. He wanted to help his friend. *Friend.* It was a word Chaucer seldom used. Chaucer didn't have friends. Not anymore. Not in years. His new reality called for a downsizing of life to its essentials. He had one friend. One family member. That was all. And between the two? He felt closer to Fitz. After all, Fitz was the only reason Chaucer was still among the living.

Chaucer said, "Sit back down. Let me help you."

"Would you? I'm dying here."

Fitz sat on the edge of the chair. Chaucer came in behind him, his fingers probing the old man's spine. Chaucer suppressed a wince at the pain of physical contact. Fitz noticed him flinch. "You don't have to—"

Chaucer saw it in his eyes; Fitz realized exactly how bad his friend was. Nobody knew Chaucer well enough to notice such things. Nobody but Fitz.

"What happened?" Fitz asked.

"I got recognized, that started it. But let's take care of your back first."

Fitz looked skeptical. "But you're okay?"

Chaucer wanted to say yes. More than anything, he wanted to set Fitz's mind at ease. But yes would be a lie. "I haven't been okay for a long time, and you know it. Come on—let me do this."

Chaucer felt the ravages of age in the man's skeleton, sensing the tiny incongruities that added up to agony. "You need a professional to see you twice a week."

"They're all witch doctors. You're the only one I trust."

Chaucer found the problem spot, a slight protrusion indicative of a bulging disk. He wrapped his arms around Fitz, taking in a deep breath to hide the agony passing through his body. He began slowly rocking Fitz from side to side.

"Count to three. One—"

Snap! Chaucer rotated the old man around swiftly, lengthening his spine in the process.

Fitz's eyes opened in shock. "Ow! You son of a bitch! You never do it on three! I thought you couldn't lie."

Fitz jumped out of the chair, steamed. Chaucer replied, "I never said I'd do it on three."

"Who doesn't do it on three?!" Fitz walked around in a circle, flexing and stretching.

13

"You tense up when it's coming. That's not good. You're a very tense man, Fitz, you know? Now, how do you feel?"

Fitz twisted himself around and stood up straight. He frowned but couldn't keep himself from laughing. "You're a miracle worker, but you're a sadist."

"No. I'm not." Chaucer was deadly serious.

"No, you're not. Now tell me what happened."

Chaucer frowned. He didn't want to relive the minor inconveniences of his day that brought him to the brink of ruin. He didn't want to face the tightrope he walked each day. "A miscalculation. I forgot that the World Summit is in town."

Fitz smiled. "Ah, the UN's big shindig. One hundred and ninety-three countries officially, and another ten or so disputed territories. Each country averages a dozen dignitaries, each dignitary averages two security personnel, nine support staff, and twelve of—well, us. The intelligence apparatus. That's more armed men than stormed Omaha Beach, all packed into Manhattan. Of course you were recognized."

Chaucer stared at the ground. He hated this, admitting to his vulnerability. "I saw one of them crossing the street, coming toward me. Triggered a flashback—when the Ministry of State Security came for me. Put me into a panic attack."

"That can be the top of a very slippery slope. How far'd you fall?"

"Maybe a five on the scale. Nothing more. Then there was a thing on the subway."

Fitz looked intrigued. "Thing?"

"A pimp preying on a young girl. Lying to her—" Chaucer caught the amusement in Fitz's eyes and had to look away.

"Lying! Well, we can't have that, can we?" Fitz smirked through his sarcasm.

"It was a ... brief altercation." *Every word true: check.*

Fitz's nostrils flared. *Surprise. Anger.* "I asked you to stay in Brussels after the job. I begged you to stay. That guy at that clinic? I paid for a month. A month's ... vacation. You could use a vacation, Mal."

"I have to work."

Fitz wouldn't let it go. "Do you have any idea how much all that cost?"

"I thought he reimbursed you."

"He's a goddamn miracle worker, Mal. Miracle workers don't reimburse."

Chaucer hated this. It wasn't pity, exactly, but it wasn't far removed. Fitz was a well-meaning person trying to fix him. But Chaucer realized a truth he wouldn't allow. "I've been to miracle workers, Fitz. The guy in Nepal. The woman in Finland. That team of people in Minnesota. And the only thing they have helped me with is to realize there may be no miracles. Not for me anyway."

Fitz's anger grew. "Cut that surrender shit out. I didn't spend years working to get you out of that hellhole—years more getting you a job, *functioning*—for you to give up now. You can still change."

Lie. Chaucer looked his friend in the eye and he knew that Fitz didn't believe it. Not really. Chaucer tried to soothe his friend. "It's okay. Really. If this is all there is—if there's nothing better coming—I'm still thankful for everything you've done for me."

"You know what really steams me? Not only aren't you trying to get better, you're actively putting yourself in danger of an episode that could end you."

Chaucer said, "The subway thing? No. I had to do that."

"From where I'm standing, that was reckless behavior. Your ... condition—it's precarious. So enlighten me. Why'd you have to do that?"

Chaucer looked away. He didn't want this conversation, but Fitz asked a direct question. Everything in Chaucer compelled him to answer. "Suicidal ideation. Very common for torture victims, yes?"

Fitz grew instantly uncomfortable. "Yes."

"Mine? It's very particular. When—if—you know, I'll be a jumper. So every time I'm staring down from a height, I count to myself. I see how long I can look out at a vista, a cityscape, whatever, before I think about jumping. When I first did it, I could barely make it to ten."

"And now?"

"I made it to forty-five yesterday. Today, after the incident on the subway? I made it to sixty."

Fitz looked confused. "I don't understand."

Chaucer took a deep breath. "My life is alienation and agony—and the only reason I keep going, is because I can help people who can't help themselves."

"Like on the train?"

"Like on the train."

Fitz shook his head, "I just want you taking better care of yourself."

Chaucer shrugged. "I'm doing what I can. I'm seeing my brother tomorrow."

Fitz was surprised. "Terry? Really?"

"He's been promoted. Detective First Grade. He wants me at the party."

Fitz laughed. "Malcolm Chaucer at a party? You're serious? You said you'd go?"

"It turns out I'm not impervious to guilt."

"How is he?"

Chaucer thought for a moment, how best to answer that question, "It's been a while since I've seen him. He's got his friends, his wife. I don't really fit."

"Told you that, did he?"

"Terry would never say anything like that. He doesn't think like that. The problem is, I do. I just can't shake the feeling he'd be better off without his damaged brother hanging around."

Fitz shook his head, "I've met Terry, what? A dozen times? He loves you. I think he loves you far more than you're able to handle right now."

"Don't get me wrong. I love Terry. I just … maybe I love him enough to let him be."

Fitz laughed. "For the world's greatest expert on human

psychology, you really are dense sometimes. Lucky for you, you shouldn't have any trouble making the party. Tomorrow's job should be a quick one."

Chaucer relaxed as they got to business. "What do I need to know?"

"The interrogation's about as simple as they come," Fitz said. "A civilian who may have witnessed an assassination."

Chaucer was surprised. "Somebody is paying my rate to question a civilian?"

Fitz nodded. "The victim's the son of a South Korean VIP—a minor titan of business over there, I'm to understand. He'll spare no expense to get this done right. And you know how the Koreans feel about you—you're a god to them."

For a brief second, Chaucer was no longer at Fitz's home but back in a hole, three by three feet and eight deep, at the bottom of a cave at the foot of Mount Kuwol. He shivered from the memory as a spike of remembered pain shot up through his body, radiating from his spine to every limb.

He closed his eyes and breathed through the agony, burying it deep. When he opened his eyes, he was back on Long Island with Fitz.

Fitz was staring at him. "You went there, didn't you?"

Chaucer gritted his teeth and shook his head. He wouldn't talk about it. He couldn't talk about it. And Fitz nodded, letting Chaucer know it was okay.

Chaucer took a deep breath and changed the subject. "And if the civilian knows nothing? Is the client aware that I will not harm a civilian?"

"They wanted you and only you. They're aware of all that comes with that."

Chaucer didn't like interrogating a civilian. Even with his methods, which more often than not involved no physical harm whatsoever, he knew all too well the psychological damage of that level of fear. But better him than one of his competitors who might do actual injury.

17

"Are you sure there's nothing more here? I can't remember the last time I did an interrogation of a civilian for a civilian."

"This isn't exactly that. The businessman's well connected in places the US would love to have connections."

"China."

"And Myanmar. And the DPRK."

Chaucer got a sinking feeling. "Arms?"

Fitz waved the concern off. "Hardly. Textiles—a business that still relies on the absolute lowest labor costs to turn a profit. But nonetheless, the man is connected in a lot of places where it's hard to be, so when he wanted to know who killed his son, the CIA was only too happy to facilitate."

"I'll be working for the Company?"

"Not officially, but yeah, they're running the op, if you can even call it an op. For you? This is gonna be a simple Q and A. If she knows something, you'll get it. If she doesn't, you'll assure the father there's nothing there. End of story. Come on. I've got a dossier for you in the house."

Fitz started up the lawn, and Chaucer followed a step behind. "How's Nan?"

Fitz tilted his head to one side and bit his lip. *Fear. Sadness. Something else? Something buried deep.* "Good days and bad. More bad maybe. She'll kill me if you stopped by and didn't say hi."

CHAPTER 4

The interior of the house was dead silent, the last remnants of light casting long shadows over the slices of Americana within. Fitz led Chaucer through the cozy living room and up the long flight of stairs to the second floor. The house had no food smells whatsoever. Just the scent of bleach and a faint whiff of something cloyingly sweet.

Fitz paused at the door to the master suite and tapped. He got no answer, but opened it anyway. On an electric hospital bed lay Nancy Fitzgerald. Nan to her friends, which numbered many. She was the picture of late stage cancer. In her mid-sixties, her honey-blonde hair had long since fallen out, and her warm, inviting eyes had sat deep in their dark sockets, but there was still something soft, something noble about her, even as she lay there in agony. The cloying sweet smell doubled in strength, and Chaucer realized what it was. Ketoacidosis. Her breath, her urine; it was all sickly sweet because her pancreas was no longer creating beta cells. No beta cells, no insulin. It meant she was nearing the final stage of the disease.

The lone tube in her arm was familiar. Morphine. The drug of last comfort. Nan stirred. She turned her head and saw Chaucer standing in the doorway. She struggled to smile and prop herself up in the bed better. "Mal, it's so good to see you."

Chaucer returned the smile. He had to force it on his face and then tell himself it wasn't strictly a lie. "Hi Nan, how are you feeling?"

"Ugh. It's like I'm on fire from the inside, and then I take a drip and I'm freezing. Tell me—nobody will be honest with me—tell me, truly, how do I look?"

Chaucer grimaced. A direct question. *Always answer a direct question. Always tell the truth. Concealment is death.* Chaucer wanted to tell the kind lie with all his heart. But his mind, conditioned by years of torture, just couldn't do it. "You look like you're dying, Nan."

Nan smiled and laid her head back down against the pillow. "Thank you, Mal. Everyone else is a bullshit artist, but you? I can always count on you."

"You're in good spirits. Considering." Chaucer was already running out of pleasant truths.

"Oh, well, you know how it is. Hope springs eternal." Chaucer stared at her and was surprised to see it clear as day. *Hope.*

"Hope?"

Fitz stepped in. "More like hoping for a miracle."

Eyes darting away. Holding a breath. Fitz was more than simply nervous. *Scared.*

Nan closed her eyes, as if the act would shut out Fitz's words. "I believe in miracles. We live in an age full of them. You'll see. Yours is coming, too, Mal. What does your therapist say?"

Chaucer frowned. "I'm not seeing a therapist right now."

Nan tutted. "You can't do this alone. You're not strong enough. No one is."

"We're all alone."

Nan winced as Chaucer witnessed a fresh jolt of pain pass through her body. She fumbled for the round cylinder on her stomach with the red button. The morphine drip. She hit it, and in a moment, she was at peace.

In another moment, she was asleep.

Back downstairs, Fitz searched the kitchen counter for his car keys. Chaucer asked, "Any update on her condition?"

"They say it's in her pancreas now. Fully metastasized. No turning back."

"It's amazing that she still holds out hope."

"Yeah. Amazing." Chaucer watched his friend as a hundred different micro-expressions flashed across his face. *Hiding something. Behind a wall of pain.*

Fitz found the keys and headed to the side door to the garage. He stopped there, turning back to Chaucer. "Mal, do you think God will punish us for all the things we've done?"

Chaucer was surprised. He had never heard Fitz talk like this before. "I don't know. I don't know if you've done enough to warrant punishment."

Fitz grimaced. "We're the bad people, Mal. We do things—moral men would call us monsters."

"But why do we do those things? For king and country. Remember that."

"It hasn't been for king and country for thirty years and you know it."

CHAPTER 5

The next day, Chaucer walked crosstown along 4th street, staying far south of the UN until he reached the Westside, and then proceeded north. The plan was largely successful. On his walk, he spotted a dozen people in his profession, but none recognized him.

By the time he reached Eleventh Avenue, traffic was nearly gone, both foot and car. Twenty-Seventh Street between Eleventh and Twelfth Avenues was an uneven brick roadway, a bowling alley hemmed in by block-long warehouses. The neighborhood had changed radically in the last decade, with all kinds of upscale businesses moving in. But it remained quiet. Removed from the bustle of the rest of the city. The smell of rotting urine that one encountered in much of Manhattan became overpowering here, as a sizable homeless population used the street to transit from the Hudson River Greenway to the city proper.

He reached his address: a nondescript sliver of a warehouse building like so many on this block. This particular stretch of building looked unchanged from a decade ago. Windows were blacked out, boards over the street-level doors and windows promised a renewal that might never come. But it was a facade. One flight up, on the other side of a slightly mirrored window, a high-tech security camera recorded his face and matched it with an enormous database. It took half a breath to come up with the proper match. *Chaucer, Malcolm.*

Chaucer looked left and right out of habit, but the truth was they would not let him in until the security system verified his identity and saw that there was no surveillance in place on the street.

The large steel shutter over the garage door gave way in an unexpected direction, swinging open electronically like a bank vault would. And as Chaucer passed through the door, he could see that the bank-vault analogy wasn't far off. The door was eight inches thick, filled with both armor and the densest sound-proofing materials available.

The interior of the space was hollowed out; a large empty warehouse floor, save for a dentist's chair in a spotlight, and a small mirrored room along one wall.

Three people glowed in the spotlight. Two of them were standing. Large, muscled men in simple black suits barely hiding shoulder holsters and 9mm pistols with generous ammunition magazines. One was Rodgers, the other Lane, but which was which, Chaucer could not be certain. They were blue badge all the way.

Chaucer used to be blue badge, the color of ID you wore at Langley if you were a direct CIA employee, as opposed to green badges, outside contractors. With each passing year, there were more and more green badges at Langley, until one day Chaucer himself went freelance. But not Rodgers and Lane. They were Directorate of Operations men through and through.

The third person was the civilian, strapped down to the dentist's chair. A woman, approximately twenty-seven years of age, with a duct-tape gag over her mouth and tears streaming down her face. Chaucer stood over the woman, examining her with the trained, efficient manner of a doctor.

There was something wrong with her eyes. Anger prickled at Chaucer's temples. Her pupils were too dilated for the harsh light. Something in her struggling movements, too. A sluggishness. A lack of coordination.

They'd drugged her. Despite his explicit instructions for all interrogations, they drugged her. A civilian, whose only possible crime was being a witness to a murder.

One of the large men wheeled something else into the light. A state-of-the-art polygraph machine, which to Chaucer was like saying "cutting-edge bloodletting." Chaucer detested the polygraph, a crude machine that was all too easy to fool and even easier to manipulate to say whatever the interrogator wanted it to say. *Tea leaves for the modern age.*

Chaucer stared angrily at the man who'd wheeled it out. The man outweighed Chaucer by fifty pounds and had five inches on him, but under Chaucer's stare, he backed away a step. Left hand twitching. Eyes darting down and right. Lips pursed. *Fear.*

No one said a word. *At least they followed one of my instructions.* Chaucer left the spotlight, walking straight to the small mirrored room.

The man in the spotlight said, "Wait, you can't—"

Chaucer did not stop. No instructions followed. Amateur hour. Time to abort.

As Chaucer entered the mirrored room, everyone inside was already looking at him. The entire room was constructed of two-way mirrors hiding a vast array of video cameras, audio recording equipment, and computers parsing the incoming information in every spectrum and manner. In the business, such a room was called a blind.

Chaucer scanned the faces in the room. Six people in all. Three CIA, all blue badge. Three visitors. Two of the CIA people were youngsters running the room's tech. The third was Vincent Roma, whose squat face was reddening fast. The book on Roma was a short one: hot-tempered, ruthless, workmanlike. He intercepted Chaucer as soon as the door clicked behind him.

"What do you think you're doing? You know protocol. You don't look behind the curtain. You do your job and you leave."

The room's other three occupants turned as one: three Asian men who swiveled in their observation seats up by the two-way glass. Two wore expensive suits tailored in a conservative and mannered fashion. It was that perfect combination of wealth and modesty the elites of communist nations had to master. Myanmar was unlikely. These men were either mainland Chinese, or from the DPRK.

But the third, the man in the center? This was the father, no question about it. Chaucer took the man in. His suit had a touch of shine to it. Not sharkskin, but not terribly far from it either. This was someone who lived where capitalism was no vice. His eyes were sunken, pupils dilated. He was on something as well. A mild sedative of some kind. Likely to calm him in his grief. He stared at Chaucer with a combination of hope and awe. Chaucer hated that look, the pressure it placed upon him. Without a word, the man was begging him: *Find my son's killer.*

Chaucer turned back to Roma and spoke matter-of-factly. "My conditions have not been fulfilled. This terminates our working relationship. I will return your retainer within twenty-four hours."

He turned to leave out the door he came through. Roma put a hand on his shoulder, causing pain to ripple through Chaucer's entire body.

Roma was oblivious to the impact of his touch. "Listen up, asshole. I didn't want you. I had Mathers all lined up for the job."

Colton Mathers. Chaucer knew the name well. A sadist. A butcher. A distant number two in their profession, with all the resentment that came with it. Colton Mathers destroyed the people he interrogated, often simply because until he did, he had no idea if he was hearing the truth.

"The clients insisted on you," Roma said, "So you're gonna fulfill your contract or you'll never work for us again."

Chaucer shrugged off Roma's hand and waited a moment for the pain to subside. "I've been green badge for years, freelancing at will. The Company has always been free to contract with me

25

or not, at their discretion. I've terminated other Company contracts for a lack of attention to the conditions I require, and yet your people still see fit to hire me frequently."

Chaucer took another step toward the door. The Asians stood abruptly. Shoulder tension. Clenched jaws. Eyes rapidly shifting between Roma and Chaucer. *Worry. Fear.* The father took a step forward. Roma noted it, putting out a hand to hold the man back. Roma's brow furrowed. Hard swallow. *Anger. Embarrassment. Capitulation.*

Roma said, "What conditions did we not fulfill?"

"Your man beside the subject. He talked."

"An unforgivable sin. I'll have him shot immediately."

"My methods require total control of the psychological space surrounding the subject."

"Fine, I'll have him removed. That it?"

"The larger problem is that your men drugged the subject. I rely on the body's natural responses, and drugs obscure them. That is why all my subjects must remain clean."

"Yeah, I know, but there was a complication." Roma's nostrils flared. *Frustration.* But there was something else in there as well. *Fear.* He was hiding something he didn't want Chaucer to pick up on. "A problem with acquisition. My guys needed to use a tranq stick."

Chaucer knew the technique. It was the standard means of kidnap. Swarming the victim and hitting them with a tranq stick: a small, baton-like auto-injector loaded with a fast-acting concoction of tranquilizing agents.

"Then we can try this again, in approximately six hours."

Roma looked back at the father. He shook his head no. *Fluent English.*

Roma said, "Can't. We're on a timer on this one. That's why we revived her ourselves. We had one of our docs look at her. He says she's close enough to normal for you to work your voodoo."

Chaucer wanted to say that no doctor could understand what he required for his work. Chaucer wanted to say a lot of things, but chose instead to focus on the problem. "I need to know exactly what she has in her system."

"The tranq stick was standard. Etorphine hydrochloride paired with a biological accelerant. And the doc gave her a dose of Benzedrine to bring her back up again."

Chaucer referenced each drug in his mind, working out the effects and counter-effects. The drugs mentioned would explain the girl's pulse and pupillary response. But her breathing still troubled him. Something was off, even with all those drugs coursing through her system.

"Is that everything? Are you sure?"

Roma's nostrils flared again. Hard blink. Sweat forming at the brow. *Stress. Worry.* The man was under a great deal of pressure. This was certainly not business as usual today. *What is going on here?*

Roma said, "Yeah. I'm sure. Now can we get on with the show?"

Chaucer shook his head. "No. One more violation of my conditions. There is a polygraph next to the subject."

Roma pursed his lips. "Yeah, that one is nonnegotiable."

"Then we have nothing to talk about. I do not use the machine."

The father cleared his throat. He waited for eye contact and recognition from Chaucer before speaking. Roma and Chaucer gave him both.

"I am Sim Se Yoon, and you are the Oracle, Mr. Chaucer. I understand your methods and apologize for the machine's intrusion. I need you to find my son's killer, Mr. Chaucer. Were it up to me, your word alone would be all that was needed. But I am a business owner in the middle of a major deal, and a primary investor is holding up the deal until he can be assured that my son's death is not due to some family flaw or secret."

It was a simple story. It made sense. But every inflection, every facial tic told Chaucer a very different story. *Terrified.* The father was scared for his life and desperate for answers. Chaucer realized there was more at stake here than a father's need for closure. Sim Se Yoon was a man in pain, but also a man in the grip of a great fear. A fear Chaucer's diligent work could possibly relieve.

"It is a problem beneath mention. I will do as you have asked," Chaucer replied as he bowed his head.

The simple fact was that someone was going to interrogate that young woman, and only Chaucer could protect her from whomever they would bring in next. If he refused, she would be harmed, in a way she may never recover from. Everything about this interrogation told him to leave, but that one simple fact sealed his decision. When he turned to the door this time, no one stopped him. But upon reflection of all the compromises he just agreed to, he certainly wished someone had.

CHAPTER 6

His subject was about to break. Chaucer knew the signs. Even beneath the drug-induced haze. Even with the wild-card responses that a civilian always gave. She was about to yield her secrets to Chaucer. It had taken two hours to get here, but Chaucer was not about to damage Isabel Marcano, office assistant to the graduate biology department at NYU. She was an innocent bystander under his care.

Chaucer could almost sense Roma smirking back in the blind; the mighty Malcolm Chaucer, having trouble with a garden-variety civilian with zero training.

But then that was the problem. Subjects with military experience were prepared in some small way for this eventuality, to face a hostile interrogator who would exhibit no mercy in his quest for a closely guarded truth. And, paradoxically, that was what made them so easy. Their preparation, in essence, greased the wheels. It formatted them and gave their reactions a unity that formed Chaucer's baseline for judging responses. Plus, they were already in a resigned psychological state. They'd already accepted the process that was about to unfold.

And acceptance was a long way down the path to Chaucer's goals.

Intelligence officers were tougher nuts. Better training, sure, but that wasn't the only reason. There was an inherent duplicity; a schism between persona and reality that most such officers possessed, extending down to the bone. It was a lightly guarded fact that pathological liars would beat polygraphs every time. The reason? That if they believed their bullshit, so did the machine. Intelligence officers were of a similar ilk.

The machine. There it was again, invading Chaucer's concentration. He stared at the machine, slowly drawing electronic ley lines across a graph of time, supposedly a record of what was occurring.

An audio pickup was recording and time-coding every word, every grunt either Chaucer or his subject made. Video from several angles was being recorded. A grand circus servicing nothing.

Chaucer's disdain for the machine existed on a subatomic level. In his professional opinion, the machine was a scam. In fact, a common amplification technique involved an actual scam; a magic trick, to be more precise. A trick so hackneyed, Chaucer was shocked to find it was still in occasional use. The interrogator says they need to calibrate the machine, and they fiddle with the nobs and settings. They have their subject draw a card from a deck and tells them to answer "no" to each of the next thirteen questions. And so the dance begins. "Is your card a two?" Of course, the deck is marked, and the interrogator knows full well what card their subject looked at. And so, when they get to their card, and the subject replies "no," the machine goes crazy. A simple manipulation of the various adjustments, visually the same changes he had been making all along, but there it is for the subject to see: the omnipotence of the machine.

If only it were so. Even with the most advanced zone-comparison techniques, the machine was beatable to the point that most interrogators using it were reduced to the status of mediums reading palms. "He seemed evasive on this answer." "He broke rhythm here—possibly a concealment." To Chaucer, the words were all the same: "Who knows?"

But Chaucer knew. There was nothing in the field of interrogation, and of torture, that was a mystery to him. Because he knew what it was like to be in that chair. Under the lights. And worse. As bad as any subject ever had it, Chaucer knew worse. Personally. That's why he was the best. That's why he was sought after, the world over.

That's why he was a mess. An exposed nerve to anything and everything. A graduate course on PTSD. Except for now. This moment. When no one could touch what he could do.

He stared down at his subject with his owl eyes and sold her on his determination. "This is it, Isabel. This is the moment. The one you will look back on for the rest of your life. If you tell me, I will administer a sedative, and you will awaken in your bed, and if you try as hard as you can, you will convince yourself this was just a bad dream. You will find a good therapist. You will work your way through sleepless nights and panic attacks, and in a year or so, your life, your normal life, will be restored to you."

Eyes flicker right. Eyes flicker up. Half breath. Hold. She was still showing ghosts of deceptive behavior, deep within the muddy shoals of the drugs.

Again, Chaucer had to reevaluate. She was a civilian. No training. And she seemed like it. Her answers were not programmed. And yet—they didn't seem exactly natural either. There was something he couldn't put his finger on. Almost like anticipation. Almost like she knew where this was going. That was the problem Chaucer was facing. She was a civilian, and so her responses in isolation could mean anything. And they'd drugged her. Every clue Chaucer was used to relying on was buried under a blanket of amphetamines.

Chaucer put these thoughts out of his mind. Despite these hiccups, her behavior was consistent. She was just a terrified witness. Someone scared her to death, convincing her that to reveal what she saw would mean she would be killed, just like the grad student with the powerful father.

"If you do not tell me, I will turn you over to the next shift. Whoever comes after me will have one method and one method alone: torture. Plain and simple. They will ask no questions.

Their lone goal will be to place you in a state of pain and panic. Until you beg to tell them what they want to know. And once you've done that, I can't be sure what they will do with you. But your return to a normal life? Some victims of torture succeed. Most don't."

Twinge. Rapid breathing. Good. Exactly the response desired. And then Chaucer noticed his own body reacting in the same way. *It never fails.* After all these years, the words still worked on him. He still wished he had made a different choice. He also hated this part of his performance. He needed to instill fear in a young woman who deserved no such treatment. But everything Chaucer read on her face told him she needed this one last push, and then it would be all over.

Cough. The subject, Isabel Marcano, was about to make her decision. "What did you see, Isabel?"

Eyes dart right. Eyes dart left. Return gaze. Again, Chaucer was struck by the sense that something was just a little off. It was like—it was like she was waiting for this moment too. *Damn amphetamines, throwing everything off.*

She blinked the tears from her eyes. "I was ... I was getting coffee. Going around the back. I left a brick in the ... in the fire door. It's faster to ... It's faster to the coffee shop. But the door, the door was already opening. She ran right at me. But then stopped. She looked at my badge. She knew, she knew where I worked. She knew my name! She told me ... she told me if I ever spoke to anyone, she said she would kill me. Just like Tajo."

The tears fell harder, the memory still fresh. Chaucer softened his demeanor. "What did the shooter look like, Isabel?"

Isabel looked right into Chaucer's eyes. Like she was desperate to say this part. "Red hair. Long ... wavy. Blue eyes. And she had ... she had a tattoo on the back of her neck."

Chaucer straightened up, looking for a better grasp of gravity. Dizzy. He was actually dizzy. He could feel it. His entire world was changing. Isabel's next words could change everything. "What sort of tattoo?"

"It looked like ... what you see through a rifle. Through the scope."

Crosshairs, thought Chaucer. An old joke from an old friend.

Back in the blind, Roma typed madly on a laptop. "Jesus H. Christ! The Widowmaker! Tempest MacLaren! She's talking about Tempest MacLaren!"

The two men in the conservative suits regarded Roma carefully. The taller addressed him in halting English. "She is one of yours?"

"*Was*. Strictly was. The Widowmaker went freelance over a decade ago. Listen, the last thing we would want is your people getting the idea that one of ours popped the kid. We want to extend to you every advantage of the Agency. We will hunt her down and we will eliminate her."

"You will do nothing of the kind. We prefer to handle our own affairs."

"You can't expect us to just let one of your hitters run free in our country—"

The tall man didn't flinch. He didn't blink. "Yes, Mr. Roma. That is exactly what we expect. If you wish, you may supply an observer, but our man will deliver vengeance."

"There is one more thing you should know—after all, you were the ones who insisted we bring the Oracle in on this."

"Yes?"

"Tempest MacLaren, Back in the day. She was married to Malcolm Chaucer."

A flurry of Korean erupted between the three men. Roma couldn't follow it, but it was beyond agitated. Less than a minute later, they stopped speaking, and whatever it was, the matter was settled. One of the men left the room abruptly, via the back door.

Sim Se Yoon bowed slightly. "Thank you for enlightening us, Mr. Roma. We will take it from here."

Roma couldn't help himself, "Hey. Your guy, the one you're sending to take out Tempest MacLaren. He's good?"

The tall man in the conservative suit stopped and turned back to Roma, "Of course. Why do you ask?"

"Because if he's gunning for the Widowmaker, he needs to know that bitch has killed more men than prostate cancer."

CHAPTER 7

Sung In Su's helicopter ride to the diplomatic terminal at New York's JFK airport took just ten minutes. As he was climbing out of the helicopter, he saw Vice Marshal Kang's plane taxiing toward him. Sung clutched a briefcase full of the polygraph results from the interrogation.

He considered it a rare honor to watch the man they called the Oracle at work. Chaucer reminded Sung of the master artisans at the base of Mount Paektu; patient beyond measure, revealing truth with each gesture. Sim Se Yoon, the father and business owner, had great respect for the Oracle, but no appreciation of what he was witnessing. As would be expected. The man had never witnessed an interrogation before. He had no frame of reference.

Waiting for both Sung and the Vice Marshal on the tarmac was a lone man. Sung In Su took him in. His name was Min Gun, and he was nothing much to look at. Solid but seemingly unremarkable. One would think he worked as a store clerk or some sort of junior manager. One would not think he was the finest killer his nation had ever turned out.

A sociopath. That was certain. Min Gun tortured and killed his family's cat when he was five years old. In the province he grew up in, cats were nearly sacred, being the eyes and ears of their ancestors. Further, they were a status symbol in a land where such symbols were exceedingly rare.

Here in America, such behavior would be met with counseling. Drugs as well. The Americans did love their drugs, their quick fixes. But in their homeland, such a rare and dangerous trait was to be exploited.

They placed Min Gun in a special school with others of his kind. A school in the mountains north of Kapsan. A school where fighting was encouraged. Each year, at least two of the students in each grade would die. Sometimes many more. But the survivors would grow exponentially stronger. They were taught Mandarin, English, Russian, Spanish, and math practical enough to be adept at everything from sniping to demolitions.

But above all, they were taught to love their country.

These boys and girls did not love easily. Something inside was broken and their understanding of love differed greatly from their fellow citizens'. But they did understand need. They did feel desire. And in them was cultivated a need to serve their homeland, and a desire to outdo the bravest acts of the patriots that went before them.

What a glorious civilization we are. We teach even our sociopaths to love.

The Boeing 747 came to a halt, and the ground crew rolled a long stair up to it, ending just feet from where Sung and Min Gun stood. The vice marshal was the first man on the rolling stair. It was a major breach of both decorum and security, but Sung expected it. Today decorum would be jettisoned in favor of speed in order to avert a crisis.

Stone-faced, Vice Marshal Kang marched down the steps briskly. Sung gave him his most respectful bow.

"What do you have for me?"

Sung handed him the briefcase. "Inside you have video, audio, transcripts, and the polygraph of the witness. She gave a positive description of the assassin. A rogue American asset. The Widowmaker."

For just a second, Min Gun shifted his stance, as if swayed by the name alone. Vice Marshal Kang paid no attention to the man.

"We know this woman. She has been a problem for us in the past. Can you be sure of the information?"

"The interrogator was the Oracle. Malcolm Chaucer."

The vice marshal's face softened. Malcolm Chaucer was a name above reproach. He was a great mystery to them, but they never dared question his skills. "Then our friend has his target."

Sung knew to approach the next matter delicately. "He does, but we must discuss the note."

Vice Marshal Kang's lips pursed. He did not want to discuss the note, but acknowledged the need. "Where exactly was it found?"

"The sniper's nest in the rafters. Where she fired the shot."

The vice marshal nodded. It was not a message for just anyone. It was a message for him. "It's exact words?"

"It simply said, 'The Year of the Rabbit is coming.' I thought perhaps—"

The vice marshal's raised hand cut Sung off. "How many know of the note?"

"The Americans, obviously. Us. Two State Security men who first responded. And the father."

Vice Marshal Kang rubbed his chin. "Sim Se Yoon and State Security? That's it for our side?"

"Yes, sir."

"Good. I want to see them at once. The father as well. And we will not be staying at the embassy."

"Sir?"

"Today we have no friends there. Not until we learn more."

The vice marshal turned to Min Gun, who was as still as an Easter Island statue. "You have your target?"

Min Gun nodded.

"I have questions for her. Bring her to me."

For the first time, Min Gun's face showed expression. Discomfort. "Sir, my target, The Widowmaker, is like me. She possesses … superior training. Killing her is a great honor and a great challenge. Bringing her in alive is almost impossible."

The vice marshal's hand lashed out to slap Min Gun's face, but the man's reflexes were three times faster. He dodged the blow, allowing it to pass harmlessly an inch in front of his nose.

Vice Marshal Kang's eyes were filled with fury, Min Gun's with understanding. Min Gun stood still for the second blow, overriding his instincts and accepting a frightened man's slap.

For the man, for the Democratic People's Republic of Korea, Tempest MacLaren would be held to account.

CHAPTER 8

Chaucer didn't remember the last hour of the interrogation, the verification of details. He didn't remember leaving the interrogation site. He didn't remember the long walk back to his apartment. He didn't remember climbing the four flights to his spartan walk-up on the Lower East Side. All that Chaucer could remember was the name: Tempest MacLaren.

His ex-wife's name was never very far from his thoughts, but after the events of the day, it positively consumed him. He looked down and saw the ash-colored receiver of his landline in his hand. He didn't remember picking it up.

He kept the old phone for security reasons. No scan could intercept its signal. It pinged no cell tower. A physical tap would be necessary to overhear his conversations on it, and he had managed to route that physical line to the next building over, so planting such a tap would be an endeavor. Chaucer stared at the phone in his hand, listening to the faint sound of a dial tone ringing through the empty air. He placed it back on its cradle.

The sun poured in the windows of the narrow space, turning floating motes of dust into a suspended field of golden light. The light, the dust: none of it moved. Frozen, just like Chaucer. The one bedroom itself was frozen as well. The kitchenette, the living room, even the bedroom was populated by furniture in varying tones of beige. None of it had Chaucer chosen. No, the unit had once been temporary corporate housing before an enterprising landlord bought the place during the tumult of 2008. He remembered the landlord, a sharp woman of Polish descent, who was mystified when he told her to leave the furniture. He wanted the unit as-is. The agonies a fully furnished apartment would spare him, she had no idea.

Chaucer stared back down at the phone. His hand was on it again, as if his body was fighting his mind. If he did not pick the phone up, if he did not call and warn her, Tempest MacLaren would be dead. That was close to a certainty, even given the woman's seemingly superhuman abilities.

Tempest MacLaren. He thought back to the last time he spoke with her. When he returned to the States, she was already remarried, but the situation wasn't as awkward as it could have been. Because it was very clear to everyone involved that the Malcolm Chaucer that returned from North Korea was not the Malcolm Chaucer who left. And he certainly wasn't the Chaucer Tempest had married.

They'd stayed in monthly contact in the intervening years. Neither her marriage to another man, nor her subsequent divorce changed that pattern at all. Chaucer could tell that it pained her whenever they talked, but still, she would reach out. She was always the one to reach out. He wasn't quite sure why. There were still tiny corners of human behavior which the Oracle's spotlight could not illuminate.

Their marriage, such that it was, lasted only three months. They married on a whim, a romantic gesture when Chaucer discovered the Company would station him in Pyongyang, making their relationship more complicated than simply long-distance. And then one day, Chaucer crossed a Pyonyang street, heading for a Mercedes that would take him to the Pyongyang airport, and a man crossed that same street to intercept him.

Never again would Tempest see the Malcolm Chaucer she once knew.

Chaucer lifted the receiver. He knew she had a landline, very much like this one. He wouldn't need to say a word. Just calling that line, and letting it ring once, would be enough. It would be the warning she needed. But to do so, Chaucer knew it would be committing a cardinal sin. He wouldn't say a word, but still he would betray a confidence. He would take something from the interrogation, something from his secret world, and he would act on it.

A loud, repetitive beeping filled the room, signaling the end of the deliberation. Chaucer put the receiver back in its cradle and the phone fell silent. *The Widowmaker. Spotted by a civilian. Left alive. How the mighty have fallen.*

It made no sense.

The Tempest he knew was as hard and cold as a granite mountain when she was on a mission. No question, the Tempest he once knew would have killed Isabel Marcano rather than waste one word on her. So then why?

Chaucer picked up the receiver a third time. With the same hand, he dialed a number he had not dialed in years. He typed quickly, his middle finger stabbing the keys. The seventh, the eighth, the ninth—

Chaucer's middle finger hovered over the last digit. The tenth. Once he pressed that, the phone would connect, and hers would ring. He swore an oath never to reveal the information obtained in an interrogation. But surely this wasn't that?

What it was, was close. Close enough that he would bear a heavy price if he just—

Chaucer's finger pressed the tenth digit, shocking him. Somewhere deep inside him, there was a remnant of the old Chaucer. The man that loved Tempest enough to risk everything.

The phone on the other end rang once. Chaucer hung up. That was it. That was the signal. *Danger.*

He only hoped it would be enough. He felt his heart race as a sense of vertigo overcame his emotions. He felt like he was falling. And in fact, he was falling. Collapsing into darkness and dread.

Chaucer awoke in the cave. He smelled the fire in his nostrils, the acrid-sweet aroma of Korean red pine burning. Needles pricked in his back as he lay paralyzed over a bamboo rack, his back in the air and his head upside down. He felt an agony that seemed to go on forever. And he heard his master, Po, laughing at him. He heard his gravelly voice in the darkness. "All pain, all misery comes from the lie."

Chaucer saw only flickers of shadows on the cave wall. He could feel another needle pressing into a gap in his spine. Between his T10 and T11, he thought. This had been done to him thousands of times. He knew what it meant. But all that knowledge did was stoke his fear all the more.

Chaucer cried as an electric bolt of pure agony rocketed straight to his head. He pissed himself from the pain, snot flowing out his nose and dripping into his eyes. He screamed. He always screamed. And the cave was a place of deep echo. He heard the scream coming back to him, again and again as wave after wave of pain consumed him.

Through snot-covered eyes, he saw his master, Po, his face upside down from Chaucer's point of view. In the firelight, the worn creases of his face deepened into black holes. His eyes were empty, bottomless pools of malice. "Why do you lie when only the truth will set you free?"

"I don't know … I-I-I don't know." Chaucer had no dignity remaining, sobbing from the agony that racked his body.

Po smiled, his yellow, crooked teeth mocking him. "I believe you. You tell the truth now, yes? Good. Good. And yet—"

Po reached back and touched the newly placed needle. Instantly the lightning bolt of electricity was back and Chaucer shook from its effects. The shaking of his body disturbed the other eight needles as he felt wave after wave of pain. Pain of burning, of freezing, of shock.

Chaucer cried out. "Please, Master Po—"

But Master Po was impervious to any and all entreaty. Master Po had a job to do. "Shh. Shh. We must work together now to find the answer."

"Answer?" In the agony, Chaucer forgot what they had been talking about.

"Why do you lie when only the truth will set you free? You do not know. I do not know. But the pain. The pain knows all. We must simply invite it in and wait for its wisdom."

The last thing Chaucer saw was a grin on his master's face, a moment of sadism before the old man pushed the needle further into his exposed spinal cord.

———

How had it all gone so wrong? Tempest MacLaren stood in her shower, letting the hot water blast away at her aching neck and shoulders. She whipped her red hair around to the front to give the stream better access to her shoulder blades, where her left sported a knife scar she picked up in Khartoum, and her right sported a nine-millimeter entry wound she picked up in Poughkeepsie. She felt—old.

More than that, she felt bitter. For a brief, shining moment in her twenties, she felt like she had risen from her difficult childhood into a bright future full of possibilities. Now, just twenty years on, it had all gone to shit. She was twice divorced—no, of course it was more fucked up than that. Her first husband was declared dead until one day he waltzed out of the Korean Demilitarized Zone, so while she had two ex-husbands, she was only a divorcee once. Technically, she was also a widow. Or at least, widow-adjacent.

Her second marriage resulted in a child. Tyler, now five. Her joy. And—in moments of brutal honesty—the locus of anxiety in her life. Twenty minutes ago, she hung up on a child psychologist of impeccable credentials who told her his diagnosis of her special boy. Oppositional defiant disorder.

She told him to fuck right off.

He told her it sometimes ran in families.

Tyler was just—misunderstood. Oftentimes even by her, or by Dennis, his father. The shrink, of course, was Dennis's idea. Early intervention was always Dennis's idea. Child counseling, couples counseling, divorce attorneys: if there was a problem, Dennis was ahead of it, and had the person to call.

She didn't hate Dennis. Her emotions toward that particular ex weren't strong enough to metastasize to hate. No. She knew what Dennis was: a fantasy. Dennis was an escape plan from a profession she had soured on. And when her housewife fantasy bit the dust, so did the marriage.

Oppositional defiant. It was a truly shitty diagnosis. If it was true, then her amazing little boy wasn't going to just grow out of the tantrums, the low impulse control, the strange, strange behaviors. The road ahead wasn't just long. It was unclear there was a road.

She took a mouthful of hot water and spit it against the blue tile wall. She imagined she was spitting in the shrink's face. Fuck that asshole. If she were Tyler's age now, they'd probably say the same thing about her.

"*It sometimes runs in families.*" She just now got what he meant by that. *Touché, Doc. Ten points for Slytherin.*

She slapped the shower valve and it shut off. She grabbed a plush Turkish towel and dried herself off. The house was quiet. She hated that. It made her tinnitus stand out all the more, but beyond that, it was just ... lonely.

Her first husband, Malcolm Chaucer, crossed her mind at that moment. Why when she was lonely was it always Chaucer she thought about? She was not about to go down that particular memory lane, so she left the bathroom for the living room and turned on her Bang & Olufsen stereo, set the turntable spinning, and chose a record from the nearest pile.

She cranked the volume knob to 80 and let the raw attitude of Joey Ramone bleed away her worries.

And then the strangest thing happened. The old phone—the landline sitting abandoned and forgotten in the corner of the living room—rang. Just one solitary ring. And suddenly Tempest had a whole new set of worries.

CHAPTER 9

The Ramones' "Blitzkrieg Bop" lit up the sensor like a Fourth of July fireworks show. Cuddy, a lean, unambitious CIA case officer, couldn't help but admire the tech from his vantage point behind the wheel of a black Suburban. The tech wasn't the Company's. It was from the RGB, North Korean foreign intelligence. The stone-faced Korean sitting next to him, the man he was babysitting, stared at it as it pulsed with multi-hued light, studying carefully. The brightest spots were clearly coming from two speakers of a stereo, pulsing in fast rhythm. The music and its reverberation clearly outlined the room, and the lone figure in the room. The target: Tempest MacLaren.

Min Gun handed the device to Cuddy and opened to door to the SUV. He looked at Cuddy a long moment and finally spoke, "You do nothing. No calling. No backup. Nothing."

Cuddy was about to respond when Min Gun shut the SUV's door, ending the encounter. Cuddy shrugged and examined the foreign tech in his hands. The device was a small package, no bigger than a radar gun, with a flatscreen mounted on the rear of the device; it gave a complete sound profile of the little house at the end of the suburban Mamaroneck street. The house was at the end of a cul-de-sac, bordering a small wetland. It was a good choice, Cuddy thought. Private.

The sonar gun showed the entire floor plan of the house, measured out in sound reflections off hard surfaces. The living room was the brightest, with two supernovas of sound, probably high-end speakers blasting the house with anarchic rock and roll. From there, the light show and the colors grew more muted.

He turned his attention to Min Gun, stealthily approaching the house. The man was a walking arsenal: a H&K MP7 strapped to his back, a Fostech Origin-12 short-barrel shotgun in hand, and a Beretta pistol holstered at each hip. The man was armed to the teeth.

Min Gun used every tree, every shadow as he approached the Widowmaker's home. From his sonic scan he knew exactly where she was, and had a reasonable certainty that she would remain there for as long as it took him to gain entry.

He chose the front door. The distance from it to the living room where his prey awaited him was the shortest, the path the clearest. Tempest MacLaren would not employ a security system that overlooked any point of access, so there was no inherent advantage to another entryway.

On her porch he assessed the door. It was solid, reinforced most likely. The security system was one Min Gun was familiar with, a solid company with a good reputation, but there was no security system that was impervious. Min Gun pulled a tiny magnetron from his pants pocket and placed it up near the contact sensor at the door. Activated, it would maintain the electric circuit his entry would otherwise cut.

The lock was a Schlage Primus, a dual pinned lock that was particularly difficult to pick. It took Min Gun the better part of a minute to defeat it. With that he slipped inside the foyer and closed the door silently behind him.

The hallway was old hardwood, far from ideal. Creaks and cracks abounded on such floors and it was nigh impossible to detect which spot might emit those sounds. Min Gun stuck to the edge of the hall, his feet nearest the wall, to minimize noise.

The rock and roll coming from the living room was loud to the point that the precaution was almost unnecessary, but Min Gun was about to face an operator of legendary status. There was no such thing as too many precautions. He readied his Fostech Origin, releasing the safety silently.

Click. It was barely detectable over the music, but he was sure he heard it. He looked down at the shotgun. It was not what made that noise. No. The noise came from the other side of the wall.

Impossible. That was his thought. His mind went over every aspect of the last two minutes. There was no alarm, no cameras, nothing to betray his presence. A shiver went through Min Gun's body as he brought the Fostech around to face the wall beside him, suddenly certain that Tempest MacLaren was on the other side, aiming a weapon at him. An explosion of plaster and lead a half-second later confirmed every dread rising in the man.

Cuddy watched as the fireworks started. It was like one of those laser shows at a planetarium. He saw showers of sound erupting inside that house, but out here? Nothing. Cuddy was amazed at the soundproofing.

But after a minute, when the fireworks failed to subside, Cuddy realized his mistake. *"No calling. No backup. Nothing."* But what if Min Gun, elite warrior of North Korea, didn't come back?

Suddenly, a flash of light nearly blinded Cuddy, and an instant later, he saw the rear of the house blow clean off, a single bang reverberating into the night.

He looked around the sleepy neighborhood of dark houses. Waiting for a neighbor to stir. None did. Not one. He looked back at the Widowmaker's house. The sonar gun registered nothing. Not a creature was stirring, not even the proverbial mouse.

No calling. No backup.

Cuddy quickly got on his phone.

CHAPTER 10

Chaucer was not well. He awoke on the floor of his living room, his body cold and shaking. He discovered he had soiled himself from the intensity of his flashback. He checked his watch. An hour had passed. His brother's party would be starting now.

Chaucer was in no condition to go, but he had promised his brother he would attend. To not show would be the same as a —*lie*. Chaucer shuddered at the thought of another flashback, of another visit to the cave. No, Chaucer would attend, no matter what. He pulled himself to his knees and crawled to the shower.

An hour later, Chaucer entered the Social fully prepared for war. It was a large dance club, decked out in prohibition-era style, right down to the waitresses in flapper dresses. Instantly, he saw the party he was here to attend. A baker's dozen of New York's finest, four women and the rest men, were dressed up and yet still completely giving off the aroma of "cop." They were already getting sloppy, and that shook Chaucer to his bones. He steeled himself for the maximum physical contact his condition would allow.

And then things got worse. "Malcolm! Hi! I'm so glad you made it!" The voice rang out across the dance floor, a slightly nasal Long Island twang that could only belong to Sheila, Malcolm's sister-in-law.

Sheila was nearing forty, and a few inches shorter than the other cops' wives, with wavy auburn hair and a bright smile. Tonight, she was all dolled up, as she would put it, wearing a silk dress with purple horizontal stripes. She did not wait for Chaucer to cross the dance floor to the party. No, Sheila did not wait for such things. She tottered over to him on four-inch heels that her gait suggested she was not quite accustomed to.

"Hi Sheila, thanks for the invite."

"Are you kidding? Terry would kill me if I didn't invite his big brotha!"

He saw her fight the urge to come in for a hug. She knew the rules, and for that, at least, Chaucer was thankful.

"You're looking good, Malcolm."

"Thank you, Sheila." It was beginning. Chaucer liked Sheila. He thought she was a kind woman, and a great match for his brother Terry. But Sheila was a woman who relied on the niceties of the world to secure her a place in it. She stared at Chaucer, waiting for him to reciprocate the compliment. But there was no kind truth coming to Chaucer in that moment.

Sheila twirled around, showcasing herself. "Well? What do you think of the dress?"

Chaucer cringed. Direct question. He could not lie. That was impossible. Evasion? Evasion was as good as a lie. He paid a steep penalty for those, avoiding such moments if at all possible. "The horizontal stripes," he said, "they are not good for you."

And there it was. Sheila swayed there as if a sudden indoor gust had caught her off balance. Tears welled up in her eyes.

Chaucer wanted to do anything to soften the blow. "I'm sorry—"

"No, Mal, I know you—you have to tell the truth. I understand." And then she broke down sobbing, rushing into the back in search of the bathroom. Shocked, a table full of cop wives followed her.

"Jesus, Mal, every time with you."

51

Chaucer turned to see Terry. Terry was Chaucer's younger brother by three years, but at the moment, Chaucer looked at least a decade older. Terry's smile was broad and there was mischief in his eyes. He put folded arms up across his chest, the sign for a hug he knew not to give. Chaucer did the same.

Chaucer said, "I feel terrible."

Terry laughed. "It's just the way she is. You and her are like oil and water."

"Please tell her—"

"I will. And it won't change anything. Don't worry about it."

Chaucer shook his head. "Is there anyone else you'd like me to alienate while I'm here?"

"As if you need encouragement. Hey, are you okay? You look a little ... Let's just say worse than usual."

Chaucer didn't want to get into it, but direct questions must be answered. "I had an episode today. I'm fine now." Chaucer felt more questions incoming and sought to circumvent them. "Detective First Grade, that's a big deal." Chaucer made an awkward wave of congratulations. Terry accepted it.

"Thanks, man. And thanks for coming out. I know this kind of thing isn't for you."

"It's because I feel like I have to."

"It's because you love me."

"I do. I just— It's not easy to show. I don't think it ever will be."

"Bullshit, big bro. You're just messed up. We all are. But broken? No way. Nobody breaks Malcolm Chaucer."

Chaucer smiled. He looked in his brother's eyes and saw no lie. Terry truly believed in him. "Mom would be so proud of you. I mean, dad too ..."

"Except there's no way that flinty asshole would show it you mean."

"Something like that."

Terry smirked, "This is probably bullshit, and you probably already know, but I see these things and I can't not say 'em."

Chaucer knew what was coming. Another 'cure' for his

condition. Terry's main hobby these days was fixing his big brother. "What did you read, Terry?"

"Microdosing. Magic mushrooms. There was this guy, serious PTSD case, nothing was working, and then he just …" Terry saw the smile on Chaucer's face and stopped himself. "Like I said, I can't not say 'em."

Chaucer nodded, "High dose ketamine. No effect. Low dose ketamine. No effect. High dose psilocybin. No effect. Low dose. No effect."

"I know, I'm annoying. Like mom mailing us those articles about joining the postal service."

"You're trying to help. Just like she wanted us in safer jobs. I get it. And I appreciate it. I really do."

Terry bit his upper lip, "I'm not gonna stop, you know. Not until I find something you haven't tried."

"I know. The Chaucer boys … "

Terry smiled. He joined his brother in their shared motto, "Do not quit!"

Sheila appeared out of the dark hallway in the back, eyes puffy and red. She took one look at Chaucer, and again, she burst into tears, retreating into the darkness. Her committee of wives took the opportunity to throw Chaucer their darkest death stares before following their fallen comrade.

"You are in deep shit now, big guy." Valerie Spinoza walked up to the Chaucer brothers, putting an arm on each of their shoulders. Chaucer swallowed the wince that came with such contact, but in his eyes, the pain showed. "I'd rather have the Westies put a contract on my head than incur the wrath of the wives of the Four-Three."

"Let him go, Spinoza," said Terry.

Spinoza did as she was told. Chaucer had met her a half dozen times and knew her to be smart, loyal, and a force to be reckoned with. Everything you want in a Sergeant. "I'm just messing with him. Grab a seat, Mal. Maybe just not near the significant-others table. Over there, table three. Oh and Terry? We got to wheel a cake in here in a minute, so be a good boy and disappear for five. Then look shocked." Spinoza winked, and Terry headed for the restrooms.

Two of the cop wives and a cop husband kept their eyes on Chaucer as he found a seat at the table Spinoza sent him to. Chaucer had seen less intense malice in the eyes of terrorist masterminds. Chaucer wanted to leave. Now. Sooner than now. But he obediently sat down at table three, which turned out to be the kids' table. He sat himself next to the only other adult there, a wiry young man with haggard features, rocking himself left and right and sitting on his hands. His face and body language were all over the map, and Chaucer began to realize he was in some sort of distress. Chaucer turned to him, but the man lowered his head and only glanced at Chaucer out of the corner of his eye.

"Hello," said Chaucer.

The young man's agitation immediately increased. The pace of his rocking sped up, and Chaucer could hear him saying under his breath, "No, no, no, no, no, no ..." *Autism. Quite possibly a panic response.*

"Are you all right?"

The man's rhythmic "no"s got louder.

"Is something wrong?"

"Bad people." Chaucer noticed his elevated heart rate, his staccato breathing pattern. *Definitely panicking.*

"Bad people? Who?"

"You." The young man risked a glance up at Chaucer's face before lowering his eyes once again.

Chaucer was confused. "Do you think you know me?"

"Chaucer, Malcolm. 2017: suspect, kidnapping, and torture. Released without charge. 2006: suspect, double homicide, Belorussian diplomats. Released without charge. Bad people."

Chaucer was floored. Whoever he was, he knew of both times when Chaucer was questioned by the NYPD. The young man pulled up the hood of his hooded sweatshirt and pulled on the drawstrings, creating a cocoon around his face.

Spinoza came to the rescue. "Mal, come on over here."

Chaucer left the strange young man and got to Spinoza's table just in time to see the cake, a large gold detective's shield with the words "TOP DICK" spelled out in blue frosting. Spinoza smirked, "You spooked the Mug."

"Who is he?"

"Manny Spitzak. But some of us call him 'The Mug.' The human mug book. So the city's got this program, giving the disabled jobs. Manny's one of them. He's a janitor, cleaning the precinct. Then one night, he's yelling. Turns out one of our John Does in lockup is a federal fugitive. Manny spotted him right away, even though the guy's wanted poster hadn't been up for six months."

"That's an excellent memory."

"That's not the half of it. We moved him to Records, had him look through our entire criminal database. And guess what? He memorized it. Autistic savant syndrome or something like that. He's got, like, a hundred percent recall for faces, but he can't tie his shoes without help. For us? He's a godsend. We haven't needed to wait for fingerprints in years."

What must it be like, Chaucer thought, to know by sight every person ever to make it into the NYPD databank? To walk down the street and know half the people and the sins they may or may not have committed. He stared back at Manny, who was now back to a slow rocking. He wasn't so different from Chaucer. Damaged, but still of use.

"Light it up, everybody," said Spinoza. Twenty lighters sprang into action to light the yellow candles on the periphery of the cake. Chaucer caught a few dark stares from the wives of the Four-Three, but nobody confronted him. They were probably as uncomfortable around him as Manny was, or close to it.

The music changed, and the serious dancers took to the floor. Older couples mostly, and a few younger, athletic pairs, tanned and lean. Likely dance instructors. One such couple caught Chaucer's eye.

The woman was raven haired and a bit more compact than most dancers. The man was blonde, but with deep olive skin tones. Spanish perhaps. He was tall, almost too tall for his partner. Chaucer thought they looked like an odd match.

"Oh my God! No, you didn't! Guys!" Terry came out of the bathroom making a big show of the surprise cake waiting for him. He winked at Chaucer, whispering as he passed. "See. Little white lies. How hard is it?"

If he only knew, thought Chaucer. An enormous woman with electric blue eyeshadow appeared with a cake knife. "All right, you animals, you want some cake, you sit down."

Chaucer thought about skipping out on the rest of the festivities until Blue Eyeshadow stared right at him. "Sit down. Now."

Chaucer obeyed, reclaiming his seat next to Manny the Mug. Manny's rocking accelerated again, this time even faster than before. "Bad, bad, bad, bad, bad …"

Chaucer felt terrible. He wanted to ease Manny's suffering. He wondered if reasoning would work. "Manny, you know I'm Terry's brother, right? And Terry's a good guy, right?"

Manny nodded quickly. Chaucer continued, "So maybe I'm not such a bad guy after all."

Manny shook his head. "Not you. Sergei Grigova: Wanted. Interpol. Mass murder in Bucharest. Wanted. FBI. Murder of Czech diplomat in Washington, DC. Wanted. Homeland Security. Reasons unknown."

The hairs on the back of Chaucer's neck rose. A flush passed over his skin. Not knowing Sergei Grigova, he sounded like an assassin. But here? Something was very, very wrong.

"Manny, where is Sergei Grigova?"

"He's coming for you."

Chaucer spun around to face the dance floor. The mismatched couple. The tall blonde Spaniard. On second glance, a bit more Slavic in appearance. Perhaps from Odessa. And as Chaucer's eyes found him, he saw Sergei was also stealing a glance at him.

For just a moment, time froze. Sergei and his dance partner performed some kind of hand flourish. Only Chaucer knew the truth. They were drawing their weapons. Not just one assassin.

The smaller woman was a hitter too, and an even faster draw. Their mark had made them and the element of surprise was gone. Time to strike.

Chaucer's old field operative brain fired up in an instant. *You're sitting. You're flat-footed. You've got zero cover. You're going to die now.*

Fall and kick. An old whisper of an instinct, but Chaucer followed it blindly, he fell out of his chair, in the process planting his back against the cold floor. With all the strength he had, he kicked up the round-top banquet table, aiming it for the oncoming assassins.

Two shots went off in rapid succession, both piercing the flying tabletop, but deflecting the bullets just enough to miss Chaucer. Chaucer scrambled to his knees to run. The assassins pushed the tabletop aside. They had him completely at their mercy.

Or they would have, if not for the detectives of the Four-Three. The moment the first shot rang out, the off-duty officers drew their pieces. Long-drilled instincts came to bear. The assassin couple cleared the round-top, focused on their target. Chaucer. Only to find, once the table fell away, six shooters drawing a bead on them.

Sergei bailed, diving under another table. But the female shooter was hungrier. She thought she had time for the kill. She lowered the barrel of her gun, lining up a five-foot head shot. Chaucer could see her right eye perfectly over the iron sights.

Blam! The shot sounded twice as loud as the previous two. And it was. The assassins used 9 mm subsonic rounds, quiet but effective. But this shot was from a .45 automatic, and it ripped open a chest wound in the woman shooter that killed her instantly.

"Freeze, NYPD!" The shout came from the other side of the room. The front door. Sergei froze as two late-arriving officers of the Four-Three blocked his exit. Sergei's gun was facing the wrong way, covering his retreat from the table of cops. The officers at the door had him sighted, center mass.

Only Sergei's eyes moved, assessing, reevaluating, looking for the angle of attack that afforded him the best chances of survival. But then a scream echoed through the room. Sheila, Chaucer knew instantly. Sheila was screaming.

"Terry?! Terry!" A few of the cops' eyes fell to the floor, where Terry Chaucer lay. One of the two deflections, the bullets meant for Malcolm, had found Terry's chest. He lay in a widening pool of his own blood, his eyes dead and lifeless.

Sergei saw the momentary distraction. It was his opportunity. He bolted to the right, past the maître d's podium, going for the large glass window that overlooked the city street.

"Fuck you," said Spinoza as she emptied a magazine into the fleeing assassin. Her buddies followed suit. They peppered Sergei with bullets, making his body dance one last time before he fell to the floor of the Social.

CHAPTER 11

Chaucer stared at his brother's dead eyes. Waves of emotion coursed through his body, each wave bringing on pain and panic. Terry, his baby brother. Terry, the Boy Scout. Terry, the last connection Chaucer had to the person he once was.

Terry was gone. Chaucer felt a grief so raw it gnawed at his stomach. That rollercoaster feeling of falling, over and over. He fought against his swelling emotions, willing himself not to black out or dissociate. He forced himself to look into his brother's unblinking eyes. He choked every ounce of mourning out of his mind and body, placing it in some hidden holding place deep inside him. A place he promised he would return to one day. Terry deserved to be mourned.

"They only had eyes for you, Mal," Spinoza said, coming up behind Chaucer. It was part observation, part accusation, and all true. Two assassins from Eastern Europe just tried to murder him.

Why? Why would someone put out a hit on an interrogator? In a second, the thought came to him. The call. The one singular ring. *Could that be it?*

"What's going on, Mal?" Spinoza was between two worlds. She was a friend of the deceased, but she was also a cop.

"I don't know."

"And you're not lying to me?"

"I think you know that's not possible."

Spinoza was fighting to keep powerful emotions bottled up. "So how about you tell me what you do know?"

"They're assassins. Eastern European. Manny ID'd the guy a second before the hit."

"Why you?"

"It makes no sense. They saw you guys. They could've waited. They're pros. They would have waited until they could kill me clean. Unless …" Chaucer's mind raced, pulling together disparate facts into a narrative that fit them. "Unless they couldn't wait. Whatever their reason, I had to die tonight."

"You gotta go. Get outta town. You got someplace safe? Some people to protect you until you get this sorted?"

Chaucer thought about it. A whole new world of hurt was about to descend upon this place and these people. He had to protect them as best he could. Terry would've wanted that. "I'm not leaving town. I'm gonna fix this. For Terry."

Spinoza shook her head. "Those two were pros. You know what happens when pros miss? Somebody sends more pros. Look, I know you're hurting. We all are. But Terry wouldn't want you sacrificing yourself for this."

Chaucer knew Spinoza was making sense. He knew it was the right call. The smart call. But Terry died because of Chaucer, and somebody had to pay. Chaucer couldn't see any way that happened if he didn't get involved. "Thanks, but this is something I gotta do."

Spinoza looked him over, assessing him. Chaucer could see her make up her mind. "What do you need us to do?"

"Nothing. You let whatever precinct we're in handle the investigation."

"Terry is ours." *Pain and anger.*

Chaucer said, "I need you to trust me. The only thing you can do right now is become a target. I will find out who is responsible."

"You can do that?"

Chaucer nodded, forcing himself to be sure. But deep down, he knew how this was going to go. Chaucer just needed to survive long enough to make sure everyone responsible for this attack died. To do this, all he needed to do was discover the truth.

And there was no one on the planet better at discovering hidden truths than Malcolm Chaucer.

"There will be a lot of people in here, people with complex credentials, coming to ask you questions. I need you to do two things for me. Can you do that?"

Spinoza was staring at Terry, lost. "What?"

"I need you to get Manny out of here. And spread the word. He wasn't here." A needle of pain shot up Chaucer's back. Even suggesting someone else lie had consequences.

"Manny?"

"He ID'd the shooter. They could view him as a liability."

"Got it. The Mug wasn't here. What else?"

"About everything else, tell the absolute truth."

"What do you mean?"

"I mean everything. That they were coming for me. What you suspect of my background. That after the attack, I ran out of here."

Spinoza was surprised. "You're leaving? What about Terry? What about Sheila?"

"I'm no comfort to her. And Spinoza? If I stay, they will take me somewhere I don't want to go, and I won't be able to find the people that did this."

Spinoza thought about it for a long moment. "Get out of here. First responders are en route."

Chaucer glanced around. No eyes were upon him. Everyone was engulfed in the shock and tragedy before them. Chaucer headed out the back way.

Spinoza called to him. "Mal. You need any help to get these guys, you let me know."

Chaucer nodded and disappeared out the fire door.

CHAPTER 12

Gabriel Asher was going to miss the plane crash. He knew it from the very moment his phone rang. He was in the last stages of a complex op in that strange Neverland that was Mexico City, and his phone never rang in the last stages of an op. His people were simply too well trained to put a call through unless the op was experiencing catastrophic failure, or he was about to receive an offer he could not refuse.

Asher picked up the phone, ready to hear the offer, because failure was not something Asher had experienced in some time.

"You're needed stateside." The voice was modulated. Disguised. One of the new models that you almost couldn't detect. Almost.

Asher thought about how to play this. "You've caught me in the middle of something."

"Well aware. And yet, you are needed. Now. There is a Citation X gassed and waiting for you at the private terminal."

"That's awfully presumptuous. Also, I assume you're aware that there are complications with me working stateside?"

"We're aware that Gabriel Asher is persona non grata as far as the Company is concerned. If only you had an alternate identity you could use."

Asher smiled. Whoever this was had quite the sense of humor. "Give me the elevator pitch."

There was a pause on the line. For a moment, Asher wondered if he had committed some kind of error. Then the voice said, "A young man was assassinated. A man with an important father in Korea. It is crucial that interested parties tie that killing to Tempest MacLaren, a woman with quite the history of exterminating people from that corner of the world."

Boilerplate, Asher thought. He waited for the good part. He didn't have to wait long.

"The plan was to ensure Tempest MacLaren's death, thereby buttoning up the story. But we ran into a problem."

Asher smiled. "The Widowmaker didn't just roll over and die?"

"She's still alive, out there. And so is Malcolm Chaucer."

Asher knew that name as well. "What's the Oracle got to do with this?"

"He was the interrogator of the witness who pinned the assassination on MacLaren."

Asher was impressed. "Some day, you'll have to tell me how you pulled that one off. Okay. And if I remember, Chaucer and MacLaren have a history?"

"Exactly."

"And if they were to find each other alive?"

"This is why you are being pulled out of Mexico City. Immediately. That must never happen. We need them both dead. Preferably yesterday."

This one would be a challenge, Asher thought. Two pros surviving hits within an hour of each other, now at large and possibly working in concert, and it was happening in New York, right when the entire world was watching. "It's going to cost you."

Buzz. A silent alarm alerted Asher to a deposit being made to his main offshore account. It was double Asher's usual jaw-dropping quote.

"That, of course, is a half payment for engagement. Another half will be delivered upon success."

Asher smiled. He liked the way this guy did business. "I've got some standing orders, a few details to happen immediately," he said. "Number one: you're going to post a million-dollar bounty on the Ghost Board. A million dollars each, confirmed kills only."

"We were hoping for something lower profile."

"I'm going to get you all the cover you'll need. You've got thousands of operatives in town for the World Summit. The best chance to put this to bed fast is to get them working for us."

"It'll be done."

"You better be writing this down, because I've got another ten things that need to be done."

Minor details, one and all, but that was why everyone hired Asher. He perfectly combined meticulousness, audacity, and ruthlessness, buying his employers nights of restful sleep. Because when Gabriel Asher cleaned up a mess, it never came back to the people that made it. Ever.

He thought of one last important detail. He needed an operator, an assassin, immediately upon arrival. He wanted the woman who shot Tajo. Anya Sergeyev. A young woman from the Baltics with great promise. She would be immediately useful to him.

Fifteen minutes later, Asher buckled himself into a swiveling leather recliner aboard a Citation X as it lifted off from Benito Juarez International Airport, racing north and east. As the Citation banked in the night sky, Asher glanced out the wide oval window beside him and witnessed a Dassault Falcon 2000 with thirteen passengers and crew tumble from the sky, erupting in a fireball that rained debris all over the airfield. The trail connecting a powerful banker to the leader of a Filipino death squad was broken, for good.

He loved it when things just worked out.

The relevant dossiers were transmitted via secure connection to the device beside his seat. The Athena device was a very secret, very state-of-the-art piece of Company tech. Essentially, it used deep brain stimulation via a headset to help new information plant itself in the short-term memory center of the brain. Operatives could use it to become conversant in Turkish in the time it took to fly to Istanbul, or as was the case here, become extremely familiar with a complex mission in just a few hours' time. The knowledge didn't last for long, but for short missions, the tech was very impressive.

What Asher was about to implant in his brain were two dossiers to be specific. Tempest MacLaren and Malcolm Chaucer. He knew them both, and not just by reputation. He had hired the Widowmaker himself in the past, though she was unlikely to know of his involvement in that particular op. The Widowmaker was simply the one you went to when you absolutely, positively needed a protected target dead in a limited time frame.

The Oracle, on the other hand, Asher knew under less pleasant circumstances. In a single two-hour interrogation, Chaucer had unraveled an incredibly detailed false-flag operation under Asher's command, sending the entire subterfuge crumbling to dust. The fact that Asher designed the op to seem like a Company-sanctioned affair was not lost on the higher-ups in the CIA. It got him on their ban list, and the no-fly list to boot. Yes, though they had never officially met, Malcolm Chaucer was the reason Asher hadn't had a US-based op in the last five years, and was the lone blemish on an otherwise perfect career.

And now Asher was being called home. Most people in his position would be worried about the first dossier, Tempest MacLaren. But as exceptional as she was, Tempest MacLaren was still just an assassin. Assassins were killed every day. But the second dossier was an enigma. True, he was no longer a case officer, per se. True, he was riddled with weaknesses, psychological and otherwise. But something about Malcolm Chaucer worried Asher.

Malcolm Chaucer. The Oracle. The broken man. The lost operative. The man who came back.

In another life, he was a case officer, an exceptional one by all accounts. He worked his way up to the North Korean desk—no simple task in an agency full of hotshots gunning for the highest priority assignments. Within three months of starting, he had uncovered a North Korean bureaucrat who sought asylum, who, in trade, offered the location details for every aspect of the Kingdom's nuclear program.

But the mission to retrieve the bureaucrat went horribly wrong. So wrong, in fact, that when Chaucer was captured fleeing the country, he simply disappeared. There was no news in the papers of a capitalist spy captured. No back-channels offering a trade. No recognition that a Malcolm Chaucer ever existed, let alone that he had been captured. In this way, the North Koreans made it clear they were keeping Chaucer, and that was that.

They moved him to Mount Kuwol, to the compound of a man only known as Po. Some say he was a Chinese mystic. Some say he was the descendant of the royal torturers of the great dynasties. But in time, the Agency would know Po. Perhaps not understand him. The thinking was that no one could, but they would know the man and his contribution to the darkest corner of their profession.

Po did not simply interrogate Chaucer. Po did not even torture Chaucer, for that would imply the goal was information. No, what Po did was far worse.

Po was a scientist, deconstructing a human being to his smallest mental and emotional components, ripping him apart, dissecting him, and then reassembling him according to his whim. And then he did worse.

He repeated the process.

For eight years, the sadist known only as Po would torture Chaucer, break the man down to nothing, then slowly nurse him back to health, changing his personality, his very nature at will. He didn't just attack Chaucer's body, he attacked his mind. His personality.

Po painstakingly located each and every pleasure Chaucer ever had and tortured him in the midst of those pleasures, rewiring him to experience only agony whenever he encountered what the old Chaucer loved. He meticulously took away every joy Chaucer ever had. Every reason for living.

And then he wrote about it. In a magnum opus of human destruction, he meticulously, scientifically recounted every experiment on the white man so unlucky as to be delivered to him. It was a statement from the regime: we will not play by your rules. You attack us, we will destroy you utterly.

Known only as *The White Book*, at most a hundred people outside of North Korea had actually seen it. Fewer still had read a translation. Word had it that the Agency burned through three translators in its transcription, each requiring mental leave.

But for every person who had actually read *The White Book*, another thousand had heard of it. It was the horror story of the profession, and Po, its ultimate boogeyman.

And then one day, a hobbled Westerner appeared in Blue House Number 3, one of the conference rooms that straddles both North and South Korea at the DMZ. No one knew who he was, but when he crossed the demarcation line, it would be discovered that Malcolm Chaucer had come home.

Of course, it was immediately apparent that Chaucer never made it home.

The Chaucer the Agency knew, the one his friends loved, ceased to exist. "He was an alien in a Chaucer skin-sack," joked one Agency higher-up. Medical took him for three months, and the write-up was brutal. On the surface, Chaucer looked intact. Any scarring from incisions and such were carefully healed, but the PET scans showed what was hidden.

Po had inserted needles directly into the pain centers of Chaucer's central nervous system. The slightest stimulation of those needles could mimic almost any torture imaginable. He dislocated Chaucer's spine in eight places to cause unspeakable agony. All of this was beyond the comprehension of the doctors who evaluated Chaucer. Any one of those tortures should have killed the man. And yet there stood Chaucer, somehow intact, if not quite whole.

The psych boys took Chaucer for six months, trying to figure out the puzzle that was his psyche. Or at least that started off as the goal.

Within the first four weeks, they abandoned that goal as unrealistic, defaulting to a simpler objective: determine if he's dangerous. Chaucer had become a ghost story in the Agency. They were worried about a *Manchurian Candidate* scenario, that Chaucer was irretrievably turned and just waiting for activation. The North Koreans, for their part, never said a word.

Chaucer was deemed psychologically unfit for field duty. And that would have been the end of it, if not for some higher-ups who felt they owed Chaucer more than a boot into the civilian world.

The director of the North Asia desk, James Fitzgerald, arranged for Chaucer to transfer to his choice of non-field duty designations. The thought was to give him an analyst's desk somewhere in the bowels of Langley. To let him sit and wait until his retirement benefits vested.

But Chaucer fooled them all. He chose interrogation. Technically, it was a non-field designation. Internally, it sent a panic through the ranks. How? How could a man who endured what Chaucer had, suddenly turn around and study the art of what Po did to him?

Of course, in retrospect, it was hardly like that. Chaucer was more an instructor than the best of his teachers. Quietly, respectfully, he would correct their misperceptions of what a subject's behavior meant, what the resulting psychological state of a certain protocol would be.

And invariably, Chaucer would be right. The division said he rewrote their entire program. Not a text was left standing. And the program became better. Results more reliable.

But Chaucer himself? He was the best anyone had ever seen. So much so, he seemed less an interrogator than a mind-reader. The Oracle was born. Even the hardest subjects, he barely had to touch to get information from them. And reliable information.

Perfect information. None of that fountain of garbage most subjects spewed to stop the torture.

In fact, though the perception was that Chaucer was the world's greatest torturer, a careful review of his case file revealed that he hardly ever needed to resort to anything like other interrogators did. A clear 80 percent of his subjects broke down with no torture technique employed. And of the other 20 percent, in nearly every case, they left their ordeal with exceptional long-term prospects.

It was as if Chaucer was doing for them what no one would do for him. He was doing his job in a way to cause the least amount of collateral damage. He knew so well what it was like to sit strapped down to that chair. He knew what to say to them. He knew how to read them. And he never, ever lied.

That was the most intriguing conditioning aspect that Po left him with. Chaucer had been tortured for so long, conditioned so heavily by pain and reward, that he was psychologically incapable of telling a lie. Even a lie of omission. Even telling someone he would prefer not to answer them would bring about a relapse of agony.

Asher closed the dossier. No, the Widowmaker was a world-class assassin, and clearly a problem. But Malcolm Chaucer, the man who came back, was more dangerous by far. That was why he needed to die. And quickly.

The fact that such a result was so pleasing to Asher was quite beside the point.

CHAPTER 13

Every fiber of Chaucer's being told him to run. In the first five blocks, he spotted two women and a man, all in intelligence. For a group of people trained to be undetectable, it was shocking how easily Chaucer could pick them out. For him it was simplicity itself. Normal people were blissfully unaware of their surroundings. These were not. Were they here to kill him? Or were they just here for the World Summit?

Chaucer ruled out hostile intent, one by one. He made up his mind. He couldn't run. If he was to run, Terry would be buried without anyone knowing why. The thought of his brother in that cold, cold ground brought on another wave of grief, an onrush of emotion so powerful it threatened to bring Chaucer down.

Chaucer fought back. He got angry. He would not run. He promised Spinoza he would find answers. And Chaucer would not be a liar. No. Chaucer would find the people responsible for his brother's murder, and he would make them pay.

But to do that, Chaucer needed answers.

He couldn't go home, that was certain. They could have followed him to the Social, or the hitters could have had detailed information about him, in which case his drops were also compromised.

He went to an old payphone on the lower level of Grand

Central Station, one of the few still intact in the city. A useful location. From here, he could travel in eight different directions at high speed in a matter of two minutes. He could make a couple calls, discreetly. Modern tracing technology, especially the high-speed NSA stuff, only afforded him thirty seconds before his location was given away, but it would be enough time to at least tell friend from foe.

He pulled out his cell phone and realized his first mistake. He hadn't removed the SIM card yet. *Rusty, Chaucer, rusty.* Virtually no one knew his phone, but it was still a major security risk. He removed the SIM card and broke it in two. But his cell phone still had one more use. His was a modified unit, with a line tap built-in, capable of detecting nearly every form of wiretap and trace.

He attached the alligator clips of the tap onto the pay phone, and he dialed the contact number Roma gave him. The case officer in charge of the interrogation. Whatever his personal opinion of Roma's talents, he could get the full force of the Agency behind Chaucer. They could protect him.

Roma picked up on the second ring. "Yeah?"

"It's Chaucer."

"What the hell time is it?"

"A little after eleven."

"Then I'm gonna assume you've got a good fucking reason for calling me this late?"

A red light on Chaucer's cell illuminated. TRACE IN PROGRESS. Chaucer cut the line. Not good. Not good at all. It was almost as if Roma was expecting the call. Even his vocal stress wasn't right. He wanted to seem to be asleep, but he had been up for hours. He heard it in his tone. *Anxious.*

Roma was a part of this. That made things very tough. If the Agency wanted him dead, then soon he would be, and his brother would remain unavenged.

His next call was to the CIA. He asked to be put through to whoever was answering calls to New York station. The pleasant-sounding receptionist put him on hold. A moment later, the red light came on again. TRACE IN PROGRESS.

Chaucer cut the line. Oh for two. One last call to make. The one guy Chaucer always trusted. Never had that fact been more necessary than right now. Chaucer called Fitz.

The phone rang six times before Fitz picked up. Old fool, thought Chaucer. He left his answering machine off. "Fitz here."

He didn't sound like he was just awakened either. Warning bells sounded in Chaucer's head. "Sorry to call so late, Fitz."

"Don't worry about it, buddy. I was up anyway. Nan's having trouble breathing. What's going on? Is everything okay?"

Chaucer stared at the cell phone in his lap, staring at the red light, willing it to stay off.

And as luck would have it, it did.

Chaucer filled him in with just four sentences. Fitz responded with just one. "I'm bringing you in."

A few minutes and a couple of phone calls later and Fitz was in charge and decisive. In this mode, he brought a multitude of crises to successful resolution over his career. It was when he was at his best. He was a planner, a calculator. Meticulous to the point of causing operatives under him to tear their hair out, trying to meet his exacting standards. But at this moment, it was what Chaucer loved most about the man.

"Roma traced my call. How can you be sure the Agency is safe?"

"I checked with my people in the Agency. Roma's been on leave for a week. He lied to me. Today's op was off the books. Freelance. All you need is to come in, and we'll nail that slimy bastard."

Chaucer still wasn't sure. There were too many unanswered questions to feel secure that anything was what it seemed. Fitz was always an Agency man. No matter what he was doing, he believed fully that somewhere above his station, a moral equivalency had been worked out to make sure that his actions served the greater good of the red, white, and blue.

Chaucer labored under no such illusions. This was an amoral business that used perceptions of morality as leverage to guarantee outcomes. Nothing more. And as such, he was far from secure in the idea of the Agency taking him in with open arms.

"I don't know, Fitz. Something's not right here."

"Everything's not right. We're gonna sort this out, and we're gonna find the bastards behind this."

Chaucer thought again about Tempest. Could he tell Fitz? But it was hopeless. His mind had long been twisted into its current configuration, and somewhere in the labyrinth, there was a stone blocking Chaucer from anything that could be a lie. And a violation of his oath would be a big lie indeed.

"When and where?"

"There's a self-storage building on Tenth Avenue and—"

"No. If I'm coming in, it has to be the front door. Minimizes the risk of ambush. I'll come in to a field office."

Fitz paused, no doubt to weigh the benefit of arguing with Chaucer. He opted against it. "Fine. Grace Building. Forty-Second between Fifth and Sixth. The offices of The Groton Group. Seven a.m. work for you?"

Chaucer checked his watch. Seven a.m. was eight hours away, but given all that Fitz would have to arrange, it made sense. "Will you be there?"

"I can't, Mal. Nan — I can't leave her."

"That's okay. I'll be fine."

"I'm sorry."

"Don't be. You're a good friend. Without you, I'd have nobody." He suddenly realized how true that was. With Terry's death, Chaucer was well and truly alone. Fitz was Chaucer's lone anchor to the world.

"Be safe. And get your ass in at seven sharp."

Chaucer returned the pay phone to its cradle and looked out at the concourse. He had eight hours to kill. Sleep was out of the question, and he felt his mind spiraling toward dark places. Places where he risked losing his precious control. For Chaucer, that could mean the end of him.

He thought of Terry. For some reason he couldn't get a memory out of his mind. Terry at age five, on a metal trash can lid that doubled as a sled. Terry laid at the bottom of a snowy hill, bloody-nosed and smiling. It was, Chaucer realized, the first time he had ever feared for Terry's life. And now that fear had become reality. Nausea rose in his stomach.

He had two choices. He could walk for eight hours and hope to avoid overstimulation. Or he could investigate the interrogation he had just conducted. He could begin his journey to the truth.

Fifteen minutes later, Chaucer stared at the screen of his sim-free burner phone in the back corner of a Sichuan noodle house. He used the noodle house's internet to do some preliminary digging. He had the name of the graduate student murdered the day before. Tajo, otherwise known as Sim Ju Won, son of Sim Se Yoon, an apparel magnate from Seoul. A man with factories in China, Myanmar, Bangladesh and the DPRK.

Chaucer dug into the student, Tajo. He was a promising researcher in the field of virology, according to a handful of mentions in academic articles. To Chaucer, it was the clear favorite for what might bring Tempest MacLaren to your door. Virology was a potential Pandora's box of nightmares that men, and women, would kill for.

Chaucer looked up Tajo's faculty adviser. Dr. Mira Patel.

Thirty minutes later, Chaucer stood across from the Biology department faculty offices for NYU, a red-brick building on Lafayette Street that was lit up invitingly. Chaucer took it as a good sign. It was nearly midnight, so the odds of finding Dr. Mira Patel in her office were slim. But they weren't none.

A student exited the building as Chaucer approached the door, and he caught it with one hand. Inside, he found a wrought-iron staircase in a brightly lit atrium, and a more modern retrofitted elevator. Dr. Mira Patel's office was on the second floor, and Chaucer elected to walk.

The offices on the second floor were small: a row of doors

spaced six feet apart and extending down the length of the hallway. He knocked twice on Mira Patel's door and waited a long moment. *Struck out, Chaucer.*

A moment later, a soft voice bid him enter.

Mira Patel was a tall Indian woman in her early fifties. She wore a tweed suit—fashionable without drawing undue attention—and her prescription glasses magnified her already striking eyes. She looked up from her cramped desk, and from her expression, she was clearly expecting someone else. "Can I help you?"

"Sorry to bother you, Dr. Patel, but there were a couple outstanding questions I need to ask you about Tajo."

Chaucer felt the pain rise in his spine. He felt that lightness in his head as the panic rose. Nothing he said was a lie, but his words implied he was with the police and that was enough.

Mira noticed nothing of this. There was already a sadness in her eyes, and that sadness only intensified. "Of course. Please, have a seat. What do you need to know?"

Chaucer swallowed the pain, letting it wash over him as he sat. "I need to know a bit more about what Tajo was working on. His research. My understanding is that it was viruses?"

"Yes, it was. Tajo was a promising biologist. He was a quick study. Not the most gifted student I've had, but he made up for that with his work ethic. Many of us felt he would do great things."

"In layman's terms, could you tell me what he was working on specifically?"

Mira Patel's eyebrow raised a quarter of a millimeter. Pupils dilated. A hitch in her breath. *She's starting to suspect you, Chaucer.* She asked, "Do you think what he was working on might have something to do with his death?"

"I'm just looking to get the complete picture, ma'am. Viral research could be weaponized, isn't that right?"

At that Mira smiled faintly, indicating Chaucer's comment was naive. "It is true that certain small branches of virology could have—antagonistic applications, but I've never met anyone who got into this field and was interested in anything other than helping humanity. Tajo—well, he was even more dedicated to that than most."

"More dedicated?"

"He was the hardest working student I've ever had. Sometimes he would go days without sleep. As a PhD candidate, of course, he had coursework to teach as well, and he always did it without complaint. But every second he could, he was in that lab. I asked him once why he was pushing himself so hard. He simply said he wanted to make a difference— You're not taking any notes?"

Mira's body tightened up. Fingers tensed. Nostrils flared. Chaucer tapped the side of his head. "I've never needed to. Dr. Patel, I'd say I have just one more question for you, but it's actually the only question I've asked you. What exactly was Tajo working on?"

Chaucer allayed her suspicions enough for her to answer. "Phages."

"Phages?"

"Yes. Bacteriophages are their full name, but we're finding they're not exclusively hostile to bacteria. A virus is an amazing molecular machine. In a sense, you're right, every virus is a weapon. But not all viruses attack us. The bacteriophage is a virus that attacks single cells, often bacteria. Tajo had been studying them his entire academic career. He interned with a team that found a phage that attacks a variant of C. diff, a very dangerous bacterial infection of the human intestinal tract."

"Aren't there antibiotics for that?"

"Fewer and fewer. Bacteria adapt. Surely you've heard about antibiotic resistance? Such resistance could plunge us into a new medical dark age if we don't come up with other answers. Phages could well be that answer. Phages attack and consume the deadly bacteria, and there is no known adaptation against a phage. You know what my students called Tajo?"

Chaucer simply shook his head.

"Dr. Dolittle."

Chaucer shrugged. The name meant nothing to him. Mira continued. "His lab was always full of animals: guinea pigs, rabbits, mice, rats. They would come in sick, and sometimes Tajo's phages would make them well again. Now, does that sound like a weapon to you?"

"It does not. Thank you for your time, Dr. Patel."

CHAPTER 14

At 5 a.m., Chaucer was in position. He occupied the copier up at the front window of the twenty-four-hour copy shop across the street from the Grace Building, slowly copying yesterday's *New York Post*, one page at a time. Standing at the copier gave him a clear view of the comings and goings of the building and the parking garage.

Whatever reason he was targeted for death, it was unlikely that it had anything to do with Tajo's work. But that left far too many other explanations. Most prominent in Chaucer's mind was the question of why a South Korean business owner would draw the attention, and assistance, of the CIA. Sim Se Yoon had factories in China and North Korea. If he were connected to the Agency, he could be a valuable asset. Was it possible that Chaucer entering the blind and seeing the man had made him a threat? Chaucer had to entertain at least the possibility that the Agency itself wanted him dead.

He figured if there was to be an ambush, he would see some sign of commotion, some change of personnel. In truth, he knew it was a long shot. If the Agency or those in its employ wished him harm, he was dead. Simple as that. And if they were, in fact, going to help him, such paranoia wouldn't help at all. That said, he still had two hours to kill and at least this activity fed his need for diligence.

At 5:30 a.m., two cars pulled out of the garage beneath the building. A dark sedan and a blue minivan. The minivan was likely a group of cleaners finishing their shift. The dark sedan could be anyone. A car service for a prostitute or a fast ride for a high-level executive, there was no way to tell. The futility of Chaucer's makeshift surveillance was becoming more and more obvious to him.

The vehicles stopped at the curb just a hundred feet from the building entrance, one behind the other. Maybe not a cleaning crew after all. The cars seemed to wait together.

The lobby doors of the building opened, and two men and a woman exited the Grace Building. They all wore suits; the men in gray, the woman in black. They headed right for the vehicles.

The hairs on Chaucer's neck stood to attention. Something was clawing at the back of his mind. Something familiar. Against plan, against training, Chaucer stepped out of the copy shop, crossing the empty lanes of Forty-Second Street and coming up behind the men and the woman.

The move drew eyes. The men glanced back, marking him. Chaucer marked them as well. They were the two men stationed around the interrogation chair this past afternoon. Lane and Rodgers.

The woman sensed them slowing. She took the slightest glance over her left shoulder. A wisp of brown hair moved out of the way and Chaucer glimpsed her face.

It was Isabel Marcano. The woman he had just interrogated.

CHAPTER 15

The sirens saved Chaucer's life. Lane and Rodgers were drawing their weapons when three NYPD police cruisers raced down Forty-Second Street, sirens blaring and lights flashing.

Indecision. Confusion. The operatives looked toward the waiting cars. The revolving doors of the Grace Building were just behind them, and the police cruisers were coming in fast.

At first, Chaucer thought the operatives were simply going to wait until the police cleared the scene. But they were acting way too skittish for that. That's when it hit him. They thought the police were a part of this. They thought they were in the middle of an ambush. A blown op.

They holstered their guns and waved to the waiting cars, which pulled away from the curb. The three then sprinted back toward the Grace Building's entrance.

Isabel Marcano remained hidden between her escorts. Chaucer only had a split second to decide on a course of action. He had to be sure. He had to know.

Chaucer ran right at them. It was a calculated gamble. If they still thought the police were coming for them, they wouldn't resort to deadly force. They would risk too much if they allowed the police to witness the murder of an American citizen on the streets of New York.

They saw Chaucer coming. And they were ready.

Isabel hustled to the revolving door while Lane and Rodgers planted themselves just beyond arm's reach of each other. Perfect technique. The goal would have been to tempt Chaucer to run between them, to intercept the girl on the most direct route. Then, with both his flanks exposed, they would attack in a coordinated fashion. One blow to the temple, the other to the solar plexus. Chaucer would have zero chance to defend against both blows and whichever landed would incapacitate him and still give them time to make it back to a high-security zone within the building.

They thought Chaucer was an amateur. They knew who he was, but not who he had been. That was their first mistake. They were faster than Chaucer. They were stronger than him too. Chaucer hadn't been in a physical fight in ten years, but still held one card he could play.

He had a torturer's knowledge of the human body.

Chaucer feinted at running between them. They bit. They spun and attacked the space where Chaucer was supposed to be. But Chaucer stopped short a second before his momentum would doom him. The two blockers were now throwing blows at nothing but air. Worse. They were practically engaging each other.

And they both showed him their auricular nerves. That was his one chance. A blow to the nerve would cause a feedback loop to the brain that would render the subject instantly unconscious. Chaucer had his fist ready, two house keys barely exposed beside the thumb. He struck the bigger of the two, the one that moved first, the alpha of the group.

The keys impacted the side of the operative's neck, pressing hard against the nerves and soft tissues underneath. Like a marionette with its strings cut, the big man instantly went limp, flopping to the pavement.

His partner was shocked. This was not how it was supposed

to happen. He searched for Chaucer's hands, looking for a stun gun but finding only keys. Keys headed right for his own neck. He twisted away, but a moment too late. Chaucer found the same spot, and the second man folded the same as the first.

Isabel was at the revolving door. Chaucer threw his body at it, wedging himself between a revolving pane and the curved glass wall. She was trapped, not able to make it into the building.

Behind him, the police cars raced past. The woman looked right at Chaucer. It was her. It was the woman he interrogated. Her eyes went wide when she saw the police cars disappear down the street. In an instant, realization bloomed across her face. The cops were not there for her. In less than three seconds, she drew a pistol and opened fire.

A three-shot burst. Grouping was a two-inch spread, at most. *Agency training.* Chaucer's next thought: *So why aren't I dead yet?* Then he saw the bullets lodged in the glass pane between him and the girl. The Grace Building's exterior doors and windows were bulletproof.

Chaucer pulled himself out of the door. It swung free, depositing the woman inside the building. She sprawled to the floor, then rolled back to standing and raced outside. But by the time she got there, Chaucer was out of sight. She methodically searched every possible near hiding place. Nothing. No sign of Chaucer whatsoever.

Rodgers, one of the suited men stirred. He shook his head, trying to knock the cobwebs loose. Isabel took charge. "Call it in."

"He's gotta be close. We can find him."

"He saw me. He knows. Call it in. And then check on Lane."

Rodgers looked behind him, to the spot on the pavement where Lane fell. There was just one problem. Lane wasn't there anymore.

Lane was nowhere to be seen.

CHAPTER 16

Lane awoke to the smell of blood and axle grease. He was gagged, his arms bound tightly behind him at the wrists and elbows. He was on his back in a narrow dark space, putting pressure on his hands and wrists as his body forced them down against small sharp rocks.

There was no sign of Chaucer.

It was too dark to know for sure, but Lane felt he was alone. And so he got to work. Following his training, he began flexing and compressing the muscle groups of his arms, wrists, and hands, slowly testing every anchor point of his bonds. Every confinement material, even steel shackles, has an angle of attack. Most have some give as well. Combine the right angle of attack with the maximum material give, and that just might spell your freedom.

But Lane quickly realized Chaucer was going to make him work for it. The elbow tie was the clincher. Without it, Lane could've gotten his hands in front of him where he could potentially remove his gag and get his teeth to make quick work of the problem. But the elbow tie prevented all of that, and it severely restricted his arm rotations as well. Wherever Chaucer was, Lane hoped he would take his time coming back.

The paramedics had Rodgers sitting on the marble floor of the lobby of the Grace Building. A paramedic shined a light in Rodgers's eyes. For the third time, they asked him the same questions about his name and address. Rodgers's answers got shorter and surlier. "I'm fine. Will you leave me alone?"

"Sir, your coworker said you collapsed straight away. We have to check for brain damage."

"There is no brain damage. He got a lucky shot in, that's all."

"Sir, just allow us to do our job—"

The lobby doors opened. Roma stormed in. "You two. Out."

The paramedics realized he meant them. They considered objecting, but something about Roma's demeanor helped them to change their minds. They packed up their boxes and hustled out.

They loaded their boxes into their ambulance, idling at the curb, when one of them noticed a defibrillator device was missing. "Goddamnit. Can't leave anything out in Manhattan without nailing it down."

Chaucer worked his way down the dark steam tunnels, lugging the defibrillator behind him. He swung open a heavy iron door, then closed it behind him, throwing himself into total darkness. He opened his cell phone and used its light to descend a set of dark stairs that led to nothing but a pile of stones, a sealed-up passageway to an old, long-forgotten subway line.

At the bottom of the stairs, Lane had turned himself over and was writhing like a worm after a heavy rain. He was almost a third of the way through the ballistic nylon tie around his elbows. A rage rose in Chaucer. He was lied to. Profoundly. And it resulted in the death of his brother. But he forced his anger back down. This was to be an interrogation. He needed to be calculated, dispassionate. He needed to be the Oracle. But pieces of a grieving older brother kept leaking into the facade.

Using the toe of his boot, Chaucer rolled Lane. The man's face was red and sweaty with exhaustion. He tried to yell at Chaucer, but the duct-tape gag held firm and all that came out was a muffled groan.

Chaucer stared at his face, his eyes. He gathered information. He saw both fear and confusion in equal measure. The fear was good. The confusion, less so. It suggested that perhaps Lane might be privy to less information than Chaucer had hoped. Then he asked a single question: "Did you know they killed my brother tonight?"

Lane shook his head furiously. *No!*

Eyelid flutter, deep swallow, fingers tensing. *A lie.*

Chaucer pulled out the defibrillator and opened it in front of Lane.

"You know what this is, Lane?" Chaucer said as he opened the back panel of the machine and removed a small chip, one that prevented the defibrillator from operating on a healthy heart. Next he charged the machine, and it emitted a high-pitched whine, rising as it acquired more and more power.

Lane paused, considering what his next move should be. He nodded.

"Good. In a person suffering from a cardiac arrest, the heart's electrical activity is all over the place and the heart muscle is no longer pumping so no blood flows. The brain dies quite quickly. This defibrillator shocks the heart into resetting its electrical rhythm back to normal. Do you understand?"

Again, Lane nodded, questions in his eyes.

"But in a healthy heart, it can do the opposite. If one knows what they're doing, it can trigger a dangerous heart rhythm, resulting in cardiac arrest. That's what I'm going to do to you, Lane. You're going to die for me."

Lane was confused. Something didn't add up. Chaucer wasn't even asking him any questions. Which was exactly the point.

Chaucer could see Lane gathering resolve, steeling himself for the battle to come. And so it could not happen on his terms. There were, no doubt, teams searching for them at this very moment. Chaucer put the odds of them realizing the purpose of the missing defib at about one-in-three. And if they did that, there were only so many places Chaucer could be.

No, this had to be an abbreviated interrogation. Chaucer used the paramedic's scissors to cut open Lane's shirt. Lane's eyes bulged. He screamed into the duct tape. Two short syllables. Chaucer recognized them immediately. "I'll talk." It wasn't true, of course. It was a stall. Lane wasn't ready yet. But he would be.

Chaucer placed the paddles expertly. One on his right pectoral muscle, below the collar bone, the other at the lower left of his chest, below his armpit. The cold metal made Lane flinch as if he had already been electrocuted. Chaucer silenced Lane's last scream as he depressed the trigger and 200 joules of raw electricity shocked Lane's heart.

Lane's body stiffened and arced up off the gravel floor. A fine sheen of sweat covered every inch of skin. His eyes bulged. An agony unlike anything he had ever experienced ripped through his body.

Chaucer moved up to Lane's face, so he could see him clearly as panic set in. "Lane, you're the lucky one. I gave you the first chance. I have to go now. When I come back, you will have a second chance to tell me everything I want to know. Unless I get my answers before I return. Think about that as you die."

Every statement true, and yet calculated to make Lane think Chaucer had another captive. A misdirection. Chaucer felt a twinge of agony pass up his back, his penance for the near-lie.

Chaucer quickly packed away the paddles, the scissors, and left. In truth, he simply climbed twenty steps to a landing, shut off his cell phone light, and waited for Lane to die.

He waited exactly one minute. There was no chance of brain damage at the one minute mark, but at two minutes it was a possibility. Of course, Lane would not see his absence as a minute long. Chaucer knew all too well how time stretches in certain psychological states. From Lane's perspective, Chaucer had gone and let him die five to ten minutes ago.

"That took a while, Lane. I'm sorry about that."

Lane writhed in agony, his whole body feeling like it was catching fire. Chaucer pulled out the paddles again and gave him a second jolt. A jolt that reset the rhythm of his heart, as it began to start pumping properly again.

Instantly, Lane's body collapsed to the gravel. He had no energy left to fight. Chaucer pulled off the tape over his mouth. "Lane?"

Jonathan Lane, trained case officer of the CIA, started talking. Every secret he ever kept from childhood onwards he revealed to Chaucer in the next twenty minutes. And patient, owl-like Chaucer sat over him, listening to every detail, waiting for the bits of information that mattered.

CHAPTER 17

It was 6:30 a.m., and Roger Atwood had visions of murder on his mind. He heard the crash, the tinkle of glass in the private courtyard garden behind his brownstone on West Ninety-Seventh Street, and he knew what he would find.

A squirrel.

His war with this one particular creature had been an ongoing affair since he moved his family into the brownstone six months earlier. He was a dedicated soldier in this war because Roger Atwood was a birder, and birders, especially urban birders, have strong animosities toward the squirrel species.

The war was a strictly tactical affair. Roger would install a bird feeder, each of which, he was assured, was absolutely squirrel-proof. Then the squirrel would spend night after night on maneuvers and penetration tests until it achieved its objective: the seed cache that was its own personal fall of Berlin.

Roger put on a blue-and-black flannel robe—the early morning was cooler than average for April—and slipped sandals over his bare feet beneath the gray cotton pajamas he wore. He slunk out of his own home onto the back deck in search of the perpetrator that had once again destroyed his bird feeder.

But the enemy awaiting him was not a squirrel.

Sitting on Roger's bench, next to the gently bubbling bird bath, was Gabriel Asher. Roger blinked hard, clearing the sleep from his eyes, trying to will the apparition away.

But the face of Asher only grew clearer. "Morning, Roger. Sorry to meet like this."

Roger felt foolish in his pajamas, robe, and sandals, but he wouldn't give Asher the satisfaction of seeing that. "What the hell are you doing in my backyard? I mean that in both senses of the word, Asher. Aren't you required to notify the Company if you step stateside?"

Asher waved a hand through the air between them. "Gabriel Asher's still in Mexico. I'm Theo Reynolds today."

Roger assessed the man on his bench. Asher always had an air of dilettante about him, the idle rich amused by mere mortals. Today was no different. "Here for the summit? You're a little late if you've just arrived. It ends this afternoon."

Asher put his hands together, as if in prayer. "Sadly, no. I'm doing a small job in town. And I need your help."

"If you think I owe you something, you're mistaken. You'll get no favors from me."

"Bad blood. I get it. But my job? It's your people involved."

"Bullshit."

"Roger. After all these years? You think I'd bullshit you? No. A few of your people contracted a side gig. A freelance job that they made look official. And, well, it went south."

"How far south?"

"Tierra Del Fuego."

Roger paced on his own deck, feeling Asher's eyes on him. "You want official cover for your side gig?"

Asher smiled. "That's exactly what I want. I can't tell you how much that would be appreciated."

Roger shook his head. "I'm the deputy head of station here. If you think I'm going to risk my career to help you—"

"I know it's a big ask, but I'm desperate. You have no idea how life or death this situation is."

Roger was confused. Asher was always so self-possessed. So sure. But now? Here? He was nearly prostrating himself. "Your desperation is not my problem. You seriously thought you could convince me to drag the Agency into your mess? You're delusional."

Asher's hands left their prayer pose. They spread wide as he leaned back on the bench. "I felt I had to try."

Roger detected a half-smile on the man. It unnerved him. "Head out the way you came. And, Asher? Never come to my home again."

Roger turned back toward his home when Asher spoke. "I mentioned my situation was life or death, right?"

Roger spun on his heels. Here it was. Everything so far had been early-game gambits. Here was the game itself. "And?"

"You're gonna do me a huge favor. You're gonna mobilize Agency resources to track down and eliminate Malcolm Chaucer and Tempest MacLaren."

Roger knew the names. He knew them personally. Both were ex-Agency. Both were practically legends. He wondered what they could've done to earn Gabriel Asher's wrath, but he wiped that question from his mind. "And how the fuck do you figure to make that happen?"

"Life. Or death. When the deputy head of New York station falls to an assassin's bullet, I'd suspect the Agency will give Roma anything he needs to find your killers."

Roger felt just the whiff of a breeze sneak down past the collar of his pajama top, chilling his spine. Asher expected him to react. To gasp. To run. To dive for cover.

But Roger knew it was already too late. "You've got a gun on me?"

Asher nodded. "A very talented young lady named Anya Sergeyev. Estonian, but her mother was a Finn, I believe. And you know the Finns and their long rifles. She killed a Korean grad student the other day at nearly point blank range and I promised her a bit more of a challenge this morning."

A crisp snap pierced the quiet of the backyard. Roger felt a sharp and piercing pain in the back of his head.

He glanced down at the birdseed scattered along the ground at his feet as his vision faded to black. His last thought: *At least it will soak up the blood, and tomorrow, the squirrel will feast.*

CHAPTER 18

Tempest MacLaren was pissed. She hid behind the passenger seat of a silver landscaping van that smelled of fertilizer, manure, and bad coffee. She curled a stray strand of red hair behind her ear and willed her wounds to stop hurting. She took a couple grazes and a single through-and-through, nothing but soft tissue. Not a bad outcome from the visit with Captain Quiet. It was the name she had given to the Korean assassin who nearly killed her.

Was he dead? He triggered the grenade she left for him in the kitchen, so he could be. But he was good. She had seen few who could go toe to toe with her for more than a round, and their gunfight? It was way longer than that. Yes, she thought. He had probably survived the encounter.

Amkae. The only word Captain Quiet spoke. He said it when she shot him in the stomach. She knew the meaning. More than a few North Koreans over the years had said it to her. "Bitch." She said it now to the through-and-through on her flank, trying to get it to stop complaining so loudly.

Her wounds didn't listen to her. They ached in a way they never used to. Tempest was in her forties, but she swore her mind and body had lost no more than a single step. Even in her most relaxed state, her mind was vigilant, on the lookout for threats, escape routes, and improvised weapons. Her ten-mile morning run was her body's religion. But her wounds told a different story. Age, the greatest assassin of them all, was coming for her.

But the Korean came to her home, and that simply could not be forgiven. If her five-year-old son Tyler had not been with his father—if he had been home when the attack happened—fear gripped her. She immediately shoved it down into the place she buried all her fear, and replaced it with a fresh dose of rage.

She had called her ex, Dennis, and got assurances that nothing out of the ordinary was happening at his place. She had moved heaven and earth to protect Dennis's identity some years back, but when an assassin shows themselves into your living room, it'll give you pause to think whether any of your precautions were worth a damn.

She would probably be dead if someone hadn't called her landline. Who did that? Why? How did they know? The more she thought about it, the more Tempest realized she was truly in the dark, targeted for death for reasons unknown.

This was far from the first time Tempest MacLaren had been under fire. It was far from the first time she had been shot. It was, however, the first time she had been shot in her own home. It felt like a … a violation. In her younger years, Tempest had apartments in various cities—staging pads, for whatever job was next. When she struck out on her own, the apartments were places she bought herself. But staging pads they remained.

She had tried for a more normal life. Her marriage to Chaucer was her first attempt, and despite it going up in flames, several years later she tried again. But it wasn't until her pregnancy, until the birth of her little Tyler, that Tempest realized she wanted something more than a holding pen between jobs. She wanted a sanctuary. She wanted a *home*. And now, everything that word represented was gone. She was out in the cold again.

She adjusted her stance so her legs wouldn't go numb. Through the hole between the passenger seat and the headrest, she watched her target outside the van.

The guy pretending to walk the dog wasn't half bad at his job. All in all, it was a pretty good cover, but the dog gave him up. That was one cold, tired-looking dog. Most dogs look like it's the highlight of their day when out for a walk, but this mutt was over it. The guy had to practically drag the dog down the street to continue his patrol.

The fact that there was an operative patrolling outside the kid's place told her she had guessed right. In reality, there were a number of reasons a Korean assassin might show up at her door, but most of those were the better part of a decade old, and in her experience such angers cooled over that time frame. No, the assassin had something to do with the kid. With that stupid kid who wanted to hire her as protection.

The guy with the dog came close to the van. She knew she could take a shot right from here, but Tempest felt a pressing need for a fistfight to blow off the rage rising inside her. And besides, gunfire in broad daylight was never a good idea, even on a sleepy little side street like this one.

Tempest scanned the street for a third time. No backup. Just one operative on a lonely watch. Whatever was going on, OpFor was stretched thin. *OpFor.* Tempest smiled at the use of the word. Opposing forces. *That's right, motherfuckers. You attacked my home. That's a declaration of war.*

She suddenly realized she was being very ... oppositionally defiant. Despite everything that had happened in the last ten hours, she laughed, then winced as she paid the price.

She considered the guy's dog and ruled him a non-factor. That dog looked like it would run for the nearest warm café if his master would so much as drop the leash. No, she just needed the operative to come a bit closer.

And then providence arrived.

The guy turned and walked right toward Tempest. Walking right along the curb, his path bringing him within inches of Tempest's stolen delivery van. If only the door swung open, she would get a KO without laying a finger on him, but since the door was on rails, she would have to get physical.

Tempest smiled in anticipation as she tensed. The guy arrived. She slid the door open, startling him. Biggest benefit of surprise: the long second of immobilization during the shock reflex. Tempest went for the quick KO. The guy looked up at her as she jumped out of the van, his Adam's apple in full view. Tempest delivered a jab, throwing her shoulders into the punch to guarantee maximum damage. She heard the snap, crackle, pop sounds of a trachea collapse and the operative went down without a sound, even landing quietly on a pile of green garbage bags.

He tried to scream, but found that impossible. And before he could come up with a second idea, Tempest delivered another blow, this time to a small indentation in his temple, just below the hardest skull point, a place Tempest liked to call "Lights out."

The dog made no sound. For the first time since Tempest saw it, its tail wagged. It looked at its unconscious master, then the strange woman, and ran off into the morning light.

The dog walker awoke funny. For most people, it's a slow stirring to consciousness. This one came back with a jolt. Tempest was, of course, expecting a rapid return to consciousness given what she had done, but even she was surprised. The dog walker yelled, but it came out as a muted bleat, due to the duct tape across his mouth. He writhed his entire body, only to find one wrist bound by handcuffs to the steel frame inside the landscaping van, and the other wrist fastened to the cuffs with a plastic zip tie.

She watched him for a minute. It was always better to let them figure out their situation themselves before the questioning began, and Tempest didn't have time for idle questions. She was on a clock. He whipped his head so he was looking forward to where Tempest crouched, watching him. That was her cue.

She moved until she was in front of him, staying in a crouch. His legs were duct-taped together, so him kicking her was pretty much out of the question. Tempest was reasonably happy with her jury-rigged setup.

"Hey buddy. Look, you're just doing your job, right?" She plastered a sympathetic smile on her face. "I don't want you to suffer any more than you do. We're in the same biz. At worst, we're temporary adversaries, right? So that burning in your crotch? Neither of us want that to continue."

His eyes went wide and he screamed again. She watched him realize that the pain and discomfort he was feeling wasn't some byproduct of the attack. This was something planned. This was something that might get a whole lot worse.

"Yeah. I'm not a hundred percent sure about the burning exactly. I'm improvising here, you understand. I smeared this concentrated glyphosate on your junk about three minutes ago. You know this shit? It's the stuff that's in Roundup? Nasty, I'm told. Real evil stuff. Like, in twenty years we'll be looking back at it like it was Agent Orange. Anyway, in concentrated form, it's supposed to give one hell of a chemical burn."

Another scream. Sweat beaded all over the dog walker's skin. Panic was setting in.

"Now, like I said, at best we're temporary adversaries, adversaries who are usually on the same side of things, so I have zero interest in burning your junk off, right? So, in a minute I'm gonna pull off that gag and I want you to tell me four things. One thing is non-negotiable: You gotta tell me if you got another man inside Tajo's apartment, and you gotta make sure I believe you. And then, you gotta tell me three other things I really want to know. I mean, think hard, and make them really good. Because I gotta be honest, I was having a pretty shitty day and then some Korean motherfucker came into my home and tried to kill me. And I got zero idea why, except of course, that it had something to do with Tajo, who I should add, I barely know. So among the things you could tell me that I'd find real good would be: who ordered the hit on me, why they did that, and what the ever-living fuck is going on? Got it?"

Rivulets of sweat poured down his cheeks. The glyphosate

must've been really working its magic. He nodded. Tempest held up a small plastic jug. "And if you do that, if you really tell me four things I want to know, I'll cut one hand loose and I'll give you this big jug of aloe vera. It'll probably stop the burn, you'll save your junk, I'll learn what I need to know—a real Hollywood happy ending. So, what do you think? You got my four things?"

He didn't nod instantly. She could see him racking his brain, trying to be sure he could deliver. His eyes never left the jar in her left hand. Thirty seconds later, he nodded. She put the jar down and leaned forward to remove the duct tape over his mouth. "Okay, here it is. Your one shot. I don't need to tell you to speak quietly, do I?"

He shook his head vigorously, no. She ripped the tape off. And the dog walker spoke. Quietly. Intently. Quickly. "It's just me. There's nobody inside. This is a Company job. I work for Vincent Roma. This Tajo, you assassinated him the other day and he's connected to people who want you dead—"

Tempest didn't let him finish. "Tajo's dead?" The dog walker nodded. "And you—the Company—think I killed him?" Another nod. "Why the fuck would they think that?"

"There was an interrogation. An eyewitness fingered you as the shooter."

Tempest felt her anger growing. "And you assholes believed that?"

The dog walker could see her anger growing. He grew scared. "It was the Oracle. the Oracle did the interrogation. The guy's never wrong. Never."

Tempest felt her whole world shift. Malcolm fucking Chaucer. How the fuck did this happen? How the fuck could Malcolm fucking Chaucer be wrong?

The dog walker spoke up. "Um ... was that ... four things?"

Tempest looked back down at the guy. His shirt was already soaked in sweat. "Yeah. You did good. Now, you gotta wait fifteen minutes before you start yelling, or I'll have to come back in here and shoot you, and neither of us want that, do we?"

The dog walker nodded. Tempest pulled out a karambit, a short curved knife that she loved like it was her second child. She advanced on the dog walker, who suddenly squirmed in terror. She moved behind him, cut the zip tie, freeing his left hand, and then she handed him the jar of aloe vera.

As she exited the landscaping van, she saw him take a huge handful of the stuff and shove it down his pants.

———

Tempest entered Tajo's apartment and found it empty, as promised. She looked around and quickly realized the futility of her plan. An man outside meant they'd already been in here. They'd surely gone over the place with a thoroughness she couldn't hope to match.

Tempest surveyed the minimalist one-bedroom apartment. It looked as sparse as most grad students' places, but the few items Tajo had were all quality—the mark of a rich kid.

The place was sanitized. Everything was in that not-quite-clean, not-quite-messy state that had the appearance of unstaged reality, and yet screamed to Tempest "arranged." Everything in this room had been photographed and sent to analysts in some well-ventilated room where Ivy Leaguers would work shifts studying it all, looking for anything trained specialists might miss. Tempest had no facility for this aspect of the trade. She would miss more than most. *So what are you doing here, Tempest? And how does Chaucer fit into this mess?*

All the usual hiding places would have been gone over by now. The water tank in the toilet, behind the heating grates, in the back of the freezer. The sweep team simply would have taken anything incriminating. But there was one hope. Tempest met the kid right here, three weeks ago. And even though the paranoid little shit wouldn't tell her why he contacted her, she did learn something in their time together.

The Year of the Rabbit. He said it was happening, and he needed protection. She told him that wasn't what she did. He said … She didn't exactly remember what he said. She mostly came to find out how the little shit got her number. He wouldn't say. He wouldn't say a lot.

Tempest got the sense the kid was scared. But also excited. He said he was being followed. He thought someone had tapped his phone. She asked him to describe who was following him, and he frowned at her. He said it was a different person every day.

This part—this part, she remembered. She asked him, if one of those people were in his flat, what wouldn't he want them to see? His eyes went right to his desk. And not just the desk. Tempest was pretty sure he had been looking at a red flier with a Korean symbol on it sitting on the top.

But searching the entire apartment did not turn up that symbol. Tempest felt strangely impotent, a feeling she neither relished nor knew much about. She had already burned fifteen minutes in the apartment. She was pushing it. Sleeping Beauty had probably missed a check-in already. A response team could be on their way. Or they could be right outside the kid's door.

Why didn't you listen to the little shit? He needed your help.

Tempest took the back way out, passing through the building's basement laundry room and heading for the casement window leading to a narrow alley behind the building.

Tempest froze before she reached the window. Above the washers was a bulletin board. On it: a notice mentioning there would be no hot water between ten and three on Tuesday, fliers advertising nannies and seeking bassists, and a red flier consisting entirely of Korean characters, arranged vertically. And in the center of the flier, bigger than the others, was the symbol Tajo was looking at. The one thing he wouldn't want the enemy to see.

CHAPTER 19

Chaucer stuffed himself into an archaic phone booth on the lower level of a midtown shopping mall and hooked up his phone again. He called Fitz. Fitz picked up on the first ring. *Not good*, thought Chaucer. It meant Fitz was on high alert. At least the trace light didn't illuminate.

"Chaucer? What the hell happened? The station said you were a no-show." There was a tremble in the voice. A pitch shift that indicated extreme stress.

"It was a setup," Chaucer said. "The meet. The interrogation. Everything."

"What? The interrogation?"

"Fake. They took a trained CIA impersonator, drugged her to the gills so I couldn't get my normal reads, and fed me disinformation."

Fitz sounded even weaker. "How do you know all this?"

"I saw her exiting the CIA station, just two hours before I was due to report. And I may have questioned one of them."

"One of them?"

"Lane. He was there, in the room. He knew the impostor's name. Miranda Ross. She went through the Farm with him a few years back."

"They're all CIA?"

"So far as Lane knew. And there was something else. The assassin who killed the Korean kid? They left a note: 'The Year of the Rabbit is coming.' Whatever the hell that means."

"Somebody tried to kill Tempest last night as well," Fitz said. "Is she mixed up in this?"

"I can't talk about it."

"Damnit, Chaucer, they played you. It wasn't a real interrogation. You don't have to protect their secrets."

Chaucer knew he was right. But he had a hard time talking about the interrogation, nonetheless. Old habits. "The impostor IDed Tempest as the shooter. I served her up on a plate."

"Year of the Rabbit. When even is that?"

Chaucer said, "The next Year of the Rabbit's in four years. Hardly urgent."

"Maybe it means something else?"

"Likely, but it's not really menacing. The rabbit in Chinese and Korean culture represents elegance, nobility, good fortune."

There was a long pause on the line. Chaucer could hear Fitz breathing. *Stress. Increasing.* Suddenly Fitz blurted out, "Shit, Chaucer, I just got an alert. Somebody's put a broadcast bounty on the Ghost Board."

Chaucer reeled as if hit by a phantom punch. The Ghost Board had existed since the first days of the internet. In the early days, it was a dial-in bulletin board where operatives could pick up work outside of official channels. With the rise of freelance spying in the modern era, the need for the Ghost Board only grew.

It was a hidden, electronic job board. To the untrained eye, it would look like any of a million obscure fan websites with an active forum dedicated to that niche. The board floated, so one month it would be poodle fanciers, the next it would be fans of Italian horror movies. But encoded in the seemingly harmless forums would be handlers seeking operatives, operatives seeking handlers, and every other form of connection in the business.

Chaucer asked, "How much is the bounty?"

"Don't. There's no point in knowing that."

Big, then. "I need to know. It's threat assessment."

Fitz said, "It's a million dollars, Chaucer. Somebody's paying a million dollars for your scalp. Tempest too."

A million-dollar lottery ticket on the Ghost Board, broadcast, all applicants welcome. Paid to the first man or woman to bring down Chaucer, dead or alive. And this week, with the UN Summit crowd in town, ten thousand people minimum had that lottery ticket.

Chaucer needed to be gone. Now. Yesterday. No place in the city was safe. "You're saying I need to run."

Fitz sighed. "I'm saying you shouldn't still be on the phone. All hell is after you, Mal. Give me an hour to come up with an exfil strategy for you."

Suddenly, the red trace light ignited. Chaucer stared at it, confused. "Are you tracing me, Fitz?"

"Me? No. Why—? … Wait, wait … No, no!"

Suddenly, the sound of an explosion battered Chaucer's eardrum, and the line went dead.

CHAPTER 20

"Homicide," Spinoza barked into the receiver.

"It's me."

Spinoza straightened up in her chair. "Yeah?"

"Are they still there?"

"No. They questioned us for six hours, then let us go, just in time to punch in."

"And you did as I said?"

"Yeah. We kept it straight, except for the Mug."

"Good. I need him."

Spinoza scratched her forehead with the eraser from a pencil at her desk. "Manny? You're telling me you need Manny?"

"I'm blown. I'm worse than blown. I need to disappear, and I need Manny to help me."

Spinoza thought about it for a minute. Chaucer never asked for help. Chaucer never asked for anything. Whatever trouble he was in, it must have been really bad. Of course it was. It killed Terry. The question was, should she help the man who got Terry killed?

In truth, Spinoza always liked Chaucer. He was a weird dude, there was no question about that, but he seemed harmless beneath the harsh exterior. No, Terry died as collateral damage. To blame Chaucer would be finding a scapegoat.

"Where and when?"

Manny sat on the narrow metal bench of the bus shelter, playing with the strings of his hoodie. He would pull one side down, watching the other side rise. Then he would reverse the process. Chaucer watched him for a good five minutes. It was a gamble to contact him, but Chaucer had no one else to go to. He rolled the dice that the opposition wouldn't have the resources to tap the entire precinct's phones. Or at least not yet.

When Chaucer accepted that if Manny was being watched, he would likely never spot it, he made his move. He crossed the street. Manny marked him at the double yellow lines, pulling down on both sides of the string, tightening his gray hoodie around his head, like a turtle retreating into its shell.

"Hi Manny."

"H-hi."

"Come on, Manny. I need your help."

Manny popped up off the bench, ready to follow Bad Chaucer anywhere he wanted to go.

They walked just one block to a shaded, empty courtyard with a bank of vending machines. The courtyard looked out on a gargantuan post office. The central Manhattan branch. It was an imposing neo-classical structure: a row of thick columns forty feet high; themselves sitting atop twenty white marble steps that spanned the entire block.

It was quitting time. Around three dozen office workers sat on the steps, waiting for friends, dates, and roommates to join them.

"Manny, I have a safe-deposit box in that building. There are many important things in there that I need. But the bad people may know that I have a box there. I need you to look at all the people over there and tell me if there are any bad people."

Manny looked over at Chaucer. "Terry is dead, isn't he? Nobody will talk to me."

Chaucer looked into Manny's innocent eyes. He honestly didn't know. "My brother died last night."

"Some people fall down when they get shot. But some people, when they get shot … they get back up. I wanted Terry to get back up."

Chaucer could see Manny was processing this, mourning Terry in his own way. Chaucer ducked into the shadows as a large group of financiers moved past. That damn broadcast bounty—he could be picked up any minute. That's why he needed Manny to focus.

"Manny? The bad people?"

Manny moved over to the fern planter, concentrating on the scene across the street. "Jamal Anjou, possession with intent to distribute."

"No, not him."

"Anthony Ferraro: cocaine possession."

"No."

"Lawrence Zales: marijuana possession and DUI."

"Manny, how about only the bad people like me? You know? Not drugs?"

Manny concentrated harder, squinting to make out all the faces in front of him. He opened his mouth to speak, then shut it.

Chaucer knew he saw something. "What Manny?"

"I almost made a mistake."

"What mistake?"

"I thought I saw a bad person, but he's not."

No evasion. No concealment. Manny was telling the truth.

Manny looked back at Chaucer. "No. No bad people like you."

"This is very important, Manny. Are you sure?"

"Yes, I'm sure."

The relief washed over Chaucer. In that safe-deposit box were multiple new identities and fifty thousand dollars in cash. Once he got that, he had a fighting chance.

"Thank you, Manny. Thank you very much."

"Are you going to be a postman?"

Chaucer nearly laughed. Must be wonderful to be in Manny's world. A man going to a post office. Maybe he'll become a postal worker. "No, Manny. People like me don't become postmen."

Manny was already walking away. "Yes, they do. Edward Christensen did."

Chaucer froze. It struck him that he was missing something. "Manny?"

Manny turned back around, engrossed once again in his hoodie string.

"Who is Edward Christensen?"

"Edward Christensen: breaking and entering, carrying forged documents, possession of an illegal weapon modification. All charges dropped."

The hairs on the back of Chaucer's neck rose. "Where is Edward Christensen, Manny?"

"He's right behind you."

CHAPTER 21

Chaucer turned just in time to see the postman make his move. As his hand reached into his letter-carrier's satchel, it dropped a five-dollar-bill. Chaucer realized Christensen was caught as flat-footed as he was. He had simply come over for a coffee from the vending machine behind Chaucer and had recognized Chaucer just as Chaucer recognized him. And he was too close.

Chaucer raised his right foot and stomped down at the satchel. The gun inside, a submachine gun by the heft of it, stayed inside. And as Chaucer kicked down, it threw Christensen to the ground, dragged down by the strap around his neck.

But Christensen wasn't through. He turned his momentum into a roll, scissoring his legs up and around Chaucer's torso, pulling him to the ground as well.

Manny stood motionless, paralyzed with fear.

Christensen was fast, strong. He knew grappling. He had already moved into position behind Chaucer, going for an arm bar, a submission hold designed to cause maximum pain and immobility. In an MMA tourney, it would result in a quick tap out.

But this was not an MMA tourney. This was to the death. And Chaucer was no normal opponent.

Christensen overpowered Chaucer's defense and applied the arm bar expertly, twisting and pushing until tendons strained to their breaking points.

Agony. Total agony washed over Chaucer. Not pain. Pain is a highly undesirable data input for the human body. Pain is something a body and mind responds to. Agony is something else entirely. Agony is the capitulation of the psyche to the intolerable.

For anyone but Chaucer, that was true. Agony was an old companion for him. Agony was a walk in the park.

He turned toward Christensen. He could see it in Christensen's eyes. How is this guy moving? Why hasn't he given up? Christensen tightened the arm bar. Chaucer's elbow was nearly out of its socket. But still he turned toward Christensen.

He just needed to see where he was striking. Christensen realized the same, just as Chaucer made his move. He lashed out with his free thumb, going right for Christensen's neck nerve cluster.

Christensen responded with a head butt. Hard, fast, effective. Chaucer may have been somewhat immune to agony, but a forehead to the nose has certain unavoidable physical symptoms. Chaucer's vision tunneled. He was losing consciousness. He was going to die. So Chaucer did the last thing he could. He went for one last nerve strike.

His vision went black before he could know if it worked.

"Mr. Chaucer. Mr. Chaucer. Mr. Chaucer. Mr. Chaucer." It was less a conversation than a mantra. Chaucer came to, staring up at Manny hovering over him, fear and panic in his eyes.

"I'm okay, Manny. I'm okay."

"I thought he was good. I thought—"

"I understand, Manny. Can you help me get him off me?"

Manny gingerly reached for Christensen's limbs, pushing them away. The man was out cold. Chaucer glanced around the courtyard. It was still empty. No witnesses.

"I'm sorry. I'm sorry."

Chaucer freed his arm, somehow both numb and throbbing in pain at once. He would have limited use of it for a few days. But he was alive. Christensen lost. It was the second fight against trained operators that Chaucer had survived that day. The odds of a third success were longer than that wall in China. The safe-deposit box was out of the question. Christensen would undoubtedly have backup. They'd be looking for him any minute. It was time to get scarce.

Chaucer grabbed his mail-carrier's satchel. Inside he saw an MP5 with mounted suppressor, and a SIG Sauer P226 lying in the bottom. He left the submachine gun and took the pistol, stowing it in his waistband after checking to see that there was a bullet in the pipe. He grabbed three spare ammo mags as well, fully loaded.

"I'm sorry." Manny trembled visibly. Chaucer couldn't hope to follow his thinking, but Manny somehow thought this was his fault.

"It's okay, Manny. You helped me. Understand? You helped me. Everything's going to be okay now." It was a true statement, as it had to be for Malcolm Chaucer. But it was only the truth for Manny.

For Chaucer, he had to face the fact that all of his drops were compromised. He had no money, no alternative ID, no resources to speak of, and an army out there looking for him. He needed help, but everyone he could call had a million reasons to turn him in.

And Tempest was in the same boat.

Tempest. If anybody could survive this, it was her. If anybody might know what the hell was going on, it was her. He needed to find her, and that was not gonna be easy.

Chaucer was gonna need a little backup.

CHAPTER 22

Hunts Point was changing. A lonely peninsula to nowhere, Hunts Point had been the epicenter of the narcotics and streetwalker professions for decades. Now it was showing signs of life. A massive produce market and fish market brought badly needed jobs to the area, and that made all the difference.

But traces of the old Hunts Point remained, and it was his search of those traces that brought Chaucer here. Manny pulled his hood tight around his face, so only his eyes and nose peeked out. "Why are we here?"

Manny was a book of tells, all of them fearful. Chaucer said, "We're here to find a bad man. But a particular kind of bad man."

Manny looked up at Chaucer. "This is where the bad men are?"

"No, Manny. Bad men are everywhere. But in other places, the bad men can hide better, and we would never know about them."

As Chaucer led him past truck repair shops, machinists, and bodegas, Manny's nervous tics multiplied.

"It's okay, Manny. I'm here with you."

Manny nodded, but his eyes kept darting to and fro. Chaucer

realized what was happening. He was clocking everyone in the neighborhood, and more than a few he recognized. People with long criminal records. Manny was scared.

"Do you want something to drink? A soda?"

Manny looked up at Chaucer, hopefully. "Cherry Coke."

Chaucer headed for the nearest bodega when two young men entered first: one skinny and pale, one broad-shouldered and tatted. Manny tugged on Chaucer's shirt.

"No. No Cherry Coke."

Manny's nervousness was clearly spiking, but getting a read beyond that was impossible. He shrugged and kept walking down the street. "I need you to find me someone specific, Manny. Someone suspected of murder, more than once but never convicted."

Just then, a gunshot rang out. Chaucer spun in time to see the two young men running from the bodega and fleeing to the north.

Chaucer looked at Manny. "Did you know—?"

Manny stared at the ground and swayed rhythmically. "Clay McDermott, Benny Sykes. Armed robbery, armed robbery."

Someone screamed back in the store's direction. Chaucer marveled at how useful Manny was turning out to be. "Okay ... like I was saying, we need to find—"

"A murderer."

"No, Manny."

"No convictions. A murder suspect with no convictions. Why?"

Chaucer wasn't ready for this. "What?"

"Why?"

Chaucer thought a moment about how to answer. "Because most murderers aren't smart. Most murderers just have bad impulse control. I need someone who can kill, but has very good impulse control. I need a smart murderer."

"Albert Farr."

"What?"

Manny extended a thin finger and pointed at the man

111

crossing the street. Albert Farr was Black, early thirties, wearing gray wool pants and a slightly wrinkled white dress shirt. He appeared lost in thought, and those thoughts didn't seem to be happy. He was a man having a bad day.

"Tell me about him."

Manny bit his lip and inhaled through his nose, "Albert Farr. Three arrests. 2014: suspicion of murder. 2014: suspicion of murder. 2014: suspicion of murder. Released in all cases with no charges filed."

Perfect, thought Chaucer. Mr. Farr was a killer. A killer who knows how to get away with it.

"You can go, Manny. Do you need me to walk you to the—?"

Manny was already gone, hustling down the street somewhere between a power walk and a low jog, making a beeline for the subway stop six blocks away.

———

Chaucer approached Albert Farr carefully. He shadowed him, falling in behind him and to his left, remembering bits and pieces of tradecraft. Keeping good distance, watching for changes in direction or behavior, blending into his surroundings.

Albert Farr entered a coffee shop on the far corner of the intersection. When Chaucer reached it, he saw it was well lit and clean, but aging. The décor was Greek, but there wasn't a Greek to be seen behind the counters. Central American, Chaucer guessed, assessing the waitstaff and manager.

Albert looked tired. He walked up to the long Formica counter and sat down. A motherly Guatemalan server with a warm smile nodded to him, and a steaming cup of coffee, black, appeared in front of him in seconds. Another sweep of her arm and three packets of Splenda appeared there as well.

Albert Farr was a regular here.

Chaucer sat down on the next stool over. Albert shifted on his seat, glancing left and right at the many empty chairs at the counter. He didn't make eye contact with Chaucer, but he was clearly perturbed that someone chose to crowd him.

"Albert, I'm wondering if you might be interested in a job."

Albert turned, suspicion on his face. "I know you?"

"No. My name is Chaucer, and I need a special kind of help today."

Albert blew on his coffee, taking this in slowly. He only looked at Chaucer out of the corner of his eye, not sure he wanted to engage with this stranger. "What kind of help?"

"There are people trying to kill me. There are a lot of them, and they're very good at it, and when they come for me, it's likely I'll never see it coming. So I need an X factor. An ace up my sleeve, so to speak."

Albert stared at Chaucer with both eyes, trying to suss out exactly how crazy this unwanted visitor was. "Why are people trying to kill you?"

"I don't know. That's my job. Find out who and why. Keeping me alive long enough to learn that information, that would be your job. If you're up for the challenge. I would estimate the job will last twenty-four to forty-eight hours and I will pay five thousand dollars a day."

Squint. Hard swallow. Jaw tension. *Interest. Suspicion.* "Why me?"

"Because you're a killer, Albert. And because the people gunning for me will never see you coming."

Albert stands up abruptly. "You got the wrong guy—"

Chaucer put his hand on Albert's wrist. Albert's eyes went right to it. A confrontation was building. "No, I don't. You are Albert Farr. In 2014, you killed three people, and you got away with it. I am not in any way connected with anyone who wishes you harm. I am exactly what I said, a man who needs someone who could kill if they had to, and who is smart enough to do it well."

"Bullshit. How'd you know who I am?"

"I have a friend with a photographic memory."

"Bullshit. You're a cop."

Albert stepped away from the counter. Decision time. He pulled his wrist away from Chaucer's hand. Chaucer rose and twisted, putting Albert Farr in a simple arm bar, sending his head slamming to the Formica. He swiftly drew the pistol he took off Christensen and put it between Albert's eyes.

The diner's patrons and waitstaff froze. Several people in the booths near the door bolted outside. Police would be along, but being that this was the Point, they wouldn't be here too soon.

"I'm not a cop, Albert. Do you see this pistol aimed at you?"

"Y-yeah. Yeah!"

"Do you see the barrel extension on the end of it?"

"Yeah!"

"Can you tell me what that is?"

"S-silencer! It's a silencer."

Chaucer kept his eyes on the patrons, fixing them with his gaze, keeping control of the room. "A suppressor, that's right, Albert. Now, have you ever seen a cop with a silencer?"

"No."

"Who uses them?"

"I don't know ... mafia ... spies."

"Do you think a spy would give a damn about what you may or may not have done in the past?"

"I don't—no, no."

"Good." Chaucer leaned in for this last part, speaking quietly. "I am exactly what I have said: a man offering you a job. I can get you a thousand up front. If you are in, I will be at the Columbus Circle subway newsstand, the one right by the B and D trains, in one hour. Goodbye, Albert."

Chaucer released the arm bar, stowed the gun, and swiftly exited the coffee shop. No one made the slightest move to impede or follow him. In Hunts Point, people had their own problems.

CHAPTER 23

Fifty-eight minutes later, Albert Farr came looking for Chaucer. He had his hands in his pockets, shoulders hunched, looking furtively for anyone else who might be here to surprise him. When he saw nothing out of the ordinary, he approached.

"I'm not who you think I am."

Chaucer replied, "Could you shoot a man in cold blood if you had to?"

"Bad guys?"

Bad people. First Fitz, then Manny, now Albert Farr. Must be something in the air. "Yes, Albert, they will most certainly be bad guys."

"Then yeah. I can do that. You really a spy?"

"Step into my office."

Chaucer led him down a narrow corridor beside the newsstand and through a propped-open door marked "DOT Access Only". On the other side, a long access tunnel. At the first branch, Chaucer turned left and opened the door at the dead end of that tunnel.

He led Albert into a small, windowless room. A row of ancient CRT monitors sat above a simple metal table, showing washed-out security camera views of the labyrinth that was the

Columbus Circle subway junction. Albert looked around. "What is this place?"

"Used to be a security post until New York got its 9/11 Homeland Security money. The new security office is a wonder to behold. And this? Pretty much a forgotten relic. Now is the time to ask any questions if you've got 'em."

Albert took a moment, letting the questions pile up. "How exactly do you become a spy?"

It reminded Chaucer of an Agency joke. "Test smart, then make horrible life choices."

"I'm smart."

"That's why I chose you, Albert."

"So I'd be, like, a spy?"

"Of a sort. You'd be my protection."

"How would it work?"

"You'd be following me. About a half block behind me. If we're on a subway, you're at the far end of the car."

"You want to pay me to follow you?"

"You'll have a gun. You'll be watching. If anyone tries to kill or capture me, you will move on them and kill them first."

"Is that all?" Albert's words dripped with sarcasm.

"It's not. The people you will be shooting are trained killers. But they will most likely not see you coming. Everything they're trained to look for, you're not."

Shame. Anger. "That an insult?"

"It's a fact. Your walk, your demeanor, everything about you rules you out as a threat, at least in the category they're trained to look for. But you are a threat today. And when you make your move, if you ever have to, you need to use three bullets on each person you shoot. Two center mass in the torso. One in the head. Always. Repeat it, please."

"What?"

"Repeat what I just said."

"You're kidding, right?"

Chaucer stared at Albert. He was sweating. Pulse visibly

pounding at the neck. Pupils open wide. He was scared. *Good. This should give him pause. It means he's not a psycho.*

Albert quickly withered under his gaze. "Three shots. One to the head, two to the chest."

"No. Two to the torso. One to the head. That order. Can you tell me why?"

Albert struggled. "Look, man, I got turned down for a mall security-guard job today. That's how bad things are out there. So, do me a favor and just tell me what I need to know. I'm a fast learner. I'm just not in the mood for another interview."

Chaucer nodded. "It's because your adrenaline will jack your nervous system. You're aiming for the torso because it's big. If you put two slugs in that direction, you will probably hit something at least once. You're hitting them center mass with a P226. Even suppressed, it's got some good stopping power. It should knock them down. But most operatives these days wear some form of body armor, so they're a few seconds away from returning fire. So you put one bullet where they have no armor. The head."

Albert looked away from Chaucer. Chaucer knew he didn't want to visualize doing the deed. Albert said, "That's it? That's the job?"

"That's the job."

Albert bit his bottom lip. "Stomach cancer."

Chaucer didn't follow. "Beg your pardon."

"My uncle, kinda the man who raised me. He's got stomach cancer. Spends his days in agony. There are things they can do for him, but only if you're rich. That's the only reason I'm doing this."

Chaucer knew now he picked the right guy. He needed justification, and he had it. "That's comforting to know."

"You got any idea what those meds cost? You want me for this? The price has gotta be ten grand a day. Half up front."

Chaucer frowned. "I can only get whatever the ATM maximum is, but I can show you the account has plenty to pay for your services. Is that acceptable?" Albert considered it a moment, then nodded. Chaucer continued, "Good. I've been meaning to gauge our opposition anyway."

Chaucer withdrew a thousand dollars from the ATM beside the newsstand in the Columbus Circle subway labyrinth. He would've withdrawn more if he could, but that happened to be the limit for this ATM's transaction. Chaucer then got the receipt and checked his watch.

He retreated to the abandoned security post where he handed Albert the thousand-dollar stack, the receipt showing a six-figure balance remaining, and Christensen's pistol and silencer combo. Albert handled the gun gingerly, turning it over in his large hands, taking it all in.

"You know how to use it?"

In answer, Albert racked the chamber, checking that a round was in the pipe. "No. How?"

Chaucer smiled. Albert had a sense of humor.

"Mind if I ask you a few questions?" said Albert.

Chaucer nodded and turned his stare to the monitors, glancing down at his watch. One minute since he put his card into the ATM.

"So you're some kind of spy?"

"I'm an interrogator."

"And you work for the CIA?"

"Once. Now I'm freelance."

"Freelance spy? There's such a thing?"

"Did you know for the last eight years of the Afghan war, there were more private contractors in Afghanistan than regular army? The same thing is happening in the espionage community."

"And these people who may be coming for you? Who are they? Who wants you dead?"

"That's what I'd very much like to figure out."

"Good, 'cause if it turned out I was killing CIA agents—"

"Oh, that's what you're asking. Yes. You will probably be killing CIA operatives. Or the operatives of a foreign government." Chaucer checked his watch. Two minutes.

Albert blanched at the prospect. "Wait, what?"

And then they appeared. They swarmed onto every monitor, seemingly simultaneously. Dozens of operatives. Chaucer watched as, in seconds, they secured exits and shut down every train in the station.

Two minutes and ten seconds. An insane response time. They had to have rovers operating, roaming response units in several sections of the city, ready to pounce at a moment's notice. And the sheer number of operatives. There had to be at least ten or twelve locking down the station. Multiple rovers with a dozen plus men each. This was no small-scale operation. These guys were loaded for bear.

Chaucer pointed them out to Albert. "Them. You may kill a handful of them. But don't worry. Now that you've talked to me, it will be self-defense. Because each one of them is going to want you dead as well."

"Oh ... wait, what?"

"Come on, we have to evac. They'll find this place soon enough."

Chaucer calmly left the room and disappeared down the long, narrow tunnel. Albert Farr shook off the shell shock and rushed to follow his new employer.

CHAPTER 24

Asher entered the buzzing room quietly. A dozen operatives paced back and forth in the open bullpen of a former bond-trading firm, now an empty shell waiting for a new occupant. The operatives alternated between their phones and animated arguments with the man in charge. Roma.

In all the commotion, no one noticed Asher. He grabbed a seat at a desk near the wall and took in a mental transcript of events for the next fifteen minutes. For Agency regulars, they weren't doing too bad. Horribly inadequate for the task at hand, but that resulted from the mismatch between their training and the demands of the op.

Roma was clearly out of his element. From his file, Asher knew him to be a political creature, hanging onto his position more by bureaucratic judo than his skills as a field man. The rest of the operatives in the makeshift command center were divided in the usual way: the thinkers and the meat. For a command center, the meat ratio was way too high.

"I want Rovers Three and Four to converge on Columbus Circle, sweeping inward from ten blocks out. Three sweeps north to south. Four sweeps south to north," Roma barked.

Asher stood. It was time. "I wouldn't do that."

Roma spun, pinning Asher with his furious stare. "And who the fuck are you?!"

"I'm Quilted Pampers. I'm here to clean up your mess, and keep it off Mommy and Daddy's hands."

Roma was incensed. "Get out of my command center before I kick your ass."

Asher checked his watch. He ignored Roma, addressing, instead, the rest of the room. "As of 4:15 p.m., I am assuming total operational control—"

Roma yelled, "The fuck you are!"

Asher pressed a button on the cell phone in his hand. He tossed it at Roma, who caught it out of the air. "Answer it."

Roma was confused, but he put the phone to his ear. "Yeah."

He said nothing else. He just listened for a minute, his anger slowly turning to confusion, then resignation. He hung up the phone without saying another word.

"Everyone, this man has operational control. Give him your attention. Give him your best."

"Thank you, Roma. All right. We've already made enough mistakes to sink this op, so we have to move fast. My name is Gabriel Asher."

A shudder went through the room. All of them had heard of Gabriel Asher. The name filled them with a mixture of hope and fear. Gabriel Asher was used to that reaction.

"First, call off the rovers."

Roma didn't understand what was happening. "Chaucer was at Columbus Circle fifteen minutes ago. We locked it down two minutes later. We got him. You pull those rovers and he could get away."

Asher smiled broadly. "So you're telling me that the Oracle withdrew money from an ATM without knowing *exactly* what our response would be?"

"What do we care why he did it? He did it! We know where he is!"

"We know where he *was*. He was ready for us. He was counting on it."

Roma stuttered. "Why? Why would he risk exposure?"

Asher took a deep breath. This one would take patience. "Let's see. First, he got a thousand dollars. That's useful to him. Second, he got a look at our response. He timed it. He likely counted men, estimated his opposition forces. By taking the bait, you've told him nearly everything about the level and scope of this operation. And if you give him a look at two more rovers, you might as well just email him the dossiers of everyone on this op."

Roma had no response. He stood there, trembling slightly with anger and shame, but he couldn't find a single fault in Asher's logic.

"Mistakes, one and all. Those end right now. Your training will not help you through this one. You are offensive weapons. They trained you to take the initiative, to generate plots, to manipulate assets. And what training did you get for when it all went down in flames? Did you get any training beyond evidence destruction and extraction? No."

Asher looked around the room. Every eye was on him, waiting for his next pronouncement. He had them right where he wanted them. "Okay, now what is this operation's cover?"

All eyes turned to Roma. "Training op. An exercise finding a rogue operative in a target-rich environment."

"Incorrect. We are hunting the assassin and accomplice responsible for the death of Roger Atwood."

A murmur went through the room. Confusion. Roma took the bait. "Roger Atwood? Deputy head of New York station? One problem. Atwood isn't dead. I talked to him last night."

Asher smiled. "Then you may have shared his last conversation. Atwood died early this morning. Everything you've done today has been in the valiant search for his killer. The CIA takes care of its own."

Shock. Awe. Roma sat down. "What happened?"

"I thought that was obvious. The Widowmaker killed him with a long-range rifle shot."

Roma tried to wrap his head around what Asher was saying. "The Widowmaker?"

"That's the official report. When a committee ends up looking into this, they'll tie it into the murder of Tajo. It'll look like an ex-asset lost it. Settled unknowable scores."

"You're insane." Roma felt all control slipping away. He was on the verge of panic.

"Listen to me, people. A few of you may be under the illusion that this is a sanctioned op. It is not. You are freelancers, cleaning up a busted rogue op. Every crime you commit here, you are completely exposed to. So I'm reading you in. Giving you the big picture."

He saw it in their eyes. Fear. They were in deeper than they could imagine. Asher spoke calmly, matter-of-factly, "I'm trying to give this op official cover. To fold it into Company business. Whether or not that works will depend on your actions over the next hours. If we plug these leaks fast enough, you'll be free and clear. If this problem lingers, not only will the op not stand scrutiny, but the people funding the actual operation will likely kill you all to cover their own tracks."

Asher paused a moment, letting it all sink in. The activity in the room stopped altogether. He had their complete attention. "That's the bad news. Now for the worse news. In order to save your asses, you have to capture or kill a top-level asset and a support specialist. The asset, Tempest MacLaren, is generally considered an even match for a small army. The specialist, Malcolm Chaucer, is not. He's extremely smart both tactically and strategically, but it's been years since his case officer days. His toolbox is rusty. It is our job to find him before he cleans off that rust."

Asher moved over to the large whiteboard in the front of the room. He wrote three words. "Our targets are on the run. When a person is on the run, they take on one of three aspects: The rabbit, the rat, or the cat. The rabbit runs, trying to get maximum distance between itself and its pursuers, but it risks maximum exposure at exactly the time when the opposition is concentrated fully on its capture. Rabbits get caught first. Now, the rat chooses the opposite tactic. The rat burrows. It finds the deepest, darkest hole it can find and waits the opposition out. Tactically sound, but these are the days of electronic surveillance nets and fast-response teams. Rest assured, most of the time, when that rat peeks its head out in the open, it goes down just like the rabbit. Which leaves us with the cat."

Asher poured himself a cup of coffee, sniffing it. He dropped it right in the trash. "Somebody here know where to get good beans nearby?" He looked at the assembled operatives hanging on his every word. One Pakistani woman in the back raised a hand. "Good. You keep this room supplied with good coffee and you get a ten percent performance bonus, got me?"

She nodded. Finally, Roma couldn't take the suspense. "So? What's the cat do?"

"Near as I can figure? Eat, shit, and shed." Asher waited for it. No one laughed. "It's a joke, people. You gotta lighten up if we're gonna get through this. The cat starts off like the rat, going to ground, burrowing, finding a spot to hide. But the kitty doesn't wait long. It waits just long enough for you to overpursue, and once you're past her, with your back exposed, the cat strikes. She hits hard, carves you up, sows confusion, and then she escapes."

Asher grabbed a container of non-dairy creamer and tossed it in the trash as well. "The Widowmaker we have a lot of information on. We have reports of her under threat of pursuit. I have logged her responses in the field. Tempest MacLaren is a rat. She burrows and waits. The Oracle, on the other hand, we have next to no information on—except for what he has already shown us in our one day of pursuit. Ladies and gentlemen, Malcolm Chaucer is a cat. The baddest kitty you're ever gonna see. In the last twenty-four hours he's ambushed an ambush team, captured and interrogated one of your men, and has gotten a comprehensive look at your operation in terms of scope and response. In layman's terms, thus far Malcolm Chaucer has kicked your ass."

Asher took a printout picture of Tempest and attached it with a magnet to the whiteboard, right next to the word "RAT." He took another with Chaucer's picture and attached it next to "CAT" before turning to face the assembled operatives. "Which leaves us with the rabbit. I am now going to divulge to you the operational details of our hunt. Since all your necks are on the line, you might as well know why."

The room went dead silent. Asher knew they were hanging on his every word. "The Year of the Rabbit. In 2011, Kim Jong Il died of a massive heart attack. He was seventy. It was sudden, but it wasn't like there wasn't a succession plan in place. He had six kids. He sure as hell better have had a clear succession plan. But the country was in year twelve of a brutal famine, and two years after a devastating attempt at currency devaluation, there were more than a handful of Party leaders who had a different succession in mind."

Asher grabbed a water bottle. "The commanders of the Korean People's Army realized that the hardliners in Pyongyang could lose control of the situation. So they came up with a contingency plan: The Year of the Rabbit. It was a military coup of North Korea, should the wrong side win out. Back in 2011, the hardliners won and the Year of the Rabbit never came to be, but the plans never went away. For the last decade, North Korea's military has been kept fed and happy, with its commanders living a life of luxury unparalleled in the Hermit Kingdom. The Agency believe this is because Kim Jong Un has knowledge of the Year of the Rabbit. You remember those stories of Kim executing relatives by artillery bombing? Those were his attempts to defang the rabbit, so to speak. So analysts have been of the mind that the Year of the Rabbit is no longer viable. Until three weeks ago, when a British SIGINT station picked up an encrypted North Korean military transmission, mentioning the Year of the Rabbit. It is now believed that certain elements of the world's most dangerous nuclear regime are preparing a coup, likely with the aid of a wide diaspora of defectors to the West. Operatives in this room were tasked with applying pressure to certain key North Korean officials to prevent that occurrence."

Eyes darted around the room. Everyone looked surprised to be involved in an op *preventing* a North Korean coup. Some of those looks were even genuine.

"In order to preserve deniability, a scapegoat assassin was needed, as well as an unimpeachable witness. That is why we are in the mess we are in. Because somebody thought it was a good idea to burn Tempest MacLaren and Malcolm Chaucer."

Roma cleared his throat. Clearly, he felt attacked by this last point. "Well, that's a lovely history lesson, but how about we get some orders?"

Asher stared at Roma, unblinking, for a long moment. He waited beyond that moment of comfort, beyond civility. He stared at Roma, willing him to back down and accept what was going to happen. "We're pulling back the rovers. We are going proactive. Together, we're going to find out where our rat and cat are going, and when we know, we'll be waiting for them. I want deep biographies, people. I want to know their sixth best friend from grade school, and the high-school teacher that inspired them. I want to know more about them than their own mothers did."

Roma said, "There's a problem with that, you know."

Asher nodded. "Yeah. Tempest MacLaren's CIA file is light."

"More than light. Compromised. Records think she hacked them on her last day. Even what little's in there we're not sure is reliable."

Asher smiled. "You let me worry about that for now. Focus on the Oracle, and every possible location either of them might want to visit."

CHAPTER 25

Chaucer didn't see the Bolivian until too late. His hypervigilance was off the charts, ticking off everyone in his field of view, scanning and clearing everyone on the narrow Spanish Harlem side street. They'd been walking side streets like this for hours now, avoiding any and all street cameras that could track them.

The Bolivian, however, was not in front of Chaucer. The Bolivian was inside a building on Chaucer's left, glancing out a window at a particularly opportune time. So when he exited onto the street to get a better look, he was on Chaucer's seven, behind him and to his left.

Chaucer sensed him before he saw him. He felt eyes on him. But as he turned, he realized he was far too late. He saw a squat, muscular man of Incan ancestry with dark eyes that had a single focus. Chaucer. He saw recognition, and then he saw the pistol rising, the look of surprised excitement in the Bolivian's eyes, the tensing body preparing to fire.

"Don't." The sound came from behind the Bolivian. It was close and insistent enough that the Bolivian snapped his head around to assess the threat.

The threat was Albert Farr, pistol out and aimed, a look of trepidation on his face. He opened his mouth to speak again.

Chaucer knew this was a deadly mistake, but he had no time to warn Albert.

Albert said, "You don't have to—"

The Bolivian was a blur when he spun around, his own pistol covering the 180 degrees with breathtaking speed. Albert's eyes went wide in shock.

And then the shot rang out. Albert's mouth dropped open. He looked hurt, to the degree that Chaucer wasn't sure who it was who fired the shot.

The Bolivian dropped to the pavement. Albert snapped out of whatever trance he found himself in and stepped forward, squeezing the trigger a second time, pumping another round into the Bolivian's torso and expanding the growing pool of blood beneath him.

Chaucer was dazed. Albert stepped up, glancing right and left at the few people on the street. People who were now running away. He raised the P226 for the third shot, exactly as he had been instructed. Chaucer reached out and pushed the pistol down. Albert met his eyes, his own full of questions.

"He's dead, Albert."

"Three shots you said."

"That's assuming body armor. Always assume body armor, but this guy?"

Albert looked down and saw the Bolivian's blank, shocked stare. The man was no more. Albert's gun hand shook visibly as the adrenaline overload kicked in. His eyes remained wide, in a kind of half-shock. "He was gonna kill you, right? He had a gun. I ... I told him. I said don't ..."

Chaucer picked up the Bolivian's pistol; a reliable Czech model, the CZ75. Chaucer looked back at Albert. He could see Albert needed a response. He needed to hear that it was what cops called "a good kill." Chaucer said, "He raised this gun to my head. Another second, and I'd have been dead. You saved my life"—Chaucer saw a couple of braver men heading this way, cell phone cameras out—"but now we need to be gone."

They turned on their heels and headed back the way they came.

As Chaucer approached Tempest's suburban home in Mamaroneck, New York, he knew there would be a watcher. That was why Chaucer and Albert came in on foot, entering the small, forested neighborhood from the rear side, crossing a Little League field to reach it.

But on the quiet suburban street, with well-spaced houses and well-kept lawns, there were too many places to hide. Too many porches, bushes, cars, even treehouses, any of which could contain the watcher. But when Chaucer couldn't spot them, he grew nervous. The old poker adage came to mind: *If you cannot spot the sucker at the table — he's you.*

Albert closed in on Chaucer after ten minutes of stasis. Chaucer crouched behind an RV, scanning the cul-de-sac. "What's going on?"

"The gray house at the end of the street. That house belongs to my ex-wife."

Albert nodded. "Stalker, huh? Been there."

"No. She's a part of this. Which means that the chances of someone staking it out are very high. Almost guaranteed. So I'm trying to find the watcher. And I can't."

Albert nodded. "What do you look for?"

"Good hiding places with clear views of the gray house."

"A lot of those."

Chaucer nodded. "Exactly. So then I'm looking for something out of place. Something not right."

Albert pointed ahead and to his left. "He's in that bush over there."

Chaucer sighed. "This isn't *Where's Waldo*. You're not gonna just—"

"See those birds over there, going nuts on that bird feeder?

129

Those are finches. Greedy bastards. But there isn't enough room for all of them, so they keep knocking each other off."

"You know something about birds?"

"My pops was a bird watcher. He had high blood pressure, and a doc told him once it could help. So every weekend, he'd watch his birds. Guess it rubbed off."

"Great story, but I don't see how—"

And suddenly Chaucer saw it. There was a second bird feeder, on a pole beside a large bush. And there wasn't a single finch at it.

Chaucer said, "Second feeder."

Albert smiled. "Second feeder."

Chaucer turned to Albert, surprised. "You are a man of many talents."

"I don't do handouts. You promise me two grand, I'm gonna earn it. And for your part? I want you to keep teaching me things. You know, I wanna learn to fish not just get given a fish."

Chaucer nodded. He didn't have a clear read on Albert, something that felt novel to Chaucer. The man was a puzzle to him.

Chaucer dropped to the pavement where he could just barely see under the boughs of the bush. He saw two feet in black boots, facing away from him. It was a sniper's blind, cut right into the neighborhood foliage. The operative had perfect 360-degree camouflage and a clear view of Tempest's home. The only direction he couldn't see was directly behind him.

Exactly where Chaucer and Albert were.

"We can take the shot from right here."

Albert looked uneasy. "No warning, nothing?"

Chaucer saw a flash of emotion across Albert's face. *Unease. Fear. Disgust.*

"He's likely an operative. A trained killer. Something neither of us are. Any warning at all could cost us our lives." Albert's unease only grew. "You killed for me earlier today."

"He had a gun on you. That's different."

Chaucer started to get the strange sensation that his smart

killer bodyguard might not be who Manny touted him to be. Chaucer reached out his hand for Albert's gun. Chaucer now had the Bolivian's pistol and Lane's but Albert's was the only silenced weapon. Albert handed it over without protest.

Chaucer fired three shots, crisp snaps emitting from the suppressor, and the operator in the bush slumped forward. Albert's hands shook slightly when Chaucer handed the pistol back to him. *He's not a killer. Who did I hire?*

Chaucer checked the watcher, confirming the kill, then took his rifle, a Barrett MRAD, slinging it over his back.

At Tempest's door, Chaucer drew his P226. There was always a chance that another operative waited inside, or, far more dangerous, Tempest could be in there. But once Chaucer surveyed the scene inside, he knew the operator in the bushes was alone, and Tempest was long gone.

Albert came up behind Chaucer and took it all in. "Mother of God—"

Chaucer held a hand up. "Don't come any closer. And give me your phone."

Sean Keery was lanky and young, with garish arm tattoos and a pierced lip. He looked more like a bassist than a ballistics expert, which was surprising since Chaucer had called Spinoza asking for the latter. At first, Chaucer thought Spinoza sent the wrong guy. "Who are you?"

A smirk. Not the first time Keery received this kind of reception. "Keery. Recent graduate of the John Jay College of Criminal Justice, and lifetime guns and blood freak. You got something I should take a look at?"

Chaucer ushered him inside. In the front hallway, there were over two dozen bullet holes and shotgun blasts. Keery smiled. But that was nothing compared to the main room and beyond. The place looked like a target range. Shell casings everywhere, holes in nearly every vertical surface. It didn't look possible that anything survived what happened here.

"Holy shit. Holy motherfucking shit! A virgin?! You're giving me a virgin?!" Keery's eyes were wide in awe. He bounced on his heels with abject glee.

"I don't follow …" Chaucer replied.

"A virgin crime scene. No responding officers kicking casings around, no amateur Dick Traceys poking around in blast holes. Full on anatomy of a gunfight, right here. And what a fucking slaughterhouse this place was!"

"I want to know what happened here, in as much detail as you can give me."

Keery glanced at Chaucer for a quick head nod. He was already engrossed. His fingers caressed bullet marks in the wall, his eyes ogled spent shell casings on the hardwood floor. He bounded into the back room, letting out a surprised laugh, then bounded back. The look on his face was one of ecstasy.

Keery let out a guffaw when he saw the kitchen in the back. He returned a moment later, rubbing his chin. "I think I can give you a play-by-play. Hey, dude, do not step in here!"

Chaucer looked up to see Albert standing in the hallway, looking pissed. "Who you think you're talking to?"

Chaucer approached Albert and whispered, "Albert, the guy in the bush. He'll have to check in with his superiors at frequent intervals. I need you watching the cul-de-sac. Any movement, you come get us fast."

Albert got the message. He opened his mouth to respond, but nothing came out. Instead, he headed back out the front door.

Keery rubbed his hands together. "You're not gonna believe this, but there are only two shooters. This whole thing is a man on man, only the one in the house's a woman, right?"

Chaucer glanced around the room. There wasn't a single item in it that suggested a woman lived here. "How would you know that?"

"I'll get to that later. Okay, here's how it began." Keery crossed the sparse main room. Only two pieces of furniture occupied the ten by twenty space, a leather club chair, and a low table housing a top-end stereo system. Keery pulled a record from the turntable on top of the destroyed sound system. He looked down at the floor around the lone chair, noticing the faint discoloration of water droplets.

"So Rock Chick just got out of the shower and is cranking the Ramones up to about a hundred decibels. My guess? 'Blitzkrieg Bop.' Killer track—really kicks ass."

Keery hopped back to the front hallway, his eyes taking in every detail. "Anyway, the neighborhood NRA representative stops by and lets himself in, probably picking the lock."

Chaucer closed his eyes and visualized the scene. Tempest in the chair, a white towel working its way through her long red locks. The front door opening slowly, quietly. An intruder painstakingly entering without a sound.

Keery continues. "She's on alert. But it's more than that. She realizes someone's in the house. How?"

Chaucer walked to the club chair and sat down. "Come in the front door as quiet as you can."

Keery did as he was told, working his way down the hall. Halfway to the main room entrance, his foot pressed against a loose floorboard. On the other side of the wall, it caused another floorboard to move, one directly beneath Chaucer's foot.

"Floorboards. She felt him in the hall."

Keery nodded, impressed. "You think she got that lucky?"

"I think that floorboard is no accident."

"Bitchin'." Keery pulled out a penlight and examined a slug lodged in a nearby wall stud. "All right, Rock Chick! She's packin' more than just home defense. We're talking an FNX. Forty-five caliber and fifteen rounds in the mag, this girl came to play! She pops off three, gut high with one-foot spacing, giving her a great shot at flat-out takedown before the fight even begins, but NRA guy's lucky, 'cause the second shot lodges in the support beam and doesn't perform elective surgery on his totally caught ass."

Keery jumped over several shell casings, his narrative

picking up. "Not to be outdone, NRA guy unleashes the monster, a Fostech Origin 12—the fastest cycling tactical shotgun in the world. And he's packed it with cannonball load that'll chug right through a wall, a PTA meeting, and usually another wall. Good for the kill, bad for the wound. Misses Rock Chick by millimeters with the first blast, and then he's just guessing with the next five rounds. And NRA guy pulls the trigger just a bit too fast, and the Origin jams. You just can't throw that much shot that fast without the mechanism clogging."

Chaucer watched Keery move excitedly through the destruction, like a kid in a candy store. He dared not say a word. This kid was seeing it all happen in his mind's eye.

Keery tilted his head, examining the destroyed stereo, "But, not to worry, NRA guy's got several other beauties to demo before this is over. He ... he slings around his primary backup, an MP7—nastiest thing to come out of Germany since Hitler. Only Rock Chick hears him drop the Origin."

Keery's smile faded. He headed back into the hallway, examining a blood splatter on the floor. "But how the hell does she get behind him to tag him in the leg?"

Keery looked all around the room until his focus fell on the stainless-steel floor lamp at the end of the entryway. "No way! Holy shit! This one's good. This one's very, very good. She goes for the bank shot. Off the lamp. And she tags him in the back of the leg. Just a three-shot volley and she actually gets one in!"

Keery bounded back into the living room again. "And now comes the interesting part. Like they say in boxing, everybody's got a plan until you get hit. NRA guy's just been hit. So does he get smarter, or does he get dumber? He takes the leg wound away as a factor by going prone. That's smart. But he goes through the magazine on Rock Chick's previous position. And Rock Chick's too good to stay in one place. And so he's exposed, his gun's empty, and he's looking the wrong way. So he's got a left-leg injury, a right-arm injury, and he's realizing he's severely, severely fucked. She tags him twice, but only gets him in the body armor and her mag's spent. And either he counts good, or he hears the chamber empty. Either way, he's got an out. He can limp back out the front door and probably make it. But does he bail?"

Keery got down on the hardwood floor, in the killer's position, feeling what happened. "Nope. The guy pulls a Beretta M9 and goes for broke, opposite hand snapshot, around the corner. And he actually tags her arm, most likely, because she doesn't bleed much. But she's out of ammo and now she's been hit, too. So she ducks back into the kitchen for the denouement. Come on, you gotta see this. So you wanna know how I know Rock Chick's a chick?"

Keery bounded into the back of the house. Chaucer entered the kitchen only to find it entirely destroyed. Blackened by fire and explosion, and there was a huge hole in the rear wall of the house. "Right here's what gave Rock Chick away. You can tell a lot about where a person keeps their 'home defense options,' and I gotta say, I've seen guys stashing pieces in all manner of places —but hiding a hand grenade in the vegetable crisper?"

Keery's smile broadened, happy with his analysis, "That's all woman. And that's the story. She takes the window exit, leaving a present for NRA guy. He's pretty good. Probably recognizes the sound and only catches a piece or two of shrapnel. He limps his way out the front, but by then she's gone."

Chaucer nodded. Keery was an odd bird, but his analysis was dead on. Still, Chaucer pressed him, "So she's alive, you're sure?"

Keery smirked. "You keen on her, dude? Because I gotta say damn! Any girl who can do what Rock Chick did? That's a keeper, man."

"I want to hear you say it. She's alive and at large."

Keery nodded. "Yeah, both got bloodied, but NRA Guy took the brunt of the encounter. He called no joy and bailed. Now I can't say what happened after they left, but I'd say the next time someone wants to bring down Rock Chick, you better bring a brigade."

"Thank you. Do I need to tell you that you never saw this?"

"I got it. And I should be thanking you. Hey, can I stay here? I'm just gonna hang out for a while. Y'know, take it all in? This is like … my own personal Graceland."

Chaucer headed out of the burned hole in the back of the house, where Albert joined him. Albert asked, "What now?"

Chaucer thought. "My ex-wife needs new digs. We should go see a real-estate agent."

Albert stared at Chaucer blankly, not knowing a joke when he heard it.

CHAPTER 26

ittle Tyler Raymer took a workmanlike approach to his toy plane's destruction. As Chaucer and Albert waited to see his father, Dennis Raymer, they silently watched five-year-old Tyler smash his toy plane into several painstakingly detailed architectural models of high-priced condos, battering the models and his toy with equal abandon.

The middle-aged office secretary rolled her eyes as she entered the waiting room and ushered Chaucer in to see Dennis. Chaucer said, "Albert, maybe it's better if you wait here."

Albert shrugged. He was a man lost in thought. Perhaps shooting the Bolivian had messed Albert up more than Chaucer had expected. He began to reconsider his plan to recruit a killer as a bodyguard. Albert didn't seem to be the cold, calculating killer he was expecting. He set the concern aside. Right now, he needed to find Tempest. Find Tempest, and then a bodyguard will be superfluous.

Dennis Raymer's office was simple. A wall of bookshelves filled with real-estate binders. A heavy steel desk from the fifties, probably valuable as an antique, but Chaucer knew nothing of such things. Three simple office plants, lush and cared for. And one wall of nothing but glass; a window looking out at the thousand other windows of the skyscraper across the street.

Dennis Raymer was the ex-husband of Tempest MacLaren. Tall and handsome, in that vaguely unkempt professorial style, he was what turned out to be a brief flirtation with the straight life for Tempest, an experiment that both began and ended during Chaucer's long ordeal in the DPRK. Little Tyler was the unexpected result of the experiment, and the only thing keeping Dennis in Tempest's life. Chaucer only hoped that he was in her life enough to be of help today.

Dennis was visibly nervous. Under Chaucer's stare that was far from unexpected, but Chaucer sensed a sharpness to his state. Dennis was not simply nervous to see an unsavory character from his ex-wife's past. Dennis was worried about more than that. Chaucer felt a wave of relief pass over him.

Dennis knew something.

Dennis put his hands in his lap behind the desk, a smart strategy. Hands were tremendously revealing to an experienced interrogator. "Long time, Malcolm."

"You look well, Dennis."

"Thanks. I'm seeing someone. She's got me in the gym three days a week. Um—actually don't tell Tempest that. I kinda want to break it to her on my own schedule."

Chaucer shrugged, "I haven't seen our mutual ex in a long time."

"I wouldn't know. You're literally the only person from her—double life—that even knows I exist. She likes to keep her worlds separate."

Chaucer nodded. He let the conversation die and the silence build. A simple technique, but the simple ones are often the best. Dennis's agitation level amplified. He was blinking in quick triplets, his entire body becoming a tuning fork for Chaucer.

Chaucer began a slow tour of the room, a casual pacing back and forth, forcing Dennis to follow him with his eyes. "I'm looking for Tempest."

Dennis cleared his throat. Tension point. "I didn't think you two saw each other much anymore."

"We don't. But this is business."

Suddenly, Dennis's tension markers spiked. Jaw tension. Nostril flare. A lone bead of sweat formed on his left temple. Chaucer noted it all and continued his pacing. Dennis responded, "I can get you her address. She's in Westchester. Mamaroneck, to be specific."

"Thanks, but she's not there anymore."

"No?" A conscious eyebrow raise, uneven vocal stress. *A clear lie.* Chaucer was certain he already knew that fact.

Chaucer shrugged. "Would you have any idea where she would go if she needed another place to lie low for a few days?"

Dennis shrugged back. He was trying to mirror, to imitate his inquisitor. A major deception cue. People with nothing to hide tend not to think about their behavior. Those with secrets constantly seek to match the energy, even the posture of their interrogator; a subconscious response attempting to elicit sympathy. "She might come stay with me, but like I said, I'm seeing someone now. I doubt she would subject herself to that."

Again, Dennis's tension markers spiked. Something was odd. He was pinging all over the place, burying Chaucer's internal needle of tension detection, but the spikes seemed only mildly related to the questions he was asking. The timing was off.

Dennis shifted in his chair. Another hit. But Chaucer hadn't even asked a question this time. All Chaucer was doing was watching.

And pacing.

Of course, it wasn't the questions he was asking. It was where he was walking. Every time he neared the left side of the bookshelf, Dennis's agitation went off the chart. He decided to test his hypothesis. He ratcheted down the tension while approaching that side of the bookshelf. "Okay, then. It was worth a try, right?"

A dry swallow. Dennis's tension still spiked, even as the questioning seemed to be winding down. Chaucer stole a glance at the binders on that side of the bookshelf.

Listings. Recent listings. But which book? There had to be twenty in the immediate vicinity. And then Chaucer saw his

139

answer. Dust. There was a fine layer of dust settled on the shelves, completely undisturbed, except for one narrow line.

The line where binder number 221 was recently slid out.

Just then, little Tyler burst into the room, crying. Dennis wasn't annoyed. He was relieved at the interruption. "What is it, Ty? What happened?"

"My plaaaaane! It broke!" Tyler cradled his plane in his hands. Its fuselage was split clean in half from one too many impacts.

"Oh, I'm so sorry, baby boy—"

But Tyler wasn't having it. Rage filled his face as he shouted up at his father, "No! Fix it! Fix it! Fix it! Fix it!"

Dennis looked to Chaucer. "I'm sorry, but I really have to take care of this."

Chaucer nodded. Smiled. "No problem. We'll wait."

"I have a lunch."

"Take care of your son's toy. I have maybe three more questions and I'll be out of your hair."

Dennis paused, thinking of some way, any way, to get out of a second round with Chaucer. Failing to find any, he took his crying son out of the room in search of glue.

Chaucer quickly removed the binder. Inside were pages of real-estate listings in plastic coverings, all of them bank-owned foreclosures. Most of them had pouches containing keys. These houses were clearly marked as unoccupied. Others had empty pouches and slips of paper indicating the name and personal details of the renters currently occupying the home.

Chaucer moved quickly from page to page, checking each renter, hoping to discover a potential alias match for Tempest. But only three of them were single, and only one of those a woman, and unless Tempest had a cover of the seventy-year-old Jewish divorcee, that one was not her either.

Chaucer moved on to the unoccupied listings. He was three quarters through the book when he hit pay dirt. Roslyn, NY. A three-bed, two-bath home on the edge of a medium-sized development. There, in the pouch below, were two keys.

Chaucer flipped to another unoccupied listing. Three keys. All the other listings had three keys. One, the original door key; one, the original deadbolt key. The third key, missing from the Roslyn, NY listing, was the real-estate key to the lockbox on premises. Where a duplicate set of keys was stored.

Tempest was in Roslyn.

CHAPTER 27

It just wasn't his day. Chaucer walked out of Dennis Raymer's office building and right into the path of three Middle-Eastern assassins. Hag-Omer, the largest of the three, was wiping the remains of chicken grease from his mouth and hands when he spotted Chaucer. Completely unprepared. Exposed.

Chaucer froze. Hag-Omer froze. Out of the corner of his eye, Chaucer could see Albert, dutifully following directions and following at a safe distance. He was still fifty paces back in the building lobby. He would never get there in time. And if he did, Hag-Omer or one of his trusted associates would kill him when he exited the building. The timing was all off.

Hag-Omer reached into his sport coat. Chaucer tensed. His mind raced, but it was all too sudden, his instincts far too rusty to leap into the proper gear.

Hag-Omer pulled out a business card. He bowed his head and offered the card to Chaucer. "Call this number on Monday, and we will place forty thousand dollars in an account of your choosing. Hag-Omer always pays his debts."

Hag-Omer's associate on his left questioned him in Arabic. Hag-Omer waved off his concern. "This man found my father's killer, and I am in his debt."

Chaucer was still reeling at the turn of events. Then he recalled a particularly difficult interrogation, three years ago. In tracing an Al-Qaeda financier, he had uncovered an Iranian mole in the Saudi Intelligence Service. A man responsible for numerous assassinations of high-level Saudi intelligence personnel. Including, it would seem, Hag-Omer's father.

Hag-Omer held out the card a second time. "I offered my people forty thousand dollars if they could find his murderer. This is a token of my debt to you."

Chaucer shook his head. "I knew nothing about it. And it wasn't your father's killer I was looking for."

Hag-Omer smiled. He laughed a deep belly laugh, causing Chaucer to flinch and look around. This scene was becoming far too public, drawing too many other eyes. "None of that matters. You found my father's killer. Anyone other than you, and he would still be out there, breathing free air. Please, you must take it. We must become ... even."

The man was utterly sincere. It pained him to be in Chaucer's debt. Arab honor was a beautiful trait. Chaucer suddenly saw an opportunity. He took the card. Money in two days might be useful. But an indebted Hag-Omer might be more valuable still. "I may ask one favor of you instead. I would consider it payment in full."

Hag-Omer was surprised. It was clear neither he nor his associates had checked the Ghost Board in the last day and a half. Of course. Half of the intelligence personnel in Manhattan probably hadn't. This was a convention atmosphere for these far-flung men. A rare opportunity for revelry and reminiscence. Checking the Ghost Board would be work, and for these few days, once their official duties were done, many of them considered themselves off the clock.

"What would you have need of from me?"

Chaucer stuck a hand out, signaling Albert, who was closing in on them. He signaled him to stay back. Hag-Omer caught it. Made Albert. A realization dawned. Chaucer was in some kind of trouble.

143

"Check the Ghost Board. You'll know why I might need your help," said Chaucer. And with that, he turned and walked away.

For three blocks, Chaucer checked to see if Hag-Omer was following him. On his phone, Hag-Omer could've checked the Ghost Board in one minute. And the bounty on Chaucer's head might well have triggered a reconsideration of debt. When Hag-Omer never came, Chaucer knew he had purchased another survival option. Possibly a one-time Get-Out-of Jail-Free card, if the right situation arose.

Chaucer ducked into a small bodega, waiting for Albert to follow. "I need a car."

"Yeah? Good luck with that." Albert fidgeted with his fingers. *Evasion. Worry.*

Chaucer read Albert like a big print book. "Albert, I need your car."

"I don't have a car."

True. But also an evasion. "Albert, we both know you have access to a car. I need it."

Albert bit his bottom lip in frustration. Chaucer could see that his new boss's ability to read the man was driving him insane. "It's not an option."

"I can't be on the street any longer. And by now, our pursuers will have access to the subway security cameras. I need that car."

Albert shook his head. "You don't understand. It's my girlfriend's. And it's not a car. It's her business. She'll rip me a new asshole if I take it. And if I damage it, she'll fucking kill me. Seriously. I love her, but the woman is … beyond."

Chaucer turned on the ice. He stared into Albert's eyes like he was one of his subjects. "Albert. You need to understand me. You are going to bring me that car."

One hour and twenty minutes later, Chaucer couldn't believe his eyes. Driving down Lexington Avenue was the glossiest hot pink Caddy he had ever seen. On every quarter panel, in sparkling silver script, were various accolades singing the successes of Nyala Morris, evidently the greatest Mary Kay saleswoman the Bronx had ever seen.

All eyes were on a thoroughly embarrassed Albert as he stepped out of the driver's door. Chaucer didn't let his embarrassment linger. He hurried into the passenger seat.

Albert scowled at Chaucer. "I have half a mind to kill you right now."

"I have half a mind to let you."

Chaucer thought out the peculiar wrinkle this car brought. He was now sitting in the most conspicuous vehicle in all of Manhattan. But that was just to the layman. In truth, the spotters looking for Chaucer might well rule the car out immediately.

A group of three teens cracked up and pointed at Albert, who could only sigh. "Where to, Miss Daisy?"

"Midtown tunnel. We're going out to Roslyn."

CHAPTER 28

Grover's Corner, Roslyn, was situated in an idyllic little pocket of Long Island. Long Island was a haphazard quilt, a patchwork of communities ranging from rich to poor and everything in between. Roslyn occupied the social class its denizens would call "modestly well-off." It was hardly ostentatious, like the far-flung Hamptons, but was equally far from the working-class grime of Hempstead.

As the last glow of the sun faded from the sky, Albert pulled up a little further down the street to 1138 Grover's Corner, another dead end at the far edge of a large upper-middle-class housing development. It was clear that Dennis hadn't picked this house for Tempest; she knew what she was doing. Like her own home, this one was at the end of a cul-de-sac, a wooded glen behind the house. Escape options. Sight lines. Good defensibility. Chaucer also realized that the Mary Kay car would surely get Tempest's attention if she was still in the yellow-and-white two-story facing them. She would likely discount it as a threat, but that did not ease Chaucer's problem.

If she was there, Tempest was alone. Even Tempest was human. Even Tempest got bored. A Mary Kay car in the neighborhood was a welcome relief from staring at the same nothing for hours. She would be watching.

There was only one option. He would have to go in himself. He put the odds of getting shot at a modest one in four.

"Stay in the car."

"I'm not your chauffeur." Albert was bristling more and more at Chaucer's orders. An hour drive in which Chaucer said nothing will do that to a man.

"No, you're my bodyguard. But you can't help me with what's in there."

Chaucer stepped out of the passenger side of the Mary Kay car and walked slowly, deliberately, to the house at the end of the cul-de-sac. The sky had transformed in the last few minutes from pink to purple to a quickly darkening blue. In the air lingered the scent of burnt alder or cedar.

Chaucer kept a steady pace, his hands at his sides, but away from his pockets. He climbed the white porch stairs, only to see Albert coming up behind him, hand on his gun.

"What are you doing? Put that away. You'll get us both killed."

"I thought I had the gun to keep us from getting killed?"

Chaucer was fed up. "That's it. Give it to me."

"No."

"Give it. Now."

Albert protested. "I'm cool! You need backup. I got this."

From the eave overhead, a dark figure dropped to the path behind Albert. A solid crack echoed, and Albert's eyes rolled up in his head. He collapsed on the stoop without a sound.

Chaucer froze.

"Open the door. Take five steps inside. Any other movement and you're dead."

―――

Tempest's voice was as cold as January in Novosibirsk. Chaucer did everything exactly as Tempest said. Inside the front door was a dark and empty hallway extending to the living quarters in the rear. On Chaucer's fifth step, he heard a thud. In his peripheral, he could see that Tempest had tossed Albert's unconscious body in the foyer next to him. "So what now?"

He felt Tempest's hand on his neck, his skin burning in response. She grabbed him and threw him against the wall, spinning him so he was facing her. He noticed the agony of touch with her was still there, but less than usual.

Her gun, a Ruger Mark IV Lite, was in his face, her other hand still on his throat. The long, narrow barrel of the Ruger didn't waver a millimeter. The gun had little range and no stopping power, but it was as quiet as a gun could be. It was an assassin's weapon, in the hands of one of the best of all time.

"Hiya Mal. Long time no see."

Her grip on his throat tightened and moved. She spun him around and kicked his legs apart, performing a professional one-handed pat down. Her hand slowed when it reached his crotch.

"Did you miss me?" he asked.

"I don't miss."

Tempest's hand came away from him and he felt the cold barrel of the gun against the back of his head.

"You still on that truth thing?" she asked.

"Yes."

"So, is this a long story or a short story?"

"Both."

Tempest considered the answer before she replied. "You got one minute before I start the fireworks."

"You've got teams looking for you. Hitters. Both a dedicated Company operation and every freelancer who saw the bounty on the Ghost Board."

The gun barrel pushed harder against his head. "And you know why, don't you?"

Chaucer braced himself. If she was going to kill him, this would be when and this would be why. Tempest's gun didn't fire, but neither did it lower.

"I was called in on a last-minute interrogation," Chaucer continued. "I was looking for the murderer of the son of the South Korean businessman. The guy had factories in North

Korea. I figured he was an asset of some kind. The son was just some grad student."

"Tajo."

"You know him?"

The gun barrel pressed harder into the back of Chaucer's head. "I've got the gun, asshole, which means it's Chaucer's Story Time. And you've got about thirty seconds left."

"There was a witness. She saw the shooter flee the scene. She gave a description. A description of you."

"Bullshit."

"Correct. And I missed it."

Tempest said nothing. Chaucer took a chance and turned his head to glance at Tempest. His first thought betrayed him. *She's still so beautiful.*

Tempest shook her head in angry disbelief. "She beat you? You?! The goddamn Oracle?!"

"She was a highly trained specialist. They doped her up on a specialty drug cocktail designed to mute her natural responses—made it look like the result of a tranq stick and amphetamines they supposedly used to revive her."

A slight brow furrow told Chaucer that Tempest was struggling with the decision before her. He braced himself. If her decision went the wrong way, he would have zero warning.

"Is my time up?"

Tempest bit her upper lip, deciding. "Depends. Answer me this: What did you do when you figured out they were coming for me?"

Chaucer didn't so much as blink. "My contract states I cannot divulge any information gained during an interrogation. To do so … would make me a liar."

He could see Tempest's anger surge. He continued, "But I wondered if I simply called you—if I didn't say a single word, but just let your phone ring, I considered the possibility whether that would make me a liar exactly—"

"So that was you."

Tempest thought for a long moment. Chaucer read a panoply

of emotions on her face, unsure of which one would take hold of her. Then she put her pistol away. "Must've been hard."

"I paid a price."

Tempest shrugged and headed into the kitchen. "Drag him with you," she said.

The house's kitchen was lighter than the hallway; beige wallpaper reflecting the last glow of sky out a bank of windows. Tempest sat at the cozy breakfast nook while Chaucer dragged Albert's body onto the white tile floor.

Tempest let a half-smile escape her lips. "Thanks for the heads-up. Probably saved my bacon."

"I figure my mistake is what got you into this mess."

Tempest shook her head. "They played you. That's not your fault. I'm just amazed it worked."

"My gifts lie significantly short of telepathy, it would seem."

Tempest asked, "So what have you found out?"

"I know a few names. Roma, a few Agency middle relievers, a hitter or two in the bunch. But as far as 'why's go, I've got barely more than nothing. Evidently, the shooter that took out the grad student left a message. The Year of the Rabbit is coming."

"The Year of the Rabbit?"

"Does that mean something to you?"

Tempest locked eyes with Chaucer. She knew he already had the answer. "Yeah. It does."

CHAPTER 29

Albert moaned, shifted, then passed back out.
"Who's the bozo?"
"Albert Farr. Temporary protection. Until I found you."
"What makes you think I'll protect you?"
"Because we've both been set up. When you got away from the North Korean hitter, they sent a team after me."
"So, why are you here? Why didn't you run? There have to be a dozen countries that would love to offer you asylum."
"They killed Terry."
Tempest's face softened for just a moment. "Shit. I'm sorry. I really, really liked Terry."
Chaucer could only nod. "Everyone liked Terry. Even people he busted liked Terry."
"So what? This is a revenge mission you're on?"
Chaucer thought about how to explain what he was feeling. "Someone went to great lengths to lie to me. That lie marked you for death, and it killed Terry. I don't think I can live with that."
"So you're going to find the truth, is that it?"
"It is what I'm uniquely good at. What about you? I suppose you could run."
Tempest shook her head. "They sent some bastard to my

home. I don't think they knew if my boy was with me or not. And now that I hear they did Terry? No. These assholes are breaking the only rules I've ever followed. They gotta pay."

A smile creeped on Chaucer's face. "That's the ex-wife I know."

Tempest flipped a strand of red hair out of her face. *Attraction.* The realization shocked Chaucer. He quickly changed the subject. "We should probably start with the Year of the Rabbit. What do you know about it?"

"It was just something Tajo said. The Year of the Rabbit is coming."

"How did you know Tajo?" Chaucer asked.

"A few weeks ago I got a call from him, out of the blue. For a protection gig."

"You do protection?"

"Not exactly. But if you got my number, you're usually worth a sit-down."

Chaucer stared at the ceiling, lost in thought. "Is that why they set you up? Because you met with him? I don't know. Seems … flimsy. They could've set up a hundred other hitters. Why you? How did Tajo get your number?"

"He wouldn't say. I figure he got it from his father somehow. Anyway, the kid was real nervous. Made me think something might be going on."

Chaucer pressed. "Excited nervous or scared nervous?"

Tempest considered the question, remembering the incident. "Both, I think."

"Why was he looking for protection?"

"He wouldn't go into it," Tempest said. "Not directly, anyway. He talked real scattered about knowing something. Something that was about to happen. His English was pretty bad. But he definitely said there were people watching him. Then, at the end, he mentioned—and I remember this part exactly—he said there's a revolution coming and he was looking to make sure no one stopped it."

"The Year of the Rabbit?"

"I suppose. I didn't get much further. I turned him down. First, protection ain't exactly what I do. Second, he was too paranoid to tell me what I needed to know."

"Like what?"

"Why his father had my number, what made him think he was being watched, what this revolution was, who else was involved."

Chaucer knew Tempest was leaving something out. "You went on an interview, but you didn't do any research?"

Tempest bristled at the suggestion. "Of course I did, but I just didn't find much. The kid was on an FBI list. Not quite a watch list, not exactly not one. That kind of thing. But a lot of foreign-born grad students are, especially in STEM."

"Or maybe because he was a threat."

Tempest shrugged. "Maybe, but that wasn't my bead on him. Look, I'm not exactly the Oracle, but he seemed … sweet. Paranoid, but sweet. My guess was he was having a bit of a breakdown. Real common in the sciences, right?"

"And now?"

"Well, he took a sniper's bullet, didn't he? I keep thinking about the whole 'revolution' thing he said. I didn't peg him as interested in anything unless it was under one of his microscopes. But there was a … a look in his eyes when he said that. Passion. True believer. That kind of vibe. But in a million years, I'd never have picked him as a legit target."

Chaucer smirked. "So you came up empty."

"Maybe not entirely empty," Tempest said. "When he mentioned the Year of the Rabbit, he shot me this look, like he was worried that something had slipped out. There was a piece of paper on his desk, like a flier, with Korean characters on it. He immediately put a clipboard on top of it. Whatever it was, it felt like it was related."

"If you saw it again, would you recognize it?"

Tempest reached into a kitchen drawer and pulled out a red flier with Korean writing on it. "Yup."

Chaucer took the flier in his hands, treating it gingerly, like

153

an object of great value. Tempest asked, "Says '*Jibsa*,' which means 'butler' and the writing around it are a bunch of animals and Western-sounding names, but weird. Like 'Daedalus' and 'Chopper One.' Can you make head or tail of it?"

Chaucer studied the flier. "It's mostly Hanja."

Tempest crossed her arms, waiting for Chaucer to dumb it down. "Korean's like Japanese. The language has more than one alphabet. It has an alphabet of Chinese characters— Hanja—and a native Korean alphabet—Hangul. In Japanese, it would be Kanji and Hiragana. But in Japan, the Chinese characters are used fairly often. In Korea, they've mostly disappeared. The DPRK basically outlawed Hanja when they declared independence."

"Thanks, Professor. How about what does it say?"

"It's a flier for a club. Called—the word you translated as 'butler' has another meaning. It can mean 'pet owner.' And the context here? With the animal names? It's called the Pet Shop Club."

For a brief moment there was a brightness in Tempest's eyes. *Attraction, again.* A pain rocketed up his spine as the joys of the past became programmed agony, courtesy of Po. Chaucer quickly broke eye contact, staring down at the floor.

"Why'd you do that?"

When he glanced back up, there was a sadness in Tempest's eyes.

Chaucer said, "There was a year when I was with Po when he subjected me to stimulus that made me think of everything I loved in life, accompanied by escalating agony. Kind of like aversion therapy. He … he stripped me of every joy in my life."

"You have an aversion to me? Is that what you're saying?"

"Not exactly. Look, it's my problem, not yours."

Tempest shook her head. "I don't know if this is gonna work, Chaucer. Being around you isn't easy for me. You're like an alien wearing the skin of my ex-husband."

"I wish it were different. I wish *I* were different," Chaucer said.

"Yeah, wishes and dishes, the most fragile of things."

Chaucer smiled, surprised to hear such a dainty phrase from tough-as-nails Tempest. She continued, "You know I miss you. Sometimes. Dennis? He thinks I'm still in love with you."

Chaucer barely could hide his shock. He could only blurt out, "The old me. That's who you miss."

Tempest shrugged. "Not sure. Haven't been around this Chaucer enough to really know."

A shock of pain zipped up his back as feelings flooded in. Chaucer changed the subject. He nodded toward a corner of the room where a pile of yarn sat. "You got a roommate?"

Tempest's jaw softened just a millimeter. "They're mine."

"You knit? You?"

"It's Tunisian crochet, it's hard as hell to do well, and it beats meditation."

"I could use a pair of mittens—"

"You shoulda kept in touch then. There's a lot you don't know about me, Mal. I contain multitudes."

Chaucer couldn't help but agree. "Obviously."

An odd look crossed Tempest's face. "You still like me, don't you?"

"What?" Chaucer felt the panic rise in him.

"You, Truth Boy. Still like ... fancy—love—me. Right or wrong?"

Chaucer was caught, unable to do anything but tell the truth. "Right." Beads of sweat covered his forehead.

Tempest laughed. "Huh. You got a funny way of showing it. You pretty much ghosted me when you got back."

"I-I'm not capable—"

She saw him dying inside and changed the subject. "Keep your shirt on. I'm messing with you. Anyway, analysis isn't my strong suit. I need action items. I assume you have some kind of plan?"

Albert moaned.

Chaucer asked, "Is he going to be okay?"

Tempest looked hurt. "I'm a professional. I hit him in the

right place, with the correct amount of force. He won't be happy, but he'll be okay."

Chaucer nodded. "The Year of the Rabbit is years away. That's not exactly urgent. So why, just a few weeks after Tajo contacts you, does he end up dead? That's the first question we need an answer to."

"So?"

Chaucer stared out the window, trying to put it all together. "So? So we're going to the Pet Shop Club. And the scene of the crime."

"Tajo's lab? That's risky."

Chaucer smirked. "We've got million-dollar bounties on our heads, broadcast all over the Ghost Board. Everything's risky. But you and me? Together again? I'd say we'll make them earn it."

CHAPTER 30

The teak treatment room smelled of jasmine and sage as the herbalist removed the array of acupuncture needles from Min Gun's back.

His "team" was working on getting him the where and when that would allow him to regain the face he lost in his first encounter with the Widowmaker. Gremlins. That's how he thought of his team. He envisioned them in a windowless room somewhere scouring the city's millions of cameras, looking through thousands of near matches, hoping to find two needles in a haystack the size of Manhattan.

The gremlins had other uses. They provided him with Tempest MacLaren's file. Her Ministry of State Security file was scant, but Min Gun devoured every detail. To know one's enemy was to take their power. Or so he hoped.

The file was unambiguous. Tempest MacLaren was the best female wet-worker of her generation. She had amassed over one hundred confirmed kills, and nearly another hundred unconfirmed but suspected. Min Gun couldn't help but feel a twinge of jealousy. His leash was considerably tighter than hers. His opportunities fewer. Tempest MacLaren also was at her peak a decade earlier, when enemies were clearer, and the rules of engagement more liberal.

In detailing her work, the dossier laid out a picture of the consummate professional, skilled in every possible art of dispatching a human being from this mortal coil. The majority of wet-workers were specialists. Snipers were ill suited for close-up work. The close-in operators further focused their talents. There were knife men, poisoners, hand-to-hand specialists. Tempest was a generalist. She was a world-class sniper, thought to be the deadliest female at range. But her close-in work was equally impressive.

The dossier tried to offer hope. Tempest was old for the profession, it said. Her skills could no longer be at their peak. Further, the dossier said that she was impulsive, and reckless, and had emotional issues that had only gotten worse with age.

Min Gun wondered if Tempest were a man, would the analysis be so flippant. No, in their first encounter, Min Gun learned much. Tempest MacLaren had not lost a single step in her age. She wasn't just sharp. She was prepared. Ready for anything, despite the fact that her employment in recent years was spotty at best.

That told Min Gun a lot. Human behavior tends toward inertia. That's why human guards are so ineffective over the long term. They can stay sharp for several hours, perhaps for a day. But week after week of nothing happening? They simply can't maintain their focus, their edge. Even with all the training in the world, those edges dull.

But not Tempest. Min Gun had the drop on her. Every advantage, save terrain. And in seconds, she seized not only the initiative, but the advantage in their conflict. Min Gun found that astonishing. He wanted to know how that could be.

He found his answer in her biographical work-up. Tempest was a foster child. Biological father and mother unknown. They placed her with several families until she had the misfortune to find herself in the custody of the Lanes, of Wheeling, West Virginia. From age six to age twelve, they abused Tempest mentally, physically, and sexually. Her one stroke of luck came about when her screams one night were heard by a passing patrol car. The sheriff, John MacLaren, did far more than respond to a noise complaint. He freed Tempest and had the Lanes brought up on charges.

Rather than put Tempest back into the foster system, John MacLaren arranged to adopt Tempest as his own. It couldn't have been easy, Min Gun thought, an ex-marine and widower raising a troubled girl by himself. But raise her, he did. By all accounts, the girl's turnaround was remarkable. She became a decent, if not exceptional, student.

On her eighteenth birthday, she enlisted in the Marines. She took the ASVAB military aptitude test, and her score was flagged as unique. Special.

A hidden metric within the test tripped the flag. An algorithm seeking moral flexibility. The ability to profoundly compartmentalize both emotions and morality. To potentially do a terrible thing for a greater good. Less than one soldier in a hundred thousand flagged that particular metric. Of those, 80 percent immediately washed out as sociopaths. Another 15 percent were transferred to the Air Force and placed in silos at air bases from Nebraska to Alaska, those special few who could turn their key should their nation demand it of them.

But the last 5 percent of those specials. They were plucked out of their enlistment offices, flown in planes with blacked-out windows, and disappeared from the world. They would become the actual tip of the American spear, silently striking out at her enemies foreign and domestic, without need of declaration of war, congressional oversight, or hand-wringing.

Min Gun understood the selection process. He knew that for a victim of childhood abuse to make it through that program, Tempest MacLaren had to be beyond exceptional.

Min Gun shut the dossier. There were volumes more about her professional career, but he had learned everything he needed to know about his target. Tempest MacLaren would not just disappear into the night. No, she was here to stay.

The herbalist finished her work and silently stepped out of

the room. Min Gun rose, testing out his body. Range of motion. Speed. Power. The improvement was measurable.

It would be enough. It must be enough. Because Round Two was coming.

The door before him opened. Sung entered and handed him a single piece of paper. Min Gun looked at the man, waiting for further explanation.

"It would seem your mission has expanded once again."

CHAPTER 31

Asher bit into the day-old bagel and closed his eyes, savoring the taste. A thin line of lox-specked cream cheese dotted his upper lip and with a flick of his tongue, he licked it off. He didn't quite finish chewing before he spoke. "Greenberg's, right?"

Sitting across from him in the spacious living room of a Brooklyn brownstone was Hillel Abrams. Hillel couldn't speak as he was well bound to a cushioned wrought-iron chair and had a rudimentary cloth gag in his mouth. Hillel had the wild eyes of a man who had already been through the wringer, but knew that far worse could be in the offing when you were facing Gabriel Asher.

Asher shrugged. "Yeah. Greenberg's. I hear they boil their bagels for twice as long as Shelsky's before they make them."

Asher finished the last morsel and wiped his hands on the periwinkle kitchen towel beside him. Then he sat in the chair directly in front of Hillel. He looked the man up and down. Hillel was fit. Muscular. A very well put together Jew in his late forties.

During his reconnoiter earlier in the evening, Asher saw many pictures of Hillel and his beautiful wife and children. Pictures from all around the world. "Now, Hillel, your beautiful family will be coming back from dinner in about thirty minutes, and if I'm still here, well—I'm sorry to say, they'll be dead. But the good news is, you are entirely capable of preventing that tragedy from occurring. See, I have a problem, and I feel you're the solution."

Asher picked up a few garlic crumbs and tossed them in his mouth. "I'm hunting two people. The Oracle and the Widowmaker. Now I've got file after file on the Oracle, but the man's a monk. He's got no one and nothing in his life, so I've got no trail to follow, and I've got no soft points to target. But the Widowmaker, on the other hand, she's got soft points. An ex. A kid. But there I ran into a problem. The bitch erased her CIA file on her last day. The Company is still steamed about it, but it means I've got just shy of nothing on her. So here's what I'm gonna do. I'm going to free one hand so that you can type on my computer over there and you're going to get me a file I'm just dying to read."

Hillel spurted out a random assortment of vowels. There was an urgency to his words that suggested to Asher that he was nearing the useful part of the conversation, when all but one or two useless objections were left. He pulled down the cloth gag so Hillel could speak.

"I don't know what you're talking about," Hillel said, gasping for breath.

Asher gave him the slightly amused look an owner gives a new puppy who's made a mess on the carpet. "Now, now, Hillel. We are way past the 'I don't know what you're talking about' phase. You're gonna have to do a lot better than that. Twenty-nine minutes until I cut your beautiful family up beyond all recognition."

"Cut up" provoked a visceral response. Hillel tried again, forcing himself to speak slowly and calmly. "Look, I know the Widowmaker, okay? Tempest MacLaren, right? But I only know the name. I don't know her. I left the CIA ten years ago. I've got no access, no clearance—"

Asher sighed. Playing dumb was such a boring tactic. "You,

sir, are Mossad. You're an active agent on their payroll. And you were during all those years at the Company."

Hillel shook his head vigorously, but Asher put up a hand. "I don't care one bit about that. You know the Company and I have no love lost. I have no interest in sharing that information with them. In fact, it's a great thing that you have this other, deeper loyalty, because I have no interest in the Widowmaker's file at the CIA. I want the file the Mossad has. The one you stole from the CIA a decade ago, before she did her vanishing act." Asher could see Hillel's jaw tighten as he tried to find the resolve to deny him what he needed. "But you're obviously not ready. Tell you what: I'll give you ten more minutes to think about it. I sure hope with only eighteen minutes left and one hand to type, you'll be able to get me those files."

Hillel shook his head. "No, no!"

Asher simply slipped the cloth gag back into place as his head thrashed around violently. He yelled into the gag, but no one was listening. Least of all Asher. He flipped on the TV and found the local news. The story of the hour was the ending of the UN World Summit, peppered with man-on-the-street interviews of New Yorkers of various stripes complaining about the traffic headaches and voicing different versions of "good riddance."

Ten minutes later, Asher left the gag on when he freed Hillel's right hand. He marveled at how quickly Hillel's fingers hunted and pecked their way across the keyboard, navigating from secure site to secure site across a digital ocean. He entered an obscenely long and complicated password to access an offshore Mossad database, getting Asher exactly what he asked for.

He finished with two minutes to spare. In truth, the family's return was not set in stone. It was merely an estimate, a gamble on Asher's part. If the family had come in, Hillel would know that they were all dead and he might have stopped helping.

But Asher knew that hope was a pernicious beast, and even highly trained operatives weren't immune to its effects. He figured it'd be an interesting experiment to have that pretty wife's throat at the end of a knife, to see if he would keep typing just to save her from suffering, if not to save her life.

Hillel stopped typing. His eyes found Asher. They said, "Done."

Asher looked over the file, leaning forward as he did so. A smile broadened on his face as he saw the name and address of Tempest's second husband and their child. The gold standard of leverage that would bring Tempest to her demise.

Hillel saw his moment. With his free hand, he made a move for the gun in Asher's waistband.

He never got close. Asher had expected it. With the knife in his left hand, he stabbed Hillel's free hand, center palm, pinning it to the wooden desk.

Hillel screamed in agony. Asher watched the warm blood flow across the desk and onto the floor. It was beautiful, in a way. Blood often was. But now was not the time for such things. Asher checked his watch.

One minute left. He had no time to make a meal of it. He pulled out the knife, pinning Hillel's hand to the desk, and instantly buried it in his chest. Hillel's eyes went wide in shock and pain. They would not close again until the coroner arrived.

Asher exited the brownstone, feeling better than he had since he left Mexico City. A moment later, a white BMW pulled up to the curb and a very familiar, beautiful family exited.

Asher thought to himself, *You're a hero, Hillel. You just saved your family.*

CHAPTER 32

It was a speakeasy, or was a long time ago. The front of the basement establishment was a pet store. Min Gun entered and breathed in the earthy sweet smell of hay and scat. It reminded him of the animals around his parents' farmstead. The animals that fascinated him to the point of murder.

A single Korean clerk looked him up and down. It was the bandage across his face. Min Gun was used to being a nondescript face in the crowd. That advantage was gone. Likely forever. He drew his silenced Beretta and, with a single snap, the clerk was no more.

In the back, he found the black door his briefing said would be there. Beyond it, he found the black stairs leading down into the sub-basement. He heard EDM music blaring ahead. He put away the Beretta. It was ill suited for crowd work. He adjusted the sling on his right shoulder and brought forth his JS 9, a suppressed submachine gun and one of the best weapons China ever produced. The loud snap it produced would register as little more than a drumbeat in this environment.

Min Gun climbed down the stairs to the vaulted brick sub-basement. The walls were covered in exposed piping and ancient neon lights advertising brands he had never heard of. A black wooden stage dominated the back of the room, where a DJ held court.

Dancing on the aging wooden floor were a dozen kids. The oldest was perhaps twenty-five. Min Gun saw their faces and felt at home. Koreans, one and all.

A rail-thin boy turned to look at Min Gun, alarmed by his face, his age, and the shadow that loomed around his presence.

Min Gun spoke not a word. The JS 9 spoke for him.

Albert swallowed four ibuprofen tablets as the scent of brewing coffee filled the small kitchen. One arm braced himself on the maple table while the other held a dishrag filled with ice at the meeting point between his skull and neck. The sky outside the window above the sink betrayed the soft blue of an impending dawn.

Tempest and Chaucer shared a glance, filled with silent communication. Chaucer spoke first. "Albert, you've done everything I've asked of you. Your job is completed."

"What? What are you talking about?"

Tempest chimed in. "We've got it from here, chief."

"So that's how it is? You cave my head in with a shovel—"

"Fist."

"—and you think you can just get rid of me?"

Tempest squared up. "You saying I can't?"

Albert tossed the dishcloth on the table. "You got my money then?"

Tempest glanced at Chaucer. "How much?"

"Nine thousand," Chaucer said.

Tempest whistled and shook her head in amazement. "Nine grand? For this?"

"Hey!" Albert objected. "We were doing just fine until you came in and ninja'd me!"

Tempest laughed. "Did he just say 'ninja'?"

Chaucer smiled. "He did. Used it as a verb even."

Albert's eyes narrowed. "Mock me all you want, but pay me in full, motherfuckers."

Tempest looked to Chaucer. "You got that much cash?"

Chaucer shook his head. "My drops were compromised."

"All of them?"

"Yeah. What about you?"

"If yours are blown, mine are long gone. Except … I do have one, but no cash."

"Why would you set up a drop with no cash?"

"It's my 'just in case.' I haven't been in it in twelve years."

"I understand."

Albert grew frustrated. "I don't understand."

Tempest shot him a glare. "Yeah, we get that."

Albert stood; he towered over Tempest, and yet he still looked small. "Look, until I get paid, I'm on you like glue. And you're gonna start telling me what's going on. Teach me some of this stuff. Maybe I can make a career of it."

Tempest opened her mouth to retort, but Chaucer cut her off. "That's fair. The reason Tempest's stash has no paper currency is that cash is only good in the short term. The average paper bill in US circulation has a lifespan of eight years. If Tempest suddenly tried to spend a bunch of bills that were all twenty years old, she would be arrested before she got much more than a cup of coffee."

Albert said, "You really think cashiers notice the dates on bills?"

Tempest and Chaucer responded, "Yes."

Chaucer continued, "Especially since US paper's undergone redesigns in the last few years. Think about it, who walks around with a wad of twenty-year-old bills?"

Albert thought for a moment. "Bank robbers."

"Exactly."

"So you're saying you owe me, but you're both flat broke."

"Not exactly broke. But we need all the cash we have to survive. And we'll need to fence the diamonds."

"Diamonds? What diamonds? Nobody said anything about diamonds."

Tempest said, "A long-term drop can't have cash, but it can have money. Uncut diamonds. There's no way to trace them, and their value almost never changes. But they're not the easiest thing to unload. And Roma knows that. They'll be watching everyone in the diamond districts."

Chaucer asked, "So is it worth hitting your long-term drop?"

Tempest nodded. "Oh yeah. It's worth it."

CHAPTER 33

Asher returned to his crisis room where he was instantly intercepted.

"Where the hell were you?" Roma demanded.

Asher's good mood quickly faded. "I was being efficient. You really should try it sometime. What's the update?"

"Did you really halve our watchers covering Port Authority?" Roma said.

"That's not the Oracle's style. He'll know it's a low-percentage play, so he won't entertain it. I'd pull everyone off Port Authority if there wasn't a chance he would scout it to be sure."

"Well then, a lot of us would like to know what the hell we're doing exactly. We've got eyes on police precincts, hospitals, and … a graveyard?"

"He's got cop friends. He may be injured. And the graveyard? It's where Tempest's adoptive father was buried. It's a low-percentage play, sure. But they're all low-percentage plays. Welcome to our reality. They've both avoided capture now for almost two days. Did you just think we were unlucky? No. They're good. We're going to work our asses off until we get lucky—or until we get as good as they are."

Suddenly, Asher whistled. It was as piercing as it was effortless. Everyone looked up from what they were doing. Asher locked eyes with a young South Asian woman wearing over-the-ear headphones. He tossed her a thumb drive. "Pick four people to work with you on this. Dig through all of that file. Somewhere in there are bread crumbs that could lead us to MacLaren's family."

The South Asian woman nodded and immediately set to work.

———

"Rearview, not side view," Tempest said.

Albert pulled his eyes away from the side-view mirror. He glanced in the rearview. Tempest frowned. "Wrong. Flick your eyes. Nothing more. You stare like that and they know you're watching. Now call off as many details as you can of the cars behind you."

Chaucer sat in the back while Albert described his one-second snapshot of the rearview. It wasn't bad. He was able to describe three cars reasonably well.

Tempest wasn't so generous. "Useless. The car directly behind us you can ignore. That will never be a follow car. Try again, and this time, I want four cars back."

Albert tried again. "Silver minivan, grey cube van, white sedan —"

"What kind of sedan?"

"Luxury. Lexus I think."

"You think?"

"Look, what is the point of this, anyway? We made a left a while back and all the cars are different."

Tempest's anger grew. Chaucer threw her a warning glance. She took a deep breath and said, "Parallels. Modern tailing technique is to uses parallels. A minimum of three cars, often five if they have the resources. One car follows, the others race up parallel streets, getting ahead of us. Then the follow car peels off and another intercepts."

To their left, Chaucer saw white stones gleaming in the first rays of the sun. "We're here." Calvary Cemetery approached. With over three million internments, it was the biggest cemetery in the nation. They were at New Cavalry, three times the size of Old Cavalry, which reached capacity in 1867.

Albert pulled over at the east entrance gate. Chaucer could tell Tempest was agitated, despite her attempts to hide her state. Tempest said, "You two stay here. I need a moment alone."

Tempest exited the car and stepped through the gray gate arching over a low-slung gray granite wall. She headed over to a stone shed to her right and entered.

"What's she doing?" asked Albert.

Chaucer didn't respond. A moment later, Tempest exited the shed, shovel in hand.

"Oh damn. You gotta be kidding me."

Tempest climbed the barren hill, passing row after row of cold, gray stone. A lone, bare tree sat atop the hill like some melancholy memorial to the dead below. To the left of that tree, Tempest found a simple gray slab standing erect on a plot of yellowing grass.

JOHN MACLAREN
1944–2008
"Fortune favors the prepared mind."

Tempest stood still, feeling the cold east breeze on her face. She fought a silent battle before finally speaking. "Dad—I know. I haven't been around for a while. I've been busy—bringing you company. And I guess the only reason I'm here is I need your help again. One last time. Because, Dad, there's a better-than-even chance I'm gonna see you real soon, and no offense, but I'd like a bit more time before that comes to pass."

She kissed her two middle right fingers and touched them to the stone. "Love you. And thanks." She drove the shovel into the cold, hard ground. It yielded. She dug quickly, not a wide hole, but a deep one. She paid no attention to the few elderly mourners watching her from a distance, too uncomfortable to intercede.

Her shovel made a soft sound. Something other than the shaving sound of metal on packed earth. Beneath her shovel was a huge olive duffel bag, easily the size of a body bag. She wrestled with the bag a few moments before prying it free and lifting it from the grave. She unzipped it, revealing a black plastic-coated nylon bag within; a dry bag protecting its contents.

Tempest zipped it back up and marched down the hill toward the pink Caddy. The eyes of the elderly mourners followed her every step.

One of those mourners turned away from her and spoke quietly to seemingly no one at all. "Target acquired."

CHAPTER 34

Tempest pulled the duffel into the Caddy. "Let's go."

Albert stared at her. "So we're not gonna talk about this?" Neither Tempest nor Chaucer reacted. "You're not even gonna tell me what's in the bag?"

"Drive," said Tempest.

Albert couldn't contain his frustration. "Well, where to?"

Chaucer said, "Midtown tunnel. We're going back to Manhattan."

Albert pulled out of his parking space and merged with the light traffic of the early day.

"Mirrors. One glance. Four cars," said Tempest.

Albert flicked his eyes up to the rearview and then back down. "White delivery van, silver minivan, blue SUV, yellow taxi."

Albert looked pleased with himself, glancing over at Tempest. She paid no attention, staring instead at Chaucer. "I've been thinking. I wanna go to that nightclub first."

Chaucer stared out the window in thought. "I'd be fine with that, but it'll be empty at this hour."

"So? That makes things easier."

"I find people give better answers than places."

Tempest shrugged, then glanced at Albert. "Mirrors."

Flick of the eyes. "Black SUV, yellow taxi—"

"Skip the taxis and buses."

"They don't use them?"

"They sometimes use taxis, but you're not ready to be memorizing taxi numbers."

Albert's brow furrowed. "Then black motorcycle, red Corvette."

Chaucer asked, "What was the kid's demeanor when you were with him? I'm looking not for what he said, but how he acted."

"Like I told you, he was excited and afraid. Like he knew something big was coming down the pike, and he wanted to be ready for it. He wanted to hire me to be sure he didn't miss that show. That's the feeling I got."

"If there was a North Korean coup in the works, that could fit the bill."

Tempest frowned. "He didn't seem the coup type. But even if he was, why would the CIA cover up the assassination of a coup plotter?"

"Maybe they didn't. It started as a private enterprise. Roma and his men subcontracted out."

"Private? What private interest would be involved in any of that?"

"Private could mean anything. It could be a foreign entity that wants to cover its tracks. Picture this: operatives freelance for an assassination op—the pay's good enough that they don't go digging to find their bosses. The op goes sideways and draws major heat. How hard would it be for those very same operatives to make sure they were assigned to the actual Agency response team?"

"I guess it's possible." She turned to Albert. "Mirrors."

Albert flicked his eyes again. "White SUV, green pickup, silver minivan, red—"

"Wait." Every muscle in Tempest's body tensed. "That's the third time we've seen a silver minivan."

Albert shook his head. "Uh, no. There was just one a while back, but it turned off."

"There was also one right around the cemetery."

"I don't remember."

Tempest sat up, suddenly extremely alert. "I do. At the next intersection, hit the brakes hard for two seconds. Swerve a bit, as if you're avoiding a pigeon or something."

Chaucer didn't move. "Something?"

Tempest bit her lip. "Maybe."

Albert flicked his eyes into the rearview. Tempest hissed. "Stop right now. Don't check that mirror again."

The next intersection approached. Tempest turned her head to the right, just a small quarter turn. As Albert crossed the intersection, he hit the brakes hard, swerving away from an imaginary obstacle.

As he resumed, Tempest caught a glimpse one block away. A fast-moving taxi. Racing up the parallel.

"We're blown."

CHAPTER 35

Ten minutes later, the situation had not changed, but the landscape had. Asher triggered his comms to the entire team. "They're headed for the Brooklyn–Queens Expressway. I want four units ahead of them in each direction. And another four on the Manhattan side of the Midtown Tunnel in case they divert that way."

"M1 reporting. Manhattan's a problem, sir. We're out of position."

"Then get in position."

"The UN Summit, sir. It's over, and the roads are jammed with diplomats heading to JFK."

Roma broke in on the comms. "We can take them right now. Tempest and Chaucer both. Why are we waiting?"

Asher interrupted. "They're headed for the BQE. We hit them there, when they're boxed in."

Asher switched channels on the com. "Where's my air unit?"

The driver up front responded. "On site now."

"Is my sniper on board?"

The driver nodded. "With a Barrett fifty caliber, sling mount."

Asher gritted his teeth. A shooting war with Tempest MacLaren might not be avoidable, but a helicopter with a gun mount? That was more attention than this operation was supposed to generate. A CIA op on US soil was bad optics, even with the murder of the deputy head of station. An aerial gunfight was another matter entirely. He hoped their ground units could handle things without resorting to Anya Sergeyev's assistance.

Asher zoomed out on the digital map, thinking ahead. Plotting moves and countermoves. The Brooklyn–Queens Expressway, a six-lane highway cutting through some of the densest population on the Eastern seaboard. To pull off that feat with minimal disruption, large sections of the roadway were lowered into artificial concrete canyons, keeping the road noise to a minimum. These canyons were what Asher was counting on. Stop the Caddy there, and even Tempest couldn't simply go to ground and disappear.

The only complication was the Queens Midtown Tunnel. If the Caddy turned in that direction, heading into Manhattan, there was a chance that they could lose surveillance. The steel and glass mountains of midtown were the perfect foil to his air unit, and the congested streets were conspiring to poke holes in Asher's carefully constructed net.

He keyed the com. "M1, status."

"Fucked. We're twenty blocks from the tunnel."

"Is the congestion both ways?" Asher guessed that if the tunnel was jammed both ways, they'd be trapped as sure as they would be on the BQE.

"Negative. Traffic inbound is flowing."

"I want two units to get ahead of them in the direction of the tunnel. Air One. If the Cadillac gets past them, you're cleared to engage."

"Air One copies."

So much for clandestine, thought Asher. He focused on the rapidly moving digital map, silently willing the dot representing the Cadillac onto the BQE.

"What do we do?" Albert asked.

It was a valid question. The very same question Tempest and Chaucer were silently mulling. Neither of them consulted a map. New York was their home. They knew the terrain. And they knew the enemy. *Sun Tzu would give us decent odds.* Tempest smiled at the thought.

"BQE?" proffered Chaucer.

"Into Brooklyn? Death trap. They'll get us in one of those canyons."

"On and off then, make them think we're running and we go to ground."

Tempest grimaced. She didn't like any of the options before her. "I think the tunnel's the play."

"Even worse than the BQE, isn't it?" said Chaucer.

"Why? Why is it worse?" asked Albert.

"They want us contained," Chaucer replied. "They want to control the environment, so there's no chance of escape. That means stopping this car, and giving us nowhere to run."

"Then why are you thinking about the tunnel?"

Tempest gritted her teeth. "Air. They've got to have air support, don't they?"

Albert leaned forward in his seat, trying to scan the sky. A stiff arm by Tempest put him back in his seat. "You won't see them. All you'll do is tell them we're looking for them."

"Then how the hell do we know what they've got?"

"SOP," said Chaucer. "Standard operating procedure. Best practices. For sure, they've got an air asset on site. But the tunnel—"

Tempest cut him off. "We've got to roll the dice one way or another. Air? Too easy to get in place. That's for sure. But the tunnel's in play if they don't have enough units ahead of us. That's harder. They don't know where we're going. It's likely most of them are behind us, trailing."

"And the other side of the tunnel?" Chaucer asked.

"I'm not worried about the other side of the tunnel. We just need to make sure none of them are in the tunnel with us."

Ahead, the roadway forked, the left lanes feeding onto the BQE, the right lanes feeding to the Midtown Tunnel. Albert drifted right until Tempest put her hand on the wheel, forcing the car left.

Albert's frustration peaked. "What are you doing? The tunnel's on the right."

Chaucer broke it to him, "That's why we go left. We make them think BQE. We let them get as many units ahead of us as possible. Then we double back and run for the tunnel."

Albert said, "Just one problem, super spies. I used to live in Queens. Took this exact road a lot. There ain't no quick way back to the tunnel from here."

Asher exhaled deeply when he saw the dot representing the Caddy pulling onto the BQE feeder. "We got 'em. B1 through B4, they're heading right for you. Don't let them get past. Air One, you're eyes only. B7 and B8, pull back from the Tunnel, and make your way back to the BQE pursuit units."

The dots ahead of the Caddy converged, preparing a trap from which even Tempest MacLaren and Malcolm Chaucer could not escape.

"What?!?!" Albert couldn't believe what he was hearing. He looked down to his right as he passed over the six lanes of traffic going to and from the Midtown Tunnel. He was leaving it behind, as the bumpy roadway, littered with Jersey barriers on the right side, pulled him and the Caddy toward Brooklyn.

"Now, Albert." Tempest was insistent, fixing him with that glare that had a habit of getting people to do whatever she wanted.

"Fuck that!" Albert could see traffic merging from the right, traffic coming from the tunnel.

Tempest reached over and grabbed the wheel, yanking it hard right. The Cadillac made an erratic right turn, heading right for a concrete Jersey barrier, missing it by inches and smashing through the edge of a metal guardrail separating traffic entering the BQE from the tunnel and from Queens. The Cadillac spun upon impact, but kept going, now facing the opposite direction of traffic.

"Goddamnit!" Albert's instincts kicked in and he pulled his car to the near shoulder, slamming on the brakes.

"Brake and we're dead! Faster!" Tempest punctuated the statement by reaching her leg over and mashing the gas.

"You're insane!" The Caddy accelerated down the nearly nonexistent shoulder, headed the wrong way against dense traffic.

"Two miles! All we need is two miles! Steer, you bastard!"

The stream of oncoming cars veered out of their way as they blasted down the left shoulder, heading back toward the Midtown Tunnel and hope. *Just two miles. That's not too much to ask for, is it?*

As Chaucer thought this, he spotted the burned-out hulk of a car on their shoulder, an accident from earlier in the day, coming on fast.

CHAPTER 36

Communications discipline is the first thing to go in a crisis. Asher knew that even the best unit could fall prey to garbled comms when a plan unravels. And that was exactly what was happening. The plan, as it was, was dead and buried. Their prey had escaped their trap and was heading toward the one hole in their net. And the comms were filled with units reporting, exclaiming, declaring, questioning, and otherwise panicking. Of course, it was a very professional panic, filled with facts more than emotion. But the result was the same as it would be if twenty adolescents were screaming in the radios: chaos.

Asher let it happen. Getting on the comms would only exacerbate the problem in the short term. And in the long term, it didn't matter at all. No, Asher had only three cards to play in this scenario. One: B7 and B8 just pulled off the Midtown Tunnel feeder. There was a chance they could intercept. Two: Those Manhattan units needed to do whatever it takes to get in place. And three: Air One.

Asher wasn't panicking because he had a sniper above the scene. There would be fallout. Collateral damage. But that was a problem for tomorrow. Air One needed to take out today's problem today. And he could see on his digital maps that Air One was moving quickly to get into position.

The odds of Tempest and Chaucer outrunning Air One? Next to zero.

The burned-out hulk of a Chevrolet Suburban took up the entire shoulder ahead of the Cadillac. The line of cars racing by in the fast lane was uninterrupted. There was no path forward. Albert eased off the gas, unsure. "Well?"

Tempest was resolute. "Faster!"

"Are you out of your mind?!"

On their right, an A-Star light helicopter dropped to a height of twenty feet above the roadway, its side door wide open. Inside Tempest saw a young woman swiveling a fifty caliber Barrett sniper rifle in a door sling until it faced them. *"FASTER!"* With a snarl, Tempest jabbed her leg and smashed Albert's foot down on the accelerator. The first shot ripped through the air where the Cadillac used to be, and chewing up a Jersey barrier and a panel truck.

"Shit!" Albert gripped the steering wheel tighter as the Cadillac raced right for impact with the burned-out hulk. The chopper tilted forward in pursuit, its gunner adjusting aim to account for both the vector of the Cadillac and her own airship. Tempest knew the combined vectors of both the helicopter and Caddy made the sniper's job extremely difficult, so when she put two rounds into the Caddy, one in the trunk and the next ripping through the back seat and missing Chaucer by inches, she knew she was looking at the sniper who took out Tajo.

She fired a quick three shot sequence at the helicopter, trying to disrupt the sniper. The young woman was good. Her head never left the scope. Tempest thought she could see her trigger finger twitch —

— the very instant the Cadillac impacted the burned-out Suburban hulk. The round ripped into the frame of the Suburban, the rapid deceleration of the accident messing up the sniper's calculation. The round deflected off the Suburban, ripping into an eighteen-wheeler's cab, sending it slamming into the right retaining wall along the roadway. Drivers on the ramp panicked, some braking hard, some speeding off.

Instantly, the front airbags in the Cadillac deployed, punching Albert and Tempest in the nose. Tempest didn't waste a second. Her karambit was in her hand, and a second later she had popped her airbag, deflating it. Another second later, and Albert's was similarly deflated.

"Wake him," said Tempest. It was an order for Chaucer. He reached forward, slapping Albert in the face, trying to stir him from his daze.

She threw the Caddy into neutral and revved the engine, making sure the vehicle was still in working order. Then she put the car back in drive and jammed on the gas with her left foot, steering the Cadillac around the Suburban. Traffic cleared a bit of daylight in the left lane, enough to get clear of the Suburban. But Tempest didn't use all the room the lane provided her. She pushed the Cadillac forward but kept the right fender of the Caddy pinned to the right corner of the Suburban.

The helicopter rose sharply to arrest its forward momentum, trying to bring Anya's sights to bear on the newly slowed Cadillac. It dropped back down to a position barely above that of the ramp. Anya drew a new bead from a stable platform. The Cadillac was practically centered already.

Tempest gunned the engine, pushing the corner of the burned-out Suburban, forcing its wheels up the Jersey barrier, lifting the burnt frame up on two wheels. She jogged the wheel to the left for a brief second, scraping the frame of the Suburban against the right side of the Caddy.

Chaucer realized what she was doing. She had positioned the steel floor of the SUV as a shield between the Caddy and the helicopter. Jammed against it, Tempest floored the accelerator, dragging the Suburban with them.

Anya opened fire, and in the Caddy they heard a deafening

din as metal slammed into metal, the shield of the SUV's undercarriage keeping them alive. Albert awoke with a start, fighting to gain his bearings.

Asher heard the pilot yelling in the comms, "No joy! We need a new angle!" Asher exhaled. There were too many men in the van to let his emotions show, but there was little chance of camouflaging his frustration. Their quarry was getting away. "M1, M2, the tunnel is in play. Get in position, whatever it takes."

The Jersey barrier ended, and the Suburban flopped down on its shredded tires and spun out of the way. Albert grabbed the wheel from Tempest's control and yanked it hard right. The mangled Cadillac accelerated and smashed through a metal guardrail separating outgoing and incoming tunnel traffic. The Caddy was once again traveling with traffic, and Albert mashed the accelerator, gaining speed and distance from the helicopter. "You bitch, my girlfriend is going to murder you!"

The A-Star pilot cursed as he saw the Caddy race ahead. He had just brought the helicopter to a halt, trying to help his sniper get a kill-shot. Now the craft was the equivalent of being caught flat-footed.

He pushed the yoke full forward, willing the craft to pick up speed, but the helicopter wasn't built for acceleration that way. He would gain on the Caddy for sure, but now it was an open question whether he would intercept it before it entered the tunnel.

Tempest smiled as Albert weaved through the throng of cars headed for the tunnel. She had to admit; he was doing well. Well enough that she could roll down her window and find that A-Star. It was directly behind them, and coming on fast. Tempest drew her pistol and unloaded a steady stream of gunfire in its direction. She wasn't expecting much of a result, just to slow them down, perhaps.

It had no effect. The pilot kept his bird tilted aggressively forward, eating up the distance between car and helicopter. When it reached the car, it flew overhead and turned on a dime, giving the sniper a single perfect shot.

But giving Tempest one too. She raised her pistol a millimeter and fired one final three-round burst, catching the sling mount for the Barrett and sending it tumbling.

Anya's last shot chewed through concrete two feet above the Caddy as it disappeared into the tunnel.

———

The helicopter pilot keyed his mic. "Air One reports no joy. They're in the tunnel."

CHAPTER 37

Tempest fired four shots from the passenger seat. Inside the Cadillac, the noise was deafening. Literally. The loud ring of tinnitus echoed in Albert and Chaucer's ears, neurons screaming as they died.

"The fuck—!" Albert exclaimed.

Tempest didn't respond. The four shots she fired were through the four corners of the front windshield. She raised both legs and kicked the windshield out, watching it clatter to the hood, then slide off to the asphalt roadway. "Faster."

"What?"

"Faster! We have to catch up with the cars ahead of us!" Albert wanted to argue. God knows he wanted to. But he decided to be a good soldier. He accelerated what remained of his girlfriend's car, slowly catching up with the drivers far ahead, the ones blissfully ignorant of the chaos they just missed.

Chaucer leaned forward. "Plan?"

Tempest shrugged. "Not really. More like a notion."

"The clock is ticking."

"Well aware," said Tempest. The Cadillac approached a cluster of cars. "Get us up to that truck."

Two sets of cars were between them and the truck. The cars

were densely packed in the two-lane tunnel. Albert could see no way through. "How?"

"Be an asshole."

Albert shrugged and leaned on the horn, reaching over to the headlight controls, flashing them.

Tempest shook her head. "I sincerely doubt you've got a headlight left. Bump 'em."

Albert opened his mouth to protest, but quickly realized the futility of the action. If he survived the day, his girlfriend would make sure he didn't survive the night. That was certain. In for a penny …

He rammed the car ahead of him. It swerved into the next lane and Albert raced forward. Tempest nodded. Her protégé was getting it. Albert bumped the next car.

On the Manhattan end of the tunnel, two sedans braked to a screeching halt, one on each side of the mouth of the tunnel. Four operators exited their sedans, just another day at the office. They checked their weapons, making sure nothing more would go wrong; making sure that in the shit storm that would follow this operation, they would have the only umbrella. They took positions behind their sedans. Adequate cover. They got in their shooting stances. And then they waited for their bubblegum-pink target to emerge.

CHAPTER 38

*C*rash! Albert bumped a Smart Car too hard, and it careened into a BMW. He didn't wait. He shot into the gap and finally he had caught up with a truck from an artisanal Brooklyn bakery delivering delicacies to dozens of Manhattan's best restaurants.

Tempest didn't pause for a single moment. She fired two shots into the back of the delivery truck, the second a bullseye on the lock securing the rear cargo door.

"Climb out and get in the truck."

Albert hesitated. Tempest yelled. "Now!"

Tempest slid over and grabbed the steering wheel with her left hand. Chaucer climbed over her now vacant seat and carefully sidled out onto the hood of the car. Albert took longer to get over the steering wheel, but managed by the time Chaucer jumped onto the back of the bread truck and unlatched the catch, allowing the cargo door to swing upward and grant them entry.

Tempest tossed Albert her duffel bag. "Take it and jump."

Albert looked down and saw the dotted yellow lines racing past. He froze. Unable to stand, let alone jump.

"Jump, asshole!" Tempest had zero patience for the man, but her manner was only making the problem worse.

Chaucer spoke calmly. "Albert, if they see us, they will kill us. You have to jump. To save your own life. Jump now."

Albert locked eyes with Chaucer, fear more than evident. He slung the duffel over his shoulder, gritted his teeth, and in one swift motion, pushed up onto two feet and leaped across the narrow gap between car and truck.

Now it was Tempest's turn. She looked around the car for something to wedge the accelerator. She found nothing. Not even so much as a newspaper she could roll up. She hadn't taken notice before, but Albert's girlfriend was fastidious beyond all comprehension.

Tempest took her foot off the accelerator and tried to hustle out the destroyed windshield, but before she could even get an arm out, the truck raced out of reach. Tempest sat back down.

She stomped on the accelerator, and got the Caddy close, then tried again. Same result. She couldn't make it onto the hood before the truck was far away.

She looked up, and there were Chaucer's owl eyes, burrowing into hers. "Catapult!" he yelled.

Tempest smiled. He was a smart bastard, that Chaucer.

Ahead, the faint glow of daylight approached. They were out of time. Tempest slammed on the brakes.

But only for a moment. Her maneuver let the truck get about four hundred feet ahead when she mashed the accelerator again. The Caddy sped up quickly, its 4.6 liter V8 doing what it was designed to do: exhibiting pure power. It raced at the truck just as the truck approached the glowing halo of the other end of the tunnel. The Caddy's speed was way too fast, the distance closing too quickly. It was going to ram the truck.

"What the hell is she doing?" asked Albert.

"Watch and learn, Grasshopper."

Tempest calculated distances in her head. It wasn't altogether different from her sniper training, or her executive-protection-driving training, but neither discipline had the formula she was crunching on the fly. In her mind, an alarm went off: "Now."

Tempest lifted off the gas and scrambled out onto the hood of the car as quickly as she could. The Cadillac shot forth, aimed at the back of the truck like a cruise missile, and Tempest rode it like Slim Pickens rode that bomb in *Dr. Strangelove*.

Chaucer caught the hint of a smile on her face as she stood up. The woman did love her job at times. But as the Cadillac slowed, and the inevitable crash looked less and less certain, Chaucer could see the smile fade. Her calculation was off. Not by much, but very possibly by enough to doom her. The Cadillac's momentum was dying faster than she expected. She wanted a near miss with the bread truck. Now she could see that the car wouldn't make it within ten feet of the truck's fender.

She had one move, and one move only. She jumped atop the roof of the Caddy, and then onto the trunk, giving herself the most runway she could purchase. Chaucer figured out her play. He grabbed the heavy cloth strap at the base of the rear cargo door dangling above him, and he wrapped it around his wrist for a secure hold.

The light at the end of the tunnel was blinding now, the truck less than a hundred feet from the tunnel's mouth. The Caddy now matched the truck's speed. It would get no closer than about fourteen feet from the back of the truck. In the back of Tempest's mind, she recalled that the world record for the long jump was just a couple of inches over twenty-nine feet. She only needed to clear half that. The thought gave her no solace.

She launched into a run, planning each step. One more on the trunk. Two on the roof. Two more on the hood, and then it was out of her hands. At that last step, just inches from the hood ornament, Tempest had excellent form. Her arms were behind her, her knees and hips flexed, ready to unleash every ounce of momentum she could gather. She hurled her body both up and forward, willing herself to close the gap.

It would not be enough. She felt it the moment she left the hood. The arc was too high, eating away at her distance. She felt gravity take hold of her and pull her to the racing pavement below.

Chaucer had been doing a calculation of his own, one less of momentum and more of timing. He saw her leap. He saw she would be short. And so he leaped himself, hurling his lower body, his legs, into the gap behind the truck. His arms both grasped the strap for dear life, using it to further swing his legs up and out.

For a brief second, they looked like a trapeze act, Tempest flying through the air, falling, Chaucer swinging upward to catch her midarc. Tempest lashed a single arm out and caught Chaucer's right ankle. The move should have saved her life, but for one small miscalculation.

The cargo door. Chaucer's weight alone started sliding it back down. The added weight of Tempest saw it crashing closed, and sending them both to the pavement below. Chaucer couldn't see this, but his gut could feel the physics of his impending death. Until suddenly, something in the equation changed. They stopped falling.

Tempest looked up to see Albert holding the cargo door open, allowing her and Chaucer to swing back and into the truck. Then, and only then, did Albert let go of the door and let it slam shut. A split second of daylight hit the back of the truck as it closed.

The operators on the Manhattan side of the tunnel scanned every car and truck that exited, watching for the faces they had long since memorized. There were no matches. Yet.

A moment later, the pink Cadillac came racing out of the tunnel. As one, the four men opened fire, three blasting the passenger compartment with armor-piercing rounds, and the fourth taking careful aim at the front left tire.

It was far from an easy shot, but the fourth operative hit pay dirt and heard the satisfying mini-explosion of a blowout. It sent the Caddy careening into the left wall of the exit ramp, a bone-jarring crash just thirty yards past the operators and their vehicles.

They ran to the Caddy in the hopeful expectation of finding their targets either dead or completely incapacitated. Even once they looked inside the car, it took them a full minute to process that not a soul remained in the ghost car.

CHAPTER 39

Min Gun listened intently to the CIA chatter as his train crossed the East River into Manhattan. No smile crossed his lips, but what he heard was undoubtedly good news. His targets were in Manhattan, a thirteen-by-two-mile island with the third largest concentration of security cameras after London and Tokyo. His hunting field had just grown smaller. And he had gained improved spotters.

The gremlins were the reason he was listening to a secure CIA radio channel. The gremlins were the reason he was on Long Island, and the reason he was now heading back to Manhattan. To date, their intelligence had been exceptional. It would need to continue to be so, for Min Gun had a debt to pay.

The gremlins texted. Using the city's surveillance cameras, they had tracked the last sixteen vehicles to exit the tunnel before the Cadillac. They lost eleven in areas with no coverage and never picked up again. But of the remaining five, one, a bread truck, was spotted in Little Italy, offloading freshly baked goods, and three stowaways. A second text contained a map, and explicit instructions on how to switch trains to vector in on his targets most quickly. Min Gun, of course, could procure a car at a moment's notice, either through theft or gremlin arrangement. But the gremlins knew logistical details beyond his reckoning, and when they gave him train instructions, it was because they were certain that intercept route was faster.

Finally, after all this news, Min Gun betrayed the hint of a smile.

The din in Asher's command center van was deafening, with operatives on phones and radios, searching for some ray of hope that the op wasn't a total bust. The atmosphere was not quite panic, but his team was scrambling. They were not used to situations like this. In the modern era, a target escaping concentrated surveillance on home turf, in a major American city, was nearly unthinkable. Asher himself remained calm and waited. Fifty-two seconds later, what he was waiting for arrived.

He stepped outside the van to take the call on an empty side street on the East Side of Manhattan. At the corner, he could make out just the edge of the UN Secretariat building.

His employer's voice masker was a new model, designed to make the voice sound normal, a far cry from the horror film output of such devices in the past. "You were hired for your attention to detail."

"I was hired because my quarry is of the highest caliber. To expect a simple operation where Tempest MacLaren is concerned would be folly."

"Why have they returned to Manhattan?"

"There can only be one reason. They've elected not to run."

"*Not* to run?" The voice masker barely concealed the surprise in his employer's tone.

"It's hubris. Nothing more. They've allowed us to concentrate our units, and they've entered a high-surveillance zone. They've made my job easier."

"You still haven't answered my question. Why Manhattan?"

"You want a guess, or an answer? The latter will take a little more time." Asher grew tired of the second guessing. Surely his reputation deserved more benefit of the doubt than was currently on offer.

"You're scrambling. You have no leads."

"And you have faulty intel. I've got a lead of the Widowmaker's kid. We're gonna find him, and she's gonna come to us."

There was a long pause. Anger? Indecision? Asher neither knew nor cared.

Asher heard the snap. It sounded like a rubber band smacking against a package, but with just the hint of an echo, suggesting it came from much farther away.

Asher saw the tiny cloud of dust form on the pavement just a foot from him. It left him certain. It was the ricochet of a silenced rifle shot. His eyes scanned the buildings in front of him. He, of course, saw nothing.

"For now, we will not terminate our relationship, Mr. Asher. But we reserve the right of reconsideration. Are we understood?"

Goosebumps raced up Asher's arms as his body went cold. He had miscalculated. His employer was beyond desperate. Quite possibly psychotic.

"I'll have my quarry inside of twenty-four hours. Acceptable?"

"More than acceptable, Mr. Asher."

The line went dead. Asher took one last glance at the surrounding buildings, willing himself to see the threat. Knowing he would not.

CHAPTER 40

Grand Central Station. Penn Station. Port Authority. Six different stops for PATH trains. Eleven ferry locations. Sixteen bridges. God knows how many helipads. And those were just the exits the opposition had to cover for containment. Add to that another dozen possible destinations for Tempest and the same for Chaucer, and you were looking at a manpower drain of epic proportions, and Chaucer knew it.

There was a chance they would rely on the NYPD and transit cops to cover some of those options, but Chaucer ruled that out almost immediately. Their enemies knew their capabilities, and would know that the NYPD had about a 1 percent chance of success against trained operatives such as himself and Tempest. No, they were likely scrambling for manpower, and given that this was an off-the-books op, that manpower would be hard, if not impossible, to arrange.

The logic of the situation calmed Chaucer. The size of the task before their opponents caused the panic that had been building since they reentered Manhattan to ebb. He concentrated on his breathing without drawing attention. He couldn't afford an attack now. Neither Tempest nor Albert had ever seen Chaucer—devolve. Luckily, they took no note of his calming rituals, instead focused on the physical task before them.

Albert watched Tempest pick a door lock with studied interest. Her speed awed him, and disappointed him. She made it look easy, so easy that he did not pick up even the slightest of tips. In seconds, the door sprung open and the three of them entered the office of a professor of philosophy at NYU.

Albert glanced around at the books, the teak desk, the bust of some old bald guy. He was unimpressed. Chaucer thought it looked quite similar to the office of Tajo's advisor, in a building just six blocks away. took no note of the details of the narrow room. She headed right to the window. Chaucer joined her a moment later.

"Which building is the kid's lab?" Chaucer asked.

Tempest pulled out two pairs of binocs from the duffel, tossing one to Chaucer. "Gray stone and glass across the street. Six stories. His lab is on the third floor."

"And you've been inside? You know the layout?"

"No, but I did my homework—got one. Northwest corner, next to the falafel cart."

Chaucer focused his binocs on the woman Tempest identified. He might have missed her. Slight woman, Lebanese descent. She looked like one of a hundred falafel cart vendors. But the longer Chaucer looked, the more tells rose to the surface. It was lunchtime, and yet this woman wasn't focusing on the sidewalk next to her, where her customers would come from. She was scanning the entire corner.

On top of that, her hands were smooth and unwrinkled—hardly the hands of a food vendor. Her shoes. It reminded Chaucer of a child's joke: What shoes do spies wear? Sneakers. But this woman wore the wrong kind. Lightweight runners. Miserable in a job requiring hours of standing. Her entire build was too lean, too taut for her profession. Everything spoke of "close, but no cigar."

"Verified."

Albert couldn't help himself. "What? What's verified?"

"An operative, Albert. Posted across the street, watching," Chaucer explained.

"For us?"

"No, for the pope," Tempest snapped. She looked over at Chaucer. "You think they have someone inside as well?"

"They've got a lot of places to cover. They might be stretched too thin for double coverage."

"But?" Tempest heard it in Chaucer's voice.

"But if they're going to double-cover a location, it might be this one. It all leads back right here. The assassination of Tajo. Whatever has us on the Ghost Boards, it all comes back to my interrogation, which comes back to you, and the killing of the kid."

"Who?" asked Albert.

"Need to know, Albert. Do me a favor and check the door. Whoever's office this is could come back."

Albert scowled and posted up by the door. "Top floor, by the way."

Both Chaucer and Tempest glanced back. Chaucer asked, "What?"

"The lab is on the top floor."

Tempest challenged him. "And how would you know that?"

"Because I've worked in buildings like that one. It's not six stories. It's only three. The top floor is triple height. They used to be gyms back in the seventies."

Tempest scowled. Chaucer turned away from her to hide just the hint of a smile. Albert had hidden strengths. He turned back to Tempest. "Have to assume a school building like this has basic security."

"Key cards and guards. This is New York."

Albert shrugged. "I can get you in. All you need to do is take care of the chick at the falafel cart."

Tempest exhaled loudly, expecting to suffer a fool.

Chaucer asked, "What are you thinking, Albert?"

"Just find me the name of the best pizzeria within six blocks. And come to think of it, I got a way to deal with falafel chick too."

Tempest's eyebrows lowered, annoyed. "Enlighten us."

"Cops. Cops spook 'em, right? Call in a shooting, a bomb threat, whatever. Bring the cops right to that corner."

Tempest nodded, a gesture of respect. The rookie had an excellent idea. Chaucer got on his phone. Albert shouted afterwards as he left the office, "Don't forget the pizza."

CHAPTER 41

At the Forty-Third Precinct homicide bullpen, a phone rang. At first, nobody did anything. After all, it was a cell-phone ringer, not one of the department landlines. Whoever had the phone would surely answer it.

Until they didn't. After a minute of constant ringing, two detectives started searching for the source of the noise. They converged on Spinoza's desk, where the sound seemed to come from a thin padded envelope in her inbox.

They pulled Spinoza from the break room, forcing her to open the package and end the incessant ringing. Spinoza found a burner phone inside. She flipped it open and answered it. "Who the hell is this?"

"Spinoza, it's me." The hypnotist's voice was unmistakable. Chaucer.

"Mal, why are you calling me on this thing?"

"Put your cell phone on your desk and go to the stairwell."

Spinoza saw her fellow cops eyeing her. "What? What?!"

That was enough. They went back to work. Spinoza took her cell phone from its holster and put it on the desk. She crossed the bullpen and disappeared out the door to the stairwell.

"What the hell, Mal?"

"You're bugged by now, for sure. Everything you say around your cell phone, they can hear."

"Wanna share who 'they' are?"

"Wouldn't be wise. I need another favor."

"You been asking a lot lately."

"One last thing. It might just get me the information I need to find out who killed Terry."

Spinoza inhaled. It still hurt to hear his name. She replied, "Ask your question."

"What's the biggest truck the NYPD owns?"

———

The first to arrive on the scene at Greene and Waverly were a pair of squad cars, lights and sirens blaring. The woman at the falafel stand took careful note of them, especially when the officers inside rushed in her direction. But they paid her no mind. They were searching the ground for something. But what?

She was not to be distracted, keeping an eye on the building across the street. Her assignment. But the cops seemed frantic, and they kept drawing her attention, especially since their circles of focus kept getting closer and closer to her falafel stand.

Next, two more squad cars arrived. They blocked off half of the street this time, and four more officers joined the hunt. What the hell were they doing?

"Ma'am. Ma'am! I need you to move your cart."

"What? Why?" The woman was genuinely startled.

"We got a major problem here and I need you to move your cart," said the cop.

"I have the proper permits. I'm allowed to be here."

"Ma'am, you don't understand, we're responding to an automated alarm—"

Just then, a huge NYPD tractor trailer pulled into the intersection. Emblazoned on the side were the words "HAZARDOUS SUBSTANCE RESPONSE." The woman was truly flustered now and barely noticed the huge truck was blocking her vantage point.

"Will somebody tell me what's going on?"

"A Con Ed gas alarm went off, under this street. We could be looking at a gas main leak. Ma'am, we're this close to evacuating the area, and we need to find the access port," the cop said with urgency.

The operative thought quickly. She looked across the street. "Can I set up on that corner?"

The cop was frustrated. He already spent too long on this conversation. "For now, but next time? I tell you move, you move. Got it?"

"Yes, Officer. Sorry, Officer." She got out the key to the lock that secured her cart to a light pole and hustled to move to a new vantage point.

By the time that falafel cart moved, Tempest, Chaucer, and Albert were in place, outside the fire door to the southwest stairs of the building. A hundred-dollar tip bought them the promise of a young Haitian pizza delivery guy appearing any second and opening the door for them. Several labs in the building that were among the Haitian's more frequent customers. These grad students were poor, and they worked long hours, fueled by the best cheap food they could find. The lobby guards knew him well and waved him right past security.

Chaucer checked his watch. The Haitian was late. Was he spotted? Or just delayed? It wouldn't matter in less than two minutes when the spotter with the falafel cart cleared the NYPD truck. Just before genuine concern arose, the fire door swung open, a blaring alarm sounded, and in five seconds, all three of them were inside and the door swung shut.

The alarm stopped. Ten percent chance the guards would even investigate. A five-second door alarm was hardly worth it. Always some new kid leaving and not knowing about the alarm.

In any case, Chaucer and his crew weren't around long enough to find out how diligent the guards here were. They thanked the Haitian and took to the stairs.

Five flights up, Tempest turned to see Albert chowing down on a slice of the pizza. Her look of derision could cut steel. Albert shrugged. "What? We paid for it, and I haven't eaten anything since your place."

CHAPTER 42

Min Gun saw three targets enter the fire door. One was Tempest MacLaren, the assassin who bested him a day ago. One was Malcolm Chaucer, a legendary interrogator, but only a minor complication for his mission. But the third. The African, as Min Gun conceived of him, was a mystery.

He had heard reports of a third traveler from his gremlins, but he had dismissed them as unlikely. Evading surveillance as a duo is hard enough. As a trio? The difficulty increases exponentially. So who was this man? An associate of Chaucer's? Of MacLaren's? If it was the latter, Min Gun was no longer sure he could complete his mission. Looking at the African, something wasn't right. He did not move like a wet-worker. He didn't exactly lumber, but there was a lack in grace, a conservation of energy missing that years of training invariably imparted. No, he was no associate of Tempest MacLaren. But he was still a mystery.

Tempest opened the door to the third floor. It smelled of floor wax and astringent. The walls were flat white and extended up forty feet to a series of skylights. The floor was gray polished concrete. And on that concrete, Tempest heard footsteps.

She was about to close the door when a hand stopped her. A building security guard stood in front of them. Latin. Sturdy. No threat, but nonetheless, an unexpected complication. He looked at the three of them, Albert still eating his pizza. "What are you folks doing in the stairwell?"

For a moment, nobody spoke. Chaucer fought against his programming, but not answering wasn't an option. "We're visiting a lab."

And for a second, Tempest thought they were going to get away with it. Until the guard's curiosity refused to wane. "Why didn't you just take the elevator?"

Chaucer replied. He didn't want to. He had to. "We snuck into the building to circumvent security."

They could see the guard processing this all in slow motion. Tempest's hand moved as casually as possible to the hollow of her back, where her pistol awaited her. But before she could draw it, the guard laughed.

"Good one. Have a great day."

And with that, the guard disappeared down the hall. The three intruders glanced at each other.

Tempest blinked hard. "What just happened?"

Chaucer replied, "The truth shall set you—"

"Don't even." Tempest glared at Chaucer to signal her seriousness.

Albert stepped past them and into the hall. At the other end, he witnessed the guard getting on the elevator and disappearing as the doors closed.

The lab door was ajar. Tempest led the way, slipping in, scouting for any enemies that might wait inside. Instead, she found a young woman, clearly a civilian, dressed in rose and gray sweats and blowing her nose. Tempest made the slightest of motions behind her, telling Chaucer and Albert the proverbial coast was clear.

"Can I help you?"

Chaucer instantly realized who this was. "I believe you can, Isabel."

Her eyes flickered when she heard hear name. This was the real Isabel Marcano.

"I'm sorry. Have we met?"

Chaucer adopted a gentle smile, casual and disarming. "There've been so many of us in here, right? The last thing you want is more questions, but I'm afraid I do have a few more. I really think these will be the last questions you need to answer."

Jaw tension. A double blink. A hitch in her breath. Chaucer's eyes took it all in. *Stress.* It was considerably more than he expected to encounter in this circumstance. After all, a police detective with questions will bring on stress, but for an innocent bystander, it should be minimal. And it was not.

"Of course. Whatever you need."

Another double blink. Fingers flex. Stiffening posture. *Stress.* Chaucer noted the anomaly.

As expected, she assumed Chaucer was with the police, though he never overtly lied about that. Nonetheless, Chaucer's body paid the price for the lie of omission. He felt sharp jolts race up his spine. Only years of practice rendered his agony invisible to the others.

Tempest roamed about the space, eyes on the rafters. She was recreating the crime in her mind, seeing the scene through the eyes of a sniper. She paid particular attention to the hole in the box, running her fingers along the indentation in the thick plastic material. The round penetrated two different layers of thick polymer. Tempest didn't want to admire the shot, but she simply had to. This sniper was quite good.

Albert stood at a ninety-degree angle to Chaucer at a distance his employer had been very specific about. Chaucer was very particular about everything regarding this interrogation. The short of it was that he was to stay ten feet away at a minimum, and to stay as still as a statue. Nothing to interrupt the effect of his snake-charmer eyes.

Albert took Chaucer literally, standing as close to ten feet away as he could. He wished it could be closer. His temporary boss was a strange man. One of the strangest he had ever met. But Albert knew a master was at work, and that was something worth paying attention to.

It was nothing like he thought it would be. He thought it would be an *interrogation*. But this? This was just a conversation. And a fairly boring one at that. Only Chaucer's eyes betrayed it was anything more. His pupils danced to and fro, constantly sweeping Isabel Marcano for every tidbit of body language, every involuntary display of thought and emotion. Frankly, Albert thought, he didn't see how this was getting anywhere. He barely asked her anything for the first five minutes. It felt like strangers on a first date.

He made everything seem perfunctory, matter-of-fact. He was a blank page of emotion, a sponge to soak up every feeling she had to release. And she had a lot. She was the one who found Tajo evidently, dead inside the plastic cage in the center of the huge room. She was still broken up about it, and had been crying shortly before they entered.

She said she liked him, but even Albert could tell they weren't close. He was a grad student from South Korea, here to work, not to chat. He didn't let on much, if anything, about what he was working on, and certainly not about his life outside this place. She was simply his helper. Her job was to fill out endless paperwork, clean what needed to be cleaned, and occasionally to run the odd errand. He never abused that duty, as many other grad students did. She got the sense that he grew up in a home where propriety was a key value.

To Albert, this was a dead end.

Chaucer, however, struggled to contain himself. Her stress response was all wrong. Could Isabel Marcano be more than just an innocent bystander? He decided to test his theory.

"Isabel, have you ever heard the phrase 'Year of the Rabbit?'"

Another double blink. A hitch in the breath. Lips pursed tightly for a millisecond. She continued to tell Chaucer a story only he could see.

"I told the other detective—"

"Sorry, but I need to hear it for myself."

Isabel licked her dry lips before she continued. "His friend, Ji. She would say that. I heard it maybe twice. But she said it like it was some kind of joke."

Albert stirred just enough to earn Chaucer's glare. A second later, Chaucer's eyes snapped back to Isabel's. "Ji?"

"Ji-Ho, I think her name is."

"Is she a student?"

"I don't think so. She mentioned once she owned a business in midtown."

"What kind of business?"

"A pet store, I think."

CHAPTER 43

Min Gun took a deep breath and held it. It was a centering exercise, one that would calm his nerves before battle. He exhaled and repeated the process. He had never lost a battle until yesterday. Now he was injured, and going in for a second round.

Tempest MacLaren had backup, whereas he was alone. Individually, the men backing the Widowmaker did not seem to present any significant challenge, but together they were a complicating factor. Min Gun exhaled again, willing himself into a calm he did not feel.

No, not calm. Coolness. Calm was something he never felt. It wasn't even something he was trained to feel. Calmness was a state for civilians. No, what he was looking for was something closer to numb. Alert, ready, amped, but numb. The adrenaline coursing through him would be focused. It would not make mistakes. It would be a weapon of the motherland, delivering righteous justice for the enemies of the eternal dynasty.

After his third exhale, Min Gun readied his HK CAWS, an automatic shotgun particularly lethal at close range. Then he opened the door to the lab.

Before the door even fully opened, he saw the Widowmaker raising her pistol at him.

Blam! The CAWS fired its first shell, filled with steel balls, choke set wide. Half of the shot caught Tempest, and threw her backward over the desk of Isabel Marcano. Chaucer was caught out of position, his back to the door. Albert was ten feet further to the left, staring right at the intruder, but similarly unprepared.

Albert reached for his gun, fumbled it, and it clattered to the ground. He ducked down to retrieve it, and the move saved his life as Min Gun's CAWS continued to spit steel as he rotated toward the armed man on his flank. Albert ducked right before the barrel reached him, disappearing behind a lab bench. A swarm of steel balls passed overhead harmlessly.

Chaucer leaped over the assistant's desk, landing on top of Isabel Marcano. He shielded her with his body as he reached for his own gun, but his eyes found Tempest, twenty feet further into the room. She lay on the smooth white floor, bleeding in four places on the right side of her body.

She did not scream, or yell, or do much more than grimace. Chaucer started toward her, but she held up a hand, holding him off.

"Stay down. I got this bastard."

Min Gun couldn't see the Widowmaker, but he could see the spray of her blood on the floor of the lab. She was wounded, evening the playing field. The Oracle was completely defensive, and the mystery man dropped his own weapon. Things were looking up. Min Gun knew that the rest of the shots in his gun were buckshot; steel balls designed to rip a human body apart. He switched to semi-auto, ready to pick off his targets one by one. He retreated and circled the center of the lab.

Tempest popped up and put a tight grouping of three rounds in the general location of where Min Gun had been. But he was gone. There was no sign of him. Tempest tucked and rolled behind another lab bench.

In her sweep, she caught no sight of the North Korean. This was bad. She looked at Chaucer and realized that it was all she could do to stay alive. She couldn't protect him. "Chaucer, you and her get in the box."

Chaucer glanced behind at him at the thick plexiglass box of the virus lab. He looked back at Tempest, many questions in his eyes.

"A sniper rifle barely penetrated it. A shotgun's got no chance. Do it! In three, two, one."

Tempest popped up and fired blindly. She peppered several of Min Gun's most likely hiding places with several rounds each, emptying the mag. She heard no indication of success. Chaucer helped Isabel Marcano up, and the two of them ran from the desk to the box. Isabel knew how the airlock functioned, and opened it, just as Min Gun rose from his hiding place, directly behind them.

Tempest spun to see that Min Gun's weapon was aimed right at Chaucer and the witness, and Tempest herself was in a straight line behind them. The man was good. One pull of that trigger, and he would potentially kill all three of them in one shot. She willed her body to move faster than it had ever moved before, spinning her gun arm around. She had feet to go. The North Korean had inches. A sickening feeling permeated her gut, like she was swimming in quicksand, unable to stop what had become inevitable. The shotgun round was incoming.

Blam! Tempest didn't understand what she was seeing. She expected a bright muzzle flash and then to feel the searing heat of blistering projectiles entering her body. Instead she saw the North Korean assassin turn his head to one side abruptly, as if identifying an unknown threat. Then she saw the blood spray out Min Gun's ear. Min Gun went down hard. Emerging under a desk was Albert, his hand shaking lightly as he lowered the pistol.

Tempest returned her pistol to her waistband. Her hand shook as she did it. It wasn't something that Chaucer saw very often, Tempest MacLaren rattled. But that was what was happening.

"Is that it? Are there any more?" Albert said.

Tempest snapped out of it and headed into the hallway, drawing her gun once again. No, just like before, the North

Korean assassin had been acting alone. She returned to the lab and checked on him. Albert's was a beautiful shot. Into his ear and right through his cerebellum. The bullet hit the back part of his skull, and likely bounced around. Nobody comes back from that.

She looked up at Albert, surprised.

"Well? Is that it?"

Tempest nodded. "Yeah, Albert. That's it."

"Hey, you called me by my name."

Tempest looked back at the body, then back at Albert. "Did I? Guess I did. Good job."

Tempest lifted her shirt, exposing three wounds from the shotgun blast.

Chaucer saw the blood. "You okay?"

"Superficial. All of 'em. Don't need more than a few Band-Aids."

She got to work, plucking out the round steel balls that sat just beneath the skin.

Albert sat down on the desk nearest him. Both his hands shook violently. "I'm sorry. I can't stop shaking."

"It's the adrenaline," Tempest responded. "It's just working its way out of your system."

"Then why aren't your hands shaking?"

"You do this long enough, you get past the shaking stage."

Chaucer searched Min Gun's body, and on it, he found a phone. He used the dead man's thumb to open it and saw a string of text messages in Korean. Luckily, Chaucer could read them.

"Tempest, look at this."

"What does it say?"

"The North Koreans found the Pet Shop Club. They gave this guy directions."

CHAPTER 44

Chaucer wanted more time with Isabel Marcano, but that was no longer wise. Tempest told her to run home and never to come back here. She seemed to follow those instructions to the letter.

Chaucer, Tempest, and Albert exited the building via an emergency door to an alley in the back of the building. They wound their way to a side street out of the falafel peddler's view.

A block ahead, Albert stopped. "Wait. Can you guys just wait?"

Tempest could see that Albert was having a tough time. His hands were still shaking just as violently as before. He sat down on the hood of a car and took deep breaths, gulping for air.

Chaucer and Tempest returned to him. Chaucer asked, "You okay, Albert?"

"You …When we met, you said you needed somebody who could kill a man and get away with it."

"Yes?"

"The thing is, until yesterday, I never killed anybody in my life."

Chaucer was surprised. "Your arrest record showed that you

were the primary suspect in four murders, and you were never convicted."

Albert shivered uncontrollably. "There was a gang in my neighborhood. When I was growing up, half the neighborhood ended up in it. My best friend growing up? He joined. I didn't. Ten years later, he was running that gang. And he was running it all wrong. It was like he wanted it to be the baddest gang in the world. So initiations, jumping people in, they got brutal—a couple of them died. So he changed up the nature of the initiation. A bunch of his new recruits, they took my fifteen-year-old niece. Kidnapped her. They did things to her. Thing is, she was special. Beyond smart, kind. It was like they destroyed something beautiful. Don't get me wrong, I wanted to kill them. I wanted to kill all three of them that did it. I wanted to kill my friend for making them do it. I had the gun. Loaded it."

He paused, fighting off a wave of emotion. Chaucer and Tempest said nothing. "But I couldn't do it. My cousin was with me. The idea was supposed to be that he was the driver, and I was the shooter. But it didn't work out like that. He took the gun from me, and one by one, he killed them all."

Chaucer said, "So yesterday, that Bolivian who came for me?"

"My first." Albert dropped his head and stared at the pavement beneath his feet. "And now another."

Tempest spoke up. "Albert, you saved my life. You saved Chaucer's life. You saved that poor secretary's life, who never did a thing to anyone. I'm not sure that makes you the hero, but it sure as hell doesn't make you the villain."

"See, I took this job for the money," Albert said. "A lot of money, and I need it right now. But I was also kidding myself that maybe, maybe this could turn into something for me. A job. But I don't think that anymore."

Tempest shook her head. "Nobody thinks that after their first kill. But you know what I saw? I saw a man in a heightened situation. With bullets flying everywhere. I saw a man do the right thing. At the right time. You gotta choose what's right for you, but let me tell you, I underestimated you."

Albert nodded in thanks, but he was still distraught. Tempest glanced over at Chaucer, nodding to him. Chaucer thought of what to say to Albert. "Albert, you know I can't lie, right?"

Albert nodded.

Chaucer said, "Look at me, Albert. You are a good man. I haven't met many people I can say that to, but I can say it to you. You're a good man."

Albert locked eyes with Chaucer, seeing the truth of it on his face. And slowly, his breathing returned to normal.

Tempest broke the spell. "Now are we past our fucking kumbaya moment? Can we get to this pet shop, hopefully before the North Koreans do?"

Albert smiled, and a half laugh escaped his lips. "Yeah, I'm good."

CHAPTER 45

The police tape was the first sign there was a problem. The pet shop was called simply that, with signage in English and Korean. It was a basement shop, with eight steps leading below street level. The smell of long-cooked pork wafted over from the noodle shop next door as Tempest descended the steps.

Across the doorway was yellow police tape, and along the seam of the door was a police seal. Tempest slipped underneath the tape, and in less than a minute, she picked the lock on the door, breaking the seal.

Inside were the black remains of a fire. It smelled of kerosene and burnt wood, but with just a faint hint of something more. Something—meaty. A reminder that animals died here. They searched the area, cramped aisles with cages and tanks containing black masses. Chaucer caught Albert's eye. The man looked unwell.

"You want to wait outside?"

Albert didn't need to be asked twice. He spun on his heels and hustled up the stairs to the street.

Tempest continued her search, but it quickly became apparent that there was no use. Even forensics teams rarely found much at the site of an arson.

"The North Koreans are nothing if not thorough," said Tempest.

Chaucer nodded. "But no bodies. At least, not yet."

Tempest headed into the back, where she found a stairwell leading down to a sub-basement. Chaucer followed. They descended the dark stairs and emerged in a large underground space with vaulted brick ceilings two stories high. It became instantly clear that this was the Pet Shop Club. The remains of a lighting booth, DJ stand, and dance floor were all there. But the dance floor had chalk outlines of seven bodies.

Tempest frowned. "Dead end."

Chaucer nodded. He took a long look at the chalk outlines. The arrangement of the bodies was problematic. This was not some assault or raid. These people were not shot dead where they stood. The bodies were laid out methodically, in rows. There was only one reason to do that. These people were tortured before they were killed.

Whatever they knew, they gave it up. It was worse than a dead end. Advantage: bad guys.

Suddenly, Tempest raised a hand. Chaucer knew what it meant. Don't move. Don't breathe. Tempest had a sixth sense, an ability to pick out a pattern from the background noise of sensory input. Far beneath conscious construction, it sometimes misfired, but it had saved her life dozens of times.

Chaucer followed her eyes. She was staring into the dark recesses of the lighting booth. There was nothing there. Chaucer was about to ask Tempest what was going on, when she sprinted, leaping off the DJ stand and hurtling the lighting console.

Chaucer rushed after her, hearing sounds of a struggle in the darkness. He did not vault the console like she did. Instead, he peered over it to find Tempest with a sleeper hold around the neck of a young Korean woman.

CHAPTER 46

Chaucer stared at the unconscious Korean for a long moment. Tempest had gone through her pockets and came up with no identification. Just cash and keys.

"Did you have to knock her out?"

"Yes, I fucking did. We've got a whole army of assholes after us."

"She could be Tajo's friend. A non-contentious interrogation would've been better."

Tempest shook her head. "That's one hell of an assumption. You notice the layout of the bodies?"

"Yes. They were tortured."

"All of them. They didn't torture a couple of them. They tortured each and every one. It means they never got the answer they were looking for."

"Meaning this could be who they were looking for—Tajo's friend, Ji-Ho."

"Or she's one of them, waiting for us to show."

"One of who?" Albert asked as he descended into the dark club. He looked better. More composed.

"DPRK, Agency, third parties," Tempest said. "Take your pick."

Chaucer examined the unconscious woman. "Was that an airway choke?"

"Who do you think I am? It was a blood choke. She'll probably come to any minute now."

The three sat there in silence a long moment.

Tempest turned to Chaucer. "While we're waiting, I got something I've been meaning to say to you. You know you're not as bad as you think you are. You're totally ... functional ... when you want to be."

Chaucer replied, "Then I've fooled you."

"Bullshit. You're able to deal. You could be even better. You just gave up is all."

He looked at her with his owl eyes. "It's a mask. If you knew what was going on inside? You'd be horrified."

"I don't horrify easily."

"I know."

"Try me."

Chaucer sighed. He knew she was a dog with a bone. She wouldn't give up this line of inquiry without a fight. He gave in. "A couple hours ago, I didn't lie to Isabel Marcano. But I did let her believe I was with the police."

Tempest smirked. "You're not gonna give me that 'lie by omission' bullshit?"

"That's what it was. So, for the last two hours, I have counted every single breath I've taken, just to keep from the worst panic attack you'd ever see."

Tempest didn't believe him. "Really? Every breath? Even when the North Korean was attacking?"

Chaucer held her suspicious gaze. "Especially when he was attacking. In high-stress situations, I'm closer to the line."

"The line?"

"I've had a few ... involuntary stays at mental health facilities. All recoverable. But one day, I'll hit the line, and that'll be that. I only came close once."

Albert couldn't help himself. "What happened?"

Tempest fixed him with a murderous stare and he backed

away. Chaucer answered, "Fitz found me a day later. He got me admitted somewhere ... discreet. The meds barely did anything. The doctors, even less. I just had to rebuild my defenses, one block at a time. In forty-five days, they released me."

A second silence descended upon the three. This one was far more weighty. And awkward. Tempest raised a hand for a moment, wanting to reach out and comfort Chaucer. But it was hopeless. She never finished the motion.

The Korean coughed. Immediately, Albert moved out of Chaucer's line of sight. He was learning. Tempest brandished her pistol and stood behind Chaucer.

The girl was petrified as she regarded the three people in the room. Pupils like pinpricks. Elevated heart rate. Shallow breathing, even after choking. Her brain was in pure fight-or-flight mode.

Chaucer offered a vague smile. Not happy, so much as reassuring. "What's your name?"

She didn't respond verbally. But her fear was far from abating. It was a good sign. She seemed like a civilian.

Chaucer tried again. "We need to know your name."

She felt her throat where bruises were already forming. "Ji. Ji-Ho."

Tempest pursed her lips behind Chaucer and backed away.

Chaucer softened his posture noticeably. Everything he did in these moments was for effect. "I want you to know we didn't do this."

Ji muttered something under her breath. Something Chaucer couldn't catch.

"What was that?"

"No shit," said Ji, bitterness in her tone.

"How are you so sure?"

"You don't exactly look North Korean."

So it was the North Koreans. The message on the assassin's phone was old. He had been here earlier. "Fair. We need your help."

"Not exactly in a helpful mood." She glared at Tempest.

Tempest took two steps toward her, but Chaucer stopped her with a raised hand.

Tempest growled. "Come on, Chaucer. We're burning time. Do this the fast way."

Chaucer centered himself. Tempest was not making this easier. Chaucer said, "My friend over there? Her house blew up yesterday when a North Korean assassin came to kill her. Probably because your friend Tajo tried to hire her."

Ji's eyes betrayed her. The mention of Tajo's name gave a deep emotional response.

Chaucer continued. "Yesterday, contract killers killed my brother when they meant to kill me, because I conducted the interrogation of a witness to Tajo's murder. Now I look around here, and I can see you've lost even more. But we are all in the same boat. We are all being hunted. The only difference is, you might know why."

Ji laughed. It was a mournful laugh. "You know exactly why. Because the most paranoid people in the world found out that Tajo and I were friends."

Chaucer made no movement. His body and face neither agreed nor disagreed with the statement. He said, "The Year of the Rabbit."

Ji looked surprised. She glared at Chaucer. "You know about that? Yeah, that's what did it. That's what got everybody killed. And worst part? The worst part is, for Tajo? It was a joke."

CHAPTER 47

"A joke?" Chaucer asked.

"I mean, do you even know what the Year of the Rabbit is?"

Chaucer had a hundred ways to turn the question back on her, but he sensed no evasion in her. Instead, he chose to build affinity. "I think it was a plan for a coup inside the DPRK."

Ji laughed. "Everything is a plan for a coup in the DPRK. You kiss your husband on the wrong cheek, you're plotting a coup. You cross the wrong street, you're plotting a coup."

"Then what?"

Ji shrugged. "I mean, yeah. We want to change back home. We want to wake up our people, to show them the lies they've been told their whole lives."

She stopped herself. Her cheeks blushed. Chaucer knew she was blushing at her own naivete.

"It must be hard. To affect change in the Hermit Kingdom."

"It's not hard. It's impossible. That was why I came up with the Year of the Rabbit. It was a good goalpost. Far enough away that it didn't seem impossible. Close enough that it gave us urgency."

Chaucer nodded. "You came up with it? The Year of the Rabbit?"

"There was this con man, early twentieth century. Napoleon Hill. He said a goal is a dream with a deadline. That's all it ever was. A goal."

"But the Korean People's Army—"

"I never even knew there already was a Year of the Rabbit. Never knew that some KPA generals planned anything. I just ... picked a date on a calendar."

"So, what was your plan?"

Ji shivered slightly. "You got a smoke?"

Chaucer shook his head. He looked back at Tempest. "I quit five years ago," she replied.

Albert stepped forward and pulled a hard pack from his jacket. Ji took it. He lit it.

She took a long drag, grimacing as she did it. "Menthols? Who the hell still smokes menthols?"

Albert frowned. "Well, fuck you very much."

Chaucer got her back on point. "What was the plan?"

Ji stared at the black ceiling. It pained her to say it. "The goal is simply to penetrate the Kingdom. There are so many of us. And we know things. First, we know how we got out. And if you can get out one way ..."

Chaucer figured it out. "Then maybe you can get in that same way."

Ji looked down, dejected. "Something like that. And we figured a couple of the ways out could work both ways. But the next problem was information. The Kingdom is totally compartmentalized. Moving anything from one region to another is almost impossible. And most of the people? At least the ones that aren't in the regime's pockets? They don't even have VCRs. They have nothing. So how do you get them information? How do you make it real and not make it seem like propaganda?"

"You came up with something?"

Ji shook her head. "Fuck no! We came up with ideas, notions, plans. One by one, we ruled them all out. I realized years ago what the Year of the Rabbit really was."

Chaucer stayed calm. He asked in an even tone, "What was that?"

"It was the first-ever branch of the NKA. North Koreans Anonymous. People came trying to figure out how to change the Hermit Kingdom, but we were really here to talk about what we experienced. It was a good thing, you know? When you escape the DPRK, you're the most alone you've ever been. And nobody but a fellow refugee understands what you're going through."

Tempest's brow furrowed, her frustration rising. "You're telling us there is no coup? That all this is bullshit?"

"You don't understand how paranoid these people are. They sent fucking agents to infiltrate us. Tajo helped us smoke a few out."

Chaucer asked, "What was his connection?"

"What do you mean?"

Chaucer took in a hundred signals of genuine confusion. "Tajo was South Korean. What was he doing here?"

Ji nodded. "Yeah, we thought that too, at first. We thought he was some kind of infiltrator. By then, we knew how to deal with infiltrators. We treat 'em like mushrooms."

"Meaning?"

Tempest interrupted. "You feed them shit and keep them in the dark."

Ji smirked. "She gets it. But Tajo kept coming. And when we'd talk, he'd participate. Never telling his story exactly, but he said enough to know. He was there."

"How did you two meet?"

"It was random, really. He needed guinea pigs and his supplier was out. So he came into my shop."

"Guinea pigs?"

"He's a biologist. They need lab rats and stuff like that. I became a kind of secondary supplier for him once I saw how he treated the animals. We bonded over it. Animal lovers. You know what his NYU friends call him?"

Chaucer nodded. "Dr. Dolittle."

"So we were friends for the longest time. I liked him. He was this great combination of hopeful and cynical. And then one day he saw my people gathering for a meeting. After that, he was always here. But no, I can't say he was ever a part of it. Not really."

"Hopeful and cynical."

Ji laughed. "Like, he told me once he was going to make a difference—no, no, he said that he *had* to make a difference. Like, to pay a debt or something. But every time we talked about anything concrete about the Year of the Rabbit, he would leave. He said … he said we could never change that place."

Chaucer paused a long moment, considering how to phrase this next bit. "Ji, you say there was no Year of the Rabbit? Not in any real way. From what you're saying, even if there was, Tajo was never a part of it. And I believe you. But then why did Tajo contact my friend here for protection? Why did he tell her 'The Year of the Rabbit is coming'?"

Ji-Ho took a deep breath. "I don't know. But a month ago, he said the same thing to me. But—he said it—kind of like a joke. He got that way, kinda giddy, when he got excited."

"Excited, or scared?"

"I think … excited. I'm not sure. You have to understand, Tajo was the most buttoned-up dude I ever met. Like, impenetrable. I could have it wrong. I mean, he was acting weird."

"Weird how?"

"He got paranoid in the last month. Thought people were following him. He said he wasn't gonna let anyone stop him."

"Stop him from what?"

"He would never say. It's like … I worried if he was losing it. He started doing weird things. Like staying on my couch for, like, a week. He left stuff at my place."

Chaucer said, "We'll need to see that. Whatever he left for you."

Ji laughed. "You think that's still there? My apartment exploded yesterday. Killed the landlady next door. If they were looking for anything, they found it. That son of a bitch, sitting on top of that cuckoo-clock tower, is probably laughing right now."

There it was. New information. Chaucer didn't let a single tell get out. "What bastard? What tower?"

Ji stared at Chaucer like he was an idiot. "Sim Se Yoon. Tajo's father. One of my friends found out he was here. They reached out to him for help."

"What did he do?"

"Nothing. Not a damn thing. Now he's in a protected suite on the top floor of that building at Fifty-Seventh and Fifth, with his North Korean friends. They're probably sifting through everything right now."

Chaucer sat back. There was nothing more to be gained here. "You need to get out of town."

Ji shook her head. "That's the thing about North Koreans. Comes a point we get tired of running. Sure, they burned this place down. But I got a life here. I got other businesses. Friends they never heard of. I'll be fine."

Tempest spoke up. "Don't ever come back here. This was a mistake. You know that, right?"

Ji nodded. She looked down at the chalk outlines on the floor. "I'm North Korean. We never go back."

Tempest exited first, doing a quick scan, looking for threats. The street was empty. One side was cleared out for street cleaners, the other side was simply experiencing a lull at this time of day. She waved Chaucer and Albert up, and they headed down the street briskly.

Tempest asked, "What do you think?"

Chaucer pursed his lips. "Maybe Tajo heard something in one of those meetings. Maybe he went from thinking the Year of the Rabbit was a pipe dream to thinking it might work. That's the thing about brainstorming. You never know when something will click for somebody."

Tempest shook her head. "How does a North Korean get … adopted, I guess, by a South Korean businessman? Did he escape when he was a kid?"

"There is one way to know. We need to see a man in a cuckoo-clock tower."

CHAPTER 48

The Callery pear trees were in full bloom at the southeastern corner of Central Park. The fragrant smell mixed with incense and fresh tar that wafted over Tempest, Chaucer, and Albert as they stood on the small lawn there. Albert watched a father and daughter play catch with a Frisbee. Chaucer watched Tempest. Tempest stared up at the penthouse of the Crown Building, a stone's throw from their current location, through a detached sniper scope.

It was a multi-story unit with a huge and opulent deck on the building's twenty-third floor. The roof was a steep, angled affair clad in pale green copper, with gold accents on its edges. It looked like a mini-castle; a decorative adornment perched atop a cake disguised as a mundane skyscraper.

Chaucer asked, "How's it looking?"

"Worse than expected," Tempest replied.

"What does that mean?"

"Think I've got at least five hitters in the penthouse."

Chaucer considered it. All in all, it didn't seem like that hard a task for Tempest. "Why is that a problem?"

"The problem is, I would need to kill them all with anyone knowing it. I'd put the odds at one in a thousand."

"What do you mean?"

"The penthouse was designed for high-security VIPs. It was owned by Ferdinand and Imelda Marcos during their exile. They beefed up security like you wouldn't believe. Stair access is heavily barricaded, nearly impenetrable. And the only elevator that goes to the penthouse has a kill switch. It's completely controllable by the occupants."

"So you're saying at any point they can lock it down and there's no way in?"

Tempest nodded. "If there's even two fewer guys, I could probably get a position of fire on them. Take 'em all out and then waltz up in the elevator because there's nobody to press the kill switch. But five? Five is just too many. There's no way."

Tempest put down the sniper scope and stuffed it in her duffle bag. "We might be at a dead end here. We need to rethink strategy."

"No. This is the play. Somebody up there has answers, and I can get them."

Albert chimed in. "Good luck with that, unless you're planning on growing wings."

Tempest stood, mouth open, staring up at the penthouse. "Goddamn it."

Chaucer knew that look. "What?"

Tempest said, "Albert, you're a freaking genius."

Chaucer didn't like the look in Tempest's eyes. "What?"

She grinned maniacally. "You ready to get crazy?"

CHAPTER 49

Tito did not inspire confidence. He drove a windowless van painted primer orange. A van that violated at least ten motor vehicle codes. The only thing he could have done to look more sketchy was to spray paint "Free Candy" on its side. Tito himself was a specimen as well. A Mexican fireplug of a man maxing out at five foot six with long curly hair down to the middle of his back and a lazy eye. But it was Tito's smile that really caused concern. It was broad as his shoulders and half-toothless. He grabbed Tempest and hugged her tight.

"Morning, *mija*!"

Chaucer couldn't believe this was happening. He didn't understand why Tito was still alive, but Tempest at least tolerated the hug. In fact, she hugged him back. "*Hola*, Tito. *¿Que pasa amigo?*"

"*Nada mucho, niña.* You know me. I'm just looking for something to fill the days." Tempest nodded to Albert and Chaucer. "Guys, this is Tito. Served with my old man. Tito's good people."

Albert raised an eyebrow, not quite believing it. Chaucer's implacable face remained still.

"You got what I need, Tito?" Tempest asked.

"I got it, but I don't know if you want it. You ever done this before, *chica*?"

Chaucer asked, "Done what exactly?"

Tito laughed heartily. "You mean you didn't tell them? Oh, you're your daddy's girl, *chica*."

Tempest shrugged. "It's nothing. People skydive every day."

Skydive? Chaucer liked the sound of this plan less and less.

Tito shook his head. "This ain't skydiving. This is BASE jumping. Way different."

Tempest shot back. "The principle's the same."

"Only that you're trying not to die. But BASE jumping? One in sixty BASE jumpers die. And that's the pros. It's got forty-three times the death rate of skydiving."

Albert and Chaucer stared at each other for a long moment. Albert replied first, "Hell, no. There's no way I'm doing that."

Tempest smirked. "As if. You were never going to do it. No, it's just me and the human lie detector."

Chaucer stared at her for a long moment. "I'm not really qualified."

Tempest grabbed him by the shirt. "Stop with this bullshit. You've done all of this. Okay? You and I did a HALO jump into Ch'o-do at three a.m."

"That wasn't me."

"Cut the crap. You're the same person. Sure, more fucked up. But which of us can't say the same?"

Tito smiled. "I sure as shit am more fucked up."

Tempest ignored him. She kept her stare into Chaucer's eyes. "I want answers. You want revenge for your brother. This is how it's got to be. You do what I say when I say, and this can work. Goddamnit, Chaucer. Believe me, this can work."

Tito dragged three backpacks, parachutes when Chaucer looked closer, out of the back of his van and handed them to each of them.

Albert dropped it like a hot potato. "Just to be clear, I'm not doing this."

Tempest replied, "Yeah, yeah. I've got a different mission for you." The words sent a chill through Albert's spine.

Tempest stared at the New York skyline and dreamed of flying.

CHAPTER 50

Thirty minutes later, Tempest and Chaucer stood outside an alley off West Fifty-Seventh Street beside an impossibly thin, impossibly tall skyscraper. It was, in fact, the tallest residential building in the world, topping out at 1550 feet —a skinny-scraper, as the neighbors called them. Using new building materials, engineers and architects could build impossibly tall structures on tiny footprints of the most valuable land in the world. Apartments in this establishment started at ten million dollars and went as high as the skyscraper itself.

Tempest threw her chute onto her back and eyed up Chaucer. "Ready for this, big boy?"

"No." Always the truth with Chaucer.

Chaucer and Tempest entered the structure from the alley, passing through a plywood tunnel painted sky blue.

The lobby was opulent: Italian white marble everywhere, although covered head to toe in plastic sheeting. Workers on scaffolds had installed all kinds of ornate fixtures on the walls and ceiling. It looked like they were about six months away from this place being show ready, or so Tempest thought. Behind the doorman desk was a plump, ruby-cheeked woman in her sixties wearing a cream pantsuit. She threw a smile on when she saw she was not alone. In a thick Queens accent, she asked, "Are you my two o'clock?"

Tempest nodded. Chaucer did not.

"I'm Donna. I'm going to be showing you the place. Could I see some ID?"

Tempest showed her the gun.

The elevator was well-appointed in dark woods and gold accents. Donna took the kidnapping surprisingly well as the elevator rose quickly into the stratosphere. "I don't know what you're after, but there's nothing up there. Finishings won't even be in for five more months. You look like good kids. Don't you know that crime is not the answer?"

Chaucer laughed. It had been a long time since he laughed, but this one was a card.

Tempest replied, "We'll try and keep that in mind, ma'am. Just do as we say and nobody has to get hurt."

The elevator stopped on the 131st floor, the top of the building. It opened onto a massive empty space. In a year, it would be the most expensive penthouse in the world, with God's view of the city. But for now, it was a very acceptable jump platform. Tempest stepped out of the elevator, guiding Donna ahead of her.

Tempest stared at the skyline, spying the penthouse of the Crown Building far below. She finished strapping the parachute onto her torso and thighs. Chaucer watched what she did and did the same.

Donna was confused. "Like I said, there's nothing to steal here. What are you doing with those straps? Is this a sex thing?"

Tempest smiled back at Donna and said, "Lady, this is better than sex." And with that, she ran to the edge of the 131st floor and leaped off.

CHAPTER 51

Chaucer took a deep breath and followed suit, trying not to fall too far behind Tempest. Terror rose as he ran toward the edge of the building. He could taste it in his mouth, especially those last three, two, one steps. Chaucer leaped into the air, and instantly heard a roar of wind rushing by him, his face growing instantly colder from the gale.

He aimed his body at Tempest. She was right. In another life, he had training for this. It came back to him. Evidently, falling off a building is much like riding a bicycle.

Tempest pulled her chute, and it arrested her fall, nearly snapping her neck in the process. Chaucer fumbled for the pull tab and found it just in the nick of time, pulling it and arresting his fall just behind her. Tempest guided her streamlined black parachute with the precision of someone who'd been doing this all their life. She pulled hard on the right cord, steering the parachute up and away from the eighty-seven-story skyscraper between them and the Crown, narrowly missing its edge.

Chaucer saw what she was doing, and it gave him the extra time necessary to perform an identical maneuver. When they came around the other side of the skyscraper, the roof of the Crown, with its tailored, Japanese-style gardens and plunge pool, came into view.

Tempest let go of one toggle, removing some of her steering ability. She did it so she could draw her Ruger and take aim. She was coming in fast, and she was coming in hard. There would be no graceful landing today.

Two security men patrolled the perimeter of the Crown Building penthouse, and they were staring in the wrong direction. Down.

Pop. Pop.

The security men went down within a second of each other. Perfect headshots. Chaucer marveled at the surgical precision of the woman.

Then a shout went out.

The third security man was under the awning, and invisible to them from above, he rushed out, trying to spot where the attack was coming from. His eyes went wide as he saw Tempest and Chaucer barreling down toward him. Tempest fired off a snapshot, catching him in the leg, and then she promptly smashed into the bushes. It was a hard hit, and she got tangled in her own rigging.

Chaucer pulled hard on the toggles, slowing his descent and hoping for a graceful landing. But he overshot his target, and the wind pushed him toward the interior of the penthouse.

Two more security men rushed outside just as Chaucer slammed into them with full force. The next twenty seconds were pure chaos. Tempest dropped her pistol and pulled out her karambit, cutting herself free from her entanglements. Chaucer's entanglements only seemed to get worse. He pulled every release that he could find on his harness, finally breaking free.

The two security men Chaucer hit were tangled up in his lines as well. That was what saved him. Just as one of them got a pistol raised, Chaucer grabbed his wrist and fought him for dear life. Then the wind ballooned the parachute and pulled all three men toward the edge of the building. The security man with the gun dropped it and fought for a knife, just as Tempest had done.

The second security man was not so lucky. He didn't have a

knife. He was pulling at the cords wildly, thoroughly entangled in its web, trying desperately to solve the Gordian knot.

The first security man cut himself free at the same moment Chaucer broke loose. He smiled as he brandished the knife. Tempest searched the bushes for her pistol, but came up empty.

The second security guard screamed as the windblown parachute yanked him over the side of the building. The first security guard rushed at Chaucer. Tempest reached for her karambit, but she was twenty feet away, and the weapon was not made for throwing.

She threw it anyway. The security man fell dead just a foot from Chaucer, a karambit lodged between two ribs.

CHAPTER 52

Tempest and Chaucer stormed into the interior of the opulent penthouse, going from room to room, clearing each. In the parlor, they encountered two men cowering in a corner. The one in the olive military uniform yelled and raised a PPS 43, a Soviet-era submachine gun.

Tempest put two bullets from the Ruger in him. Then in the second man for good measure.

Chaucer scolded her, "You understand I need to talk to people. That's our whole purpose here."

"You're looking for the dad, right? They're not him, right?"

"The more people I can interrogate, the better."

"Reality check, Mal. A small army's about to lay siege to this place. You'll be lucky if you have enough time with the dad."

They pressed on deeper into the penthouse. In the back bedroom, they found who they were looking for. Sim Se Yoon cowered under the bed. Tempest pointed the Ruger at his head and said, "Give me the code."

Less than a minute later, Tempest pressed the suite's panic button, locking down the elevators and stairwell emergency doors alike. The electronic security system asked for the master code to verify that this was an emergency. Tempest entered it.

The thought crossed her mind that the dad could have lied to them. But in her experience, a civilian with a gun to his head tends to do the right thing. Sure enough, the code worked. She dragged Sim Se Yoon out to the balcony. When he passed the two dead guys in the parlor, he had a bit of a freakout, but a couple slaps brought him around.

Tempest deposited him on a bright white canvas lounge chair within sight of at least three of his dead security team. Chaucer sat beside him, getting his attention, which was not easy while Tempest held a gun to his head.

"Sir, look at me. Look only at me."

Chaucer put his hand on the man's wrist, feeling for a pulse. He didn't strictly need to do this, but he found it added a certain assurance that lies would not work. But Sim Se Yoon would not look at Chaucer, mesmerized by Tempest and her gun.

Chaucer put it to her gently. "This will go better if you're somewhere else."

"You got ten minutes. Tops."

"Should be all the time we'll need."

Sim Se Yoon looked at Chaucer, staring into those hypnotist's eyes. He recognized him instantly. "The Oracle."

"Yes. You sent someone to kill me."

"You alerted the assassin."

Chaucer shook his head. "She's not your girl. They lied to you. To us both."

Sim Se Yoon's eyes widened, but he didn't quite believe Chaucer. "Remember, I cannot lie."

The realization crossed the older Korean's face, and he was amazed. "Who? Who lied to us?"

"Everybody. The next ten minutes will decide if you live or die. If you tell me what I want to know, I promise you'll walk away from this. Who was Tajo?"

Sim Se Yoon replied, "He was my son."

"Lie. He wasn't. Who was Tajo?" He spoke in long, measured pauses, implying an impatience that was completely accurate. Chaucer could see Tempest rushing from one emergency stairwell to the next, anticipating a breach.

"I can't. I can't. They'll kill me."

Chaucer grabbed the man, slipping behind him, and with a quick sideward thrust, twisted his back. It was a chiropractor's motion. And suddenly Sim Se Yoon was in utter, complete agony.

CHAPTER 53

"I've dislocated your L5. The nerve underneath is being hit by bone on both sides. Perhaps you've felt a raw nerve in a visit to the dentist. The raw nerve of a tooth is only a quarter as sensitive as the nerves in your back. If you move a millimeter, you'll feel like you're dying. If you move two, you could be paralyzed for life. Now, tell me what I want to know. Who was Tajo?"

Sim Se Yoon's entire body poured out the sweat of abject terror. Even professionals in this situation have a hard time resisting, and Sim Se Yoon was no professional. He felt a pain he could never have imagined. It felt like he was dying.

It would be a simple matter to restore his back. The man would be in full health a minute after he finished his confession. But for now, all he could think about was some way, any way, to make the pain stop.

He cried out, "The boy was a Kim!"

It meant nothing to Chaucer for a moment. Kim and Park were surnames so common in Korea, it might as well have been Smith or Jones. But the way the man said it told him something else.

"Kim?" he asked.

The paralyzed man's eyes filled with tears at betraying a deep trust. "Yes."

"As in the supreme leader of the DPRK."

"His family. Yes."

Chaucer said, "Tell me how it's possible."

Sim Se Yoon tried his best not to move. When he spoke, he barely moved his jaw. Chaucer leaned in close to him to get every word. "It's what they do. It's what they've always done. The supreme leader himself—"

Chaucer filled in the blanks. "Kim Jong Un."

Sim Se Yoon nodded and then screamed. That simple motion had thrown his entire body into agony. It took a moment of steady breathing for him to calm down enough to continue. "He was under another identity when he went to school in Switzerland. No one knew who he was. They want their family educated in the West. And then they want them brought home."

"So who is he?" Chaucer made another adjustment to the man's back and relief washed over the man's face. He was still all but paralyzed, still in pain, but he found it easier to speak. And speak he did.

"Kim Jong Il had three sons. The eldest was always to be the next leader. He was groomed from a young age to wear the crown. But when he was educated in the West, he grew to love it too much. They arrested him in Japan, on a fake passport, trying to sneak into Disneyland Tokyo. It was the Disneyland part that finished him. Kim Jong Il saw him as weak, corrupted by the West. He saw his influence slipping away – his son even suggested that the Hermit Kingdom open itself up more to the West, to reform. So Kim Jong Il turned to his second son, the second son was not strong. He was kind, sensitive. His father tried to beat it out of him, trying to make him the leader the nation needed. But it was never to be. So the third son, Kim Jong Un, would take the throne."

Chaucer felt Sim's pulse racing up and down. He saw the layer of sweat on his skin accumulate. This man was not stalling, not biding for time. He was telling everything he knew.

"We never know who our foster child is. We don't even know who in the family has children. But Jang Bo gave it away. He was the eldest son of Kim Jong Il's second child."

Chaucer did the math. This boy had been a direct descendant of Kim Jong Il. Further, he'd been the son of the older brother of the current dictator, Kim Jong Un. The legitimacy of his claim to the throne, to the seat of power of all of North Korea, would have been beyond easy to establish. Those kids talking about the Year of the Rabbit? They had no idea they had a ticking time bomb sitting there with them.

"I was only supposed to protect his identity."

Chaucer snapped back to the interrogation. "Why? Why you?"

Sim Se Yoon stared blankly at Chaucer, not understanding the question. "Why else? Money. I do not own twelve factories in China. I own twenty-seven in the DPRK. I turn my products out at just ten percent of the Chinese labor rate. Then I ship them into China, relabel them in warehouses, and send them all over the world. It has made me a fortune. But I always knew one day there would be a price to pay. I just did not know that price would be a meeting with the Oracle."

Chaucer detected zero deception. "What about Tempest? Why did you tell Tajo about her? How did you have her number?"

Sim Se Yoon struggled to breathe without moving. Spit bubbles poured from his mouth as he spoke. "She does not remember me? No. Why should she? There were five of us. Executives. Business owners. Held hostage at a conference in Kuala Lumpur, for a king's ransom. The Widowmaker did the impossible. She freed us. She was—beyond exceptional."

It made sense. Executives like Sim Se Yoon often had huge kidnap insurance policies. Those companies would pay top dollar to a freelancer who could save them the expense.

Chaucer had just one question left, and he thought he knew the answer already. He asked, "Did your people kill Tajo?"

This time Sim Se Yoon resisted the temptation to shake his

head. "You mean elements plotting a coup? No. At least I don't think so. The first time we heard of the Year of the Rabbit, it was provided by your CIA. The security team in charge of his surveillance has been executed for negligence of duty."

Chaucer thought it through. "So the CIA knew about the Year of the Rabbit before the DPRK knew?"

Gunshots rang out. Tempest ran onto the balcony. "Tick tock, motherfucker! Wrap it up!" She hurried over to another stairwell.

Sim Se Yoon looked up into Chaucer's eyes, pleading for mercy. "The note has Kim Jong Un in a panic, the leadership are in bunkers, and everyone involved with this is being executed."

Chaucer was confused. "The Year of the Rabbit?"

Sim Se Yoon pursed his lips, the agony was becoming too much for the man. "Yes."

Chaucer didn't have the full picture, but he had everything Sim Se Yoon knew. He was sure of it. He got behind the old man and twisted his spine a second time, snapping him back into alignment. Chaucer then laid him down on the chaise. "It will take about ten minutes for you to regain sensation in your body, but you shouldn't have any lingering aftereffects. You know my friend there? Tempest?"

Sim Se Yoon nodded.

"I need you to do one last thing, and then she won't come back and kill you."

Sim Se Yoon looked up at Chaucer with the eyes of a child, full of wonder and expectation.

CHAPTER 54

Two security teams battered down the emergency fire door atop the north stair and raced into the penthouse. They found their principal, Sim Se Yoon, shaken, but entirely healthy and intact. He pointed a shaking finger out at the balcony. Several members of the security team raced out to the balcony, while the second-in-command unlocked the panic code and brought an elevator full of reinforcements up.

On the balcony, the security forces scoured the area for the intruders. They found the remains of one parachute and nothing else, until one of them looked over the side. There, in the park a hundred yards away, was a parachute stuck in a tree. He called out an alarm, "The park! Now!" The security team raced back into the building and the waiting elevator.

The elevator reached the ground floor, and the team raced through the lobby of the Crown, up one block, and then fanned out into the park.

———

Lying on the roof of the elevator, wedged between two sets of greased cables, Tempest and Chaucer listened intently. Tempest whispered, "I think they're gone. We gotta give it another couple minutes, then we make our break."

Chaucer nodded. Their bodies were touching, and he struggled against the pain of that contact. Tempest saw his discomfort. She said, "I haven't been entirely honest with you."

Chaucer looked into her eyes. "You lied to me? Doubtful."

"Omission only. Just something I didn't think you needed to know."

"But you want to tell me now?" Chaucer asked.

Tempest bobbed her head from side to side, making up her mind. "There was another reason I was chosen as patsy. Another reason I was a good choice for Tajo's assassin."

Chaucer asked, "Why?"

"There was a two-year period, when you were first taken. When we heard nothing—and I mean nothing. No trade offer. No bluster that they captured a spy. No acknowledgment of any kind that they even had you. It kinda drove me crazy."

"It must've been hard for you."

"Yeah, well, I'm a big girl, and I knew you had it worse, but yeah. So, anyway, I can't just sit on my hands. You know this about me, right? So I started coming up with … scenarios."

"Scenarios?"

Tempest smiled sheepishly. "Gambits. Ways to change the status quo."

"Like what?"

Tempest grew defensive. "Look, I'm an operator, right? I'm not a planner. But push comes to shove? I make a decent tactician."

"I have no idea what you're saying."

"I proposed killing top officials of the DPRK. Anyone out of the country would be fair game. With zero acknowledgement. Just this guy's dead. Now that guy's dead. Until they released you."

Chaucer smiled an amused smile. "The fifth floor must've loved that."

"Yeah, no shit. They shut me down, pronto. So I quit."

Chaucer was stunned. "Wait. That's why you went freelance?"

"Don't flatter yourself. I was on the way out. But … maybe that was the push I needed."

Chaucer said, "But I still don't understand. Why did that make you a good choice for a patsy?"

Tempest exhaled a long, frustrated breath. "Because I started carrying out the plan."

"You what?!"

Tempest put her finger to her lips. They lay there a moment in silence, just listening. There was nothing coming from below. Chaucer tried again, more quietly. "You didn't."

"I did."

"How many North Koreans?"

"A little more than a half dozen. Until Fitz gave me a talking to. He said one more and the Chinese would intervene. They'd sic the Seventh Bureau on my ass and I'd be dead. He said I'd created a power vacuum in Pyongyang that would take years to fix, and still they wouldn't acknowledge that they had you."

Chaucer stared into her eyes. Tempest looked away, embarrassed.

"I don't know what to say," Chaucer said. "Would it be weird if I said that was the most romantic thing anyone ever did?"

"Yeah. Super weird."

She looked into his eyes. Now it was his turn to look away. And just like that, the moment was gone. Tempest said, "I think we're good to go."

In the elevator, the service hatch on the roof popped open. Tempest and Chaucer dropped down, dusted themselves off, and calmly walked out.

They found Albert, and then they found a quiet spot down by the East River for Chaucer's debrief. Chaucer was kind enough to lay out the information to both of them, even though everyone knew Albert didn't specifically need to know any of this. But Chaucer promised Albert an education, and an education he would have.

Tajo was indeed a Kim, in the line of succession of the mighty Kim dynasty of North Korea. If a coup were to occur in the DPRK, Tajo would have been a contender. It explained the CIA's interest in the situation. Killing this kid? It was like an act of war. Chaucer knew enough about the regime to guess that the CIA was responding to a potential global threat. If Kim Jong Un took this as a personal threat, his retaliation could include anything up to and including dropping a nuke on Los Angeles or Chicago. The CIA could be trying to placate a madman.

"Could it be possible that's why they faked the interrogation?" Tempest asked.

Chaucer shook his head. "Doubtful. Possible, but doubtful. It still doesn't explain the Year of the Rabbit."

However things went wrong, the North Koreans believed an assassin was paid for by the plotters of the Year of the Rabbit, and Tajo was killed. Whoever sent the assassin also sent a message, spreading fear that the coup was still on, and that the plotters had other options.

Tempest thought a long while before she spoke. "Paints a picture, all right. But I don't know … Something doesn't feel quite right."

"It fits most of the facts, but I agree. Sim Se Yoon knew less than I was hoping. There's more to this. Even if Kim was threatening a nuclear launch, these private contractors, this unit within the unit—it doesn't feel like the way it would play out."

They wouldn't be able to ponder it any further, because Tempest's phone buzzed and when she checked it, she saw just three numbers.

911

Chaucer knew instantly what it meant. The call came from Dennis. It was his code. And the only time he would ever send it to Tempest was if the unthinkable was about to happen.

Somebody had just threatened their son.

CHAPTER 55

Dennis's Midtown office was thirteen blocks away. Tempest covered that distance in six minutes. Albert and Chaucer struggled to keep up with her. Once in the high-ceilinged art deco lobby, Albert had to grab the elevator door so he and Chaucer could get on.

The wait for the elevator to climb to the twenty-seventh floor was interminable. Tempest paced like a caged animal. Albert opened his mouth to offer a word of comfort, but Chaucer shook his head, gently urging the man away from a disastrous course of action.

Nothing would soothe the woman until she saw her son again.

Tempest burst into Dennis's office, gun drawn. She cleared the reception area in two seconds. It was empty. A bad sign. She moved immediately into the back office. Dennis's office. It was empty as well. Another bad sign. Tempest and Chaucer searched the room wordlessly, looking for signs of struggle, then progressed to searching for signs of anything, any clue what happened here.

Albert was the first to speak. "What the hell is going on?"

Bang!

As Chaucer bent down to examine a coffee stain on the floor,

Albert slammed into the wall behind him. He screamed like an air-raid siren. It was a sound of pain, shock, and abject horror.

Tempest's reaction was far faster than Chaucer's. She tackled him behind Dennis's huge steel desk.

Bang! Bang! Bang! Chaucer's head rang from what he suspected was a concussion. The world came in and out of focus. When he turned toward the desk and saw three large indentations, he finally understood what was happening.

Tempest said it for him. "Sniper! Next building over!"

The loud clanging in Chaucer's ears? High-caliber rounds impacting the steel desk, but thankfully, not penetrating.

This was a trap.

Chaucer looked over at Albert. He was slumped over, his back against the wall, a streak of blood extending overhead from where he stood a moment ago. He was still screaming in pain.

Tempest put an end to that. "Shut the fuck up!"

"I've been shot!"

"No shit!"

"Help me!"

Chaucer and Tempest looked at each other. Albert was five feet away, in the open. He was no longer a person to the sniper.

He was bait.

Asher stood over Anya Sergeyev, spotting for her with binoculars. He was disappointed, and he wasn't afraid to show it. "You missed? You fucking missed?! What are we? Three hundred yards?"

Anya lay perfectly still. Her body hugged the desk that was her firing position. She spoke softly, not wanting to disturb her aim in case there was another opportunity. "The Oracle moved at the last second. It happens."

"What about the follow-up shot?"

"The Widowmaker's fast." She scanned the room. The Black

man was slumped against the wall, bleeding. The other two were hidden behind the damn desk.

Asher was hearing none of it. "This isn't some NYU researcher this time. These people bite back. Now finish them!"

She pumped two more rounds into the desk. Nothing. She could see the dents. No penetration. "That desk is thick. Practically armored. These rounds go right through car doors, but the desk is stopping them."

"Then what are you waiting for? Finish the wounded one."

"No. They might go for him."

Asher knew Tempest wouldn't lift a finger. He was pretty sure Chaucer wouldn't either. But the sniper was right. Let's see how this plays out. "Fine, they've got nowhere they can go anyway."

Asher called out to the next room. "Roma!"

Roma came into the room. He was frustrated, and it showed. He didn't like his demotion to lapdog. And he especially didn't like the fact that he wasn't allowed in the room with the sniper, or across the street where the action was happening. But Asher was insistent. If Tempest or Chaucer saw one whiff of surveillance, it would blow the op. There was nobody over there. But that was about to change.

"Eight-man team. You're the lead. Go! Get them!"

Roma smiled. It had been a long forty-eight hours for him, waiting for an order like this. He relished the opportunity.

CHAPTER 56

Chaucer and Tempest searched the room from their crouched position behind the desk. They were looking for some hope in their situation, and they found none. Tempest said, "You know we got five minutes tops, right? We're pinned and they're flanking."

Chaucer said, "Should we see how good this guy is?"

Tempest pulled off her duffel bag, unzipped it, and reached in. She pulled out a mirror on a telescoping arm and extended it past the edge of the desk. *Blam!*

The mirror shattered, knocking the arm out of her hands. "She's pretty good."

"She?"

Tempest nodded. "Got a glimpse. Blondie. In perfect firing position. We're rightly fucked here."

Chaucer said nothing. Chaucer was staring into Tempest's duffle bag. At two fragmentation grenades. An idea was forming. "You've got grenades?"

"She's at two hundred yards plus. That's a non-starter."

But Chaucer had a different idea. He pulled out the two fragmentation grenades. "Albert, if you can, crawl over here now."

Anya saw Albert move. He was crawling toward the desk. "Wounded's on the move. What's the call?"

Asher considered authorizing her to finish him. But then he had a better idea. The Black man's wound was like one from a Bouncing Betty, a landmine designed to wound but not to kill. The idea was simple. A dead soldier takes one combatant out. A wounded soldier takes three out. The wounded man, and two to carry him.

"Let him go. He'll slow them down."

Albert made it behind the desk. Chaucer pulled him in and examined him. Chaucer's interrogator training had a significant medical component. It was essentially a mini-med-school, if the Hippocratic Oath was reversed.

Albert was in trouble. Gut shots were a real crapshoot. Get lucky, and they can be highly survivable. But they can also be among the most agonizing wounds a human being has ever experienced. Unluckily for Albert, his wound was not in a good place, evidenced by the dark blood freely flowing from him.

Albert croaked. "How's it look, doc?"

Chaucer wanted to lie to him. More than anything. "I'm going to try my best, but you're bleeding badly." Chaucer looked to Tempest. "You got an IFAK in there?"

Tempest nodded. Of course she had an Individual First Aid Kit, but she was concerned with other things. "What's your plan with the grenade?"

Chaucer ignored her, pulling out the IFAK and giving the man some morphine. He also pulled out Celox patches and applied them to the entry and exit wounds. Celox patches were bandages treated with a hemostatic agent; they could take an arterial bleed and seal it shut in sixty seconds of direct pressure. But Chaucer knew it wouldn't do much. The bleeding would continue internally, unabated.

Tempest caught Chaucer's attention with her stare. "We don't have time for this. They're sending everyone. You know this." Then she looked at Albert. "Sorry, dude."

Chaucer gave Albert a nod. He wasn't sure what it meant, but it seemed to give the man some comfort. Then he pulled one of the heavy steel drawers out of the desk. He flipped the drawer ninety degrees and put it up against the wall behind them.

"What's that for?"

"Tamping charge."

Tempest's eyes widened as she realized what Chaucer was talking about. "Yeah. Yeah, yeah, yeah. That could work!"

Chaucer pulled the drawer back. Tempest pulled the pin on the grenade. She put the grenade in the drawer and she and Chaucer both pushed the drawer so that it was facing the wall, their feet bracing against it. "Hope this doesn't rip right through the drawer."

Chaucer only had a second to panic.

Boom! The kick was violent, as if the drawer had a demon inside it, trying to get out. But the drawer held. All the explosive force of the grenade was directed into a single location: the rear wall. Smoke poured from the space between drawer and wall and filled the room. Albert screamed again as he moved away from the explosion. Tempest pulled the drawer away.

There was a hole. Not big enough for any of them. Yet. But there was a hole in the wall.

Asher saw the smoke at the same time as Anya. Anya spoke first, "Smoke, chief."

"I see it. What the hell are they doing?"

"No idea."

Asher got on the radio, "Roma, double-time it—there's action in the room."

Tempest searched through her duffel bag and came up with just one more grenade. It would have to do. They pulled out a second drawer, in case the structure of the first was compromised. She pulled the pin, Chaucer readied the drawer, and they repeated the process.

This one bucked worse than the first, kicking back at them and nearly spraining Chaucer's ankle. But the result was the same. A little ringing in the ears, a haze of smoke filling the room, and a wider hole.

Chaucer asked, "Do you think you can—"

Tempest was already crawling through the hole. It was a little tricky. She had to do a little kicking when a joist didn't give at her first request, but she made it through.

"Albert next."

She shook her head. "Try to stabilize him and pass me my bag. I'm gonna kill a bunch of people."

CHAPTER 57

Asher saw the second plume of smoke. "Ring their goddamn bell! Just keep putting rounds into that desk. Maybe one'll punch through."

Anya didn't need to be told twice. She put round after round into the huge steel desk, watching and waiting for some indication of penetration.

Tempest extricated her Honey Badger assault rifle from the duffel. It was prepped and ready to go. She only needed to chamber a round and unscrew the silencer that just wasn't called for in this instance. It wasn't the perfect weapon for the task at hand, but in a pinch it would have to do.

She considered heading out to the hallway and to a nearby office. It was the safer option, but it burned time. And time wasn't something she had right now. So she went with the riskier option. She circled back to the open doorway to the office she had just exited.

She laid herself prone and prepared herself mentally for what she was about to do. She turned onto her left side and scooted next to the door. Here she would be ten feet from Chaucer behind the desk. Close enough that she would be in the sniper's view the moment she entered the doorway. She would have a second at most to fire against a sniper already in perfect position.

It sucked. If anyone she ever trained suggested it, she would've hit them over the head and called them an idiot. And yet, here she was, preparing to try just that. She recalled a conversation with her mentor, Caleb Moss, the deadliest man on earth. Caleb once told her, *"God hates stupid, but he's got a soft spot for audacious."*

She only hoped the audacity of this move outweighed its stupidity. She heard a new volley of bullets ring out as they pulverized the desk, and she rolled into the doorway.

Anya was too close. Her dominant eye was sighted on the desk and nothing but. It was only her open, non-dominant eye that caught the movement in her peripheral. Human beings' vision is particularly good at recognizing movement in the peripheral, a survival trait that served the species well. But it wasn't until she shifted the rifle's aim to her left that she made out exactly what that movement was. A prone figure with red hair. *Shit.*

Asher saw Anya shift aim. He could tell something was wrong. It was too big a shift. He was about to ask her when another shot rang out. It sounded—different. A second later, Asher felt something against his face. A warm mist. Something was wrong, some new sensory inputs he couldn't quite order properly. He wiped his face and saw the blood on his hands. He looked down and saw the lower half of the window spidered, and his sniper's head wide open.

His cognition flew into high gear as he dove behind a partition. *Blam! Blam! Blam!* The wall behind Asher was suddenly full of holes. One bullet grazed him as he went down, but he was thankfully alive. Keeping his body low, he crawled out of the office, grabbing his radio as he went. "We're taking fire! We're taking fire!"

Roma and his seven-man team reached the lobby of the building, crossed it in seconds, and then jumped in the waiting elevator. As they drew and checked their weapons, the elevator's other two passengers wisely stepped out, deciding to grab the next car.

Ninety seconds later, they reached the twenty-seventh floor.

Ding went the bell.

The elevator doors opened and three of Roma's men died in the next second. Automatic fire filled the hallway, and as Roma dove for cover, he could barely make out Tempest MacLaren through the gun smoke. The surviving members of his team plastered themselves in the corners of the elevator. Roma mashed any button he could reach, silently willing the doors closed and the nightmare over.

Tempest killed another of his men before the doors finally did just that. Roma pressed "26."

This is just round one, bitch.

The shots had stopped. Tempest told Chaucer to stay down for another minute, and Chaucer was in no mind to argue. He checked Albert's bleeding midsection. His jeans were black and soaked in blood. Chaucer pulled up Albert's shirt to confirm the news. The Celox patches had not stopped the bleeding.

"No. No." Chaucer tried direct pressure on the entry wound, but he saw a torrent of blood escape out Albert's exit wound the moment he pressed down.

"Just stop. I feel okay. I'm not gonna die," Albert said.

Chaucer suddenly had an image of Terry in his mind, bleeding out on the dance floor of the Social. A wave of emotion consumed him. He fought it back enough to speak. "Your brain isn't getting oxygen, and it's shutting down various sensory inputs."

"I'm fine. Just leave me be."

Tears welled up in Chaucer's eyes. He fought to maintain control. "I'm sorry. This is my fault."

"You gave me a job. This ain't on you."

"If you really knew what I was up against—"

Albert shook his head slowly from side to side. "No, man. You told me exactly what the deal was. Who does that?"

Tempest opened the door to Dennis's inner office. She saw the look on Chaucer's face and instantly knew the score. "Take the elevator down to the lobby," she said. "Find a hiding spot, and I'll come get you."

Chaucer wanted to say something to Albert. Something kind. He told him the one true thing he had left to say. "You would've made an excellent operative."

Albert laughed weakly. "Stop talking like I'm dying, and listen to her. Go."

Chaucer left, but not without one last pained look at Albert. Tempest loaded a new magazine into her Honey Badger and sat down beside the dying man. "What do you want now, Albert? You want the truth? Or a beautiful lie?"

Albert coughed as he tried to breathe. "Bein' around Chaucer, kinda gives ya a taste for the truth, don't it?"

Tempest spoke calmly and softly. It was uncharacteristic of her, adopting the demeanor of a military chaplain. She approached this moment with something approaching solemnity. "The truth it is, then. You're bleeding out. If the Celox patches don't stop the bleeding, probably nothing will. So you're gonna have to move on. Can't say that I believe in God. I don't really qualify to make that call, so it's just a hunch. Reincarnation sounds like bullshit to me too."

Albert coughed as he laughed. "You're fucking horrible at this."

Tempest shrugged and accepted it. "What I'm trying to tell

you is I don't know what happens next. I don't believe in a lot. But I believe in the death flash."

Albert's eyes lifted to hers, an unasked question in them.

"I've seen it. You ask any ER doctor, they'll tell you that when someone dies and they're hooked up to an EEG or something like that, they know *exactly* when the brain dies. There's this ... death flash. A surge. Like the energy in the body decides to leave all at once. It just ... fucks off and goes. See? Now, me, I think that's your soul. The part of you that's more than just meat. I think it leaves, and when it goes, it goes together."

"Where?"

"I don't know where. I'm not a theologian, but I know it does go, together, all at once. And I like to think, well—most things that do that—most things that pack up and leave together? Those things have a plan."

Albert laughed faintly. "I feel like nobody's listening to me. You got another one of those Celox patches?"

"They're not gonna help you."

"Bullshit. I'm not dying today, so just give me the damn patch, and go. And do me a favor and take a few more of those assholes with you."

Tempest nodded, and handed Albert another Celox patch. Then she hustled out of Dennis's office, heading for the elevators, when she encountered two of Roma's men coming up the back stairwell. She was expecting this, and she let them know it. Two auto-fire blasts made them retreat double-time into the stairwell. And by the time they burst out to return fire, Tempest was gone.

When Tempest reached the lobby, it was full of reinforcements. Not the A-team exactly, but they were alert, armed, and more than a little paranoid. None of these reinforcements were prepared for Tempest to suddenly appear before them. They were kind enough to give her the first volley.

She sprayed the room wide, not looking to kill anyone, just trying to ensure that heads would be down long enough for her to affect an exit. It worked like a charm. Tempest ran to the east, down a narrow hall leading to a small door. She was glad to see Chaucer's outline opening the same door a hundred feet ahead of her.

CHAPTER 58

Chaucer burst out of the east door and into a world of trouble. Six more operatives swarmed in the door he was coming out of. A second later: recognition. The lead man, Lopez, smiled. "Christmas came early, boys."

He threw a choke hold around Chaucer while the rest of his team delivered body blows, taking the fight out of the man instantly. They dragged him to their car, a BMW 7 Series, and stuffed him in the back.

A second later, Tempest emerged out of the same door, assessed the situation in less than a second, and started firing. Two of the team died where they stood. The other four dove over to the other side of the car. These guys were smarter than the others. They knew not to get into a protracted gunfight with Tempest MacLaren. Two of the operatives emptied mags, filling the air with gunfire and forcing Tempest to take cover behind a dumpster. One fired up the BMW and threw it into gear. Lopez hopped into the shotgun seat.

Tempest popped out from behind the dumpster and fired at the last two operatives running for the BMW, the operatives that pinned her with cover fire. The Ruger wasn't made for distance shooting, but Tempest knew you go to war with the army you have.

Two shots. One found pay dirt, hitting its target in the neck. The other was a shoulder shot. The .22 caliber barely spun the man at all, but it gave Tempest just a second for another shot. Center mass. This one went down stiff as a board.

But behind them, the BMW accelerated out of the alley. She saw it happening in slow motion and was powerless to stop it. Tempest ran flat out, watching the BMW disappear to the right as it hit Madison Avenue. She reached the corner a moment later, spying the Beemer a block and a half away already, and headed uptown.

Tempest searched the four corners of the intersection for a suitable pursuit vehicle. The first thing her eyes hit was a Vespa scooter. It took her a millisecond to reject that. Next, the Toyota Prius pulling up to the light. *Hard pass.* Then her eyes spotted the Mercedes dealership showroom across the street. *Yeah, that'll do.*

The salesman's tag on his sharkskin gray jacket read "Todd." He sat in the passenger seat of the loaded S-series watching Jesse, a bond trader, slowly pick apart the best German engineering since the V2 Rocket.

Jesse said, "I don't know. Feels … dowdy. The BMWs don't feel like this. Feels more like you're in a … fighter cockpit."

Todd hated himself for needing the sale so bad, but it had been a slow month. "Sure, the BMW is great at faking you out, making you think it's a performance car. But it's not. It's all compromise. It even makes you think it's a high-end luxury car. But you don't want to know where BMW gets their leather from."

Jesse smiled smugly. "The BMW's got more horses. A lot more. My buddy Topher's got one, and if he races me and wins? I've got to eat shit for months. Literally. His shit."

Suddenly, the driver's door opened and Tempest forced her way in, hurling Jesse into Todd's lap. "Sorry, boys!"

Tempest shut the door, started the engine, and threw the car into gear.

Todd barely had a chance to yell before the S-Class smashed through the window of the dealership showroom, bounced off the curb, and peeled off down the street.

CHAPTER 59

Todd yelled, "What the fuck are you doing!?"
Tempest pulled out a pistol. She found that with civilians, non-verbal communication was often best.

"Shit!" Todd reached for the door latch, but the S-Class was already doing seventy.

Jesse? Jesse couldn't take his eyes off Tempest. He was mesmerized.

Tempest floored it, blasting through a red light and narrowly missing a bus. "We're looking for a BMW 740i. Black. First one to spot it gets a cookie."

Jesse smiled at Todd. "This bitch is crazy!"

Tempest spotted the Beemer first, ten blocks ahead and headed straight uptown.

A minute later, it was five blocks ahead. Jesse glanced at the speedometer. It read ninety-five. Ahead, a taxi cut off a delivery truck, blocking half the avenue. Tempest braked and kicked out the rear end of the Mercedes to drift through the space between taxi and truck, straightening back out as the car drifted through another red light.

"You'll never catch them," Jesse screamed. "The BMW's got more horses!"

Tempest exhaled. "The BMW's got twenty more horses, but

I've got fifty more foot-pounds of torque. Trust me, we're a match, if not better." She gunned the engine through another light, cutting off two police cars coming from opposite directions. Lights and sirens immediately followed.

"Yay. I love a parade."

The men in the BMW heard the sirens as well. Baker, the driver, checked his rearview, and saw the S-Class barreling down upon them, less than two blocks away now. "Shit."

"What?"

"Widowmaker."

Lopez drew his pistol, opened the window, and prepared to fire. Baker called out, "Hard left!"

The BMW swerved left, making a hard turn onto Fifty-Eighth Street. It was a one-way street going the opposite way. The BMW's rear end swung wide and Baker fought for control. Regaining it, Baker leaned on the horn and parted the sea of taxis and trucks working their way eastward, jogging hard left and right to avoid collisions.

Tempest saw the Beemer turn and followed suit. "See, that's another thing. See the way the Seven Series fishtails there? They programmed the differential like it's a Five Series. But it's not. Watch how this baby corners."

Her two passengers held on for dear life as Tempest kicked the back end out and executed a perfect drift into oncoming traffic.

"See? Perfect for its weight distribution. They didn't program this thing like it's an AMG. They know what it can do and what it can't. It's carrying a lot of weight, and they compensate for it. At least better than the BMW. Now sure, that's not quite fair, this comparison. After all, that BMW's a 2019."

Her unwilling passengers failed to access most of the knowledge she was imparting. They were simply trying not to scream. Tempest guided the S-series from sidewalk to sidewalk, swerving around the traffic jam of cars and trucks in the BMW's wake. Horns erupted angrily. Sirens behind them multiplied. It was utter chaos, with a growing array of pursuit vehicles gaining on them. Todd looked over at Tempest. It looked like she was having a pleasant Sunday drive through the country.

Jesse puked in the footwell on the passenger side, from fear more than motion sickness. Todd, sharing the seat with him, pushed himself into the back to escape the stench. Tempest shot off an angry glare, "Hey, dickwad. Respect the vehicle. Out the window next time."

―――――

The men in the BMW were losing ground, and they knew it, but they were two, where Tempest was only one. Baker shouted, "She's close enough! Take the shot!" Lopez popped out of the passenger-side window and aimed at the approaching Mercedes.

―――――

Tempest saw the passenger stick half his body out the window. She pulled hard on the wheel, careening the Mercedes across the street and up onto the sidewalk just as Lopez fired a three-round burst. A tree took a hit, the wall beside the Mercedes took the second, and only the third hit pay dirt, punching a hole in the top center of the Mercedes windshield. It was a clean hit, and the glass neither shattered nor spidered.

"You boys might want to get down. These fellas decided to get nasty."

―――――

"Lopez! Get in!"

Lopez pulled himself back inside just as the BMW raced into the next intersection, just a block south of Columbus Circle.

Tempest followed right on their heels, barely a quarter of a block behind.

The BMW bore down on Columbus Circle, and the chaotic counter-clockwise traffic filling it. The four lanes of traffic surrounding the small park and tall column were more than half full when two luxury sedans screamed in and whatever order had existed went straight to hell.

CHAPTER 60

The BMW tried to thread the needle between a box truck and a cargo van, only to be cut off when the van switched lanes suddenly. Baker slammed on the brakes, swerving to the inside of the circle to avoid a crash.

Tempest pulled the Mercedes alongside the BMW in an attempt to cut it off. Baker slammed the BMW into the side of the Mercedes, sending it hurling toward a delivery truck. Tempest braked hard, throwing the wheel to the right to avoid a collision. The Mercedes missed the delivery truck, but spun out until it was now facing the wrong direction. Tempest gritted her teeth, for a second considering kicking the car into reverse. Instead, she pressed the accelerator to the floor and raced the opposite way around the circle.

Baker laughed out loud. "Take that, bitch!"

Tempest bobbed and weaved as both of her passengers were sick on the floor. Honks and blasts of headlights erupted all around her, but she maintained focus as she guided the Mercedes like Moses through a parted Red Sea. The only time she had to brake was for a bicycle messenger, a fact that pissed her off no end.

Baker was twenty feet from daylight when a line of trucks ahead suddenly stopped, stuck behind a red light. He honked the horn in frustration, inching the car forward, looking for a way through. "Find her!"

Lopez was doing just that, scanning the road behind them, looking for Tempest like she was some sort of ghost. The light changed. The trucks parted just enough for Baker to surge past. He floored it, and the BMW shot forth, aiming for the westside drive. Suddenly, Baker caught something in his peripheral, and glanced to his left. He yelled something unintelligible.

Tempest aimed the front of the Mercedes at the front corner of the BMW. It gave the greatest chances of knocking the BMW out of the fight in one blow. The impact was fierce. Airbags went off all around the car, punching her and her passengers in the face. Tempest already had her karambit out for that eventuality. She cut into the airbag in front of her, freeing up her view. The BMW did not stop. She only altered its trajectory. The BMW spun in a 90-degree arc until it slammed into the stone wall marking the border of Central Park. Its nose was pointing down a walking path.

Tempest gunned the engine, aiming for a second collision. She glanced for just a split second at her passengers, verifying they were either dazed or unconscious.

The men in the BMW drew guns and shot their own airbags. The echo of the gunshots in the narrow space set their ears ringing, furthering their disorientation. But dead ahead, Baker saw the walking path. He pressed on the accelerator and the BMW lurched forward.

Tempest rammed the back of the BMW, letting them know she was right on their tail. The BMW fishtailed a bit, which forced it off the narrow path and into the woods. Tempest pursued, swerving left and right around groves of trees, large boulders, and the occasional young lovers canoodling in a secluded spot.

Baker drove like a man possessed. As his vision and hearing cleared, he blasted through a large bush and saw salvation up ahead. A large kickball field lay ahead, and beyond it, Sixty-Fifth Street; one of only a handful of streets that wound their way across the park. If the BMW could make it there, they had a shot. The BMW's steering was damaged from the crash, but its engine was miraculously intact. Glancing at the rearview mirror, he could see that the Mercedes's engine was smoking. What he needed to do was get back on city streets, so he could get away from that psycho.

Tempest saw Sixty-Fifth Street as well. She did the same calculation. If she was going to stop them, it had to be now. She gunned the engine, watching smoke billowing up out from under the hood, and hit the back of the Beemer again as it struggled to weave around another grove of trees. "Damn, he's not a bad driver," she said as the BMW righted itself and pointed, once again, at Sixty-Fifth Street. Tempest was running out of time. She had one chance left. There was a lone boulder between them and Sixty-Fifth Street. And the BMW would have to wind its way around it, giving her time to catch up to it.

Tempest slammed into the rear side of the BMW, fishtailing it. More than fishtailing it, actually. She turned the BMW completely around. Baker kicked the car into reverse, backing up the last fifty yards to launch it onto Sixty-Fifth Street. Tempest's Mercedes followed suit.

The BMW braked to a halt, now facing east. Tempest's Mercedes, with more momentum, crossed three lanes, facing west, until the delivery truck slammed into her. Tempest's head impacted the driver's window as the Mercedes spun into a light pole.

As her vision cleared, the last thing she saw was the BMW limp up Sixty-Fifth Street and out of view.

CHAPTER 61

It took about a minute for the sirens. Two more for the lights. And just shy of five minutes total before angry cops had guns pointed at her face. Tempest knew the drill. She had been arrested in probably thirty countries in the world. In some countries, the procedure was quite smooth, even dignified. In some, it was barbaric and deadly. Her home country of the USA wasn't at the bottom of the scale, but it was solidly in the lower half. She would rather be arrested in most of the rest of the world than here.

The cops got her passengers out first, rag dolls suffering from shock and concussion. The cops gave them a pretty rough treatment, not knowing yet that they were innocent victims in all this. But they reserved most of their adrenaline-fueled aggression for Tempest.

They dragged her from the car and slammed her on the hood. They handcuffed her and manhandled her over to a police cruiser, locking her in the back. Tempest diagnosed herself with a mild concussion, forcing her vision to clear, and her brain to do the same. She took in her surroundings. The cop who put the cuffs on was angry. That worked against her. Lots of cops put the cuffs on too loosely, which, about 50 percent of the time, gave her a way out if she dislocated her thumbs. Not this guy. He wanted these to hurt. And they did.

Her training kicked in. She identified all the improvised weapons she had at her disposal. She identified the methods of egress and ranked them based on difficulty. But deep down, she knew it wasn't looking good. Say what you want to about the civilian police, their cars are designed after decades of painstaking experiments on all manner of dipshits. She wasn't going to come up with something that a million criminals hadn't already thought of. No, escape would not be now. Which was bad, because Chaucer was getting farther and farther away. And the whereabouts of Dennis and her boy? Tempest didn't want to think about it. She pushed that thought out of her mind. She had to. These assholes would not see her cry.

Speaking of assholes, two suits showed up, flashing badges and talking to the police. Tempest thought she recognized one of them. Agency. Probably flashing an FBI badge and telling some cock-and-bull story. It sent a shiver down her spine. They were going to take her right now.

A moment later, that came to pass.

The operatives were a tall blond and a compact Latina. They shook hands with the police sergeants, who led them over to the car where she was confined.

The Latina put her cuffs on before the police sergeant undid his handcuffs. Smart. Tempest noticed the Latina put hers on tight as well.

The operatives held Tempest by an arm each and led her to their unmarked sedan. "What do you say? Give me a ten-second head start?"

The Latina laughed. "Whaddya think, Holm? I'd kinda like to see how that plays out."

Blondie smirked. "Dunno, Soto. I prefer a sure thing."

So Soto was in charge. And from the look Soto gave her, Tempest put the odds at 80 percent that she would be the one who killed her in less than an hour. These two were definitely not Bureau.

Soto told Holm. "Throw me your cuffs."

He did. She used those cuffs to hook into the reinforced stanchion in the middle of the back seat of the sedan. It was an anchor point to make sure prisoners didn't go anywhere. Its purpose was simple. Unlike the police cruiser, the sedans don't have a partition between the back and the front seat; they needed to lock their prisoners down better. Holm put his hand on Tempest's head as he lowered her into the seat. It was a surprisingly gentle touch. Tempest felt bad that she was going to kill the man as soon as humanly possible.

CHAPTER 62

Holm hooked the other end of the cuffs attached to the stanchion to the center of Tempest's cuffs, forming a "T." Then Holm slammed the door shut. Tempest could overhear a bit of their conversation, something about Soto smoothing things over with the cops for a minute. Holm walked around the sedan and got in the passenger seat.

Tempest asked, "Got a cigarette?"

"Those things'll kill ya."

Tempest laughed. Despite the situation, she liked this guy.

Holm said, "Sorry about all this. Just business."

Tempest didn't respond, which Holm took as either depression or resignation. He stared at the kids playing on the kickball field nearby. "I read your jacket, you know. All those kills you notched—you ever wonder what it would be like on the other side? 'Cause you're about to find out."

"Really?" Tempest paid him the bare minimum attention, because what Tempest was really doing was working the problem. With your hands cuffed behind you, your situation is entirely disadvantageous. But if you can get those cuffs in front of you, a world of possibilities opens up. Tempest used to practice that, purposely handcuffing or binding herself to various objects, to play out the tactical possibilities of that situation. That the cuffs were anchored to the stanchion didn't help, but that didn't mean it wasn't worth trying.

As Holm prattled on, Tempest held her breath, pulled her legs into her chest, and attempted to do a forward flip. She wiggled her body through her outstretched arms behind her, being exceedingly careful not to shake the car in any way. She knew she had maybe thirty seconds before Holm turned around. He made one tactical mistake. He didn't sit in the driver's seat. If he had done so, he would have seen what she was doing in the rearview mirror.

Holm noticed her silence went on a little long, and he turned to see what was going on, just as Tempest finished her somersault. She finished the move with a kick to the temple, as hard as she could muster.

His body slumped over the center console. It was another bit of luck, allowing her to use his back to get her feet up and over him. It took her another thirty seconds to kick off her combat boot and strip off one sock, so she could search him for the handcuff keys. She was annoyed to find that they were neither on his belt nor in his back pocket. She would have to flip this asshole over.

"Holm? Holm!" It was Soto coming toward them. Tempest was out of time. The keys would have to wait. She looked over her shoulder and saw that the sedan's keys were in the ignition. Not so much a stroke of luck as another bit of laziness by Holm. He left the keys in so he could put on the air conditioning. Which meant the car was running. Another bit of good fortune.

Soto walked back toward the sedan, and instantly got a bad feeling. She couldn't see Holm. She couldn't see Tempest in the back. She drew her pistol, just in case.

Tempest pushed her head up as far as she could and saw the Latina dead ahead. Her toes found the gear shifter and pulled the car down into drive. The car inched forward, even without the accelerator pedal depressed. Soto fired two shots into the windshield.

Soto made an error. She would never have a shot at Tempest.

It gave Tempest time to kick Holm's head until his body tumbled into the driver's side footwell. She kicked his head right onto the accelerator.

Soto had one thought when she saw her own sedan suddenly race at her: *Fucking Tempest*. She dove out of the way, but the sedan caught her full force, threw her up over the hood, and left her lying in the grass.

The sedan plunged blindly into Central Park. Tempest searched Holm's crumpled body, looking for the damn handcuff keys. Several times the sedan jolted and bucked, making her job even harder, but eventually her big toe found something that felt right, and she lifted it toward herself.

That's when the car hit the lake.

It was nearly sunset and a few boaters were taking their darlings on a last row around the lake when they saw the Crown Victoria launch itself into the middle of the lake. One particularly athletic boater rowed over to where he saw air bubbles rising. His girlfriend implored him not to, but he smelled a hero moment.

A second later, a wild-eyed woman with one handcuff around her wrist emerged and grabbed onto the side of his boat. He tried to process what he was looking at. "Give me a hand!"

It was an order, not a request. The boyfriend reached down, but Tempest gave him a hand other than hers. It was Holm's. Boyfriend and girlfriend pulled the unconscious operative into the rowboat as Tempest pulled herself in as well.

She looked around for any sign of police. There were none. *You caught a break, you lucky bitch.*

CHAPTER 63

Holm awoke to the sound of whirring. It was a familiar sound, but he couldn't quite place it. Before his vision cleared, he realized he couldn't speak. His mouth was wide open, gagged by some sort of cloth. When his vision cleared, he discovered he was cuffed to a chain-link fence, upright, with a pair of handcuffs securely binding each wrist. His arms were spread wide, crucifixion style. He looked out ahead but could see nothing in the darkness. Squinting, he thought he could make out the faint outline of a small circle. What it was, he had no idea.

"Hey, sleeping beauty." Tempest came into view. "How you doing, pretty boy?"

Holm tried to give her a look of defiance. Not so easy with a huge cloth gag in your mouth. It didn't matter to Tempest. She was calm as the Salton Sea. Though, given what she was about to do, she was happy Chaucer wasn't here. For an interrogator, Chaucer sure was queasy about torture.

Tempest punched Holm in the jaw, one hell of a blow, and left his ears ringing. She then unwrapped her fist in front of him, revealing a roll of quarters. This didn't scare Holm. If that's all she had, he could hold out.

But Tempest didn't keep the quarters in her fist. No, she put them on some kind of machine to Holm's left. Holm noticed the chain-link fence turned ninety degrees on both sides of him and that where the ninety-degree turn was, stood the machine. A chill ran up and down his spine as he realized where he was.

He was in a batting cage.

Tempest put eight quarters methodically into the machine and the lights came up. Holm could see a bat down by her feet.

"Do you have any idea of the force of a major-league fastball?"

Now Holm could see the sign beside him. "Warning. Fast pitch."

"Ray Chapman. You ever hear of him?"

Holm didn't respond.

"A Cleveland Indians player. Beaned by a pitch. Dead the next day. This was in the 1920s. They didn't even throw that fast back then."

Tempest smiled. It'd been a long time since she'd gotten to do this. And given the events of the last twenty-four hours, she needed the stress release. "Yeah. Those fastballs. Do you realize there were dozens of kids that died every year from them? Until they changed the balls. All it took was a simple hit to the chest. Those kids dropped dead on the spot."

Holm screamed in his gag as the first pitch blasted out of the machine, coming right for him.

Smack! Tempest one-handed it away with the bat. "Wow, that was faster than I thought. Foul-tipped it, though."

The second ball came in, and Tempest lowered the bat and let it pass. It smashed into Holm's chest. He screamed, so loud even the gag did little to muffle it. Tempest came up to him and got right in his face as she pulled down his gag.

"Ooh, that one was bad. I'd wager you broke at least two ribs. A few more shots like that, who knows where those ribs could go? Heart? Lungs? You know what, if I were you? I would tell me everything I need to know."

Whoomph! Another ball launched right at his damaged chest. Tempest spun on a dime, bat at the ready, and—*whack!* She smacked it out of the park. "It could ... go ... all ... the ... way! The crowd lets out a roar!"

Tempest was having fun. Holm, however, wasn't going to break that easy. He stared at her, defiance in his eyes.

Until the next pitch hit him dead in the chest again. His chest was on fire. Holm struggled for breath. He felt like he was dying. He looked into Tempest's eyes, now just inches from his. She stared into him, soaking up his pain, his panic. And he knew. This psychopath would be just as happy to let him die.

Holm started talking.

In one minute, Tempest had the location of the warehouse where they took Chaucer. In two more minutes, she found out that Dennis was dead, but little Tyler was still alive. They'd been searching for him, and just found out that he was at a sleepover birthday party in Mamaroneck. Holm said a retrieval team was headed there to get him right now.

That pissed Tempest off. As far as they knew, they already had her. Why fuck with her kid?

Thwack! Tempest took her anger out on one more fastball, knocking it into the lights. And with that, the machine stopped. The lights went out. Holm was plunged into the security of the darkness.

Then Tempest put eight more quarters in the machine.

"No! *NO!*"

Tempest put Holm's gag back in. He screamed, begging, imploring her to have mercy. But mercy was never something Tempest had in abundance. And right now, the shelves were bare.

Mamaroneck. One hour later.

The four operators in the SUV helped each other apply spirit gum as they put on comical red noses. They forewent the big floppy feet, judging them to be an operational liability, but otherwise each one was dressed perfectly as a birthday clown. None of them were happy about it, but they were relieved that this nightmare of a mission finally looked to be wrapping up.

They got out of the SUV and crossed the street, walking up the lawn of the upper-middle class Westchester County home of one Martin Feinbloom, school friend of one Tyler Raymer.

Each of the men had a tranq stick and a concealed sidearm. They weren't supposed to kill the kid, but the orders didn't specifically forbid it either. They continued up the lawn, practicing their smiley faces, when a sedan suddenly lurched up onto the lawn and hit one of the clowns dead on, crushing his spine against the tree. The impact winged a second clown, who smashed into the side of the house. The other two operators spun around, reaching for their sidearms. *Pop! Pop!* Two shots, two more clowns down.

Tempest rolled out of the sedan as the winged operator returned fire. This one was good. He saw the door open. He knew her options, and he went around the long way, hoping to catch her unawares.

What he caught was Tempest's knife as it carved open his throat. As he slowly died, he looked into her manic, feral eyes. It reminded him of a nature documentary, of a lioness protecting her cubs.

Moments later, the doorbell rang, and Judy Feinbloom answered it. She came face to face with Tempest, her white t-shirt covered in blood. Behind her, a clown died, impaled on the tree on the front lawn, pinned there by a sedan that was currently on fire.

Tempest put on a huge smile and said, "Hi, I'm Tyler's mom!"

The sedan exploded behind her.

CHAPTER 64

Chaucer awoke to the smell of ammonia and degreaser. Smells all too familiar to him. He didn't open his eyes, not at first. But it would only buy him a minute or two. He felt the accelerant in his bloodstream, forcing him awake. They would be watching him. Waiting for signs of consciousness that he was already displaying involuntarily. He was only hoping to hear something, a tidbit or two that might be the difference between dying quickly and drawing out the interrogation he knew was coming.

While most people would hope for a quick interrogation, Chaucer sought to prolong it. To buy time for Tempest to find him. After all, this was Chaucer's world. A world that had the familiarity of home.

He felt a band around his chest. More bands constricting his fingers. He almost had to laugh. They had him hooked up to a polygraph. Little did they know the thought of that was more torture than they would probably inflict in the first hour. But it was something. It would waste their time.

He heard someone's footsteps coming close, then a whiff of some variety of pine-scented deodorant. Chaucer suddenly opened his eyes and threw on a big Joker-like grin. The interrogator jumped back, startled.

Round one: Chaucer.

Chaucer didn't think he would win another.

The room was large. Maybe forty feet by forty feet. The ceiling was twenty feet overhead and all exposed, unpainted piping. Mercury-vapor lights hung from thick girders and bathed the room in a sickly orange glow.

Some sort of industrial building. A warehouse, most likely. The walls were covered in thick soundproofing, haphazardly nailed. This place was not a usual location for this outfit. This place was hastily put together.

He eyed up his interrogator. Young, clean-cut. Mormon, if he had to guess. He noticed the CTR ring. *Check. Mormon for sure.* He found it odd that such a kind and gentle people turned out so many really talented torturers. It was a fact that the disastrous enhanced interrogation program during the Second Gulf War was masterminded by two such Mormons. Chaucer met them once and thought them fools. They proved incapable of realizing the error of their ways. Most of the intel generated from the program proved to be utter garbage, but those men and their superiors defended each "revelation" no matter how many others proved false. Whether patriotism simply blinded them, or they stubbornly refused to reevaluate their methods, Chaucer couldn't say.

The interrogator recovered and reapproached. Chaucer kept him off balance. "Eli? Caleb? Melchizedek?"

Chaucer ran out of biblical names. But it was enough. The kid's upper lip snarled. Chaucer hit a soft spot and instantly regretted it. *Probably not a good idea to piss off your interrogator, Chaucer.*

"Come now, Malcolm, no need for religious slurs," said the interrogator. Chaucer tried to guess the age of the kid. Maybe he was thirty, but he looked younger. He had one of those faces: pale, with blond almost invisible eyebrows, and blue-gray eyes. Eternally cherubic. He tried to envision this kid's life before this. What did this kid's ASVAB reveal that sent him down this path? For most, it was moral flexibility. But for some, it was an extreme ability to compartmentalize. Patriots who were told that this would be for the greater good and believed it utterly. Blindly. He got a sense of that with this kid.

"How are you?" the interrogator asked.

"Peachy."

The interrogator smiled gently. *Oh God*, thought Chaucer, *this kid's actually trying to build rapport*. The kid flipped on the machine. He tweaked its levels as he spoke. "Now I don't want to be here any more than you want to be here. My employers, they've been lied to. A lot. And they need answers. I want you to know that you and I? We could be a team. If we are, I promise you this will go quickly and easily."

Chaucer almost couldn't believe it. *What the fuck are they teaching at the Farm*? He tried his best to smile, but a part of him, the professional in him, thought that maybe this was the worst torture of all. This kid was a rank amateur. Which was dangerous. Because when he stopped getting answers, he could do some actual damage. Not the kind of damage that a professional interrogator would do. A pro would deliver pain, but without lasting effects, if only so that the session could go on and on and on. No, this kid just could easily take out an eye. It was time to ditch him. "I'm ready to talk."

The kid smiled faintly. Chaucer thought to himself, this must've been like your final exam at Langley. Smooth sailing, preparing you for nothing.

The kid tweaked the poly a few more times until he was satisfied that all the readouts were properly set. At least the kid got that part right. Even though Chaucer hated these machines, he knew their proper operation, and at least the kid was fully briefed on that.

"Now, my employers want to know—"

"*Employers want to know?*" thought Chaucer, *Jesus Christ. If you're building rapport, it's about you, what you want to know. If you're putting the hurt on, it's about you. It's about what you are going to do. What the fuck is this "employer" stuff?*

The kid continued, "We have talked with Sim Se Yoon. We

know what he told you. We know you had contact with Ji-Ho as well. Our question is: Who did you tell about Tajo? Who knows?"

"I'm going to make this easy on you," said Chaucer. "I'm going to tell you everything you want to know. There's one person and one person only, aside from myself and Tempest, that we talked to about Tajo." Chaucer paused. As though he was having second thoughts.

He stared at the mirrored glass blind in front of him and smiled. Chaucer wasn't really messing with the kid. He was messing with those assholes in the blind. *Fuck you, Roma.*

Chaucer continued, "The one person we told …was your mother." Chaucer looked down at the electronic readout of the polygraph. Not a single line moved. *Truth.* The kid looked flustered. He adjusted several of the knobs, changed the scale on a few readouts. But the machine said: "Truth."

Chaucer felt a blast of agony ripple up his spine, the result of the lie. He allowed it in. He allowed it to pass. It was preparation for what was to come. Strangely, in this hopeless environment, Chaucer was finally free to lie.

Chaucer glanced down at the cable leading into the blind, knowing that those assembled inside would see the same readout that he saw. The kid tried to recover. "If you're not going to be serious—"

"I'm being perfectly serious," Chaucer said. "After I fucked the hell out of your mother last night, she was in a chatty mood and she asked me about my day." Still, the readouts were straight lines. *Truth.*

Another ripple of pure pain rocked Chaucer. But he could take it. They had no idea what he could take.

The kid got rattled fast, glancing back at the blind. "Fine. You want it like that? We can do it like that. Formal. State your full name."

"My name is Malcolm Chaucer." Suddenly, the poly sprang to life. Several of the indicators went haywire, whipping back and forth. *Lie.* "I am sitting in a chair under interrogation —again."

The ley lines of the polygraph went crazy. *Another lie.*

The kid did his best, tried to adjust the machine, to turn this disaster into something he could explain. But it was no use. Everyone in the blind knew it. The machine didn't work on Chaucer. He could make it say anything he wanted to.

Ding. A bell sounded clear as day. Some sort of way for the people in the blind to tell the interrogator, "Bye now. Next!"

The flustered interrogator got up and, without a word, went around to the side of the blind and disappeared inside. Chaucer hummed a few bars of Beethoven's *Ode To Joy* as he waited for the inevitable next step.

He waited to meet the man responsible for Terry's death. The man he would spend every last moment of his life making sure would die.

CHAPTER 65

The person who stepped out of the blind was exactly who Chaucer was expecting. He stared into the cold, dead eyes of Gabriel Asher. He had no idea Gabriel Asher was running this op, but in retrospect, of course he was. The op was ruthless, breaking what few rules the game had. It required a genius who was also a high-functioning sociopath. That was exactly who Gabriel Asher was.

Asher walked toward Chaucer with the calm of a man who knew all the angles. He stared at Chaucer for a long moment. "I thought you'd be taller. From the way people talk about you, I thought you'd be seven foot eight."

"Gabriel Asher. I see you're allowed back in the country. Good for you."

Asher laughed. "You are, without a doubt, the funniest guy I've ever had sitting in that chair."

"Not my first rodeo."

Asher put his hands on his hips. "That is the story they tell. Sorry about the kid. We figured we'd give him a chance to get his dick wet before our hired gun arrives. Me? I got nothing against you. But this guy *hates* you. It should be interesting to watch. Can I get you something while you're waiting? Coffee? Water?"

"I suppose a gun would be out of the question?"

Asher shook his head. "Like I said, funniest guy ever in the chair." Asher turned around and headed back into the blind, awaiting their mystery guest.

"Asher?"

Asher turned back to Chaucer, eyebrows raised in anticipation.

"You got my brother killed?"

"Afraid not. I was brought on to clean up that mess. Your friend my sniper shot in Dennis Raymer's office on the other hand, his death you can squarely blame on me."

"I'll see you die soon."

Asher turned away and entered the blind. "Funny, funny guy."

CHAPTER 66

Little Tyler squirmed in the back of the sedan as Tempest drove into a dark part of the Bronx. "Happy Meal!" yelled Tyler.

Tempest glanced in the rearview mirror, and then did her ritual scan of the surrounding cars. "Yes, baby. Happy Meal. You deserve it. Having to leave that great party!"

Tyler smiled up at his mama. "I love you, Mama!"

"Love you more." Tempest pulled off the Cross Bronx Expressway when she saw the familiar golden arches in the distance. She thought to herself, *I should probably grab a bite too. You never know when your next meal will be.* She was tense, anxious. And not the kind of tense she usually got before a mission. This was different. This was her body anticipating trouble of the worst kind.

She was anticipating her own death.

After little Tyler had finished his Happy Meal, and Mama had scarfed down a burger herself, Tempest drove on. Little Tyler was already complaining about his Happy Meal toy, which he had promptly broken. "Fix it! Fix it! Fix it!"

"Yes, baby," said Tempest. "Mama's going to make it all better. Mama's going to fix it all."

Tempest stopped three blocks away from the warehouse

where Chaucer was being held. She didn't dare go any closer, and it was a good thing, too. Because the more she scanned the dark, near-lightless industrial road, with rows of half-empty warehouses on each side, she knew that surveillance was everywhere.

Generally, surveillance for this sort of operation would be within a one-block radius. These guys did at least two blocks, as she spotted the first surveillance vehicle on patrol two blocks out. She drove on, so she could be sure they didn't make her. One more block away, Tempest found some Disney music Tyler wouldn't object to and stepped out of the car. She surveyed the skyline, looking back toward the warehouse. There weren't a lot of options for what she needed. Most of the warehouses were one-story, twenty- to thirty-foot-high-ceiling affairs. There was just one building that had a third story, and she estimated it was a block and a half from Chaucer's warehouse. *Well, I don't know what's in there, but you better be ready. Mama's coming.*

It turned out to be a marine fabricator. A strong smell of varnish and diesel filled the air. The ground floor of the warehouse was filled with boat engines, from simple inboards for smaller yachts, to huge diesel monsters for freighters. Tempest knew little about the field, so she couldn't tell much more. But luckily, this business was not a twenty-four-hour operation. There was nobody inside at this late hour. It didn't even have much of a security system, which was fortuitous, because her skills in that area were getting rusty. She figured light security made sense here. Who the hell would try to steal one of these seventeen-ton monstrosities?

"Fix it!" yelled Tyler, holding out his Happy Meal toy. Tempest glanced around, checking to see if anyone on the dark street was there to hear the outburst. She got right down in the boy's face. "Tyler, I told you. We're playing hide-and-seek, and you have to be quiet."

Tyler looked up at his mother, ready to challenge her, but the intensity in her eyes scared him and he backed down. "Okay, Mama. I'll be good."

On the third floor of the warehouse, Tempest scored. She found a window looking out at Chaucer's warehouse, as she now thought of it. It had a great angle.

Tempest found her sniper's blind.

She spent the next ten minutes ransacking the nearby offices, pulling out couch cushions and the like, repositioning desks, and doing anything else she needed, so she could craft an ideal firing position on that warehouse. Before long, she laid herself down on a couch cushion perched atop a desk, and pulled her Blaser R93, a German sniper rifle that Tempest thought of as her second child, out of her duffel bag. The bag was now empty.

She slowly opened the rifle's optics. She had a clear line of sight over the entire warehouse.

Little Tyler was an issue, since he had broken his toy and didn't deal with adversity well at all. The boy kicked the foot of the desk, annoyed that he wasn't the center of attention. Tempest was worried about him, but right now she had to give her full attention to today's problem. Chaucer.

Tyler finally calmed down when Tempest gave him her Sig. Of course, she pulled out the mag and emptied the chamber. She wasn't a monster.

Tyler ran around that small office, shooting every imaginary bad guy in sight. Tempest nestled her body into the couch cushion, letting gravity do its work, finding her point of ultimate stillness. And then she raised the rifle.

An hour later, there was a ruckus. A vehicle approached and passed through two different layers of outer security. The vehicle itself? Cherry-red Corvette, one of those brand new mid-engine models. *Sweet*.

Somebody important. VIP of some kind. Maybe the boss of bosses, maybe even the guy who contracted the job. She stared through her scope as they let the Corvette directly into the warehouse and closed the door behind them. She never got a look at the passengers. But she got a great look at everything else. From the glimpse she got through the open warehouse door, she knew the interior layout, and she had a pretty damn good idea of the OpFor.

The layout was simple. It was one wide open space with an office area in the back, the size of a double-wide. Above the office was a small second floor they used for storage. Chaucer would be in that office. There just wasn't anywhere else to put him.

The OpFor wasn't so simple. There had to be a dozen of them. All operators or officers with kinetic training. Up close, Tempest felt she had a chance. It was going to come down to the approach.

The trick was going to be the roof.

CHAPTER 67

It was an hour before someone came out of the blind again. And it was a familiar face. His name was Colton Mathers. He was widely considered the second-best interrogator in the world. That he knew it was the problem. Colton hated being number two. He did everything he could to differentiate himself. He orchestrated smear campaigns against Chaucer, which wasn't hard to do. All that *Manchurian Candidate* bullshit people whispered? That was pure Colton.

But none of it worked. Every job Colton ever had, he knew he got it because Malcolm Chaucer was too busy, or too principled to take it.

"Malcolm. Chaucer. The Oracle himself."

"That's it? Just my name? You've been dreaming about this day for years, and that's all you got?"

Colton smiled a deeply unnerving smile. He was like a magician who couldn't wait to show his new tricks. "You're right. I have been waiting for this. Preparing even. I thought many times about exactly how I'd do it. And now? Just sit back and relax, my friend. Enjoy the show."

It was an interrogator's joke, and not a very good one. But the words had the intended effect. Chaucer grew nervous. The book on Colton was that he was well versed in every one of the interrogator's arts. The book also said that there were some parts of the job that Colton loved—unnaturally.

Chaucer, the Oracle, was known for being ultra-clean, the guy who would leave his subjects in as good a state as they possibly could be. Whereas Colton liked to leave his mark on people. Some jobs, revenge jobs, nobody even bothered calling Chaucer. Those were Colton's bread and butter. And now he had the greatest revenge job of all. His own personal one.

Colton got up real close, staring into Chaucer's eyes. The look of glee on his face was uncontainable. He wanted to relish this moment. He pulled out his smartphone and took a smiling selfie next to Chaucer.

"By the way, that specialist who fooled you—who fooled the almighty Oracle—did you know it only took her three weeks of training to beat you?"

It was his first mistake. Rather than getting intel, he was giving it. If Miranda Ross, the impostor who played the role of Isabel Marcano, trained three weeks to fool him, that meant everything. It meant that the planning of the op predated the assassination. It meant Roma's unit was complicit in the killing of Tajo.

Chaucer suppressed all outward emotion, but inside he was taking the small victory. Until he realized what it meant. It meant that Colton was sure, absolutely certain, that Chaucer would never walk out of here.

"So what's it going to be?" Chaucer said. "Eastern? Western? Modern? Medieval?"

"Well, I know you're a bit of a traditionalist, so I figured, why mess with perfection? I thought I'd do it—by the book."

He let those words hang. It took Chaucer a moment to realize what Colton was getting at. When Colton Mathers saw the expression on Chaucer's face change, he reached into his bag and pulled out *The White Book*. Po's book.

There were few things in this world that genuinely terrified Malcolm Chaucer. This was the Pandora's box that released them all. Colton paged through the book, stopping on something that caught his eye in the middle Chapters. "Why beat around the bush? Let's start with … The Cradle."

There were three guys on the roof. Why? Tempest was pissed. Nobody ever put three guys on the fucking roof. Two guys patrolling covered every angle. But three? The third guy was useless.

It's like someone knew what she was going to do and purposely tried to fuck her up.

Suddenly, she felt the cold steel of a gun barrel against the back of her neck. She froze. "Ooh, ya got me, pardner."

Little Tyler giggled and pulled the trigger. "Bang! You're dead! You're dead! You're dead!"

Tempest rolled over for a second to look her boy in the eyes. "I sure am, baby. I sure am. But, baby?" Tempest lashed out a hand and ripped the gun from Little Tyler's hands. "Never let them get within arm's reach of you."

Tyler shrugged. "Okay, Mama."

Tempest handed the gun back to Tyler and rolled over, surveying the situation. Three guys remained on the roof, patrolling back and forth. *Shit, I'm so close to having a plan.* But the three-guys deal was going to be a real ball-buster. They were all throat-miked. If she shot one, by the time she adjusted to the second, the others could sound the alarm. Add in a third target, and it looked hopeless.

She thought about Chaucer in there. Subjected to God-knows-what, but also knowing that if she wasn't perfect on this, they'd both be dead. She stared at the three guys on the roof, pacing back and forth, walking the length of the building's perimeter. She waited for a change in the situation.

Or for inspiration.

CHAPTER 68

It was only hour two of the interrogation, and Chaucer felt his mind slipping away. For all the painstaking work he had done over the years, to rebuild himself into some semblance of a human being, Colton's inspiration to use Po's own work was a stroke of genius. It revealed the house of cards that was Malcolm Chaucer. He was unraveling before Colton's eyes, and Colton was in heaven.

Chaucer was hunched over in a ball, naked, in a stress position known as the Cradle. Bands of cloth constricted his wrists and legs and pulled them into a meeting point, while his back arched over a suspended wooden pole. It stretched and exposed each vertebra. And at each juncture, acupuncture needles dotted his exposed spine.

Colton read in awe about how flicking a single one of those needles could create virtually any sensation he wished to inflict. Broken back? The fifteenth needle down the left side. The sensation of self-immolation? The third on the right. But Po did more than just map these sensations. He choreographed them into a symphony of mind-breaking pain. He called it the Ladder.

Chaucer suddenly realized that Colton had yet to ask him any questions. This, thus far, was play. Colton, for his part, could tell that Chaucer was breaking and breaking early. For all his glee, for all his joy, there was a chance that this could all go south. Chaucer could become unrecoverable, and he might have very little warning. He needed to get to the questions his employers desperately wanted to know. "Tell me about the kid."

With that question, he twisted and played with the sixth needle on the left side of Chaucer's spine. The one that simulated whole-body frostbite.

Chaucer shivered and shook. *Malcolm Chaucer does not break after two hours.* Despite everything in his body screaming, Chaucer remained resolute.

"We just gotta know, buddy. You know you're going to tell me. I don't get the resistance, I really don't. We've got to know what you know about the kid. Tajo."

Chaucer thought the question was strange. *What do I know about the kid? What was there to know about the kid?* They already talked with Sim Se Yoon. They know I know about his true family. So what other secret could there be?

Colton grew restless. He realized he was allowing emotion into the equation, but he couldn't pretend this wasn't at least somewhat personal. Anyway, his employers knew that, so they were going to have to give him some leeway. "What did you know about the kid, and who did you tell about it?" With that, he dug in deeper with the sixth needle.

Chaucer felt like he was thrown into a blizzard. His skin felt like it was cracking, the nerve endings dying from frostbite, the setting in of gangrene, the so-cold-it's-hot sensation that only that one particular needle could provide. He shivered uncontrollably, drooling on the cement floor, a puppet in an evil master's hands. Chaucer got one word out. "Ra-Ra-Ra-Rabbit."

Colton's eyes lit up. In his face-down position, Chaucer couldn't see, so Colton was free to have whatever emotional reactions he wanted. And this was an emotional reaction. This was exactly the matter his employers wanted to know the most about.

"Yes, Chaucer, the rabbits. Do you know where the rabbits are?"

"Wh-wh-what?"

In a deep interrogation, subjects often lose the thread, and need things to be repeated, sometimes several times. "Do you know where the rabbits are?"

Chaucer struggled to focus. He was trying to say, 'Year of the Rabbit.' Did Colton just ask him where the rabbits were?

What rabbits?

Colton let his hand gently brush down Chaucer's spine, triggering ten different needles in succession. Chaucer's screams echoed throughout the warehouse.

Tempest finally had a plan. Not a good plan exactly. But it was a plan. And that was certainly better than nothing. She would take out those roof guys, and then she would hustle the lonely block to the side door of the warehouse. She would gain entry, take out the guys in the rafters, and then figure out where the hell Chaucer was. As long as nobody held the high ground, Tempest figured she could take out maybe eight operatives before they got her. From a brief glimpse inside, she thought it was a fifty-fifty shot that they had more. *But hell, you got to gamble sometime.*

She had repositioned herself four offices over and one floor down in the same warehouse so she could line up a shot. A shot she couldn't believe she was considering. She aimed at the roof of the warehouse, not from a height above it, but from eye level with the men patrolling it.

All she had to do was wait for all three to line up. Tempest wondered if she really was good enough to make it happen.

CHAPTER 69

Again Colton asked, "Where are the rabbits?"

Chaucer barely heard him. Agony overtook his body. Long-dormant parts of his brain awakened, and many of the areas that he relied on for cognition were shutting down for their own self-preservation.

But one part in Chaucer's brain that reawoke whispered to him: *Turn the tables.* Chaucer's lizard brain sprung back to life. And it came back with a vengeance.

It gave Chaucer a focus that he hadn't thought possible during torture. It told him what was happening. Chaucer realized he was getting more information out of Colton than Colton was getting out of him. An interrogation in reverse. He played into it. "Why do you think I know where the rabbits are?"

Colton didn't suspect a thing. All his training said questions were good. It signified engagement of the subject. Sometimes evasion, but that itself was engagement. "We know. We know you found his friend."

Chaucer focused on interrogating the interrogator. It was a game, a distraction from agony. It kept him alive another moment. "You couldn't find him?"

Colton tweaked two more needles, studying Po's book and watching Chaucer's anguished reaction with total fascination.

"Oh, they found him all right, and one of these idiots put a bullet in his brain before we could find out anything. Hey, Chaucer? Where are the rabbits?"

He tweaked needle after needle, in a sequence Po once called "Climbing the Ladder." Chaucer felt it coming. He remembered what it was and what it did to him, and his soul cried out for its own survival, "Please! Please don't! I don't know about the rabbits. I don't know where they are. Please!"

The sadist in Colton reveled in the moment. The source of all his wounded pride, all his professional dissatisfaction, was begging him. And he wanted it to continue. There were twenty-three needles left on the ladder, and he was going to make Chaucer climb every last one.

His hand manipulated the next needle. Chaucer pissed all over the floor as he lost control of his body, the agony overtaking him. "Please. I don't know. I'm telling you the truth."

Colton didn't care. When this sequence was done, he could tell his employers, once and for all, whether or not Chaucer knew a damn thing. But this was about far more than that. He would break the man that caused him so much pain. And Chaucer would never be competition again.

That long-hidden part of Chaucer's lizard brain spat at him from the darkness. It whispered to him, riding on waves of pain and its accompanying endorphins: *You fool. Nothing you've done means anything.*

Chaucer was lost to Colton for the next several minutes, writhing in agony and screaming. But deep inside, Chaucer's dialogue with parts of his old self continued. *Tell the truth and it will set you free. Tell the truth and the pain won't come again.* The mammalian brain cried out, but the lizard brain stormed back, *You're telling the truth, and still you climb the Ladder. You're telling the truth—*

And the truth will destroy you.

CHAPTER 70

Tempest gave her shooting eye another dose of OS-20, specially formulated eye drops for people in her profession. It soothed her eye that had been on the sniper scope continuously for over an hour, waiting for that perfect combination of movements, lining up the three men for one single shot. *It's like goddamn astronomy*, thought Tempest. She even had names for the three idiots. *Oh look, Mercury's in retrograde. Big whoop-de-doo.*

Behind her, little Tyler sat in the corner, playing with the safety on the gun, and drinking a juice box. He had gone through four in the last hour, most of the package she bought for him, and Tempest wondered what that would do to the boy.

Chaucer was terrified. Not because of the torture, not because he was likely to be killed tonight. No, he was terrified because years of Po's programming were unraveling minute by minute. His carefully constructed life, the way his mind clung to an ordered set of precepts, just to keep the insanity that should be his legacy at bay—it was all slipping away. That long-suppressed lizard brain, the Chaucer who used to be, was demanding to be heard.

You traded yourself for a quarter of a human being. And where did it get you? The Cradle. Climbing the Ladder. Everything you gave up was for nothing!

Colton could not suppress a smile. "I heard you called me a sadist. I feel I should clear the record. I'm not a sadist in any traditional sense. Sadism has a sexual connotation. There is nothing sexual in what I do. In the feelings I experience. No, what I experience is ... joy."

He reached out for another needle, staring at it with barely contained glee. "The twenty-sixth needle. What did Po call this one? The Well. This is going to activate the terror center of your brain, like a four-year-old experiencing a nightmare. It's amazing how Po was able to talk about meridians and ley lines in one sentence, and psychopharmacology in the next. And he wrote with such ... poetry. He was truly a renaissance man."

Colton brought the twenty-sixth needle to Chaucer's sweat ravaged body, and plunged it into Chaucer's spine.

The reaction was beyond anything he could have imagined.

Chaucer knew it was coming. The terror. He knew it was coming, and he was helpless to prepare for it. Somewhere deep within the brain, every horror he ever had sprang back to life. Not a conscious thought in the bunch. No monster under the bed, no serial killer killing Mom and Dad. But the pure, mainlined feeling of all of that. The feeling of abject helplessness, of illogical, unspeakable evil. Of total terror. It rushed upon him and ripped his mind apart. He screamed out into the night, pleading to no one and nothing. Praying to a God he no longer believed in. For what? Just to take it all away. Take it all far, far away and let him die.

Colton reveled in wave after wave of ecstatic joy, seeing the destruction of the man at his hands, without hammer, blowtorch, or knife. With just the slightest touch of a tiny acupuncture needle.

Jupiter, the biggest guy, slowly crossed Mars, the guy with the HK416, one mean assault rifle. But fucking Mercury stopped to light a cigarette. Fucking Mercury. Always the one out of rhythm. Almost as if he was trained that way. Tempest wiped the thought from her mind. It was superstition. Unordered minds trying to put some sort of pattern to an annoying randomness.

But then it happened. Jupiter reversed direction. Mars too. The cigarette. They all wanted a cigarette. They approached Mercury.

And stood in line, waiting for it.

Tempest had two of them dead to rights, lined up perfectly, with Mercury less than a foot out of position. She prayed to herself: *Please, just step a foot ahead*. And a moment after Mercury lit their cigarettes, he did just that. He took a step forward to resume his patrol, and the green light went off in Tempest's mind.

The tension Tempest had been holding in her finger, on the trigger but not pulling the trigger, was at an end. She released, drawing her trigger finger toward her. She felt the recoil in her shoulder, like a warm pat on the back. Tempest had been waiting so long for this moment that, to her perception, the bullet traveled in slow motion. The rifling spun it in tight coils as it plunged forth across the air between the two buildings.

It hit Jupiter first, right at the top of the ear, a great entry point. Little to no bone for deflection. And it continued on. It went through Mars's head next, slightly higher up, and slightly more forward. The bullet had expanded at this point, and severed his frontal lobe from the rest of his brain.

And Mercury, dear sweet Mercury, he got the rest of the bullet. Now significantly deformed, and accompanied by his two friends' brain matter, the bullet smashed into his medulla oblongata.

Tempest found his off-switch.

Tempest allowed herself two seconds to appreciate the beauty of the shot. Deep down, she knew it wasn't that hard technically, being at relatively close range. But the artistry! The artistry was something to behold.

Tempest hopped up from her shooting position and spoke to Tyler with her stern mother's voice. "Tyler, Mama's gotta go to work. You be a good boy and I'll be back in ten minutes."

Tempest gathered her pistol and assault rifle and headed down the stairs. She sent a preprogrammed text to one of her few friends. It contained instructions. If she was not heard from in the next hour, she told her friend where to pick up Tyler. Then she turned off her phone.

———

Colton stood in amazement at the transformation of Chaucer. This wasn't the steely interrogator that everyone knew. This was a snarling, ranting, raving madman who was swearing, to anyone. who could hear, what he would do to Colton and everyone else in this warehouse. Colton never knew the old Chaucer, Case Officer Malcolm Chaucer. He wondered if this was anything like the guy at all. Or was Chaucer just a box full of old Legos, thousands of pieces to dozens of abandoned kits, that would never fit together in any kind of whole. He tweaked one more needle, knowing that it would stop the raving, and drive Chaucer back into a deep, sub-verbal agony. But when he tweaked that needle, for the first time, it did not have the expected response. Po's book was specific. Sub-verbal, deep agony. But Chaucer was still ranting. "I'll get all you motherfuckers. Do you hear me? I will kill you all. You're dead! Every last one of you!"

Colton tweaked the needle again, driving it further into the spine. He could see the sweat pouring off of Chaucer. He could see the contortions of the face. It was having some of the intended effect, but no longer the psychology that was expected.

Colton wondered what it meant.

Old Chaucer was back and knew exactly what it meant. He would no longer play by Po's rule book, no longer be ruled by the fear of what was. He refused to be broken a second time. This was supposed to be a crucifixion. It was about to be a resurrection. Old Chaucer had no idea how he was going to survive, but he was suddenly filled with the deepest belief that he would. And unlike that other resurrected man, Old Chaucer wasn't about to turn the other cheek.

CHAPTER 71

Tempest threw a rug from the office over the fence, covering the razor wire atop it. She ran, jumped, and surmounted it in two seconds flat, landing firmly on the other side without a sound. She crossed the wide, empty alley, and climbed a pole beside the corrugated metal barrier delineating the yard of the warehouse. Chaucer's warehouse.

She could see three operatives at the side door, but they couldn't see her yet. They stood under mercury-vapor lights. Tactical mistake. Mercury vapor really messes with your night vision. She drew her Ruger and stepped into the light. Three firm snaps clicked in the night. The .22 had no stopping power, so each shot had to be perfect. That's why almost no pros still used it, except assassins, and Tempest was an old-school assassin.

The men went down like bowling pins, each with a neat little .22 caliber hole in their brain pan. Tempest paused just a moment, listening for any sound of alarm. There was none. But there was a security camera over their position, so it'd only be another moment or two.

Tempest opened the door and stormed onto the killing floor. The glimpse she had gotten of the inside of the warehouse gave her a basic layout, but the devil's always in the details. The stacks of crates that she saw, sadly did not extend over the entire floor, rather just the entryway. Therefore, when she entered, she was exposed, on open ground, and she was instantly spotted.

In the two-second evaluation that was her training, she counted six on the ground floor, and another four in the rafters. She calculated three different ways to tackle the problem and went for the Alexander strategy.

Take the high ground.

Her first two controlled bursts of the Honey Badger took out the two guys in the rafters who had spotted her. She moved laterally across the floor, toward a pile of wooden crates that might provide some cover, and opened up on spotter number three in the rafters above her vantage point. Two more bursts of automatic fire took him down.

But the fourth man in the rafters was a problem. He had a protected position behind something large and steel. It was dark up there, and Tempest couldn't tell what it was.

This changed her plan considerably. She immediately reversed direction, which ended up being a good thing. Because the six enemy combatants on the ground level filled the air where she would've been with a hail of lead. They were desperate to keep her from reaching cover. However, Tempest chose to avoid cover, running back the other way across empty ground. She figured she had a fifty-fifty shot of not taking a hit.

She flipped a coin, and it came up tails. She felt the hot round enter her side. It spun her and threw her to the ground. It was a through-and-through, mostly meat. She would survive, if only she could get up in time.

She reconsidered that thought. After all, prone is an ideal firing position. She returned fire—suppressive fire, not meant to hit them. Just to keep their heads down. Luck was on her side and she saw two of them go down for good. The rest dove for cover.

But while prone is an ideal firing position for those on the same level as you, it leaves you dangerously exposed to the high ground. The fourth shooter in the rafters stepped out from a steel drum and aimed straight down at Tempest. He fired a volley as she rolled away and put one in her gut. Tempest flipped over and snapshotted skyward. She caught the fourth man in the head, snapping it back. He went down hard.

Tempest tried to stand on a polished concrete floor slick with her own blood. The gut shot was bad. She was leaking. She had a med-pack back where little Tyler was, but she didn't like the odds of making it there.

The four remaining operatives on the ground level emerged from cover and flanked her. Two of them made the mistake of maneuvering themselves behind the cover of barrels of gasoline. Tempest put a volley into those barrels. Gasoline isn't as flammable as most civilians think, so the two men now standing in a pool of it didn't immediately abandon their position. They had good fire discipline and let loose a couple of volleys intended to pin Tempest where she was.

Then Tempest threw the incendiary grenade.

A ball of white phosphorous flew into their position. The two men barely had a second to dive out of the way, far too late for the cataclysm that erupted. The incendiary went up in flames, and an entire quarter of the vast warehouse with it.

Two left. The remaining contestants were in the back of the warehouse, under the rafters, hiding amid rows of shelving holding thousands of boxes. Tempest thought to herself, *Fine, you want a bug hunt. I'll give you a bug hunt.* She glanced back at the trail of blood she was leaving behind her. *Better find those bugs fast.*

The smell from the fire burned her nostrils, smoke filling the warehouse from the roof down. In a few moments, visibility would be next to zero. She peered into the darkness, saw movement, and moved in the opposite direction. *When they flank, you flank.*

What they were doing was a coordinated lateral dance, each trying to get the best position on her. Their goal was to get Tempest between them. Tempest's goal was to, well, not. Tempest reached the edge of the warehouse first, and a second later, down the aisle, she saw the other operative, illuminated by an exit sign. It was Roma.

Tempest and Roma went way back.

Neither had their weapon raised. Neither had quite lowered them either. It was to be the briefest of standoffs.

Roma spoke first, hoping to get an advantage in a situation where he knew he had none. "Hey, girl."

Tempest let loose a five-round burst that cut Roma apart. "Hey, Roma."

Tempest lost sight of the last guy. She went through her checklist, triangulating his last-known position. She quickly realized he wasn't here anymore. He didn't bug out. He had retreated into the back room.

That, she knew, was where she would find Chaucer.

Or his remains.

CHAPTER 72

The last operative standing ran into the blind, out of breath. Asher turned to him, ready to rip him a new one, but then he saw his face. Asher knew that face. It was the face of a man who had just seen death incarnate: Tempest. He also smelled the man, reeking of gas and flames and fire. "How many?"

"Just the Widowmaker."

"No, asshole, how many of ours left?"

"Just us."

Asher realized that there was a negative side to soundproofing this back room as well as they had. They were entirely flat-footed, unaware that their position was overrun, that defense was untenable. "Post up thirty feet from the door. When she comes in, finish her."

The operative did as he was told. Asher headed the other direction and out the north door.

Chaucer was only vaguely aware that something was happening. He saw movement in his periphery. Somebody else was in the room. He would never allow it. Would Colton? He thought he saw the silhouette of a man with a gun, crouched in a defensive firing position. But his mind had been playing tricks on him for hours now, and he didn't want to give credence to an illusion.

A man in a defensive position would mean hope, and hope was the worst trick his mind liked to play when in the Cradle.

But that was Old Chaucer talking.

New Chaucer had a different opinion. With fucking Tempest out there? She was going to kill all these assholes, and get him out of here.

She was always the brave one. Even before Po, Chaucer was the cautious partner. Scared, even if he would never admit it. Tempest? The way she was? Who the hell could hang with that? Not Dennis. Poor Dennis. He should have known this would be the end, eventually. But not Chaucer. Chaucer loved her. Chaucer *loved* her.

Old Chaucer brought him back to reality. *You're fantasizing about a romantic relationship from a decade ago. You're just disassociating in another form. Because your mind is dying.* Still, the phantom image of the crouched man didn't go away. In fact, it grew clearer.

Colton stepped between Chaucer and the crouched man; the man had drawn Chaucer's attention, and that was unacceptable. He wanted to complain to Asher, but Asher just left. Something was going on. He even thought he smelled smoke.

It gave him pause, but then again, Colton saw the dozen operatives outside. And when had an interrogation facility ever been breached? In the States? It was unheard of.

Tempest paused at the door to the back room. Normally, she would fire right through it. But Chaucer was somewhere on the other side. She would not chance it. So she had to breach. There are tactics for breaching a door with hostiles on the other side. Excellent tactics if you have three or more operatives. Decent tactics if you have two.

No tactics at all if you're alone.

Tempest knew she would take another shot the moment she opened that door. She didn't know if she could take another shot and live.

The last remaining man stayed at his post. The weight of his pistol was getting heavy, his mind telling him to run, but he stayed in a crouched position, gun trained on the door that was about to open.

And then it did just that, slowly creaking open. The man fired blindly, before he could really see what was on the other side, but something was wrong and he knew it. The door was supposed to explode open from a kick.

This one just slid open slowly. He saw Tempest's head at the floor, her hand raised in opening the door, and the barrel of her automatic rifle pointed right at him. A quick burst, and the man went down.

Colton saw the man fire, then get shot. He couldn't believe it. Colton had no gun, no appreciable weapon of any kind. Normally, he would have a collection of torture tools that would serve as weapons, but he had wanted to do things Po-style. And Po would never use something as crude as a weapon. He stared into the darkness where the shots came from. A darkness Tempest emerged from, a bloody, bleeding, smoking vision from hell.

"Ground. Hands and legs outstretched. Now."

Colton complied immediately. Tempest's eyes were wide, like a maniac. All joy was gone from Colton, replaced in a heartbeat by abject terror.

"Please ... Please don't —"

"Shut the fuck up."

Tempest saw Chaucer, tied in the Cradle position, hyperventilating. A wave of relief passed over her. He's still alive. She limped over to Chaucer. "Sorry, buddy. Got to do it." One by one, she quickly pulled out all the acupuncture needles. Chaucer writhed in agony at each one. She cut his hands and legs free. And then, she waited.

Chaucer didn't believe it. Chaucer didn't want to believe it. But Old Chaucer was here now and didn't care what Chaucer thought.

"What the hell took you so long?"

Tempest smirked. "Mercury was in retrograde."

Chaucer stood slowly, naked as the day he was born. After what he had been through, modesty didn't matter. So few things mattered at this moment.

"We gotta go. You've got a minute." She handed Chaucer her sidearm, the silenced Ruger.

He looked down at the ground where Colton laid cowering.

Chaucer looked at the gun, and at Colton. Chaucer thought, *No, just get out of here.*

Old Chaucer lifted the gun and fired until the action locked open.

CHAPTER 73

Chaucer struggled to stand at first, but the beauty of the Cradle was that the damage from it was primarily psychological. Tempest put Colton's coat around him, marveling at the speed with which Chaucer recovered. "You can move?"

"To get out of here? Girl, I can samba."

Tempest shot Chaucer a glance. She could tell something was profoundly altered in him, but she didn't have time to investigate. She helped Chaucer out the way she came, through the side door. They crossed the rear yard of the warehouse and climbed over the corrugated wall, landing in the alley.

At the end of the alley, an SUV was approaching fast. *Reinforcements. Shit.*

They ran across the alley and toward the fence that separated this parcel from the one where Tempest set up her sniper nest. The rug still laid over the razor wire and concertina, but Chaucer and Tempest both had problems getting over the fence. Chaucer noticed her injuries for the first time, slowly coming out of his post-torture daze. He saw a trail of blood in Tempest's wake. "Let me look."

"No time."

Sure enough, the SUV was getting close. Chaucer hurled

himself over the fence, landing hard on broken wood. The SUV stopped fifty feet behind Tempest, and its doors opened. Tempest didn't bother to look, hurling herself over the fence, pain be damned.

Shots rang out. Tempest flopped over the fence and landed on top of Chaucer on the other side. Together, they limped toward the warehouse, where little Tyler waited for them.

They heard shouting behind them, but neither took the time to turn around and look. Their sole focus was the small door at the back of the warehouse.

They got within three feet of it when it all went to shit. Asher and a second operative appeared, coming out of the darkness on their flank. Tempest dove through the door, but Chaucer got the butt of a gun to his head, and went down hard.

Inside the ground floor of the warehouse, Tempest tried to spin around, reaching for her backup in an ankle holster. But before she got there, she was too late. She had lost a lot of blood, and was far too slow for the maneuver. And they had a position.

Asher was the first man in the door, and he fired once into Tempest's back. Her backup, a simple .32, clattered across the floor.

This time, she didn't move. The second operative arrived, and Asher motioned with his eyes for him to check her body. "It's the Widowmaker. Many people shot her. Check her pulse, and keep your gun on her."

The man did as he was told. He kneeled down beside her and checked her pulse. He felt nothing. Nothing at all. He holstered his gun.

"She's dead."

CHAPTER 74

The operative heard a small sound. He turned at the same time as Asher. Eight feet from them stood three-foot nothing little Tyler Raymer, who at that very moment was picking up his mother's backup pistol from the floor beside him.

And aiming it right at them.

Neither man had a gun in their hand. Neither knew what to do. They looked at Tyler's increasingly sad, increasingly mad face as the boy stared at this bleeding mother. Something was happening. His face grew impossibly red.

Asher spoke, "Little boy—"

Tyler screamed, "You hurt Mama! Fix her! Fix her! Fix her!"

Asher found the moment painfully pathetic. A little boy demanding justice that was never going to happen, holding a gun, probably for the first time. He had a moment of pity. "Little boy? We don't want to hurt you, so put down the gun. It can't fire anyway. It has something called a safety, and it's on."

Tyler stared numbly at his unconscious, bleeding mother and flicked the safety off without so much as a blink. The two men glanced at each other. *What the fuck?*

Asher felt the situation slipping from his control and tried to calm things down. "We want to help you. We want to help your mama. But you have to put down the gun so we can help her."

But Tyler wasn't buying it. "You hurt Mama! Fix her! Fix her —or I will hurt you!"

Asher tried a second time. "Your name is Tyler, right? Tyler, we can't help your mommy if you shoot us—"

"You fix my mama!" said Tyler, his face reddening by the moment. The man kneeling by Tempest saw the med-kit. He looked at Asher, asking for permission. Asher couldn't believe what was happening. He nodded.

The man said, "Kid, I'm going to get the med-kit, so I can fix your mama, okay?"

Tyler nodded, wiping a stray tear from his eye. The man moved over a few feet and grabbed the med-kit. As he turned back toward Tempest, he used the motion to do a concealed draw of the pistol in his waistband.

Blam! Little Tyler shot him in the leg. The bullet ripped through the man's femur, the largest bone in the human body. The man screamed in utter agony and dropped his gun.

The gun kicked back at Tyler, hitting him in the nose. The .32 didn't have much in the way of recoil, but for a little boy, it was startling. A moment of fear crossed his face. But he kept his hands on the gun, and his eyes on Asher and the other man. Tyler screamed back, "You fix my mama!"

The man felt the floor grow slick with his own blood. The pain radiating from his leg was blinding. The only thing that kept him conscious was abject terror.

He did as Tyler said. He bound up all three of her wounds, knowing it was no use. The woman was dead.

Asher stared into the kid's eyes, waiting for his moment. He couldn't believe it. Held hostage by a toddler. But there was something about this kid. Something unnatural. His gun never wavered. His eyes never wandered. Every chance Asher thought he had, the kid was looking right at him, clocking him. Watching his every move.

"I've bandaged her, kid, but she's not waking up."

"Fix her!"

Asher had to intervene. "Tyler, your mommy needs a hospital. We can all go with her."

Tyler shook his head, blinking away tears. "You fix Mama *now*!"

The man felt the panic growing along with the pool of blood beneath him. He was dying. A five-year-old was murdering him in slow motion.

Not knowing what else to do, the man rolled Tempest over and began to give her CPR.

Tyler seemed satisfied. He had seen CPR on the TV, and knew it was how you made hurt people better. He stared into Asher's eyes. "Why did you hurt Mama?"

It caught Asher completely off guard. "I— She hurt my friends."

Tyler thought about that for a long moment. "My daddy says you can't hurt people just because they hurt you."

"Yeah, well, I'm not sure your mommy agrees with that."

Tyler nodded. It was the truth. The man kept up the CPR, trying to save his mortal enemy's life in the vain hope of saving his own. With each ten-count of chest compressions, hope dwindled.

His shot leg screamed in agony as he pressed on, keeping the beat he was taught ages ago, the rhythm an actual heartbeat matches: "Another One Bites The Dust." The lyrics mocked him as he kept the beat.

Then suddenly, the beat changed. At first, the man thought he skipped a beat. But then he realized what happened.

Tempest coughed. She coughed a second time, spitting out blood and gasping for air. Neither Asher nor the other operative could believe what they were witnessing.

Tyler ran to her. "Mama!" He lowered his gun. The operative and Asher both saw their moment. The operative picked up his gun, raising it at the boy.

But the operative never got off a shot. Instead, he looked down at his gut, where Tempest's karambit was now firmly planted. She twisted the knife, gritting her teeth as she drew it across his stomach. "You son of a bitch, I wish I could kill you twice." Tempest pulled out the knife and took his gun. She turned to Asher—but Asher jumped over Chaucer's unconscious body and ran out of the room.

Tyler grabbed his mom and hugged her tight. "I love you, Mama."

"I love you too. You're a good boy, Tyler."

CHAPTER 75

Chaucer's head rang from the concussion Asher gave him. Nonetheless, after Tempest woke him from unconsciousness it quickly became apparent that he was the more functional of the pair of them, so he drove. At a red light, he pulled a business card from his wallet and dialed the number on it. It was his last chance to cash in a favor.

Hag-Omer answered on the second ring. Chaucer asked, "Do you know who this is?"

"Yes. Do you need that favor?"

"I do indeed. I need a black-market trauma surgeon. One the CIA doesn't use. And I need them in the next"—he glanced over at Tempest, growing paler by the moment—"fifteen minutes."

"Where are you?"

"South Bronx, I think."

"I have a name and an address."

For ten miles, neither Tempest nor Chaucer said a word. Tyler laid across the back seat, dead asleep. As Chaucer drove, Tempest slumped against the passenger door, trying to even out her internal bleeding, and to glance over at Chaucer. She tried to assess the damage to the man, as if Chaucer needed any more damage. "You okay?"

"Me? You're the one dying of blood loss."

Tempest sat up straighter, surprise all over her face. "You just avoided a direct question."

Chaucer thought about it. It was true. And it scared him down to his bones. *What happened back in that warehouse?* "I don't know what I am."

"Yeah, well, hours of torture will do that to you."

Chaucer laughed, out loud. It was so abrupt and so sharp that little Tyler stirred for a moment before drifting back off. Tempest stared as Chaucer like he was an alien. "Okay, what the hell was that?"

"I think you humans call it a 'laugh.'"

"Chaucer, when was the last time you actually laughed?"

Chaucer thought long and hard about the question. "I don't actually know."

Chaucer glanced over at Tempest, her eyes as wide as saucers. He said, "If it's any comfort, I'm scaring me too."

Chaucer pulled into the Greenbrier Veterinary Clinic. He got out and limped around to the passenger door, carefully lifting Tempest out, putting her arm across his shoulders for support. "I can hobble. You don't need to be touching me."

And suddenly Chaucer realized that he wasn't feeling the usual pain of physical contact. And the moment he realized that, the pain came rushing back. As though it was all in his head. Which it was. Chaucer fought to slow down his breathing as a series of strange sensations came over him. Like all the limitations he had lived with for so long were suddenly in flux.

Chaucer said, "It's okay. Let's get you inside."

Archie had a long night. The woman wasn't his only two-legged late-night client, but she was the worst he had ever seen. How she even walked into his tiny four-room pet clinic, he couldn't fathom. She had three bullets in her, which itself wasn't entirely remarkable. But two of them were in the gut. One had ripped a decent-sized hole in her stomach, the other took a piece of both her liver and her kidney.

That night, under the blaze of surgical lamps, Archie earned his reputation as the best black-market surgeon in New York. It reminded him of his time as a field surgeon in Afghanistan, a time before an oxy addiction ruined a promising medical career. Archie dug out the two bullets that were still in her, and after a long battle, repaired most, if not all, the damage. Tempest refused general anesthesia, which made his job twice as hard, until she passed out from the pain while he was fishing for the bullet lodged in her liver.

The man who brought her was playing some sort of finger game with the boy in the lobby. That was a first. No one ever had a kid in tow when they came to see him.

Archie gave the man the instructions for her care. "She's got to rest. Someone's got to monitor her urine. Anything darker than pink in the urine, and she's going to have to go in for more surgery. You got to monitor her for fever. I've got her loaded up on antibiotics, but with the amount of damage she had, she's still in danger."

Sure, he knew someone like his patient would be unlikely to follow his orders, but, damn it, he was a professional. The Hippocratic Oath didn't expire when his medical license did.

The man looked at the vet and nodded. "What if she needs to be ambulatory? What if she's got some things she has to do?"

Archie heard it all before. "Don't. If you value her life, don't."

But something told Archie these two weren't going to listen.

Joan was a buxom, plump, middle-aged woman living in a brownstone in Spanish Harlem. The walls of her foyer were pastel pink, and amateur paintings of flowers festooned the room. She smiled when she saw little Tyler and held out her arms to him. Little Tyler did not run to her. He turned back to his mother, standing beside the car, and looked up into her eyes. "Mama? Did I do bad?"

Tempest felt tears rising in her. She resisted the urge to choke up. *Get tough.*

She forced a smile onto her face. "No, Tyler. You were Mama's brave boy, and I love you. I'll be back before you go to sleep again."

Tyler ran to his mother, hugged her tight, and ran to Joan.

Tempest winced from the hug. She was in bad shape. But Chaucer could tell she felt better knowing Tyler was safe.

Tempest returned to Chaucer and the car. "So, where to?"

And for the first time in a long while, Chaucer knew exactly where to go.

CHAPTER 76

"Where the hell are we going?" Tempest's pain meds were wearing off, putting her in a foul mood.

"Ji said it. We just didn't know what it meant. She said that Tajo meant the Year of the Rabbit as a joke."

"Dude, you're gonna have to dumb it down big time. I'm barely here."

"In the interrogation, they didn't ask me about revolutionaries, or coup plotters. They asked me where the rabbits are."

"What, like a code name?"

"No. He meant rabbits. Actual rabbits. Tajo's rabbits. At NYU they called him Doctor Dolittle. He had lab animals, to test his phage therapy on. And I think he had some kind of breakthrough."

Tempest shook her head trying to defog her brain. "Actual rabbits?"

"I asked you about Tajo. I asked was he excited nervous or scared nervous? You said both."

"Yeah. That was the impression I got."

"He was excited. His phage therapy must've done something … extraordinary. But somehow, someone found out. And it spooked him. Maybe someone was trying to steal his research, or strong-arm him. So he used some kind of connection, probably his real family, to contact you."

"To protect him. For just a short-term job. Why short term?"

Chaucer frowned. "I don't know. Maybe he was finishing up the experiment. Or writing a paper. Maybe he wanted to be sure and once he was—the Year of the Rabbit."

Tempest nodded. It all tracked. "Not a revolution in the way we were thinking. But a revolution nonetheless."

Chaucer agreed. "He said it because he was excited. It was his own inside joke. He had no way of knowing those words meant anything else. He was getting ready to go public."

"So this op, all of this, it was cover for, what? A theft?"

"A biomedical breakthrough. How much could that be worth?"

They both sat there a long moment, thinking of the possibilities. Something occurred to Chaucer. "Asher and Roma, they got the research, but not all of it. They have the data. They don't have the rabbits."

"Then who does?"

Chaucer felt puzzle pieces deep in his subconscious moving. It was right there, he just had to wait a moment—

"Ji! Ji has them!"

Tempest shook her head. "Her shop? It burned to a crisp."

"What was the last thing she said? She's got other businesses."

Tempest winced as she sat up straight. She nodded to Chaucer through the pain. "Yeah. That's it."

It took the better part of an hour to find the place. Luckily, some kind soul on Yelp gave Ji a shout-out at a tiny pet shop in Washington Heights. Chaucer parked the sedan a block away from the shop.

It was 9 a.m., and the shop wouldn't open for another hour. The garbage trucks, vendor vans, and street sweepers did their morning dance in front of them.

Tempest did a sweep for surveillance, then stared at Chaucer. "What happened to you?"

"What do you mean?"

"You think I don't know something's different? What happened?"

Chaucer thought for a long moment before answering. He didn't quite know himself, but he knew enough to fashion some sort of answer. He just had to put it in a way she would understand. "I've spent all of these years trying not to break down. Trying not to let those years with Po destroy me. I was … trying to build a box, to keep out everything that could hurt me."

Chaucer actually smiled. "Last night, that box failed. My carefully constructed mousetrap, it was useless. And I guess I finally learned."

"Learned what?"

"I learned that you have to have a breakdown to have a breakthrough."

Tempest stared blankly at him. "What the fuck are you talking about?"

Chaucer sighed. "I don't really know. All I know is that things are changing, at least a little."

"Is that a good thing or a bad thing?"

"Where I was? I'm pretty sure change is good."

―――

At 10 a.m. sharp, Tempest and Chaucer walked up to the pet shop just as the metal gate lifted. The Korean clerk inside paid them no mind. To him, they looked like boozehounds, looking to extend a hypothetical marathon romance just a little bit longer.

Chaucer and Tempest headed right to the rabbits. "How much are these?" asked Chaucer.

"Not for sale."

Chaucer and Tempest walked over to the clerk standing behind the counter. They stood there menacingly, glaring at him until they caught his eye. "Tell Ji we're here to see her."

The shop clerk shook his head, about to deny everything. But Tempest put her finger to his lips. "Tell Ji, we're here to see her."

"It's okay. They're friends. Isn't that right?" Ji appeared at a door at the back of the shop. She waved them into a corner of a stockroom that functioned as an office.

Chaucer said, "You said Tajo said the Year of the Rabbit is coming."

Ji shook her head. "Haven't we been over this?"

Chaucer pressed, "He said it. Over the phone. Yes?"

"Yes." Ji noticed Tempest swaying just a bit. "What's with her?"

"Long day. You also said he left things with you just after that."

"Yeah, and they blew up with my apartment."

Chaucer leaned in. "But not everything he left you was in the apartment."

Ji looked puzzled. Then, a realization dawned, "You mean—"

"Tajo had a very different Year of the Rabbit in mind."

Ji shook her head. "You're saying everybody died—for actual rabbits?"

Chaucer nodded. "He was studying phages. Viruses that attack other viruses. Or bacteria. Or other pathogens. He was studying the potential of viral phages to become cures."

"I don't understand."

"You said he wanted to do something big. To atone. What if Tajo was killed for reasons that have nothing to do with his country or his family? What if he discovered something worth a fortune?"

Ji could see it. Finally. "That means—"

"You have what everyone is dying for, right here in your shop. Don't you?"

CHAPTER 77

For the second time in twelve hours, Chaucer and Tempest arrived at Archie's vet clinic. He was shocked to see them back and deliriously tired after pulling an all-nighter. "No refunds."

Chaucer didn't respond. He simply lifted a cage containing rabbits.

In a baby-blue examination room, Archie pulled the first rabbit out of its cage, scanning it for a microchip. "Yup. This one's been tagged."

Archie pulled it up on his computer, examining the rabbit's records. "Hmm," he said. "Weird."

Chaucer asked, "Weird how?"

"Give me a second." Archie got out the next rabbit and repeated the process. Again, it had a microchip in its foot. Again, its records surprised Archie. "This is wrong."

Tempest interrupted. "No offense to the guy who patched me up, but if you don't start talking, I'm going to put a bullet in you."

Archie scratched his head. "These rabbits were in lab experiments, right?"

Chaucer nodded.

"These rabbits had stage-four metastasized cancer," Archie continued. "This one had stomach and liver. This one, lung."

A chill passed through Chaucer. "You said 'had' …"

"What these guys should have, I should have felt them on examination. Hell, the tumors should be visible. You mind if I scan these little guys?"

Ten minutes later, the scans confirmed Archie's suspicions. "Somebody's playing a trick on you. These rabbits have no cancer."

"Not detectible, you mean."

"Non-existent, I mean. And that's not how it works. Remission is a long process. And besides, these guys are supposed to have eight different cancers between them. Even supposing the lab gave them something to treat one cancer. That doesn't explain the others. Nothing works on every cancer. Somebody switched chips. It's the only explanation."

"If the chips weren't switched, what would that mean?" Chaucer asked.

Archie shook his head. "It's not possible. Cancer, as we know it today, is a blanket term for dozens of different pathologies. Each type of cancer is its own unique beast. If the chips weren't switched, it would mean somebody discovered a single cure for all cancers."

―――――

Chaucer and Tempest sat in the car for a long moment. Chaucer didn't bother turning it on. They were both working through the problem, trying to figure out how the pieces all fit.

Chaucer spoke first. "So there's this kid. From a family rich beyond compare, but the definition of evil. And he comes to the West, but instead of preparing for his place in the Hermit Kingdom, he wants to be a do-gooder. To atone. And he's smart."

Tempest chimed in. "He did strike me as smart."

"And he makes a discovery. Something *way* beyond all expectations."

"And he calls his friend Ji. He hasn't told anybody, but he tells her, in a way only he will truly understand."

They sat another moment, trying to figure out the next bit.

Chaucer asked, "How did he go from elated to paranoid?"

"He wanted me for protection. He said he was being watched."

"He's got DPRK handlers. He's probably always watched."

Tempest had an idea. "But it wasn't the DPRK. It couldn't be. Your interrogation. It was a show, done to fool the North Koreans. To put a big fancy bow on Tajo's death."

Chaucer rubbed his chin. "Another party. They learned of Tajo's discovery. They wanted just to kill him and steal it. But the kid's the cousin of a madman with nuclear weapons."

"It gives them their false story. The North Korean regime is paranoia incarnate. They'll have no problem believing some Western assassin murdered a member of the family. Especially when they tie him to dissidents. And a long-dead coup, using Tajo's own phone call."

"So the question is, how did anybody find out what he had discovered?" The realization came to Chaucer in a flood. "The witness. It has to be."

Tempest still didn't understand. "What?"

Chaucer said, "We got to go see the real Isabel Marcano again."

―――――

Asher took the call he had been dreading. This time he made sure he was in a dark room, with no sight lines for snipers. He punched the accept button. "Yeah."

"I want an update," said the voice.

"It's not good. Colton's dead. Roma's dead. And a baker's dozen more operatives. Chaucer and Tempest are still in the wind."

There was a long silence on the other end of the line. Asher felt the need to fill it. "The good news is, from the interrogation, it didn't seem like Chaucer knew shit. They were still stuck on the political Year of the Rabbit lead. I need a dozen more men, I don't care where from. I can put this to bed."

Again, silence on the other end of the line. Asher glanced over his shoulder, by reflex. The voice spoke. "It looks like we have to clean up your mess as best we can. How many men do you have left?"

"Three."

"It'll be enough. I need you to kill Isabel Marcano. I take it you have her work address."

Asher knew the name instantly. He had to admit to himself, it was the right call. The one person who could connect this blown op all the way back to its source.

Isabel Marcano, you have to die.

CHAPTER 78

As Chaucer drove, Tempest checked the bandages she could reach. She had to change one of them, but everything was looking better than expected. "That Archie's good."

Chaucer nodded. "He's not a bad vet either."

Tempest laughed, then winced in agony. "Don't make me laugh, you bastard."

Chaucer didn't laugh with her. He was worried. "This play is predictable."

"I'll be ready." Tempest frowned. "Asher's still out there. Question is, how many reinforcements can he get? I kind of burned through the A-team back there."

This time it was Chaucer's turn to laugh. "That you did."

They parked two blocks away from the NYU lab building. A block away, they surveyed the scene outside. If there was still a watcher there, neither Tempest nor Chaucer could see him.

"What do you think?" asked Chaucer.

"I think fortune favors the bold."

Getting into the lab the second time was far easier than the first. They knew the layout, the security. For two professional operators, it was a cakewalk. They climbed the back stairs to the top floor, and Tempest popped her head into the hallway first. "Empty."

Chaucer thought, *Maybe we have it wrong*.

He opened the door to the lab and stepped inside. Isabel Marcano was surprised to see them. Chaucer took in the hundred micro-expressions she offered, and realized she was more than surprised. She was scared.

And she should be.

Without a word, Chaucer and Tempest worked in tandem. Chaucer went straight to Isabel, and when she tried to stand, a simple hand motion kept her in her seat. Tempest circled around Isabel, taking a position just at the edge of her periphery behind her. It was an intimidation tactic as old as time. Hunters—and human beings are most certainly hunters—have a natural fear and unease when anyone is in their blind spot. But Isabel Marcano didn't look back at Tempest. She was caught in Chaucer's hypnotist eyes.

Chaucer could approach this a hundred different ways. He decided on blunt force. "We know almost everything, Isabel. We need you to tell us the rest."

Isabel looked down, fidgeting with her hands. "I don't know. I don't know what you're talking about."

"You got the kid killed, Isabel. Did you know that was what they were going to do?"

"I don't know what you're talking about." *Lie. Guilt. Remorse.*

Chaucer sighed. "I'm sure you thought it was a side hustle, a way to make a few extra bucks. It was actually espionage, but they paid you for a while for nothing. Because until just a few weeks ago, you had nothing to report. But then Tajo hit the motherlode."

Every twitch, every blink, was a novel. With every fact Chaucer laid out, Isabel Marcano became more and more convinced that it was over for her.

"I don't know what you think you know," she said, "but you got the wrong girl."

An idea came to Chaucer, and a thrill rushed up his spine. He was going to do something he hadn't done in over a decade. "We've seen the deposits, Isabel."

Tempest raised an eyebrow at this. Malcolm Chaucer just lied. *Holy shit*, she thought to herself. *It really is a whole new world.*

Isabel bought it. "Nothing bad was supposed to happen! They never said anything about anyone getting hurt. I liked him. If I had known, I never would've said anything!"

Chaucer looked at her with those large, owlish eyes, offering a subtle sympathy. "Who paid you?"

The resignation on Isabel's face said, "In for a penny, in for a pound."

"The CIA," Isabel responded.

Tempest practically snarled. Chaucer stayed calm and held her focus. "What makes you think they were the CIA?"

"I saw a badge. They said some of these grad students were working for foreign governments. Stealing our country's research. All I had to do was to report on what they were working on. Any breakthroughs. They said I was an important part of a government operation. I didn't just do it for the money!"

Chaucer and Tempest shared a knowing look. False-flag recruitment. A classic example. Who actually hired her would be a dead end, unless the money trail led somewhere.

Chaucer asked, "And they wanted what Tajo found?"

"No. They wanted it destroyed. That's why they were so mad about the rabbits."

"Tajo took them, didn't he? He took the evidence."

"Some of the evidence," Isabel confirmed. "They took one hard drive, then destroyed the rest of his research. Drives, papers, backups. Everything—except for the two vials."

Chaucer could feel it. The missing puzzle piece about to fall into place.

"What vials?" he asked her.

"They were very specific about it. They wanted my help destroying the evidence. But they told me not to destroy those two last vials. The last samples of the phage."

Chaucer's mind raced. He couldn't quite put it together yet. "Two?"

"Yes. One vial went with the young guy. The other went with the old man.

"The old man?"

She nodded. "At first I thought he was in charge. He had that feel. But then the young guy asked him if they were good. If the vial was—payment in full."

The room spun for Chaucer. The final piece fell onto the table and found its rightful place. Chaucer could see it. The whole picture, laid out in stark black and white. He knew who ran the op. He knew who ordered the hit that killed his brother.

Chaucer got up from his chair, nodded to Tempest, and turned to leave. Without turning back, he told Isabel, "I'd leave town. I wouldn't tell anyone where I was going, I wouldn't use credit cards, and I would never come back. You're the loose end. Got it?"

Isabel slumped back in her seat as the words sunk in. She silently nodded to no one at all. Chaucer and Tempest had gone.

CHAPTER 79

Tempest stopped Chaucer in the hall. "Mercy? You just gave that bitch mercy?"

"Isabel was telling the truth. She took a little bit of money to give a report once a month. She's not responsible for any of this."

"Chaucer the Saint," said Tempest dismissively.

The two of them walked back the way they came, toward the rear emergency stairwell. Behind them, a sound. *Ding.* The elevator opening. Tempest glanced over her shoulder, a simple reflex really.

She saw Gabriel Asher and his last two men exit the elevator.

Asher and one of his people reacted instantly. They raced across the hall and into Tajo's lab. Tempest, slowed by her wounds, drew and fired a tight volley, catching the remaining man three times.

"Shit," said Tempest. "I think I lost a step."

"You died today. Give yourself a break."

Tempest headed for the lab to finish the job, but Chaucer put a hand on her shoulder. "No."

Tempest spun around. "What the fuck are you talking about?"

"What do you think you're gonna find in there? You're gonna find Gabriel Asher with a hostage."

"Then he picked the wrong bullet shield. I have half a mind to plug her myself."

"She doesn't deserve it."

"Everybody deserves it!" Tempest spat out.

"He's here to kill her. He's here to kill the last witness. You plug her, you're doing his job for him. They get away with it. They get away with murder."

That calmed Tempest down. "What then?"

"I go in there. I do what I do best: talk. You do what you do best: you figure out how the sniper got in there, and get a firing position on Asher."

Tempest thought about it. "He could just kill you. You know that, right?"

"Just make sure you kill Asher. For Albert."

Tempest nodded, then jogged down the hall leading to the back of the building, looking for an access way to the roof.

Chaucer headed into the lion's den.

He drew his weapon and threw open the door to the lab. As much as he acted like he knew how this was gonna go down, the situation was far more fluid, and far less predictable than he let on. There was no gunfire the moment he opened the door. *That's a good start.*

Chaucer stepped inside, clearing the room as his now ancient training had taught him. He saw Gabriel Asher, or at least the corner of his head, seated in an office chair directly behind Isabel Marcano. He could see the whites of her eyes from where he was standing. She was terrified.

But Chaucer couldn't see the other man.

"You're a hard man to kill, Malcolm Chaucer," Asher said.

Chaucer's eyes darted left and right as Asher spoke, searching among all the lab equipment for the threat in hiding.

"I had help," he replied.

"That is the understatement of the century. Where is she?"

Chaucer realized he had an advantage he hadn't even

counted on. He felt a shiver pass up his spine. Pain radiated from every vertebra, but it wasn't quite like it had always been. *The pain is weaker.*

He swallowed hard and tried out his new tactic. "She's in the hallway, ready to kill you. I convinced her to let me try talking first. The civilian doesn't need to die." He felt a twinge of pain rocket up his back. It was barely half of what he would've felt yesterday telling such a bald-faced lie. He gritted his teeth and let the pain pass. He felt no episode occurring. Asher noticed nothing.

Asher put together the data points. He would've thought Tempest would pull some kind of flanking maneuver. Finding some other way in here. But if there was one thing he knew about Malcolm Chaucer, it was that he couldn't lie. *So much the better.* He glimpsed his own operative performing a flanking maneuver, slowly working his way behind Chaucer.

For Tempest, this part of the job was a walk in the park: rear stairs, roof hatch, tightrope walk along some exposed pipes, and then to the access hatch leading to the rafters. If not for her extensive internal injuries, she could've done it in three minutes. Instead it took six, and she worried greatly that those extra three minutes were time Chaucer didn't have.

Chaucer told Asher, "If you kill her, you won't get out of here alive."

Asher smiled. "I don't think your ex-wife intends for *me* to get out alive, regardless."

Chaucer shrugged. Asher was right. If he denied it, Asher would know he could lie again. "You got that right. But she wouldn't shoot you if you had me for a hostage."

"Endlessly inventive, our Mr. Chaucer. So, what? I let the girl go, you put the gun down, and I take you in her place?"

"That's the idea."

"One problem with that: I have orders to kill her."

"Well, then, I guess it's your orders, or your life."

In his periphery, Asher saw his operative disappear behind a large array of equipment that he knew was roughly the same distance from him as Chaucer. In a moment, he would be behind Chaucer, and the Oracle would be dead. But a part of him wondered if he shouldn't take Chaucer's deal. "Tempting offer, but Tempest isn't exactly the Widowmaker right now, is she?"

Chaucer said, "What do you mean?"

"I mean, when I last saw her, she was on death's door. She spotted the three of us and only capped one. I'm saying, your girl's lost a step. Maybe that's enough. I figure all I need is one good shot."

Chaucer knew what Asher was doing: buying time. Even at this distance, he could tell that Asher's eyes were uncommonly still. He was using his peripheral vision. The other operative was about to get behind him.

He readied himself. He would have to make his move at just the right moment. And he relied on Asher's eyes to tell him when.

"I thought you were Gabriel Asher."

The statement stopped Asher for a moment. "I beg your pardon?"

Chaucer pressed the advantage. "Gabriel Asher is a smooth operator. He plays all the angles. He doesn't die holding onto a bad hand for too long."

Chaucer could see the anger in Asher rise. A high-functioning sociopath was still a sociopath. The dark triad could be concealed, but never eliminated. His rage was always there, just below the surface. Asher said, "I know what you're trying to do."

Chaucer saw the micro-tremor in Asher's eye, flicking over to his left. "Same," Chaucer said as he spun around and shot the man behind him. A single round caught him in the temple.

Before the man had even hit the floor, Chaucer spun back and had his gun pointed at Asher.

Asher couldn't believe it. "You know I'll kill her. You know I'll kill you. How about this for a new hand of cards? I'll take you both hostage."

"You're already dead. You just don't know it."

"How do you figure?"

Chaucer said, "Because I lied."

Asher could feel it, every hair on the back of his head rising in unison as he realized the threat, and he realized it way too late. He turned, but he never had a chance. High above him, Tempest lay flat on a girder, her body perfectly relaxed as she squeezed the trigger and put a bullet through the top of Gabriel Asher's head.

CHAPTER 80

Chaucer put the car into park and sat there a long minute. He heard the seagulls that had always been a comfort to him. Now they were a cold reminder of what he was about to do. Tempest looked over at him. "You want me in there?"

Chaucer shook his head. "I need to do this alone."

He got out of the car and stared at the serene white and gray colonial with the large, perfect lawn, and the view of the bay. The home of his only friend these many years. Fitz.

He entered without knocking. He knew he didn't need to. No doubt they had heard the car and saw him approach. Sure enough, Fitz, alive and well, was sitting in his easy chair, waiting for him. "Hey, Mal." It was a somber greeting, full of regrets unspoken.

"Hey, Fitz."

Fitz started to speak, then stopped himself. He gathered his thoughts and tried a second time. "I want you to know it wasn't supposed to be like this."

"I know. I finished the job early overseas. You begged me to stay in Belgium."

Fitz smiled. "I knew you'd understand. But not just that. I'm so sorry about your brother."

Chaucer shook his head. "Don't, Fitz. Don't say his name."

"I tried to tell you the last time you were here. We're the bad people. We're all the bad people."

Chaucer stared his only friend down. "We can change, Fitz."

"Are you kidding me? People can change? Save it for a fortune cookie. People don't change."

Chaucer said, "I did." Fitz grimaced as he tried to adjust his position on the chair. He was obviously in great pain.

"Looks like you need another adjustment."

The growing terror in Fitz's eyes was clear. "No, I'm good."

Chaucer walked over to Fitz anyway. "Nah, it'll just take a second. I've done this a million times. Don't chicken out now."

"Please, don't."

But Chaucer did. He came up beside the chair and reached down, wrapping his hands around the torso of the older man.

"Let him go, Mal."

Chaucer turned to see Nan, standing halfway down the stairs, holding a gun on him. The gun did not waver a millimeter. She climbed down the rest of the steps and walked over toward them.

Chaucer couldn't believe this was the same woman he saw just a couple days ago. It looked more like someone created a robotic replica of the woman she used to be. She was still emaciated, but there was a glow to her skin, and a gleam in her eye.

"Payment in full?" Chaucer asked.

Fitz said, "I had to. She's my everything."

Nan smiled. "For us, it was a love story. For you, a tragedy. I want you to know how sorry we both are. That it had to be like this."

Chaucer asked, "What happened to the other vial? The last vial."

"Same thing that happened to those rabbits," said Fitz.

Chaucer felt the sting. He tried not to let it show, but he wasn't sure how much got through.

Fitz sighed, "Yeah, one of my people tracked you to Archie's. They're gone, Mal. It's over."

"Who are you working for?"

"What did I tell you, Mal? There's no king and country anymore. No black and white. Just shades of gray. I work for one of the darker shades is all."

"What is this 'darker shade' going to do with the goddamn cure for cancer."

Fitz shrugged. "If I had to guess? Use it as leverage. The most powerful people in the world also happen to be some of the oldest people in the world."

"The kid wanted to give a gift to humanity."

"And I just want my wife to live. It would've taken a decade at least for his discovery to make it through the regulatory gauntlet. No, for Nan to live, he had to die. A life for a life."

"No. A billion lives for one life."

Fitz nodded. "Bad people. I told you."

Chaucer turned to Nan. "So this is how you're gonna start your new life, killing a friend?"

Nan frowned, a profound sadness in her eyes. "You have to finish what you started, Mal. You have to eat everything on the plate."

"Good, that makes this easier."

"What?"

"Knowing that you're complicit."

Nan raised the gun, growing scared. "What are you talking about?"

Chaucer said just two words, "Goodbye, Nan."

Tempest heard it through her earpiece, sprawled out on the hood of the car, R93 sniper rifle in her hands. Nan in the crosshairs.

"Bang," said the gun.

Fitz screamed as he saw his wife fall, thrown into the wall by the kinetic force of the bullet. He tried to rise, but Chaucer had his arms around him, and gave him a short, sharp twist. Suddenly, Fitz couldn't move. He couldn't do anything but scream in agony. The nerves around his spinal cord were suddenly raw and exposed. The greatest single pain a human being could sense.

Chaucer stood back and stared at the man, helpless and in agony. "You killed my brother, you son of a bitch. I should leave you like this until you starve."

Fitz gritted his teeth, fighting his body to remain perfectly still.

Chaucer continued, "But then you'd be right. And you're not. We're not bad people. We're bad, and good, and helpless, and hopeless, and everything in between. That's what makes it hard. Deciding the right thing to do, every day. For you, today? That's gonna be mercy."

Chaucer pulled out his pistol and shot his best friend in the head.

CHAPTER 81

A gentle mist fell from the gunmetal gray sky in Valhalla, New York, as Chaucer buried his brother. The air smelled of petrichor and freshly cut grass. White stones dotted the green hills as far as the eye could see.

He sat next to Sheila in the front row. The half-smile on her face was betrayed by red circles under her eyes, and the tremble in her hands. It was a well-attended affair, with three dozen of New York's finest in their class As, and seven riflemen on hand to deliver the twenty-one gun salute. Beyond the NYPD, there were at least eighty other people, most of whom Chaucer didn't know. He wished his brother could see him now. His brother always liked the old Chaucer.

Sheila turned to him. "They're about to do the gun thing. If you need to go, I understand. I want you to know I understand."

Chaucer took her hand and held it. Suddenly, Sheila didn't understand. Such a simple gesture, but Sheila was in awe. She cried anew at the simple act of connection she so desperately needed in that moment. The honor guard fired its first volley. Reflexively, Chaucer took a glance over at Tempest, sitting two rows back and to his left. She looked like she always did, stoic. But she caught him looking at her and winked at him. Chaucer looked to his right and saw Spinoza, at attention and saluting.

Behind her was Manny, hoodie wrapped completely around his head as he bobbed back and forth. But he stayed, gunfire and all. Chaucer knew a lot about people who found the world a hard place to handle, and that was the highest honor Manny could pay Chaucer's brother. Another row back, he spotted Keery, the ballistics expert. Keery was staring right at him, nodding out of respect.

The rifle corps fired again, and Chaucer thought of all the people who died in the last week. Terry. Tajo. Albert. Dennis. The kids in the Pet Shop Club. Archie. Asher. Roma. Operatives, North Korean and American both. For what? Fitz was right about one thing. It was a new world for dinosaurs like Chaucer and Tempest. State espionage was giving way to economic espionage. New groups were forming. Hidden and dangerous.

That's when Chaucer noticed the man in the charcoal-gray suit. A distinguished-looking Black man with gray hair, sitting in the fourth row. He had a placid look on his face, staring respectfully at the service. Chaucer had marked him earlier, but then Sheila had grabbed his attention. But now, Chaucer couldn't help but have the feeling that he stuck out somehow. That he didn't belong. He talked to no one, looked at no one, seemed connected to no one. As Chaucer took a long glance in his direction, the man smiled faintly and checked his phone, typing something discreetly.

Chaucer's phone buzzed. Out of curiosity, he glanced at it.

Hello, Mr. Chaucer. We need to talk.

CHAPTER 82

After the service came that awkward time when the mourners milled around for a moment. None of them wanted to be the first to leave, but all of them wanted to go. Spinoza found Chaucer first. "So, how you doing?"

"I'm good. Clear sailing."

"Clear sailing. I don't know what that even means."

"It means you can rest easy, and so can my brother. The problem has been solved."

"You've been busy."

Chaucer laughed. "If you only knew." For a second, Chaucer thought Manny was going to pay his respects. Manny made a beeline right for him. But when Chaucer caught his gaze, he diverted forty-five degrees, and opted for a flyby instead. Chaucer could hear him muttering to himself, "Bad people, yeah. Bad people."

Chaucer took a quick glance around before realizing that the bad person Manny was referring to – was him.

Keery was respectful enough to wait until after the service to pull out a few fresh sticks of gum. He chomped down on them heartily and tried chatting Tempest up. Chaucer had half a notion to blow his mind and tell him he was talking to the shooter he so admired the other day, but what would that get anyone?

"Something's different." Chaucer turned to see Sheila had found him, and it was a statement, not a question.

"I want you to know the people responsible for Terry's death have been dealt with."

Sheila nodded. The statement made her deeply uncomfortable, but Chaucer liked to think a part of her was grateful.

"What happened to you?" she asked.

Chaucer thought for a long moment, trying to come up with a way to put it to her. "There was a guy I knew once, back in college. He had OCD. Anyway, it started getting worse. It was spiraling out of control, so bad that he had trouble leaving the dorm. Hell, he had trouble leaving his own room. We eventually took him to the doctor. The doctor said that his condition was basically a misfiring defense mechanism. Well, that was me."

"And it's not anymore?"

Chaucer glimpsed the Black man with the gray hair, standing up by the cars. "No. It still is. Maybe it will always be. But I have something I didn't have last month."

Sheila asked, "What?"

Chaucer smiled. "Hope."

"Mal, I want you to know you can totally say no to this, but I've always wanted to hug you. Would that be—"

Chaucer hugged her. He hugged her tight, and he hugged her long, and she melted into his arms, and sobbed. "I miss him so much."

"Me too."

"I thought … I thought I was alone. I thought I was the only one who was gonna miss him like this."

"You were never alone. I just couldn't show it. It's gonna be okay, Sheila. We're gonna have gray skies for a while, but it's all gonna be okay."

Sheila just hung on to Chaucer and let it all out.

Ten minutes later, Chaucer put Sheila in her limo. Tempest waited a respectful distance away.

"You okay? That was a lot of touching."

"It's ... manageable."

Tempest eyed him up. "So still pain."

"Life is pain. But I've built up quite a tolerance."

Tempest checked her phone. "You get this text?"

Chaucer nodded. "I think I know who sent it."

"The Black guy with the gray suit. Where is he?"

"I'm right here."

Chaucer and Tempest spun around, and sure enough, the Black man in the gray suit was standing less than ten feet away. Tempest laughed. "Takes a lot to sneak up on us."

"You're in mourning. Your defenses are down. I'm sorry to have to reach out to you here, but we do need to talk."

Chaucer said, "This place is as good as any. You here about blowback?"

The man smiled cryptically and said, "There will be some, that's for sure. I'm actually here with an offer. I'm offering cleanup services. You won't need to explain yourself to anyone."

"If?" Tempest said.

"Fitzgerald was on the outer rim of something new. Something dangerous. An intelligence organization whose only motive is money."

Tempest laughed dismissively. "You think that's new?"

"The way these people are doing things, it is. They're not putting themselves up for hire. They're creating disruption and profiting from it."

Chaucer could see it. Entrepreneurial spies. No longer whoring themselves out to nations and organizations, but using their skills and going into business for themselves. "Okay, let's accept your thesis. There's an organization—"

"Organizations," the man in the gray suit corrected him.

"There are organizations that have gone completely dark, and completely private. What does that make you?"

The man in the gray suit stared out at green hills dotted with white tombstones. "For the time being, let's just say this. There was a CIA, there was a KGB. There was a balance when these two organizations worked at crossed purposes. The organizations I'm referring to are profiting off of chaos, disruption, war. For now, you could say I represent a competing force. A counterbalance, if you will."

Tempest smirked. "So, a real white hat?"

The man in the gray suit just smiled and strolled away. "I'm sure you could get yourself out of your own mess. But if you want my help, just text that number." The man stopped, but did not turn around. "Oh, and, Mr. Chaucer? I truly am very sorry for your loss."

And with that, he passed over the hill and out of their sight.

Chaucer and Tempest looked at each other, neither one sure of who should speak first. Tempest took her turn. "It's bullshit, right?"

Chaucer looked at his phone, at the simple text. "Right, total bullshit."

"So what next?"

Chaucer looked ahead, at the line of cars awaiting them. Something caught his eye, causing him to smile. "A reunion."

Tempest turned to follow his gaze. Her jaw dropped. There, next to a black limo, stood Albert. The man was on crutches but there was no question it was him.

Chaucer and Tempest crossed the distance quickly. Tempest spoke first. "How the hell are you alive?"

Albert smirked. "I told both of you assholes I wasn't gonna die. You just don't listen."

Tempest turned her gaze to Chaucer. "You knew?"

Albert cut in. "Chaucer owes me a lot of goddamn money. You think I wouldn't get in touch?"

Chaucer said, "I thought it'd be a nice surprise."

Tempest shook her head. "A nice surprise? A nice surprise? Flowers are a nice surprise. Lazarus here rising from the dead? That's ... incredible."

Albert nodded. "Yeah, well I'm not out of the woods yet."

Chaucer and Tempest looked worried.

Albert continued, "You two owe me a hot pink Cadillac, or I'm gonna need a full-time bodyguard."

Chaucer shrugged, "That's only fair. But after the reception, okay?"

Tempest and Albert looked confused. Tempest asked, "Reception?"

Chaucer shrugged. "It's out on Staten Island. Will you guys be my plus-two?"

Tempest laughed heartily. Then she looked him in the eyes and saw that he was serious. "Man, this new Chaucer is going to take a lot of getting used to."

Malcolm Chaucer returns...

YEAR OF THE SHEEP: THE PREQUEL

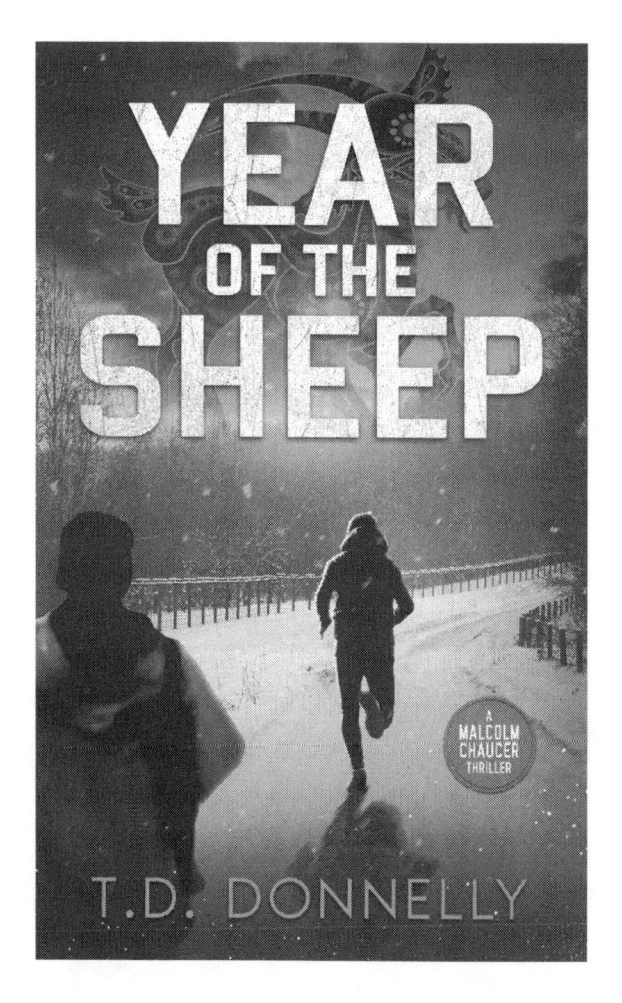

Absolutely FREE and exclusively available by signing up for my mailing list at TDDONNELLY.COM

IF YOU ENJOYED THIS BOOK

Word-of-mouth is crucial for any author to succeed. Please consider leaving a review, even if it is only a line or two. It would make all the difference and would mean the world to me.

ACKNOWLEDGMENTS

Novels are not the work of just one person. I was helped immeasurably by so many people in this process.

First, I must thank Mykala Brennan and Danielle McCarthy for their awesome transcription skills. A good half of this book was written via dictation while walking on my favorite beach, and Mykala and Danielle made sense of the noises that came out of my mouth and delivered excellence.

Next, I have to thank my fantastic editor, Rebecca Millar, for her thoughtful and detailed adjustments that made a good story better. Also, my amazing master proofreaders, Elizabeth Addison and Sarah J Russe for a level of precision and correction I could never hope to match.

I'd be remiss if I didn't mention some amazing writers who shared their expertise and wisdom with me along the journey, in particular Craig Martelle and Jo Penn, your generosity astounds.

And lastly, to every beta reader and ARC reader who took a chance on a new novelist, and provided amazing feedback. I'm truly blessed to have been surrounded by so many positive, uplifting people, and I thank you all from the bottom of my heart!

ABOUT THE AUTHOR

T.D. Donnelly is a Jersey boy transplanted to Hollywood, where he's been a screenwriter for more than twenty-five years. In that time, he has written on projects that have grossed over a billion dollars worldwide. He has adapted the classic works of writers such as Ray Bradbury, Clive Cussler, Stan Lee, and Robert E Howard. He's worked on franchises from *Voltron* to *Uncharted*, and from Marvel's *Doctor Strange* to *The Walking Dead*. His feature credits include *Sahara* starring Matthew McConaughey, and *Conan the Barbarian*.

You can find him early mornings walking the beaches of Southern California, and spending time with his wife, two mostly grown children, and two very demanding guinea pigs.

Year of the Rabbit is his debut novel.

Made in United States
Troutdale, OR
08/16/2024

Made in the USA
Columbia, SC
24 June 2019